Also by Joan Williams

THE MORNING AND THE EVENING

OLD POWDER MAN

THE WINTERING

County Woman

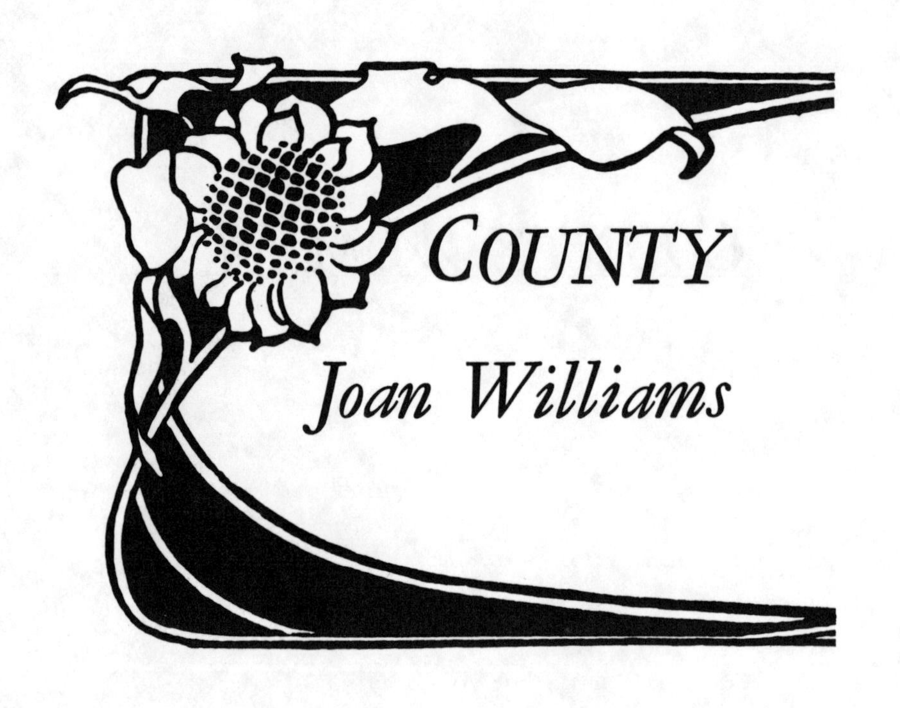

COUNTY

Joan Williams

WOMAN

An Atlantic Monthly Press Book

Little, Brown and Company

Boston/Toronto

Second Printing

ATLANTIC–LITTLE, BROWN BOOKS
ARE PUBLISHED BY
LITTLE, BROWN AND COMPANY
IN ASSOCIATION WITH
THE ATLANTIC MONTHLY PRESS

LIBRARY OF CONGRESS CATALOGING IN PUBLICATION DATA
Williams, Joan, 1928-
County woman.
"An Atlantic Monthly Press book."
I. Title.
PS3573.I4494C6 813'.54 81-18571
ISBN 0-316-94237-5 AACR2

BP

Designed by Susan Windheim
Published simultaneously in Canada
by Little, Brown & Company (Canada) Limited

PRINTED IN THE UNITED STATES OF AMERICA

To
hill country and its people;
and to
Dorothy Olding and C. Michael Curtis

County Woman

1

THE DUST was thick. It obscured the four small white stores of town when a car passed. The dust slid down the grooves in their tin roofs. In nearby pastures, trees were covered and had a hangdog look. The one smooth road through town reflected the sun. Town seemed emptied, a place where everyone was hiding. Four old men sat around a stump playing checkers on the porch of Loma Murphy's General Merchandise store, and might have been calcified — there forever.

A battered gray Oldsmobile swished to a stop beside Loma's single, locked gas pump. The old men slyly watched a thin and tired middle-aged Negro woman get out. She wore sandals fashionable for that time in hot weather, flat rubber soles held on by thongs. She did not glance in their direction, much less nod. The shoes slapped the ground and then the steps as she went up them, revealing heels whiter than her brown feet. She left behind, for the old men, the prominent smell of her cologne.

Inside, Miss Loma looked past the woman as her door's bell tinkled. "You want some gas?"

"Yes'um. I want to fill up."

Miss Loma reached overhead to pull a string, which unlocked the pump outside. "I have to have my customers wait on themselves," she said, smiling.

The woman's face had no particular expression. "I don't care to pump gas," she said. "Don't seem ladylike to me. I know I'd splash my clothes."

Loma stared at the Negro; her hand came down slowly. "Were you wanting anything else?"

"Yes'um. Ivory soap flakes. Some Vicks. Got a cold."

The door opened then with a great clatter. John Q Dobbins

rushed in with important news written all over his face, motioning Loma toward the rear. "John Q," she said tightly, "I'll hear later. I've got me a customer that can't pump her gas."

John Q stopped himself, like someone in the old child's game Statue; he froze as if he were still running. Miss Loma had a clear pleading look on her face. "Can you help me, John Q," she said, meaning she did not need to lose even one customer's business, as he well knew.

His eyes were hard when he looked at the Negro. The woman kept her profile toward him and stared toward the rear; he muttered something in a tone that was clear, but since his words were not, he could not be directly accused of anything. He let the door slam. When he stood speaking to the old men, one got up and peeked inside the store, his face pressed directly to the window. Loma thought she could hear the gas pumping violently, though the store was sealed up against hot weather. The air conditioner blew chills down her spine. "Anything else, then?"

"A big bag of potato chips. A pound of butter."

"Butter's high as a cat's back." Loma lifted her head a little. "I don't carry anything but margarine for my customers."

"Well, my goodness," the Negro said. "I just hadn't paid any attention to the price."

"Maybe I don't carry in my store what you need," Loma said. "Mose Perkins across the road has a lot bigger selection," nodding her head.

The woman's gaze did not follow Loma's gesture. "You're pumping my gas, ma'm. I don't want to have to do my shopping in two places. I'll try your margarine, and I'd like a dozen of your oranges."

"Then you'll have to step in the back," Loma said, "to pick them out."

"I trust you not to pick me out any rotten ones," the woman said, almost smiling.

"I don't ever leave the front unattended." Loma looked outside for John Q. He was still waving his arms and talking. She saw the gas suddenly rush out of the woman's tank and all over him. She clenched her fists. She was losing money.

Unclasping her patent-leather purse, the Negro took out a bill. She flattened a fifty-dollar bill against her chest, watching Loma's face. "I can pay for what I want. You get it, please, ma'm."

So Loma went to the rear and got what the woman wanted, watching her as she dropped the oranges one by one into a large opened sack, each thud sounding as if the bag would split. Then coming back she met John Q walking in, his boots splattered and smelling of gasoline. He rubbed his hands red on a greasy rag.

"How much I owe you, sir?" The woman stepped forward holding out the money.

"Me?" His voice had a surprising squeak. John Q was a large man. "I don't work here. I'm doing Miss Loma a favor." He grasped the holster around his waist. You know who I am, he was saying.

The woman's lips were lighter than her skin; they whitened turning up at each corner for a vanishing moment. She turned patiently and held out her money to Loma. "Ma'm?" she said.

Loma's hands fluttered above her cash register keys. She opened it without looking inside. "I can't change that bill. You have something smaller?"

The Negro sighed. "I guess I've got something smaller." Looking into her purse she finally brought out a twenty.

John Q was whistling between his teeth. Loma read the gas-pump meter through the front window, and then made change. "Thank you," the woman said. After proceeding to the door with her groceries, she clattered it politely shut.

"Who in the name of Sam Hill is that?" John Q said.

The woman drove away without noticing anything, but all left behind watched her car till it was out of sight of town.

"She's one of these new Negroes who've moved down here

from Memphis to work in the underwear factory that opened out on the highway. Some of them want to get away from the city and get out into the country, like white people are doing."

He stumped to the front window in his boots and stood there again, as if daring her to come back; the old men looked up expectantly. John Q only turned back around.

"What was it you were bursting to tell me?" Loma said.

"Just that," he said, nodding toward the road, "they're bringing that Negro James Meredith into the University of Miss'sippi Sunday night, to integrate the school."

"Then it's the end," Loma said, looking out the window. "The end of living the way us Southern white people have. And that woman knows it."

2

THE NUMERALS *1962* stood out prominently on a funeral director's calendar tacked near the front door. Loma felt that date imbedded in her heart. Just as she adjusted her handprinted sign in the front window, gone crooked, IF YOU CAN'T STOP WAVE, she saw Allie McCall pull up in front. Then going past so fast, so close Allie's skirt flew in the breeze, was what the townspeople called a "wop" car, since nobody could remember its real foreign name. Quad Brewster slid quickly to a stop, and got out. People in town lined the road to watch him curiously, surprised the boy would avoid a rooster. Was he drunk already, this early in the day? He mocked the rooster running in its crazy frightened gait till it disappeared by ducking under one of the two stores opposite. Letting out a long crow, Quad Brewster got into that low car to fly on toward the Delta, out of the hills, where the next county was wet.

Allie hurried inside, moving faster than she usually did.

"John Q Dobbins," she was saying, "you go out there after that boy! What kind of constable are you?"

Loma turned to stare at Allie, that she would light into John Q so; Allie was usually such a quiet woman. Loma nodded at her encouragingly. Allie said what everyone seemed to know. "He's going to run over somebody out there in the road one of these days."

John Q simply stood there like a whipped puppy. He lowered his head. "When'd womenfolks start telling the law what to do?"

Allie looked startled; some thought crossed her mind. "Why," she said, "I suppose when the law stopped doing its job."

Loma smiled.

"I have spoke to the boy," John Q said, still peevish. "He knows he's not supposed to drive through town so fast." He tried to smile. "Told him we don't have but three hundred folks and need all them."

"Spoiled rotten the whole eighteen years of his life and his daddy owning the county have ruined him. Everybody scared Mister Brewster'll call in their mortgages, or not give them any credit, or not gin their cotton if they do one thing against his precious package," Loma said.

"Oh, but surely that day is passing too — you've heard about Ole Miss?" Allie said. The others nodded. "People are going to stop worrying about some family's name. Mister Brewster is just a figurehead. Inherited everything and doesn't know how to run anything himself."

A stranger walked into Loma's store, a blonde, young, kittenish woman who looked a bit flea-bitten. She was barefoot. White people simply did not come to town like that, even in hot weather. Here at the end of September the thermometer continued to hang around ninety-nine degrees. The woman waved a frail handkerchief with change tied up in it. "You got a phone I can use?"

Loma nodded toward the back. "You'll probably have to wait for the line to clear."

Who is that? Allie asked, raising her eyebrows as a question.

Loma shrugged. Nobody knew if Loma didn't, because storekeepers knew everything.

"Well," said John Q, returning to his conversation, "if that boy gets into the university, he'll only stay as long's the marshals are there. As soon as the marshals are gone, that nigger'll go too."

"John Q! That's a very offensive word," Allie said.

"Please don't use it in my store, honey," Loma said. "You know I need my Negro trade."

"What'um I supposed to say — black?" John Q said that like a sheep bleating — bla-aack — so that it sounded as bad. When the blonde laughed in the rear, John Q swelled up like a peacock preening its feathers. Loma and Allie exchanged a disgusted look. "Honey, isn't that line clear yet?" Loma said.

The woman said, "It wadn't," and picked up the receiver and set it back. "If you bang it down hard they're more likely to hang up," Loma said. She looked in despair at the others. "I asked to be on a line with three other businesses, but I would have to draw Sudie's Klip-'n-Kurl. That's as bad as having a homemaker on the line."

"Somebody's trying to decide 'tween Poinsettia and Fire Engine Red," the blonde said timidly.

"Got to be Miss Pearlie Mae. If she'd let her hair be natural she'd look better." Allie, at fifty, had stopped touching up her own few gray hairs.

"Nothing in creation the color of her hair but the rear end of a baboon," said John Q. The blonde twittered. The other two women shook their heads in annoyance that men were such suckers for flattery. The woman had wandered back. "I declare, I wondered where such a pretty box of candy come from."

Loma lightly touched one of the fancy boxes she had carefully pyramided on a counter. She fingered some of the pretty, stiff, pink crinoline bow-ribbon around one, then a velvet flower that was tucked in to it. She said, testingly, "You had a box like this from my store?"

"I don't know where the pretty thing come from. It was give to me. Mine didn't have that pretty little old flower, though. I wished it had of." The woman dimpled. Loma's sudden strangeness made Allie remember something Loma had told her a long time ago. "You'd be surprised," Loma had said, "how many men I know driving round this countryside with a box of candy under the front seats of their pickups." "Where'd you say you stay, honey?" Loma always probed for information by pretending she knew something, but had only forgotten.

The woman said, "Over toward the government dam," which told them little.

Picking up the evening paper from Memphis, John Q tossed down a coin. "It's the university now, but Eisenhower sold out the Southland over yonder in Little Rock. A Judas to all us little Southern folks who voted for him. Now Miss'sippi's whole public school system's going to be integrated. Anybody got kids haven't eat with niggers yet, they will have soon."

The woman in back sucked in her breath; Allie and Loma both reproached John Q again. Slapping his paper to his thighs, John Q said, "Well, I hope Little Black Sambo gets hisself plenty pancakes in college."

He departed. Loma's pleasant storekeeper's smile remained frozen, while Allie stuck out her tongue behind his back. But the blonde stood at the rear of the store laughing to beat the band.

3

ALLIE COULD NOT FORGET the sudden sharp intake of the blonde woman's breath, the way she looked when John Q mentioned the schools. Red-necks were the very people who hated Negroes most — what else did they have but to kick one, the saying went. Already, after James Meredith began trying to integrate the university, people here had started talking about a private academy. In a little country town like this, that sounded absurd, but country people were good about laughing at themselves, the way they were good with their hands. They planned to remodel the large brick schoolhouse for it at one end of town. The building had been going to ruins since the county schools had consolidated.

"Honey, keep on that line!" said Loma, as a warning. She did not like strangers hanging around unless they were buying. Suddenly, asking for another town, the blonde waved to Loma to mean she'd pay, stop worrying.

"Momma, hey. It's Iona. Heard on the radio you all had a tornado down yonder. I got worried. Heard some men escaped from Parchman. You hear from Brother?" She listened hard. "It's nice of 'em to let him call."

Loma looked busy counting change. Trying not to listen, Allie went over to the front window. John Q was talking to the old men playing checkers. She looked out at pastureland belonging to her poppa, at cows standing beneath willows, which dipped into a pond that was muddy and opaque like all in the countryside. A streak of yellow was the beginning of the driveway leading to her house. Although she was unable to see it, she knew how things looked from the road. Except in the dead of night, blue/black/gray shadows were always jumping at one window, which meant Poppa was watching television; though what more could she expect of him at ninety? The window's strange glowing was an example of things not being what they appeared. As far as others knew, she was a calm matron happily taking care of her husband and home and old daddy. Yet now, without warning, she began to shake, because all her life she had fought against a feeling of nothingness, and in middle age she had the terrible fear that she was losing that battle.

She had never been content with the idea that one lived for each day. She could not live, either, believing the point was only to be good enough to meet her Maker; could not believe, as an older generation had, that this life was a testing ground, and heaven was where life began.

She wanted to accomplish something, she wanted something of her own, so that if Tate were to die, she would not be just

Allie McCall, his widow. She feared idleness and life without meaning. But how much easier it would be to give up, give in, and grow old.

Now the sky was flattening out serenely toward suppertime, yet the tornado down south could be coming this way. Peaceful times could change overnight, with the university integrating: so many changes, so quickly. An astronaut planned to orbit the earth eighteen times in one day. Why can't I change *my* life? Why can't I? Allie thought.

Loma was calling, "Allie, won't you take a cold drink with me?" Allie turned from the front window. "Too near supper," she said. "I'd better go. I left Poppa beans to string, but he won't. Ask him to put in a new roll of toilet paper, and he says that's womenfolks' work."

"Everything here cut and dried in that respect," Loma said. "Always has been and probably always will be."

"Well, maybe not," Allie said.

Banging down the receiver, Iona then threaded her way toward them around stacked cardboard boxes, oil barrels filled with trash, and some old cedar church pews Loma hoped to sell.

"Had a tornado down your way?" Loma said, accepting money for the call.

"Yes'um. My—I mean, somebody told my momma lights went out at the penitentiary, and four colored prisoners escaped. Said one's from up here."

"Up here? I don't know of a one of our Negroes in Parchman," Loma said.

"Well, if he is from round here somebody better be expecting company. I know that from experience. Prisoners are like homing pigeons, ever time." She went on to the door. As if John Q were still there bleating, she looked back before opening it. "Black," Iona said. "Child, if black is beautiful, I have shit many a masterpiece."

She went out calmly, leaving total silence after the bell's slight tinkle. Then Loma said, "Why, have you ever!" She answered herself. "No. I never." She turned toward Allie, whose face bore a look as astonished as her own. Quite clearly, they had never expected a woman to say anything so vulgar, particularly in public, and they had never expected to laugh. Then suddenly they were saying if they didn't stop, they'd tee-tee in their britches, though they were not laughing at the remark, but because it was refreshing not to be hypocritical and stand there like two old biddies with their bosoms stuck out and saying things like, My land! What is this world coming to! Because what it was coming to was being more open. Allie had long felt she strained against all the things dictated to her by being born in her time and place.

Then, sobering, she put out a hand and took hold of Loma. "Loma, do you know of a single Negro from Itna Homa who's gone to Parchman since Elgie killed Momma?"

Loma looked back as seriously. "Not in all these years, Allie. Maybe that woman was wrong. But if it was me, I'd go to bed with a gun under my pillow tonight."

4

HE HAD BEEN the uppity type. Elgie would look a white person straight in the face while he was being talked to. Some white men said they had the uneasy feeling that when he said "Mister" to them, he did not really mean it. When he was a child, his parents went to Chicago, leaving him with a grandmomma who lived in a cabin back of Poppa's house, where Allie grew up and still lived. Elgie seemed to wear a chip on his shoulder, but people in the community could not understand why. It was natural for Negroes to go off and leave their children with others: nothing for the boy to be ashamed about. Negroes weren't supposed to have feelings about things like that.

Summers he went to Chicago to visit, and each time people in the community guessed he would not come back. Yet every fall he was home wearing new store-bought clothes that rubbed people the wrong way. In all the years before World War II, country people in this part of the world wore hand-me-downs and patched and homemade clothes. Elgie wore flashy nigger clothes that everybody laughed about; still they were new.

Allie's mother, May Stewart, was called a do-gooder. She had tried to teach Elgie more than he could learn in the colored school the scanty months he could attend, when he didn't have to hoe, chop, or pick cotton. She taught him also about flower gardening and shrubbery, filling his nappy head with ideas about having a profession to get himself away from the fields and out of these dirt-poor hills.

Often Allie wondered why her ancestors who found their way here from South Carolina stopped on this poor land. Why didn't curiosity, urgency, need, or whatever their motives, send them a few miles farther south and into the black alluvial land that was the Mississippi Delta, some of the richest land in this country? Maybe they feared the mosquitoes and malaria prevalent in that low-lying land.

Needless to say, Itna Homans did not hire real gardeners. Old or feeble people might hire a colored boy to rake leaves and clean up their yards, but anybody unable to tend a garden was dependent on others for vegetables and flowers. How much Elgie learned no one ever knew. By the time he was sixteen he was what was called a "buck." That was one point on which everyone agreed, though some were uncertain whether or not he raped May Stewart before killing her. Poppa naturally claimed she was not touched, but Allie sensed some of the good people did not readily believe that, only pretending to for Enos Stewart's sake. She was uncertain what she felt in her own mind. How much did she actually remember seeing when she was five; how much had she invented; how much had she overheard, or been taunted with? That the cruelest people are children was so true, it seemed a wonder everyone was not soured on human nature early on. "A nigger killed your momma! Your momma was a nigger-lover!" The feistiest of the country kids, those wise from the beginning, made enough dirty half-remarks, jokes, that everyone got the idea her momma and Elgie had been playing doctor or playing momma and daddy or whatever it was you called it, the same thing dogs and cows did. Later, of course, when the insinuation was clear, young people were old enough not to taunt her. Still, as innocent as she tried to keep her mind, she had the feeling that everyone took for granted that the worst had been going on, or was beginning the day her mother died.

That day the shot seemed loud enough to blow off the cabin roof, though it only pierced a window. When Elgie came bursting out the door, her mother remained silently in the cabin, where she had been teaching him; then Poppa was there, and Belva Dean, whisking her indoors, away, but not before Poppa shoved aside the door crying, "The Lord Jesus!" She saw her momma with her dark head bent, one hand idly in her lap, sitting in a corner. That was the largest thing that struck her at that age: Why's Momma on the floor? Belva Dean went on saying, "Oh, Lamb of God," as she went on staring over her shoulder. Poppa came out of the cabin and watched Elgie running across the pasture, straight into the arms of some waiting men. Poppa blasted into the sky with shots remaining in the gun. Why didn't her momma yell at him, Crazy fool! the way she usually did when he shot too close to the house? she had wondered, in Belva Dean's arms. Then she buried her face to Belva Dean's shoulder, knowing there was something not only sad, but wrong, about all the commotion. Elgie had been her friend, her playmate even, despite their different ages. Long afterward, knowing what being a buck meant, she had felt betrayed by his knowledge of other things all along. Of course she had hated him, but gradually had felt that the truth was not known. Because who back then did anything but blame a Negro when there was trouble? Elgie was threatened with tarring and feathering if he did not stop yelling. He had yelled, "Y'all peoples knows Miss May. Y'all peoples knows I got mo' sense than to fool with a white woman. Somebody hep me." Allie had gone on a long while hearing his repeated cry, "Somebody hep me." Always, she would think how nobody had.

He'd had more than forty years in prison for his resentment to grow, and to grow warped in a place like that himself. So that she could believe Elgie coming back might be looking for the woman she was now, or looking for Poppa. Who knew?

Knowledge of her past came to her, it seemed, like the whistling of wind through trees, some high, thin sourceless sound that left her knowing things. Not certain exactly what she knew, she picked things up from the atmosphere the way she might pick up flu. A visitor would come to the community, or someone old whose memory was shaky, or some kid came along who didn't know the story, and she felt dogged by tidbits of gossip.

Over the years, piecing together fragments of her mother's story, Allie gathered that Elgie, sixteen years old at the time, had been swiftly tried, and as swiftly convicted. The community was proud that it took care of its own dirty linen. Not a word about the murder or the trial even appeared in the local weekly, *The Democrat*, published in Nashtoba fifteen miles away. No one knew she visited the courthouse and read through bound papers yellowing and flaking; she found nothing but her mother's obituary. It said only that the Death Angel claimed May Stewart of Itna Homa community unexpectedly. The trial took place shortly after her mother's death right out in the main road through town, between the stores now owned by Loma and by Mose Perkins. The constable set up a card table, and brought nail kegs from the stores for seats, and appointed a jury. Perhaps the landscape of lightly populated small hills bred a climate that was not one of violence or hatred. The Ku Klux Klan had never been active here, and no one had been lynched within memory. Perhaps Poppa chose to let Elgie go to prison. If so, he must have had a good reason. Nobody who witnessed the trial would ever forget how that was one scared nigger. "That didn't hep May Stewart a bit though, did it?" Of all the snatches of conversation she had overheard, Allie was not certain who said that, but she remembered it perfectly.

"Gratitude? You see what May Stewart got for her trouble, don't you?" Her mother's death was always pointed out as a prime example of the fact that Negroes are like mules. "They'll work for you as long as things are going their way, but wouldn't mind turning on you and kicking you in the end." Anybody in town could have warned May. People who hoed and plowed land of yellow clay to make a living didn't much go in for idealism.

Never to herself had she referred to her mother's death as a murder; Allie was uncertain why she shied from that. But growing up as an only child, she was alone a great deal and became reflective; also, like most single children, she was with adults mostly and had insight beyond her years, which the adults did not have the intelligence to perceive. Though she had Poppa and his mother to raise her, she became in some ways a ward of the community. Early on she realized that the unmarried townswomen offering to help take care of the motherless girl were setting their caps for Poppa, though none caught him. She sensed that neither love nor loyalty for his dead wife kept Poppa from remarrying. He was fearful of being burned twice. That was the question she had always asked herself. How had he been so burned?

5

LOMA WOULD SAY nothing else about Elgie. No one in this town would talk to Allie about what had happened, because her Poppa had ruled that long ago—and he abided by his own ruling. Allie felt walled in by this silence; she would never dare ask anyone so speculative a question as, What do you think really happened?

She and Loma stopped talking. John Q walked back into the

store with a rapscallion named Snake Johnson. They never said anything personal in front of him. Snake had a prominent gold tooth and a dark gap where a tooth was missing. His nickname came from older days when he hid near outhouses and then joined some housewife when she went into one. The old wags on the store porches liked to say a lot of husbands didn't realize how long it took their wives to start hollering, though. Snake was as sneaky as one of the wild dogs that roamed through town. Now he was laughing to John Q over one shoulder, "Nigger never has wanted nothing but a bottle of whiskey in one hand and a white woman in the other one."

"Lots of men I could say that about."

Taking that as a compliment, Snake bent over laughing. His hands were shaking, as if palsied. He had obviously been to Cottondale to drink the previous night, in the Delta where the Brewster boy had been headed. In the upcoming election in November, beer and whiskey would be important issues; each year the margin of "victory" was smaller on the question of whether their county in the hills would stay dry. Staring at Snake, Allie could only think it would be bad for Itna Homa to become a wide place in the road with beer joints.

Right now, Snake went on running his mouth about niggers, whiskey, and women. She was glad that when John Q had part of his stomach removed, and had to quit farming, he had not become an idle member of the community, like Snake. John Q had agreed to run for constable, a job no one else wanted. It paid too little, and he didn't have much to do. If serious trouble arose, something he could not handle, he was to call the high sheriff in Nashtoba.

She considered talking to him about the possibility of Elgie's being escaped, but turned cold at the idea. At this minute, she did not want to know. Not able to live in innocence, she might live without fear. Though remembering the boy Elgie from her girlhood, she could not believe he would come back to take revenge on her—if revenge would be his reason for coming back? She felt tears of confusion spring to her eyes, realizing that what had happened between her and John Q in the past made it difficult to talk with him in an intimate, secret fashion. For years she had not been able to speak to him at all. One day he apologized abruptly, but in a boyish way that satisfied only him.

"Hush!" said Loma. She always heard the door's bell tinkle before anyone else. They all greeted an old Negro woman who came in. She was wearing a stocking cap on her head: the top half of a woman's stocking twisted at the top the way a balloon is tied; no one had seen one in years. Allie watched pleased expressions cross John Q's and Snake's faces while Annie talked. "Ain't had a sanking spell in a while," she answered Loma's inquiring about her health.

"What am I going to do for you today?" Loma said.

"Came in to get them pink earrings." Annie pointed toward a showcase that displayed jewelry on cardboard cards, several Afro wigs sitting lopsidedly on Styrofoam heads, and key rings studded with rhinestones. Even when things at Loma's were not old, they somehow seemed to be. She had no easy row to hoe any longer, with most people in the community whizzing off to work in nearby larger towns, and shopping in supermarkets. "Where you going all gussied up in them earrings?" John Q said, with a beatific smile.

"Going to Uncle Lawson's funeral tomorrow."

"Why, no!" Loma said. "I hadn't heard he'd gone."

"Passed this morning."

"Died this morning and you're burying the old man tomorrow?" John Q said.

"Oh, yas suh. Us getting to be like white folks. Bury bodies, don't hold them."

Loma rang up the sale in silence, while Annie stood, asking John Q twice whether he was going to swap her some of his muscadine wine again this year for some of her honey. Once they made their usual deal, Annie said, "Miss Loma, I'm going to have me some pigs birthing soon. Could you take one as payment to work something off my bill?"

"I take payment any way I can get it," Loma said, waving toward the store. "Fence posts. Peas. Anything I can sell."

"Mister Tate headed this way from the fields, Miss Allie." Then Annie was at the door saying, "Y'all white peoples take care now. All y'all been knowing me like I knowed myse'f." And she was gone.

There was a moment's silence before Snake Johnson spoke.

"Like white people, my foot," he said.

Allie felt something as sharp as metal pierce her heart.

She thought of Tate coming in, and the evening ahead, and wondered if she could speak to her own husband about a prisoner being escaped. She didn't want to trust Iona's talk—could it be Elgie, after all these years? If so, could she take up a gun after him? She did not believe so. She would lock the doors tonight, whether she mentioned him at home or not. Elgie? She could not picture him as a revengeful, mean man. Yet he had every right, now, to be one.

She sat on one of Loma's church pews, only vaguely listening to the others talk. People did still speculate over whether her mother had been raped. Allie thought back to an article in the Memphis Sunday paper recently. A city detective who was interviewed said he knew of very few real cases of rape, that women always just hollered afterward like a stuck pig. It was enough to make anybody blow a gasket! Later when the editorial page was full of protesting letters from women, she had wanted to write one. But she could not write openly without a lot of talk in this community, and it might reach Poppa's ears, too.

Instead, she had called up police headquarters. When the detective got on the line she could not say anything. She only listened to his breathing and bellowing "Hello." Then she said, "Boo!" and hung up. The memory brought her near tears again. She stared at the sun's last dazzle on the tin roof of Mose Perkins' store opposite, thinking it the color of rain, or tears.

So much she had wanted to tell the detective about another kind of rape, besides bodily harm. Yet she sensed the man was too stupid to understand the soul or emotions, pictured him squatting on a chair like a frog. When Tate wanted to know if the call to Memphis on the phone bill was hers, she told him it was one of her foolish days. Said she phoned a radio station to give the answer to a musical quiz, that an operator told her to hold on, and she got tired of waiting and hung up. She was glad it didn't occur to Tate to ask what the question was. She had grinned and said, "Could have won us a free dance lesson at Arthur Murray's in Memphis."

"Shoot," he had said, blushing.

To her recollection they had not danced since World War II, when Tate was stationed at Camp Shelby down near the Gulf Coast. That is, if you could call dancing her stepping around Tate's shoes while he stood in one spot bending his knees back and forth. She was fond of that memory, though, as she was fond of Tate.

While thinking Tate understood that some days she went berserk staying with Poppa, she heard John Q rattle off another cliché: "Shucks," he was saying, "Negroes are happy. They're so happy I've always called them God's chosen people. If you'd ever been a nigger on Sad'dy night, you wouldn't want to be anything else."

"John Q," she said, rousing herself, "you're riding an old horse, like Governor Barnett, and whipping it to death!"

"Lord hep us, woman," said Snake.

But only recently, a Negro John Q knew turned over on another man's tractor and was rushed to Memphis with John Q right behind the ambulance, and the first to donate blood. It'll never be sorted out, Allie thought, opening and closing her eyes: the South's past. John Q wiped his chin and went on running his mouth, when men all the time talked about women running theirs. She had learned long ago that men were worse gossips than women.

They told everything to brag, while women of her generation were filled with conventions, and when they broke any, wouldn't tell it for the world. People here were still old-fashioned in ways. At gatherings, men were apt to get on one side to talk crops, and women on another to talk what men considered womenfolks' things. Only, what men here didn't seem to realize was that by her age, women were beginning to free up to talk about a lot more; particularly if they had been married so many years; no longer were they as genteel as men thought.

In this part of the world men expected nothing of women that involved using the brain. Allie often thought men didn't think they had one. Many times she'd heard a wife say, "I think—" and her husband cut in to say, "You're not supposed to think. I'll do the thinking." He would not be joking.

Recently she and Tate came home from a softball game in Mose Perkins' pasture. Tate said, "Well'd you women get it settled about how long it takes to boil a three-minute egg?"

In middle age she found her thoughts more explosive; once she wouldn't let herself even think cuss words. "Hell's bells," she'd said to herself that day.

When she said nothing, Tate didn't notice. Finally she said, "That remark hurt my feelings." He'd forgotten it, and when she told him, he said, "Oh sugar," swatting her on the behind. That was supposed to make matters all right, though she didn't know why, since after thirty years of marriage their sex life had dwindled away. There were mostly memories. Living without sex because she had to strangely gave her a sense of self-reliance. However, discovering self-reliance for a woman not used to it was a somewhat lonely business, she found.

The male ego was the most fragile thing in God's creation, she thought. If she had a daughter she'd have told her that first thing, to start her out right. Two things in the world caused more trouble than anything else: drinking and men's egos. When young, flattering a man could get you anything. She'd never been the type to do it. Was that a mistake? Might have been fun, if men wanted to be so stupid.

Women her age were beginning to discuss how tired they were of catering to men, feeling they had served their sentences.

Insinuations and jokes led her to believe in most long marriages there was little sex, if any. Divorce was still uncommon here; time could change that. Men now did not up and leave their older wives for younger ones. But subscribing to a women's magazine called *The Homemaker*, she recently read an article saying this was becoming a trend other places than Hollywood, wherever people called themselves sophisticated. They had to be richer than here, too. She wondered if middle-aged men played out on young wives, the way they had on the older ones they left.

She thought about being taught to cater to a man, and how women even covered up for husbands who mistreated them. Several here received black eyes from running into clotheslines rather often. She'd been born somehow with more backbone. If Tate raised a hand to her she'd tell him to put his feet in the road, for good.

Loma broke Allie's reverie, crying, "John Q, you been blocking my gas pump all this time!"

He jumped like most men at that half-shrieking sound in a woman's voice. "Sorry. Sorry. I need some gas." It was obvious John Q was not sure he did. His eyes seemed like the windows of a slot machine, his thoughts as visible as flowers, birds, and whatever flew past in those. Allie, having seen the machines only on TV, could not see quickly enough to catch everything. He swayed like a hound as he walked. Opening the door, he called to a Negro boy sitting on the porch's raggedy edge and swinging his feet. He had the idle complacency of a vanished time, when country people sat to watch whatever passed in the road, once a whole Sunday's occupation after church, before television came in.

"Son," John Q called, having waited till an amber light bulb in the store went on. "Miss Loma's unlocked her pump. Would you fill my truck for me?"

The child leapt down happily, grinning from ear to ear. Allie smiled at his sense of manliness as he aped exactly Mose Perkins across the way, who was filling up a car. The child set one dusty foot to the pickup's bumper and rested the hand holding the hose across that knee. His little brown bare foot and its rim of pink underfoot absurdly reminded Allie of Loma's expensive candy boxes; on their covers were halved chocolate candies with pink centers showing.

When the gas hose clunked, John Q looked relieved the truck took so much. But Loma was still frosted. "Something else I can do for you today, John Q?" He might as well have stolen money from her till, blocking her pump. Maybe cars had gone to one of the other three pumps in town. The person at Mose's might have been my customer, Loma's tone said, as she peered out to study whose car it was.

John Q turned, tyrannized, to buy something else. Her oranges were shriveled almost to the size of kumquats, and no one in the community had brought in fresh produce for Loma to sell, so he reached to the nearest counter and picked up a square box with a cellophane window, without looking inside even to see what kind of cake it was. Loma got out her gray paper pad with lines faded almost invisible from the beginning, while her eyebrows questioned: That all? John Q asked for cigarettes and then determined not to be intimidated anymore. Loma obligingly wrote on her pad, her expression agreeable, and her yellow, freshly sharpened pencil flashing busily.

Again, she reached overhead for the string above the register, which was tacked across the ceiling to a far corner. When pulled, it unlocked the gas pump and turned on the amber bulb as a reminder. Now she turned it off, and the string danced frenziedly in the air awhile. Allie watched the small light diminish, thinking how it had no effect upon the ghoulish coloring from the new fluorescent tubing. These were so wrong for the store. Yet why feel so stirred up over it? She supposed it was part of her general feeling of unrest. Tate would blame her mood on the menopause, she thought angrily.

Also, the fluorescent lighting rubbed her wrongly, she thought, because the store still smelled old inside, though not as it once did. No longer was there an open barrel of soda crackers or a potbellied stove with its pungent woodsy scent or the odor of men drying out wool clothes and rubber boots. Once, a brittle pecan tree blew down in a high wind and the part that was turned into a butcher's block was still in the store's rear; on it sat a great wheel of mousetrap cheese, which gave off a reminiscent smell. From a wire strung across one side of the room hung leather boots and rubber ones and straw fieldhand hats, which people wore now in their gardens. The ammonia-like smell of the cola case and the smell of damp wood beneath where it leaked were the same as always.

She wondered how to choose what of the past to keep and what to let go. How did you manage to let go once you decided?

Then the small Negro child came in, saying, "His gas fo' dollars."

"Whose gas, honey?" Loma did not speak unkindly.

The poor child was filled with indecision, which Allie well understood. She wanted to rescue him, but it was Loma's store. He hung his head. She imagined him at home that way, while his glistening, earnest people told him different things from what they'd learned back in their day. When he stubbed a toe into a crack in the floor, Allie remembered with shame thinking for the longest time Brazil nuts were truly named nigger toes, as she'd always heard them called.

"Mister John Q's gas," the child finally said.

"Why, I knew you knew him. He's been constable longer than you been born," Loma said.

The child gravely laid a quarter on the counter. "Can I have me a nickel and two thin dimes for this block quarter?" His hair glowed purple in the lighting, with perspiration.

Loma glanced at them all. It was too much to make him say Please, ma'm, too. John Q and Snake moved uneasily. Once that child would have been yanked home and his parents threatened if he did not know how to talk to white people. His head would have been cracked open like a walnut by his own kin. Allie felt relief that he now only left with the pitiful handful of candy a dime would buy, knowing no difference about that, either. Loma fit caps back onto her side-lying candy jars. "I don't know where the Negroes get their expressions. 'Block quarter'? But I know where they get this thing of not calling white people by their names. Don't want to have to say Mister or Missus. The child learns that at home, but older people learn it in church. It's only beginning down here in the country. Annie told me colored church is nothing but taking up money and talking against white people. The young ones want to turn Miss'sippi into an all-black state. Annie said she wouldn't live in one. It'd be too dangerous!"

"Negroes like for you to call them down. They respect you more for it!" Snake said, stomping one foot.

"No more." Loma told them all about the Negro woman from Memphis coming in earlier.

"I had a tractor driver tried it," John Q said. "I hold him my name's not 'you'—it's Mister John Q."

"He had to keep his job, John Q," Allie said, quietly. "That's the best one around, almost the only one for any Negro who wants to stay with the land."

"That's another matter," he said. "This thing about minimum wage. Worse thing the government's come up with for the little fellow. I used to hire me an old Negro to haul manure, just to hep him out. I can't pay him minimum wage to do that. A lot of wives and chirrun have lost jobs. Man can't pay minimum wage to kids. Drove the farmer to mechanization. To folks losing jobs."

"Put them on welfare, all right," Loma said. "Annie says her people who've gone to Chicago never have worked. Says their kids see them not working, so don't see then why they should. She said this younger generation of Negroes isn't worth killing. That's what the older Negroes feel."

"It's hard for misplaced people who've never done anything but look at the rear end of a mule to find jobs," Allie said. "Don't know how to do anything, too old to learn."

"All us here grew up raggedy as a can of kraut," John Q said. "You can't hep but resent the younger generation having it so easy."

"Where'll it all end?" Loma said.

"When the Negroes have broke the United States of America," Snake said.

He did not realize the others were openly thinking he'd never done a thing in this world but live off a government disability check.

Allie was glad not to be excluded when John Q mentioned everyone here having been poor; she'd had more than most growing up. Impulsively, to help out Loma, she said, "Order me a case of dog food, Loma. I'm tired of toting home cans."

Loma wrote on her ashy pad, but her eyebrows queried: Would Allie's mutt live that long? She could never replace Sweetie, Allie thought; they'd been through too much. The little black mutt was the only thing female she'd lived with since her grandmomma died, when she was fourteen. Sweetie instinctively took her side in a household of males: where Tate, after playing catcher on the town ball team, used to drop on her supper table what he called the protector of the family jewels, always smelly; where the toilet seats were always turned up; where, if Sweetie puked, the men did too, and she had to clean up after them, while Sweetie at least ate her own; where if she spent an afternoon crying about nothing, Sweetie understood, and watched her in commiseration.

The men were leaving. John Q generously said, "Neb' mind," when Loma offered him a sack. He went away swinging the cake, till the icing would be on the sides of the box when he got home. He looked young from the rear. He had the same wide shoulders as when he had been a football hero back in high school, in the days of her puppy love, when she had been so innocent.

Now that it was almost evening, the sun was behind Mose Perkins' store. Willows in the pasture were luminescent in their greenness, and Allie stood thinking about the past. Loma was too. She said, "I don't even ask Negroes who come in here direct questions anymore. I can't stand having them say yeah or naw. Hurts me to the quick. In the South we've always been taught to respect our elders. So it hurts especially to see what's happening to that little boy."

"Disrespect certainly can hurt," Allie said, thinking of something else. As John Q drove away, she wished that he might have heard her words. Did he ever think about the day he'd said, "You'll remember me, sugar. Because I was the first one there"?

Yup. John Q had gotten the old cherry, without its even being ripe.

6

SHE WAS FIVE GRADES behind John Q in Itna Homa Agricultural Grammar and High School. When she became aware of the school hero, he seemed always to wear football pads under his clothes, his shoulders were so wide. His waist tapered to a *v* and he had the tiniest hard knots as a butt she ever saw. He was a senior and captain of the football team when Allie entered seventh grade. In the upper school then, she was able to pass him in the halls daily. When she saw him, she'd find the crotch of her pants dampen unexpectedly, inexplicably, though she would not have mentioned this to another girl any more than to her grandmomma. Simply, it was not an era of shared confidences. Since John Q was her first crush, Allie had no idea how it showed, or that he and his friends were even aware of her existence. They could not help noticing and being amused by her somewhat peaked face and the sorrowful and worshiping green eyes that followed John Q's every move.

Silly to realize, but in that time both the playground and the lunchroom were divided into a boys' and a girls' side; monitors supposedly watched them but were always off yapping with one another, their backs turned. Boys had organized games, but girls were not thought to need exercise. At recess, they sat around or drew lines in the dirt and played Hopscotch and sometimes Red Rover or Statue. The fact that boys and girls were separated kept sex uppermost in everyone's mind, although the point had been to squelch it.

The agreed-upon barrier between the male and female sections of playground was where the fire escape let down; here ells of the school formed a shady corner and the ground was cindered. To dash there and escape the monitors' notice was far more daring than to smoke in the bathrooms.

One day when Allie had to go inside to the girls' toilet at recess, she glanced to the shaded area and saw poised there for all of time John Q and the newly elected May Day Queen, Betty May Spraggins. That they had slipped there at all was enough to set Allie's temples throbbing. But John Q had opened Betty May's blouse and was nursing a big white tit. Allie was blocked by shock. She had a slip, on which was written permission to use the toilet, and felt duty bound to go and sit but could not squeeze out a tinkle.

Later, she grew so pale her teacher sent her to the nurse's office to lie down, over Allie's protest. She was left alone after the nurse pulled down opaque green shades and trapped in the room a fly that buzzed ceaselessly, as if it were being tortured. While girls she knew never confided in their mothers, Allie wished at times like these she at least had one. If she had had a soft, sweet, young mother she'd have gone home. But, at home, Grandmomma would make her drink comfrey tea and would talk darkly to Poppa about all the illnesses the child might be coming down with and would belch continually because of her gall-bladder condition and want Allie to take Pepto-Bismol every time she did. Allie preferred to lie on the scratchy, black, hard horsehair lounge in the nurse's office. Her mind's eye would not stop containing that fat full moon, Betty May's breast. Tentatively, Allie felt her own hard knots. This led to a tightening and twisting of her legs, in a newly discovered way, that soon sent bubbles and stars dancing to her head, and left her drained afterward. She sensed that to cause the sensation to herself was wrong. The nurse's tapping heels came along as Allie finished, and, finding her lying in a pool of sweat, the nurse took her temperature and was astonished that she had none.

The nurse sent her home anyway. Allie went, having been given the distinct impression she was probably coming down with polio and would infect the whole school. Grown-ups in those days had little thought for the feelings of children, and no thought at all about their psyches; they didn't think of children as people.

She went on and on being haunted by that schoolyard scene. One day, lying on the living-room floor, reading comics, she thought of it again. Her legs tightened. She could not stop squeezing until the bubbles and stars began. Then suddenly she was standing, truly yanked up by the hair of the head. Grandmomma stood screaming and holding a whole long curl of Allie's hair. She screeched so loud Allie never knew what she was saying, if anything. The house dog and the yard dogs barked their heads off. With the windows open, everyone uptown could hear Grandmomma screeching, yet Allie could be certain no one would ever know why.

It would have surprised Grandmomma to know Allie had no idea the sensation she produced for herself was one she would someday look for from a man. Allie simply assumed that the sensation was wrong because it felt so good.

She went out of the house and down to the barn, since it was milking time. She did not want to see Poppa really as much as she did not want to be alone. Grandmomma's shrieking rankled, along with her own shame and disgust, without her knowing why. She went in as Poppa was pulling a swelled pink tit of Bossy-Cow's. Suddenly Allie knew what a stupid and childish name she had given that cow; losing reason, she sent the milk pail flying with one kick. The tin pail hit the barn's nearest wall and hard-won milk splattered everywhere.

Poppa jumped off his low stool and knocked her against the head. In a particular way of his, he tucked one thumb into a fist and thumped it out to the side of her head: a hurt worse than a slap and more humiliating. Someday Allie would reason out that was because the hurt was so deceptive. Coming, it didn't seem the thumb would hurt at all.

Neither Poppa nor Grandmomma asked what bothered Allie so much that she would do something so uncharacteristic as to kick the pail, something so uncharacteristic as to let her emotions show at all.

Only Belva Dean, the cook, expressed sympathy, and dared that mutely. Her face darkened, the way Negroes could make them when they were sad. Always, Negroes had more compassion for her in her childhood than her own people. Maybe Belva Dean was not surprised when a few months later Allie turned into what Grandmomma called "a young lady." She had her first period. Belva Dean knew Allie's confusions and probably her pitiful ignorance and certainly about her feeling that no one paid the slightest attention to her growing up, and that she did it all alone.

7

IRONICALLY, Poppa contributed toward the day his little girl lost her virginity. Often, Allie longed for nerve to tell him. But she supposed no father, from any standpoint, could see the funny side.

Her best opportunity for hero-worshiping was in the school cafeteria. One of the community's better-off kids, she could afford a nickel for hot lunch every day. Most kids brought their noon dinners in paper sacks that were greasy-bottomed and smelly before twelve; otherwise they brought them in tin lard pails. She wanted to take her lunch, to be like the others. Then no matter how often Allie begged Grandmomma not to do it, she cut crusts off sandwiches she fixed for Allie. It was impossible for Allie to cover that up by the way she held the sandwiches; the other kids always knew and she felt further apart. Aside from the fact that cutting off crusts seemed a waste, the others did not understand the motive behind it. Mostly, they ate hunky cold country biscuits with sometimes a teaspoon of sorghum inside to help the dryness. These lunches were common; only those who got free lunch were looked down on. At no time in this part of the world, among proud hill-country people, had getting something for nothing been a popular idea.

John Q brought his lunch in a sack. When Allie saw he creased it and returned it to a back pocket to be reused, she wished she could have remained ignorant of that fact. The senior boys came into the lunchroom boisterously. She liked to watch them fake their lunches as if they were footballs or basketballs. When they finally settled down to eat she couldn't stop watching. The sight of John Q made her feel delicious, and the crotch of her pants stayed damp.

Once, she woke up to his watching her watch him. When he began to peel a banana, she was mesmerized because it took him so long. Then she realized that he was doing it all for her benefit, the slow unpeeling, and that the table full of boys was in stitches. What'd it mean? As John Q left the room, he never stopped watching her. With elaborate movements he carried the banana peel high and let it drop from a great distance into the boys' trash basket, an oil drum.

Leaving with her friends, Allie said she forgot something. She darted back, bending below table height so that the lunchroom workers wouldn't ask what she was doing on the boys' side: or at all. From the oil drum, having to stick her hand down through the mush of discarded food, she retrieved the banana peel, then had nowhere to hide it but inside her blouse. She wore a bra she didn't need, but insisted upon, which was stitched smaller from a plain white cotton one belonging to Grandmomma. Between its small cups the peeling rode the rest of the afternoon, slimy and stinky and cold against her skin. At home, she took some of the tinfoil that came off Poppa's cigarettes. After he finished each pack, the tinfoil was smoothed flat and kept to cover sweet gum balls, at Christmastime, to be used as ornaments for the tree. While they had some ornaments that were bought, they made some, and also gave the foil to Negroes to use in the same way. Some of their tree decorations were antiques that had come down in her momma's family. Allie gathered, without Grandmomma saying a word, that only something glittery, ornamental, fragile, too expensive, and not really necessary, was a typical legacy from her mother, May.

When the banana skin was wrapped, Allie stored it among other treasures in her bottom bureau drawer, her diaries and glossy photos of movie stars she sent for, which came with signatures truly in ink; it never occurred to her they hadn't been signed by a star's own hand: if a signature arrived smeared it was even more valuable. The banana skin had no significance beyond the fact that John Q had touched it. He was as unreal and remote as Metro-Goldwyn-Mayer, Warner Brothers, or any studio she wrote asking for photos, carefully enclosing cardboard with a dime stuck to it by adhesive tape, and praying a postman along the way didn't steal the money.

One morning, almost at the end of that hot May, Poppa wasn't going to the field but to Senatobia for a dentist's appointment and would drop her off at school. At the driveway's end, he stopped at the cattle gap to wait for a Negro, a mule, and a slow wagon to pass. He glanced right and said, "Who's that?" The way John Q walked, rolling those shoulders from side to side, was unmistakable to her young eyes. He never took home books and was swinging his lunch sack and she knew had missed his ride again. "It's a Negro," she said.

Poppa squinted till the figure came more into focus. "It's not. It's a young boy, probably could use a ride to school."

She burst out crossly, terrifying herself: "It's not! It's a colored boy. You're going to make me late for school."

He gave her an unsuspected thump with his thumb against the side of her head. She could have screamed: partially from pain and partially from its injustice. "It's no nigger," Poppa said. "And don't yell at me. Tell your grandmammy to carry you to get some glasses if you can't see any better than that." He chuckled. "You bad as that boy I carried down to the Delta with me one time, deer hunting. We rounded a corner in the woods, and he said, 'Lord a'mighty, look ahead. Yonder's a nigger with a fur coat on.' " Poppa laughed again. "You know what it was?"

"No," she said meekly.

He hollered. "It was a bear!" He laughed till tears came to his eyes, repeating, " 'A nigger with a fur coat on.' " And then observing her frozen and pale face, he said, "What's the matter? You think you're Miss God that it ain't funny?" Thankfully he did not expect an answer, for by this time John Q had come running to the truck, realizing they waited for him. "It's the Dobbins boy," Poppa announced righteously. John Q heard about the Delta trip and how Allie'd thought he was a nigger. He stared down at her, having settled an arm to the seat behind her, winked, and said, "You didn't recognize me, Allie?"

He knows my name, she thought. She stared straight ahead and said, "The sun was in my eyes." They drove on. Poppa said, "You got time for me to run into the post office one second?" She cried silently from her soul, No! But John Q said companionably, "Sure thing." He and Poppa had been having a good discussion about crops, baseball, guns. Grandmomma had let Allie know early in life Poppa's disappointment that she wasn't a boy.

As soon as Poppa leapt down off the running board, Allie moved over beneath the steering wheel. John Q's large thigh still pressed against hers as it had the whole way down the road, though he didn't seem to have moved. She told herself the touching was accidental. "You ever skipped school?" He had a way of glancing down sideways from beneath dark brows that made her weak. He could be Valentino's stand-in, she had already written in her diary; now she wondered why he didn't go to Hollywood and simply be a star. "No," she answered.

"You wouldn't." He seemed displeased. She lied and said, "I've thought about it."

He said angrily, "But didn't have the nerve. I bet you're teacher's pet and get all A's. It's stupid going to school in this weather. Even the teachers have a hard time keeping awake. Set up there and drink Cokes right in front of your eyes. Jesus Christ!" He pounded the windshield with one fist. She thought him unusually angry. Everybody had a hard time staying awake when the air was thick as syrup and everybody was so sweaty that to move was to make a sucking, slithering sound; people had round wet spots on their bottoms. Dumb, failed boys sat in the back of the room, because others couldn't see around their tallness; they often caused disturbances, but really hooted the day Irene Dubose threw up in the aisle. Miss Mossy, the teacher, was furious at their lack of sympathy. Irene continued to run out of the room holding a handkerchief to her mouth every morning, then disappeared from school. When Allie heard Irene was having a baby, she was astonished. Beginning seventh grade, Allie had sternly told herself to stop playing dolls. With enormous reluctance she put hers away in boxes, the best ones in a glass case in her room, and stored their extra clothes in mothballs. She still dreamed of playing with them. And Irene Dubose was having a baby! For a while Allie was obsessed by the memory of Irene's cheap white anklets, which she wore with black oxfords, and which had either tiny yellow or pink flowers on their cuffs. Having a baby and wearing those anklets simply wouldn't work out in Allie's head.

Poppa let them out opposite the schoolhouse. "Shoot," John Q said. "We're not going to go to school." Allie was swayed by his use of the word *we*. It gave her a sense of belonging when she felt so often she belonged to no family. "With your attendance record nobody's going to check on you. And they stopped bothering about me long ago. I'm not passing anyway."

"Not passing? Not graduating?"

John Q mocked her in a tone especially meant to sound hoity-toity. She could find no way to tell him she'd swap her situation for his crowded dogtrot house; people like him were sensitive about their position. So, she decided to duck through the barbed wire he was holding apart only for a minute. Then she'd just follow him a little while across Mister Otis Murdock's pasture before she went back to school. The bell hadn't rung for taking in.

Clods of dirt were so dry they broke open beneath their feet as easily as wasps' nests, spattered in all directions. The high heat of late May shone on cow plops made iridescent with green flies. Dirt daubers were flitting, shining bits of dark blue, never still. Long grass turned silver in the sun; it seemed almost to mirror their images; the stretches of yellow land were blinding. She clutched her schoolbooks so tightly to her chest, their edges cut her wrists. She kept wanting to say, I've got to go back now. But John Q never stopped talking; she felt privileged to hear and was afraid of interrupting anyway. She was surprised to learn John Q was three grades behind himself. She calculated he was at least twenty. She found his failures disappointing and listened attentively as he said the old-maid heifers who were the teachers ganged up on purpose to fail him. He did not study for that reason: they'd fail him no matter what he did. He could copy right off the paper of somebody sitting next to him and that person would make an A, and he'd fail. Explain that one! he said.

She dared not try. Instead, having the opportunity to speak, she said she had to go back. As she turned, in the distance she heard the faint and faraway sound of the school bell, and the cessation of voices that she now realized had become fainter and fainter. She could see where the pasture rose to the road, to its plank walk, but could not see the school itself. She had no idea they had walked so far. John Q grinned. "You'll be late by the time you get back. Have to walk in with all them eyes staring at you. Think of some excuse." He watched her stare back over the long, hot, and silvery way they had come. "Shit, you don't want to do that," John Q said. "Come with me, sugar. I'll show you a banana."

The one sweet word broke Allie's lonesome little heart; endearments were not used at home. Even when ladies uptown called her honey, or sugar, and she knew they said those words to everyone, it still gave her a warm sensation and made her want to cry. The word *sugar* and the long distance to travel back won her. They walked on. "You mean in your lunch?" she said.

"Huh?" Then remembering the banana, he shouted, "Hell, no, hon!"

He clapped a hand to his mouth. They could see Mister Otis' barn and outhouse now, and soon the Baptist church and the pastor's house.

"Well, where?" she whispered, nervous in all this silence. Only a crow called raucously off somewhere.

"Under them cedars yonder." She followed him on, assuming some game, because surely he knew that seventh graders knew bananas did not grow in Miss'sippi, but in places even hotter. A picture in her geography book showed Negroes scaling trees and reaching for bananas in bunches. John Q ripped aside sturdy grapevine and shoved her into a shady nook, hot nevertheless, that boughs formed. She never had a chance to tell him how often she had played here, and that acorns were still stashed that she and her friends had used as dolls' cups.

She felt too sinful to tell him she and other girls smoked grapevine in the place, thinking themselves hellions as their tongues burned.

From his lunch sack, John Q took a bottle of orange soda and flipped off the cap. "How'd you do that?" Allie was impressed. "It's been opened before," he said. "Take a swig." He laughed when she almost gagged. It was not funny to her that she was about to throw up; her nose wiggled. "Girl, what's the matter with you? That sody is mixed with the best white lightning you can buy around here."

"You drink it in school?"

"Sure. We drink all day. Old heifers haven't figure it out yet. Pass your locker and take a swig of sody pop and they just smile, being real tolerant to you."

Fighting down the taste, she was sweating more heavily than even the day called for. "Why'n't you open your blouse and cool off some, honey bug?" he said. Suddenly he was naked to the waist.

She was not even thinking of doing it. But the thought crossed her mind that he'd be disappointed if he was expecting the same thing Betty May had. She fanned herself with her tablet and said she really wasn't hot. He finished his soda. "Ready to go, then?"

"Go. Where?" She stopped fanning.

"Well, I'm going to hitch over to Whitehill to the pool hall. I don't know where you're going."

"I can't go anywhere," she said in a wail. "I can't go to school now. I can't go home now. I thought we were playing hooky together."

"You don't want to do nothing I want to do. Got your nose stuck up in the air." He grabbed the throat of her blouse. When she fought him off, he said, "See." He rose to his knees and began putting on his shirt. She saw that he was truly leaving, that she was abandoned to the cedars till school was out, and that she'd lost this incredible chance to be with him: already she daydreamed about being his girl from now on, to everyone's disbelief; though daydreams came true. She turned terrified eyes on him and sat still. He unbuttoned a few buttons. "Now, that's pretty and sweet. You got little blue ribbons on your whatchacallit — petticoat?"

She nodded and croaked, "My grandmomma made it."

She was going to explain about all the things her grandmomma made, who was expert with a needle; but she'd guessed

John Q would not be interested. She knew nothing else to talk about. He gave her no chance to talk anymore. He kissed her mouth and seemed to lose interest; he made a stab at kissing her little breasts and quickly abandoned them, as she'd suspected he would. When he began to shove at her with something hard, she told herself she didn't really know what was happening; when she admitted that she did know, she told herself it wasn't really happening.

She couldn't scream because someone would hear. Also by this time she was terrified of John Q's beet-red face and his labored breathing. She was afraid he was going to die of a heart attack, or that he was going to hurt her with his fists if she resisted. "Now, you going to see the 'nana, honey," he kept saying, panting. He looked awfully peculiar. She wondered why he couldn't get hold of himself, but whatever was wrong with him, she was too terrified to do anything but lie still.

He did say once, "I'm sorry," when she cried out in pain, though stifling it; then he went ahead hard and for what she thought would be forever. Before her mind's eye swam images of Grandmomma, Poppa, Belva Dean, her dog, and Jesus. She asked every one of them to please help her. Curiously, after a while she had the feeling that her mother in heaven was watching. Overhead were buzzards, circling around and around beyond leaves, limbs, and boughs over something in the pasture: swooping lower and lower.

Once he stopped, and Allie thought, Sweet Jesus, the way Belva Dean cried it sometime: when the cake she thought was going to fall rose, or she had a quarter when her burial insurance man came on Fridays.

But John Q put the veined, purpled, and sticky thing in her mouth, saying, "Eat the 'nana, honey." Then in a moment he yelled, "Don't bite! Suck." She closed her eyes against humiliation that was far worse than her pain or the taste, though those were unforgivable.

He got up and buttoned his pants. "You'll remember, sugar. Because I was the first one there," John Q said.

Staring up from her back, she had felt like a squirming helpless bug that couldn't right itself, inadequate, furious, intimidated as a turtle on its back. Had she then hatched an idea to get back at men someday, without realizing it? She had had a hard time learning not to be cold in bed. She held resentments against Poppa without ever daring to spit out at him one saucy word: obedience and fear were too ingrained in her generation. Even now, she and people her age were intimidated by their parents and terrified of not pleasing them.

Behind John Q's head that day the sun was one blinding, obliterating spot of white. He stood shadowed in front of her, his head ablaze. Feeling her pitiful white nakedness, and that she scarcely had breasts and only a scrawny amount of pubic hair, she grabbed her underpants.

John Q had laughed. She'd crumpled the pants between her palms and drawn up her knees to cover herself. The pants were inexpensive, pink and sheeny, and not at all what older girls wore; these had come out of a bin at the dime store in Whitehill; they added to her feeling cheap. For all that had happened, she realized she had no claim in the world on John Q. He would not take away his class ring from Betty May and give it to her, as Allie had half dreamed. She had not become in his eyes the Queen of the May. John Q strode off kicking up puffs of yellow dust, heading toward another masculine pursuit, playing pool. Whitehill's poolroom was dingy and dark and the windows so dirty it would seem the men could not even see out. Yet girls felt creepy having to pass by the place. She raised her voice to cry out, "What about me?"

"You?" He'd looked back once. Then he had said, "Do what you want," and started off again. Couldn't he understand that impossibility? A sense of female helplessness in a male world had begun to dawn on her, as he disappeared. She could not even have threatened to tell. She would have been the one who was shamed, and not him. She could not cry out again after him, fearing her voice carrying across the silent pasture, and reaching Mister Otis', where she could see his wife hanging out her wash; how safe and peaceful had seemed then the ordinary and everyday world of being a housewife. She ran naked across the hot grass and grabbed him from the rear. When he whirled as if to fend off an attack, she felt terror again at a world so far removed from her own, where men used their fists. He lowered his in a relaxed manner when she whispered, "You won't tell."

"John Q don't kiss and tell," he had said. She never had known whether she could believe him; this part of her past had shadowed her, too. To her, her words had seemed a loud, dry scream, but nothing in the countryside had been alerted. Though feeling the unjustness, she begged: "Please, don't tell." For answer, he bent and kindly hugged her to him. Her small frame covered by his huge arms, his huge chest brought sharply against her, made her feel her fragility in comparison. Moved again by the least sign of affection, she had thought that day she forgave him.

She wanted to say, You didn't even kiss me, but couldn't claim his attention any longer. She stepped into her panties and stood longingly while John Q went on. She returned to the copse, and remained till the school bell rang much later for dismissal. John Q darted through the woods behind the Baptist church and emerged at last on the high yellow dirt road and headed on into town, cheerily whistling.

In a few months she got her first period. Way back, a girl had said her older sister told her a time came when girls bled every month. Allie had felt superior saying, "That's impossible." She had never believed it till the night she looked down at a piece of toilet paper and bleated, "Grandmomma." She had come in and taken one look at Allie's face and said, "Oh, my Lord. Why did you have to begin that mess so early? Go to bed and I'll fix you up in the morning."

She suffered over beginning before Grandmomma wanted her to and went to bed and lay vaguely wondering if it was possible to die from what had begun. She knew so little. After Grandmomma bought the right paraphernalia, Allie sent off ten cents and a coupon inside the sanitary-pad box and got back a booklet that was well worth the dime she'd haggled with herself about spending. She gathered from this material she was supposed to feel proud, but didn't.

Grandmomma let her walk home from school the first day. Belva Dean stuck out her lip and said, "She shouldn't have did it." It seemed another indication of not being truly loved that Grandmomma would let her walk a mile the first day she had the curse. Back then no one took anything but jaybird baths when they had a period. To submerge yourself into a bathtub it was assumed something terrible would happen. From the beginning it was called the curse. Though, according to the booklet she sent for, some girls referred to their period as falling off the roof. Since Allie felt no connection with that sensation, she chose to be cursed.

A lot of girls, she found out, could not afford boxes of pads and wore rags that were washed and reused; it made her sick to think about it. She daydreamed of becoming rich and famous and doling out boxes of pads to those who couldn't afford them.

John Q cured her of messing around all right, until she got that wedding ring on her finger. She could be standing here this minute an old maid if someone shy as Tate hadn't come along, so shy, kissing and a little petting won him. She'd learned far too late in life that other girls were doing a whole lot more than she'd dreamed; recently in one of her female powwows women her age were beginning to have, laying bare to one another many years' worth of confessions, a woman had said, "Men stuck that thing into somebody long enough and got confused and started thinking they were in love." That woman confessed she'd let her husband do it once and then not again; he was driven crazy and proposed. Everybody always had wondered how that woman caught the man she had.

Back then, understanding her period, she was thunderstruck that John Q could have turned her into another Irene Dubose, for all he knew. She did not yet realize that all men were made up of a certain callousness. After years of living with two of them she accepted that what made up men besides snips and snails and puppy-dog tails was a certain insensitivity.

8

THE FOUR LITTLE WHITE STORES of town turned pink with sunset; the abandoned pump shed that once sheltered horses was filled with shadows; the small yellow post office turned more golden; except for the two churches, Methodist and Baptist, facing one another like a showdown, that was all there was to town; the abandoned brick school building was around a bend, and out of sight. If not rich here in worldly goods, people were rich in nature. That seemed an inadequate way to express herself, and she might read through Psalms again after supper.

Loma was quiet too, perhaps as awed by the beauty and the melancholy air to town at evening. "It's such pretty dry weather for picking cotton, if only we had a lot to pick."

"They say it's a beautiful crop in the Delta. Even so close, they didn't get the rains that damaged ours," Allie said.

"The rich get richer. Doesn't seem there is any justice, does there?"

"Justice?" said Allie, turning to stare at Loma as if she'd never seen her before. Surely, Loma knew better than to ask that question. On her pale face, freckles and liver spots mingled indistinguishably, but she moved quickly about her store for a woman past sixty. She was quick mentally too, had apparently had only a brief lapse. "There is none on this earth, anyway," Allie answered. She thought of their earlier conversation about the Brewsters' owning everything, and Quad getting away with so much.

Loma's question, for Allie, led to another one: Would she find justice in another life, in a hereafter? "I just wonder," Loma said, obviously thinking along the same line.

How surprised others in this community would be to walk in and find two middle-aged ladies discussing the literalness of the Bible. Considering their age, the assumption would be that they took the Gospel as gospel like other good Baptists. Allie had taught Sunday school enough to know that today young people were drifting away from religion, because they had too many places to go besides church. In earlier years, the old eleven A.M. service had been the center of country people's lives; suddenly she thought how dutifully she had continued the pattern, simply out of habit. Smiling to herself she considered how, having recently weathered change of life, she seemed to have changed in more ways than one. After questioning her body's behavior at certain stages, she had now started questioning a great deal else.

Willows in the pasture turned from their luminous green to a bright yellow, symptomatic not of evening but of a weather front moving in, the storm from down south near the penitentiary. Watching the strange coloring, she had the sensation of not watching in her own real life. Was it normal in middle age to seem only to be passing through this life, waiting for a real one to begin? Was her inevitable end here, as a housewife, a dead end?

Recently Poppa went to bed early for once, and, alone with Tate, she asked a question. Did he ever think the life he was living was not his real one? He stared at her up close, as intently as an eye doctor, then said his momma was nutty as a fruitcake from her change of life to the grave. He hoped this wasn't happening to Allie.

More loudly, more firmly than usual, she had said, "Since all that mess is over with, I feel better than I have in years. I wish

I'd had a hysterectomy, even, when I knew I couldn't have children."

Tate looked whiter, sickened and disgusted. She never had been able to mention anything to him about being female, like having a puffed-up stomach or cramps, without Tate's bellowing, "Don't pull that female stuff on me!" What he wanted to say was *crap*, but that was inappropriate here for a man to say before a woman. If an occasion demanded that a man say something like *damn*, he prefaced cursing by saying to the women present, "Now, you'll just have to excuse me, ladies," then the women would smile demurely, and be forgiving about the fact that men sometimes had to act like men. She was suddenly tired of a lot of things.

Tate felt her monthly discomfort was the same as his having to put up with shaving every day; however, his main concern was that she better not try getting out of fixing meals. Nothing around here gave a woman that right except her death certificate. Even though the house was air conditioned, she often stood over the stove with a fiery face drenched in sweat. After serving Poppa and Tate, she would sit a few minutes mopping till her Kleenex fell into shreds. All their faces reflected was fury that she was having a hot flash while they were eating, never commiseration. She had found hot flashes a lonely business.

Now that evening closed in, old Mister Otis came in from the porch bringing the checkers and their board; the other players scattered toward home. He wore a self-important grin. "How you doing?" Allie said.

"All right for a old widow man," he said. "How's your old one doing?"

"He gets lonesome too," she said. "Why don't his buddies come see him?"

When Mister Otis said, "Us will," she did not try to pin him down, because people just forgot homebound people, she'd found. "What's the old billy goat been up to?" he said.

"Nothing, he's just living." Then, fearing her remark too pointed, she said, "But then, I guess that's all any of us are doing."

"Why, it is all any of us are doing," he said flatly, giving her a look that said, You gone high-hat or what? before he departed.

Allie stood a moment, lightly swinging her loaf of bread in one hand, then announced she couldn't wait for Tate any longer. Loma followed her to the door. "I'm just as sorry as I can be you won't get out of the house for your little visit to Oxford Sunday."

"Oxford?" Allie said, turning.

"Honey, it's your turn to carry the church flowers to our folks at the Sunset Rest Home."

"Why, so it is. I'd forgotten."

"You can't go to Oxford with all that trouble going on at the university. The campus is too close. Carrie Thomas supposed to go, too, certainly wouldn't go."

Allie said thoughtfully, "No, Carrie certainly wouldn't go," thinking how Carrie, her voice trembling, prefaced every opinion with a My-husband-Jake-says.

"Only got two residents there anyway," Loma said. "They can wait."

"I doubt that's what Miss Precious and Miss Birdy up in their nineties think," Allie said, smiling.

"Well, if they do bring in that boy Meredith, it won't be any place for a woman," Loma said.

"Oh, piddle," Allie said, walking out.

Alone for a moment on the splinterless old porch, its sheen as silvery as Loma's worn counters, she drew in the first faintly chilly air of the season. Mister Otis was still idling in the road before starting to his house beyond the Baptist church. The old man on his tottery legs should not always choose to walk down the middle of the road, as it was hard to see his bent figure in this light. Yet town had nearly cleared of cars, now, since it was suppertime. She supposed that just living was what most people were doing. Never had she been content with the idea of simple existence, and yet never had she known, either, what to do beyond that. When she thought about Meredith, one lone Negro going to the university, making a mark on history, she longed more deeply to make some mark of her own.

9

AN APPROACHING PICKUP grew more familiar, then Tate's red, peaked International Harvester cap appeared behind the windshield alongside the two young wives of his tractor drivers, Willson and Turner. Instantly, Allie wanted to ask Tate about Elgie, but she had little hope of being alone with him on the main road through town. When Tate stopped at Loma's pump, the amber light went on behind her, as intimate as the sun. The girls clambered down from the truck on its far side, and Willson's wife, Mattie, called, "Dressed chicken on the seat Momma sent you, Miss Allie."

"Thank her! Tell her I'm going to Senatobia soon and will bring her a can of peppermint sticks"—another equal transaction that had been going on for years. Allie went two steps down to Tate's truck. "You thank Gladys?" she said.

Tate said smiling, "Of course I thanked her, hon." He got out of the cab and reached for the gas hose. She frowned. "I know. But I just wondered somehow if you thanked her enough," Allie said.

Before he had time to answer, Mister Otis came over. "See you carried your Negro women with you today, Tate," he said.

Tate winked at Allie. "Yeah, I carried them with me again today," he said. People often made remarks about his letting Negroes ride up in the cab with him, and Tate replied if somebody asked him for a ride, he gave it to them and saw no reason they had to sit in the truck bed, eating dust and being hit by gravel or rain. Allie admired his stand and was glad others did not intimidate him.

The two wives crossing the road had the high-riding behinds so many young Negro females have, and every man in town was watching and the girls knew it. They were giggling. Mose Perkins was drawing off the young trade these days, having installed a solemn-looking machine that whipped up milk shakes; even if they were all froth, they were a novelty for out in the country. He had a new, squat oven that rewarmed prefixed hamburgers and cheeseburgers, and young people bought them like hotcakes, though they were mostly bun with meat the size of a quarter inside. Mose smartly had a white, professional sign with red letters reading ITNABURGERS. It shone a long way off as one came into town from either direction; Allie saw it as a terrible and indicative sign of the future.

Loma needed to look alive harder than ever for a gimmick of her own. Allie reached into the truck for the chicken, saying, "Plump. I guess there's time to stew it for supper."

"Hon, you and Poppa go ahead and eat," Tate said, hanging up the hose. "I've got to run to Senatobia to Brewster's garage and see if Fred's got a part for the tractor. If he doesn't, I'll have to go on to Sears in Memphis."

"Wouldn't Sears be closed by the time you got there? How come you didn't go for the part earlier?"

Mister Otis' eyes grew moist as he waited to hear. "Just broke down this evening. Willson and Turner been working on it but gave up," Tate said.

Allie said, "Mister Otis, you better hightail it home before it gets any darker. Ever since Jake Thomas lost that beautiful Walker hound, I've been afraid for anybody walking along the roadsides at dusk."

"Or at night either," Tate said. "The dog got run over after dark or someone would have seen it." He took Mister Otis by the arm. "Tell you what, old man. Come inside while I pay Loma and I'll carry you home."

Mister Otis made a little skip like a child's with glee. Once he and Tate were in the store, Allie wondered if Tate had a jacket, for evenings could suddenly turn cool and he was subject to pleurisy in the fall when the days were broiling and the evenings sometimes cool, and this was the worst time of year for a farmer to be sick. Often he carried his jacket squashed alongside his gun in its rack, but tonight he was not even carrying his gun. She knelt in the truck to check the glove compartment and put her hand into the space behind the front seat. Finding only the countryside's yellow grime, she thought possibly he had shoved the jacket under the seat when his passengers got inside, but touched only more grit. Then the back of her hand brushed material caught in the springs. She worried it out; her fingers were aware of the static, bristly feel of the material. She stared down at a piece of pink netting off one of Loma's candy boxes. And she stared at a mauve velvet flower that was a violet. Should she report to the blonde she knew where her missing flower was? Iona, Allie recalled.

Tate? she thought. Tate? The countryside swam as she looked around, and seemed more lonesome than it ever had. Town dimmed and came back into view. Nothing would seem the same again. Truly, her heart felt broken. Was her trust so mislaid: was that possible? Could a man that sweet face her daily, living a lie? The possibility was astonishing. She felt enraged to think she might have been a gullible fool for years.

Rain was on its way, because now the sky had a glow like the willows and the pasture grass, and the pinkish look to the four stores of town had a phosphorescent gleam. She leaned against the truck, thinking she had carefully taught herself not to be disappointed in people by never expecting much from anyone; then if someone unexpectedly showed good, she could be surprised and pleased. Yet she had not expected betrayal from Tate or Loma. If Tate had been unfaithful, was her whole long marriage a lie? Had he openly bought candy from Loma expecting silence, and gotten it? She stared into the store trying to see him through someone else's eyes. At five nine, neither tall nor short, he had a handsome head of dark hair with gray at the temples, but gray gave a man dignity, while a woman was simply called gray-headed; parallel lines running from the outer corners of his eyes made him seem humorous, perceptive, and kindly, when her own lines were flat out called wrinkles. The thing middle-aged men had against them was being grumpy, though they were grumpy only to their wives.

Allie got quickly into her car, and, after backing, swerved across the road into her driveway. Long ago, when she was afraid of never having dates, Belva Dean had advised her: "You got the honey. The boys going to come after it." But she had been always too shy to take advantage of her advantage when she'd had it, she thought, regretfully. Passing over the cattle gap at one end of the steep driveway, which served as a doorbell for the house, she listened to its cold clang reverberate deep within the earth, knowing now that a car had passed her while she stood in the road, stunned. On its radio an announcer had been saying, "History's being made in Mississippi!" She remembered, too, that someone had called to her, without her replying. Familiar with this countryside, she knew her lapse would be discussed on party lines and around supper tables tonight. What was wrong with Allie McCall, or who did she think she was, not to answer back when someone spoke to her? By tomorrow, word might be out from charitable folks that she was going blind from a brain tumor, deaf hopelessly and early, as that was how speculation and gossip grew in small communities.

She stepped from the car thinking again about history being made, while here she was walking along carrying a naked little chicken, pondering the everlasting question for a housewife of what to have for supper. She felt tired of nourishing other people, that after thirty years she still could not wake up in the morning without thinking first thing about what somebody else was going to eat that day. Once a woman did the shopping and cooking, she then had to make sure she had toilet paper in the house so people could void her meals. It could seem, after a while, a fruitless way to spend time. Lastly, she turned her thoughts to Tate again, wondering what he would do with a young woman if he had one, then decided she did not want anyone to give her an answer to that.

Looking toward the house, she wondered why Sweetie hadn't barked and why Poppa was not at the den window. Suddenly she felt frightened. Hearing the cattle gap, Poppa usually got up and looked out. To live with someone old was to live constantly with guilt: suppose Poppa fell, or died, and neither thing would have happened if she had not left home. Nearly always it was Allie or Tate arriving. Poppa knew that; still he popped to the window to add the semblance of expectancy to his long process of dying; if only something out of the ordinary would happen. Here, though, the only strangers who ever came to the door were Jehovah's Witnesses covering the countryside out of Nashtoba. When they arrived with their pamphlets, everybody hid, and even Poppa played dead in his chair.

If Allie went to the garden and came back in, he leapt from his chair, all fiery, fists tight with their skinny knuckles, the house's defender! A burglar would only laugh; Poppa thought so too, yet he was always ready for fisticuffs. She went up the few steps wishing life were not so burdened with pretense. They talked about when Poppa got well, but he would not get well from being ninety. Not producing estrogen any longer was not nearly so sad as a man's loss of strength and virility; she did not mind so much that her skin was drier. The den seemed filled with the black-and-white jumping shadows of television, then, entering, she saw Poppa lying on the sofa, saw first the ballooning legs of his khaki pants, his clothes growing larger as he grew smaller with age. She saw the upturned toes of his work boots, which he wore for no reason, since he went outdoors only to pee off the porch sometimes, lamenting himself that his stream lessened with age: something, evidently, a man was proud of in his young days. She had caught him with his pants down. It took another moment for everything to register, and fear vanish. Sweetie? she thought. Then she realized what Poppa was trying to do with that poor, confused old dog, for he was saying, "Hold still, you bitch."

She screamed. In that instant, Sweetie escaped. Poppa was left with his hand clasped before himself, sitting up then, outraged and purplish, because not only had the dog not cooperated, he had not either.

Sweetie darted to the kitchen, her toenails scrabbling across the kitchen linoleum sounding like a rat in the walls. When she peered from beneath the table, Allie said, "It wasn't your fault. I know that." Then she turned to Poppa and said, "Pull up your drawers, you dirty old man."

Deep inside himself he was laughing. She supposed his one compensation for being ninety was that he never felt called upon to apologize for anything. While he struggled up, she kept a straight face, knowing she would laugh when she was alone. Never would she tell even Tate, feeling reflections from the act, that something in her genes might very well make her do something outlandish, sometime. She scowled to please Poppa and said, "You ought to be ashamed," letting him believe she thought what he'd attempted was within the realm of possibility, and he was delighted.

"We'll eat soon," she said. "Tate won't be home till later." Poppa would know she forgave him, since they were blood kin. After she put the chicken in the freezer and cooked the supper she had planned, they ate companionably before TV, so Poppa could watch his evening cartoon shows.

10

Fall always had a sense of hurry. Crops, cotton and soybeans, had to be gathered before winter set in with deadly cold rains, ice, or sleet. Only this year's crop was poor. In March and April, spring rains, torrential ones, flooded the fields, washing away seed and then young plants, so that replanting had to be done, then refertilizing and poisoning again, expensive processes that ate up a farmer to start with; having to repeat them a second time, the farmer's profits were gone before the crops were harvested. In Nashtoba, Brewster's Farmer's Bank and Trust grew richer lending money. Still, the cyclic pattern of farming would continue and follow the seasons; everything in its own time, as the Bible laid out. A time to lie fallow, then to row-up, plant, and finally to harvest whatever the land gave back: or what God did. A philosophic people, most farmers looked on harvesting that way. Because no matter how hard a man worked, or how good a farmer he was, who controlled weather and insects? God did: fate did. Scientists could send men into space (and maybe even to the moon, as predicted; though Mister Otis had told everyone God would never allow that—maybe a fellow might land on the moon's base, but never on God's moon itself), but farmers had no hope that scientists might be able to arrange rain, and the right, gentle amount at the right time, and then temperate spells of sunshine when needed. Farmers turned philosophic early, or they were born philosophers and decided to take up farming. The government got their goat and they had to be philosophic about it too, or blow their brains out or quit farming: men around here had done both. Because the government telling a man he had to let his land lie fallow was bad enough, but then what was the point in not even letting him graze cattle on that land? Government directives usually did not work in the farmer's favor, not in the small farmer's anyway. People here said, the reason was that folks up in Washington making the rules never had seen a hoe, plow, or the rear end of a mule.

During fall's hurry, cotton pickers were in the fields on Saturdays; Brewster's small, old-fashioned gin in Whitehill ran from daylight till way after dark. On Saturday morning Allie went to her garden early and from there watched several red, high-riding cotton trailers rumble through town, heading to the gin and scattering cotton all along the way. All fall, tatters of it lay along the roadsides or hung from tree branches like parasitic moss. She gathered all her tomatoes, even the green ones. Last evening's chill made her wary of a frost coming unexpectedly. Some of the green tomatoes would be made into pickle relish and others she'd wrap in newspaper and store in darkness to ripen in their own good time.

Last night, the ten o'clock news briefly mentioned the slight tornado in mid Mississippi and that four prisoners had escaped from the prison at Parchman; mentioning color these days was ticklish, so that was omitted. Anyway, their news came from a Memphis station, and what happened so far from there seemed of little consequence to the announcer.

Tate had come home late, having taken the part to his Negroes and stayed to help them repair the tractor. He ate his cold supper in front of TV. Allie could not speak to him in front of Poppa about Elgie. She had not decided when the appropriate moment would be to mention Iona. The whole idea of talking to her husband about another woman was new, and scary. She went to bed recalling Elgie's copper-colored face as she'd last seen it when he was sixteen. He had such white teeth. He had been running. Then Allie buried her face in her pillow and wanted not to think about him again. Now that he was sixty-one, they wouldn't know each other if they met head-on, with her as aged.

This morning she came into the house and set her tomatoes on the kitchen sink. The cow pond had the same strange glow as it had the previous evening, while the countryside went on waiting for rain. The drooping willows shone like tinsel; cows huddled together beneath them sensing the weather to come. She envied their mute, blind belief in one another, if it was blind. Since her mother died she had hated sudden noises, and Poppa, who had insisted upon teaching her how to shoot a gun, though it went against the grain of most women here, had never known how she hated the sound, as well as that of backfire or thunder. Now thunder made her jump, rumbling way off somewhere beyond the pasture.

Poppa still slept; Tate had left early. On Saturdays, he didn't expect her to fix breakfast, as if she were a kid and deserved a school holiday. Leaving, he banged around the bathroom and the kitchen to show how considerate he was, letting her stay in bed. On Saturdays the post office closed at noon, so she would hurry to be back home before the rain began. When she went into the den for her purse, she stood a moment while it thundered again, but that was not the only thing that gave her a strange sensation. Pondering, she realized finally it was the unusual feeling that she was in the house alone. With Poppa asleep and Tate gone, she felt privacy. Crooking her arms, she began suddenly to dance with an imaginary partner, asking herself if she was not experiencing something called menopausal madness, as ladies in olden times supposedly suffered it? Though her nature was to be complacent, she had found herself recently plotting the murders of the two men she lived with, without coming up with a foolproof scheme.

While she tried not to feel resentful, it was difficult. Poppa spent his days and his evenings watching television in the most used room of the house; a thousand times a day, having to pass him, she had to make small talk, for if she said nothing, he said, "Why've you got your lip all stuck out?"

A thousand times before Saturday was over, they'd discuss the weather, whether it would rain or not. And if it rained, how soon would it slack? If she flunked, played out, lay on her bed, or ran her sewing machine, she heard him talking to folks on TV since he had much better advice for people in daytime serials than those who wrote the scripts for them. Yet when he was gone, would she not be lonesome, without even children to think about? She stopped dancing. She was of the last generation to keep an aged relative at home, she supposed; people with children said they expected to be shuffled off to the Sunset Rest Home, or the poor folks' home, most likely.

Then it was raining, though without yet reaching town. Way across the pasture, beyond an old Negro's cabin on the opposite side of the road, she saw an iridescent, shimmering curtain of rain traveling this way. When a cow bellowed at the pond, it was a lonesome and plaintive sound, as if the cow were the last creature on earth and had not the least idea what to do about anything.

Poppa was up now, coughing and hacking from his chest, groaning as his joints moved after the night. Wanting her vocal cords to rest from small talk, she went to the car, determined to stay gone till his morning Kiddie Kartoons were over. He was truly amused by the outdated antics of Felix the Cat and Popeye. She could enjoy their noise more than the monotonous drone of football or baseball games that filled the house on pretty weekend afternoons. Before starting the car, she sat a moment, thinking that the games did repeat themselves seasonally, with a rhythm, in the same way farming did, giving a needed sense of continuity to life.

In memory, voices of announcers, with their familiar nuances, could summon up the brilliance of fall, or the more delicate and gentle look to the land that was spring, with flowers not fully in bloom, and rains coming at a different angle and with less force. The announcers cried out with the excitement of Chicken Little seeing the sky falling. "Folks, there's the windup and there'sss the pitch!" Or, "Rat-a-tat's on the four-yard line, can you believe it?" Starting her car, Allie thought she could always believe anything, because she'd never once had her eye on the right person, with the ball, in a football game. She had always wondered if that was some lack in herself.

She paused at the cattle gap. Sy was outside his cabin picking up sticks for kindling; smoke was already dancing up from his chimney, which on the right wind would travel to her door, bringing the acrid scent of wood smoke that was reminiscent of other times. She was surprised he was building a fire on a warm morning, particularly since the old man usually only snacked, which was why she worried about him and took him casseroles so often. Before driving off, she glanced into her rearview mirror at her house, as if that put Poppa into safe-keeping; though it was not her house — it was his. The intention had not been for them to live together, but shortly after she and Tate married, Poppa had a massive heart attack. There had been mutterings, discussions, meetings of the eye if not of the mind, as the three of them discussed building a wing onto the house with a separate kitchen for Poppa. They kept talking, and by that time she and Tate were settled in, and Poppa's belongings in the house he had lived in so long seemed permanently in place. Time had passed as it will, and they all lived together.

When Allie entered the post office, Ardella, the postmistress, explained the mail was running late; the carrier had had a flat tire. A light mist had begun to fall. Her husband scurried inside like a gaily striped bug, the American flag over his head. Having taken it in from the rain, he folded it up carefully and properly, and went into their house, which was part of the post office, to stash the flag away. Sitting down an incline, the post office was shaded by a large mimosa, which dropped crimson flowers on the path down from the road. Those entering were still reared backward, as if holding themselves by brakes. Allie squeezed in last, the post office accommodating only five people at once. One tall Negro leaned in a corner staring at the ceiling, out of habit trying to pretend he did not hear anything the white people were saying. His presence kept the conversation from turning to the university at Oxford, or to the escaped prisoners; though that subject would be talked about behind her back, Allie suspected.

Behind Ardella's head hung a sepia photograph of Franklin D. Roosevelt, and as far as Ardella was concerned, James Farley was postmaster general, still. For all her generation, Allie supposed, the names in the cabinet in those days were the ones folks still remembered: all since had seemed to pass in a flash.

"How you today, Allie?" Ardella's husband said.

"Pretty good. How're you?"

"Good, but not pretty," he said. The Negro's lips had to move into a smile.

Since the post office opened into Ardella's kitchen, it was always fragrant with whatever she had been cooking. "Greens?" Allie said.

Ardella leaned so secretively to her barred window, Allie had to go closer. "I have to cook them," Ardella said, "then they stay in me like packed sausage. Isn't that awful." She leaned back. "But I'm here. I guess that's all we can ask."

"Is it?" Allie muttered under her breath.

"I've got yours up, honey," Ardella said. Allie scanned the inconsequential mail shoved toward her. If junk mail could be outlawed, the price of stamps might not keep going up; the post office wouldn't be nearly so busy. Suppose she could start a campaign about that, be successful at doing away with junk mail? In her mind's eye, she saw the news media dancing attendance, while she modestly posed for photographs saying, Oh, anybody with energy could have saved the postal system. Then she would drive off in a large automobile, waving the wooden hand waves of the Queen of England, and of her mother, which managed nevertheless to look gracious. This reverie was interrupted when Jake Thomas said, "I hear you gave John Q what-for about the Brewster boy, Allie."

"I don't think it did any good," she said.

Sissy Morgan said, "Nothing will till John Q speaks to Quad's daddy, or to the law in Nashtoba. He needs to lose his driver's license."

"He never will," Ardella said. "Mister Brewster has a blind spot when it comes to that boy."

"Still," Allie said, "we need a constable with a little more spunk." While the others agreed, they were silent about it.

When she went out, Jake Thomas puffed up the incline alongside her, glancing at the *Commercial Appeal* from Memphis. "I wish we had us a post office sitting on the road still," he said.

Allie laughed. "I had nothing to do with what Tate did back then," she said.

"Shoot, he had his eye on you back yonder in the Cradle Roll." Jake recalled the long-ago Sunday when Tate was a boy and borrowed the family car to teach the cook Snowey to drive. She stepped on the starter instead of the brake and shot into the post office, caving it in. It was then Ardella kindly offered her house to the government instead, fearing the post office here might be done away with, and they would be on a rural route. Today that idea was in the wind again, with farming playing out and people moving away. The only thing saving this part of the world, little towns like Nashtoba, was factories moving in, Tate often said. About to repeat that now, Allie was interrupted when Jake looked at his front page. "The bloodhounds found one of those escaped Negro prisoners in a cornfield at the prison," he said. "Those dogs know their business."

"Give the man's name?" Allie said.

He read on. "Says they don't like to give out the names till they have to. Be a lots of scared folks, I reckon. Afraid one of 'em might come back and—" Then he swallowed. "My Lord, I'm sorry."

"That was a long time ago, Jake."

"Yes ma'm! These were a bunch of smart young ones, I'll bet. Paper says one had stole pepper from the commissary. They put that in their shoes. Dogs can't scent then. Another fellow was a tractor driver and took diesel oil they could cover their clothes with. Dogs can't scent then either. It was all planned, and another fellow told it. Always a squealer in the crowd, I reckon." He went off, telling her not to think a thing about it; that moment, Allie wondered if the paper had said something about one or more of the others being from, or heading toward, north Mississippi. Tate bought their paper in a café in Whitehill, since he liked to read it there while he drank coffee and talked to other farmers. She feared knowing the worst too soon.

She was hailed by Brother Walker, the Baptist preacher, coming along the road from the parsonage, a black umbrella a bower over his head. She sat inside the car, the door open, to protect herself from the mist, falling more steadily. A young man, Brother Walker had swelled membership in the Baptist church, much to the chagrin of the Methodists, though even they were pleased by his new innovations for young boys: Peewee football, Little League, and Cub Scouts. His wife, however, was not so popular. People did not understand a preacher's wife who stayed inside all the time reading books! A committed man, Brother Walker felt that after twelve years here his work was done: he felt a call to go elsewhere, and the community dreaded his having put out that word. Soon, they expected, a pulpit committee might come calling and invite him to a larger town. In Allie, he had found an ally, quickly realizing she did not resist change. When he bought new songbooks that did not have the same covers as the old ones, some people had boycotted church for a few Sundays. Others refused to have prayer meetings changed from Wednesday nights to Thursdays, though it fitted his schedule better. Many people were skeptical about gatherings he encouraged teenagers to have at the church, though dancing wasn't permitted. He bent to Allie and said softly, "What are our diehards going to do if Meredith gets to stay at the university?"

"Accept what they can't do anything about, I guess."

"They've held prejudice a long time," he said. "Our people are, though, introspective now, don't you think? They've got to be asking themselves, What do I believe?"

She nodded. "I just wonder how it's all going to be resolved."

Allie glanced toward town, seeing the white glimmer of Mose Perkin's new sign, thinking how vacant town looked for a Saturday. Once it had been so crowded with Negroes, walking was impossible. Now Negroes all had cars too, and went where more was going on. Brother Walker looked in the same direction. "People in the community aren't so insular anymore. They've been away and come back. Brought broader ideas home with them. In their hearts, people want to do the right thing. The word *Christian* is still active in the vocabularies of people here."

Allie said, "I've sensed a difference in the Negroes since Meredith tried to integrate the university the first time."

"Oh, but Negroes have told me they've felt a difference in white people, too. It worries them."

"Integration will drive us apart in a lot of ways."

"Folks are all drawing into themselves everywhere," Brother Walker said. "The world's too complex for anybody to understand it anymore."

"Whatever wrongs we've done, in the South we've always tried to help the Negro, too," Allie said. "It's said that's one reason the South was held back after the Civil War. Poppa says, all we've ever been here is some poor people trying to help some poorer ones."

"That's true, but you and I've agreed, the Negro's been held back. He's got to resent that. Always been taught, too, that the Southern white man is evil."

Allie shuddered. "I've always been taught that Negroes don't kiss each other, but jump on each other like animals to make love. Taught that dogs don't like Negroes, and that black dogs particularly don't like them. Taught that all Negroes like nuts, and all Jews like purple. Whew!"

Laughing, Brother Walker said, "How then do we let Negroes know we don't all fit into their category for us? It's hard. If I jump into the pulpit tomorrow and start preaching integration, I'll lose the very people I want to reach. They'll all walk out. Now, though, when somebody tells a joke about a Negro, I walk off and don't laugh. People are noticing." His umbrella bobbed as he moved closer. "But to tell the truth, Allie, I do think they all have rhythm."

"So do I!" she whispered back. "I envy them to pieces. Why aren't they proud of it? I can't carry a tune in a bucket. It's been a sorrow in my life."

Then she drove off, practicing the Queen Elizabeth hand wave from the car window on the short drive to Loma's.

Inside, her earrings dangling, Loma said, "Allie, we hear it's thirteen going to Ole Miss!"

"I heard three." A tiny piping voice came from one of the church pews. Allie, looking that way, thought, Good Lord. But she said sweetly, "Somebody's been to Sudie's and is looking mighty pretty."

"Go on," said Miss Pearlie Mae, covering her face.

Mister Otis spoke up from atop a stack of dog-food sacks, where he sat gumming dry, store-bought popcorn. "I've heard they're calling off Homecoming."

"Homecoming!" Loma said.

"Oh, surely," Allie said gently, "even the university's being integrated couldn't be that serious. What difference does it make?"

"Difference?" Loma said. Allie said quickly, "Whether it's three or thirteen."

"Oh," said Loma. "I thought you meant about Homecoming."

Mister Otis turned to a Memphis salesman checking supplies and told him about a family in the Delta that everybody stayed clear of, because they were said to have Negro blood. "Is that right?" the salesman said. "I'll tell you how you can always spot Negroes. By the blue moons on their fingernails. They can't hide those."

"I've heard," Loma said, her earrings quivering, "that they have a black streak at the end of their spinal cords. Now, that's what men who've been with them in the army say, I wouldn't know." Then she and the salesman could not decide whether she ought to stock up on straight-lined or dotted-lined primary tablets. With a practical finger, Loma twirled the school-supply rack. He pushed back a sporty straw hat with a fishing-fly ornament and said, "Kids haven't said what their teachers want?"

"School supplies been moving slow," Loma said sadly.

"One thing I hate to see is somebody stuck with primary tablets they can't sell," he said.

"Loma, close up this store anyway," Mister Otis said, "and let's you and me go up to Memphis and go dancing."

"Before dark?" she said.

"It could be dark by the time we got there," he said.

"You heard about the little nigger baby up in Memphis that's two parts animal?" the salesman said. After the others cried, "No!" he said, "It's got a little dear face and bare feet." He went out then, and left them laughing. "I've always heard," Mister Otis said, "that Negroes wear makeup on TV to make them look whiter."

"Well, of course they do," Miss Pearlie Mae said.

"Oh, me," Loma said, watching the departing salesman, "I meant to ask him if he knew of a Negro church in Memphis that might want to buy my pews." She looked at Allie, who said, "I'm afraid your best bet's a country church somewhere around here, even if you haven't had luck yet." Silently they commiserated over whether Loma was going to be stuck with these she'd bought after the Baptists bought new ones: a Negro church bought the Baptists' discards; Loma took these handhewn ones from the Negroes to sell. The pews' simplicity was touching to Allie, as she thought of seeing Negroes walking miles to church along dusty, yellow roads, the women wearing old dresses to catch dust, and removing them at church, having Sunday clothes on underneath. The little country churches seemed to swell in size when the Negroes filled them with their hopeful and mournful praise of Jesus. Only recently, she'd heard old Sy singing as he rounded his cabin to his outhouse. "Jesus on the main line. Call him up and tell him what you want." She had thought at the time, poor old Sy didn't have running water, much less a telephone to use to call Jesus.

When she looked around, Loma was in a storeroom off the main part of the store, moving boxes and crates. What in the world was she doing cleaning up that place after all these years?

She thought of asking, but it was a good opportunity for her to slip away without buying anything, as bad as she felt about doing it. Loma's meat case held shriveled pork chops, and though Allie'd had ham in mind for lunch, Loma's had a dubious green cast. Saying goodbye to the others, she slipped away, wondering once again how Loma was going to stay in competition.

11

SINCE TATE WAS CARRYING his cotton to Brewster's gin today and did not come home for lunch, Allie assumed he'd gone on into Whitehill to eat at the café. The phone rang while she was cleaning up a few dishes, making her turn around fearfully. It had to be an important call because no one here made social calls at twelve-thirty during a program called *As the World Turns*. In this part of the country, nothing much moved until that show was over. In larger nearby towns, women who clerked or worked in offices went home at lunch to see it. Problems on the show were discussed as avidly as those in the community, but with more understanding. The show's people could be drunks, bigamists, divorced, atheists, or have abortions, and women here would tune up with sympathy, while in real life their counterparts would have been shunned.

She watched it sporadically, finding segment after segment could be missed and the thread picked up again when she came back to it. Usually the screen was filled with close-ups of anguished faces that made everyone seem oversized. Going to the phone, she knew it was not a friend trying to be first to find out why she'd stood outside Loma's yesterday not speaking to a soul; though it could be a random call, the kind she hated: someone wanting to know if she had a baby photo to enter in Whitehill Pharmacy's baby contest. She had no on the tip of her tongue, too, for a magazine salesman, when a stranger asked if she was Mrs. McCall? Then the woman said she was a teacher at Whitehill Elementary School and a sick child there said Mrs. McCall would tell his momma, who had no phone. "What child?" She knew no children but Negroes whose parents didn't have a phone. "The school can't bring him home?"

"It's Saturday make-up school. Nobody's here but a few teachers who can't leave. His name's Ralph Duncan."

Knowing no one by that name, she was mystified when the woman gave directions down the Glen Road, having thought that she knew everyone there. Yet she could not refuse to do something about a sick child. Though the trip would not take long, something told her nevertheless not to leave her chicken on simmer, but to turn it off completely. If she disappeared till doomsday, neither Poppa nor Tate would ever think to see what was cooking on the stove. Later, she wondered if she had not figured out from the beginning that if the child's mother didn't have a phone, she wouldn't have transportation either, or the child a father in evidence.

On Glen Road she found the house by the process of elimination, knowing who lived in all but one Negro cabin, once abandoned, and whitewashed now to look like something more than it was. Having fought her way up a slimy driveway of yellow dirt, with rivulets of water running down to meet her, she thought of tooting her horn for someone to come out, the way whites once summoned Negroes. There was something so audacious about that, of course they came outside with their lips stuck out, resentful before they even knew what the white person wanted. It was the habit, too, of some country people who simply knew nothing about manners. Somehow it lessened the person inside. Allie climbed out into the rain.

One day when she was nine, a Negro came to the front door, his cap properly in hand, asking Poppa if he had some yard work — those days people were begging for any kind of little job and a little food and coffee or iced tea to go along with it. "Go around to the back door, boy, and I'll talk to you," Poppa had said. She had watched the grown Negro pass by a window, that cap between his fingers like an animal pinching something to eat between paws, on his face a look that was neither sullenness nor rage, but some dark sense of wonder. Years later she would think about his coming to the front door in the first place, knowing the taboo — had he been a man with a single, silent protest before his time? That moment was when a social consciousness was born in her: though she had no name for her feelings till she was older.

She tapped at the door. A green shade moved aside to reveal a towheaded child who yelled, "Momma!" at the top of her lungs. When Momma came to the door, Allie firmly chastised her female intuition. Why had she not known the woman would be Iona? There in the windy day smelling of dampened ragweed, Iona stood still, not knowing what to do once Allie explained things. After Iona said blankly, "I don't have no way to get over yonder," Allie sighed and said she could take her; a small, rueful voice reminded her she really had nothing better to do. Iona disappeared and returned carrying a baby. She smelled strongly of ten-cent-store gardenia perfume, and her ears held red plastic cherries with bits of green stem, so that Allie had to swallow hard realizing the importance for Iona of a trip to town, even one like Whitehill.

After pausing at a stop sign and turning opposite from Itna Homa, they began the ten-mile trip over a narrow road, with the ditch banks covered with kudzu, and even trees and telephone poles covered to their topmost, lending an air of the jungle; different from wintertime when the vine died and remained everywhere gray and skeletal. Finally, Allie said about the dark, fussy baby, "He must look like his daddy."

"I don't know who Sammy Lee favors." Iona jiggled him on her knees. That moment the car shuddered and almost shimmied as it struck the ridged surface of the bridge over Grey Wolf River, though Allie had slowed to a minimum since the bridge was dangerous, particularly when wet. Below, the muddy river ran rapidly in the rain; in bottomland on either side the same water stood deep, managing somehow to mirror the car despite trees. "This bridge is a bugger," Iona said, looking down past its inadequate railing.

"Five people been killed going off this bridge in the past year and a half," Allie said. "When the bridge was built we thought it was something. Because the one before it was the bridge of my childhood, a few planks laid together with nothing on either side. The planks rose and fell with the car. I ate my heart every time. Now this one's too narrow, and gets too slick when it's wet, and the railings aren't worth a damn."

Surprising herself, she glanced quickly at Iona, but nothing amiss seemed to have registered. "How did you say you happened to come to this community?" she said, trying Loma's tactics.

"Well, I got these six kids," Iona said, "but I have another older girl who come to me by my first husband. I wadn't but sixteen. We lived out in Texas. I liked out yonder. But he got to drinking so bad we got divorced. Then I come home and after a while married this other fellow I had these chirrun by. But me and him are getting a divorce because he was getting so mean. Drunk, you know. My brother found me this place. He lives way round to the other side of the dam. Had to hide because my husband says he's going to take these chirrun. Says I can't keep 'em up."

"That would be terrible," Allie said. "Surely, he can't take your children."

"That's what the welfare woman says. Says long's I keep 'em clean and keep 'em in school, he can't. I lost my other girl. She run back to her daddy in Texas and told me why after'ard. Said her stepdaddy been messing with her for years and she was scared to tell me. Wadn't but thirteen when she left."

"To run to Texas?" Allie said. "That was brave."

"I don't know whether it was or not, she just done what she had to do."

"I see," Allie said reflectively.

At the schoolhouse, she lent Iona her umbrella and sat tapping her fingers on the steering wheel, telling herself that only menopausal madness would make her think that baby looked like Tate. Ralph ran out ahead of his mother and jumped into the backseat, silently. Skipping amenities, Allie said, "Son, how'd you happen to have the school call me?"

"You live in that house closest to the road down to ourn."

"How'd you know that?"

He watched his foot kick the front seat. "Because ever'body knows ever'thing in a dumb hick town like that."

Through her eyelashes, Allie watched Iona approach and said simply, "I don't."

Settling in, Iona looked over her shoulder. "You coming to make-up school for missing so much sick, then get sick." She turned around. "That boy's stomach goes back on him ever' morning of this world."

"Something he eats for breakfast?" Allie suggested, driving from the school lot.

"No'm, he don't never eat none," Iona said. "Take a aspring when he gets home and that kid'll be up and running. It beats all." At the highway, Allie paused before passing beneath the stoplight and heading on back to country. In the rearview mirror she caught Ralph's periwinkle eyes with their fringe of yellow eyelashes, and suppressed her own laughter. "Does he eat a lot of rich candy?" she said.

"Only when he can get it," Iona said. Then worn out with jiggling Sammy Lee, slobbering on his fist and fussy still because he was teething, she opened her pleated leather purse and handed him a ribbon off Loma's candy boxes. "Here's you a play pretty," she said. Allie glanced down off the bridge at people fishing below, sitting on downturned buckets and waving toward the water graceful cane poles, even in the rain. But what she saw more vividly was her oversized anxious face and Iona's puny one filling a television screen, while she spoke with the openness of people in soap operas, unlike the way people spoke on the surface in real life, saying to the younger woman, I understand you've taken up with my husband. Then rain would crash against a window harder than on her windshield now; music would swell to add to the tense, unhappy atmosphere; and the segment would cut off until tomorrow, when there would be some answers: Allie saw none in her immediate future.

She thought, anyway, it was better to talk to Tate, because she could tell when he was lying. "Do you plan to stay in our community? Do you like it?" she said.

"Don't see much of it. Have it in my craw to go back to Texas."

"Not much future for a young woman round these hills," Allie said. "From what I hear about Texas, it's a growing place. Lots of opportunities. I'll bet somebody young and pretty could grab herself off an oilman."

Iona giggled. "My first husband did work on a oil rigger."

"Kids need their daddy."

"Yes'um. But the one there ain't most of mine's daddy."

"I see what you mean," Allie said.

Suddenly Ralph shoved his head between them. "I bet you her rad-jo don't work." Flipping it on, Allie let him know with a glance she knew when she was being coerced. However, she found the radio a wonderful answer to end her stint as a television soap-opera actress. ". . . James Meredith," said an announcer. "More news. In Boston today, a pediatrician said that babies do as well on bottles straight from the refrigerator as on warmed ones."

"A lot of important news," Allie said.

"In Mississippi today," the announcer said, "one of three escapees from the state penitentiary was found in a barn on a Delta plantation. He is Floyd Hayes, from Clarksdale."

In her ear, Ralph breathed, "Her rad-jo don't play nothing no account." Though Allie said, "Hush!" she'd missed what else the announcer said. "North," she said.

"Huh?" said Iona.

"The man traveled north from the penitentiary. How do they get by at all in the daytime?"

"You're thinking about old-timey convicts in them striped

ringarounds," Iona said, laughing. "Regular prisoners wear blue with a white stripe on their pants. Trusties wear white with a blue stripe. They could be delivery men. Ice-cream-truck drivers, no telling what all. The stripes is sewed on, though, so if they take them off, the pants falls apart. My—I mean, I heard of a convict didn't know that. Escaped and pulled his stripes off on the highway. Was standing there bare-assed, and got 'rested for in-decent exposure 'fore the cops even knew he was a 'scaped prisoner."

Ralph snickered, then kicked the seat behind Allie's kidneys. "I seen a nigger in one of them white suits over to the dam last evening."

"You never," Iona said.

"I reckon I know I did! He 'as creeping into one of them men's rooms, fixing to sleep, I reckon. The dam area was closed."

"Son," Allie said, "I'm going to carry you to our constable."

"Ralph never seen that, he'll tell you anything."

He flew upright on the backseat. " 'Sides, I couldn't have seen it. It wadn't me in there after dark shooting gov'ment squirrels."

"What'd he look like?" Allie said.

"Was a little old gray-haired nigger."

"Was old if he had gray hair," Iona said. "Niggers don't show it till then." Allie sighed, thinking that was what she'd always heard. "Maybe fifty?" she said.

"I don't know if he 'as that old," Ralph said.

"Last man Ralph seen was green," Iona said, proudly. "Creeping round his bed. Got so scared he wet his sheet."

Ralph leapt forward between them again. "Come the dawn, I ain't the only one with something wet spewed over my bed! What about your company!"

"Boy," said Iona, quietly, "I brung you into this world and I can take you plum out of it. I'd hush if I 'as you."

All along the soggy road to their house, crushed gravel spewed up in soft patters beneath the fenders, a staccato sound that told Allie she had to say something to someone about Elgie. But about Iona?

Having watched Iona tiptoe through mud to her steps, Allie reached back to close sharply the door Ralph left half open, and drove off. Tate did not have an ornery bone in his body, yet in middle age perhaps needed, too, something to change the long-held pattern of his life. She settled down to the drive over the rutted road, holding the steering wheel steadily. Tate's gentleness with animals showed his true nature, she believed. His cows often came to the fence and began bellowing as soon as his truck struck the cattle gap, sending out its clang — they came when it was not feeding time. In the beginning, Poppa had given his opinion: Tate was a good man who would never set the world on fire. Maybe he was too passive and unaggressive to get ahead; though was it not better to be loved by everyone the way he was? Peering ahead through the rain with narrowed eyes, she remembered Tate's being asked once to run for justice of the peace. He'd said he couldn't because he could never fine anybody, but only ask if they couldn't try to do better?

Poppa, though, had a mean streak like most men. When it showed, his eyes turned the color of dimes, the same color as wetted tree trunks in woods on one side of the road now. Back when they used to milk, he would watch Tate bringing the cows from the pasture to the barn, some feisty dog running behind their hooves, Tate only lightly waving a stick and sometimes calling, "Hoo, cow." One day Poppa suddenly hollered, "Call louder, son. Let me hear you yell." When Tate came on with a shamed grin, Allie saw that truly he could not raise his own voice and yell. Was he afraid of something, possibly of everything? Having thought him content with his lot, she was surprised another day when he said hesitantly, Maybe they shouldn't have come back to these hills after the war? Maybe he could have done something out in the world better than he could farm? Maybe, he had said, his gray eyes having a sweet expression, he should have stayed in the army, the way she had wanted him to at the time? Afterward they said nothing more about it; they did not sit that day filled with recriminations that did no good. She felt they both wondered, however, what other life they might have had if Tate had not had the unquenchable desire to get back to the land, a desire that dies hard in men born to it. Suddenly slowing as she neared the main road through town, Allie admitted she wondered about that other life occasionally, still.

The rain was mist again, the dusk turning into pitch black. Her parking lights picked out horses and cows behind barbed wire watching her with quiet curiosity. They seemed to propel her out of the car; she ambled toward them. Some retreated to a distance and watched her from there, while one horse let her rub its muzzle. During their quiet communication she felt tears; the horse, sensing an end, went away to crop pasture grass, smelling strongly of its sour-sweet but pleasant odor. She feared open land being sold off as lots for small bungalows, for people were moving out of Memphis to seek refuge from its problems in the country. All the problems would come with them, in time. Late evening added its voluble say-so when, from great dark oaks, locusts screamed and screamed their age-old and unsolved warnings. She went off and left them to themselves, feeling commanded to do so.

A car approached from town as she stopped at the battered tin stop sign before entering the main road, a blue light atop it going around and flashing glitter like mica flung everywhere. This was a station wagon with wire forming a neat cage in its rear. On the driver's side a red emblem had words she could not read, though it was not a Mississippi Highway Patrol car. Turning right and toward home, she saw nothing unusual happening in town. No one was on the road, and, except for Loma's, the stores were closed. Against everyone's advice Loma stayed open until ten P.M. Nearing her driveway, Allie's headlights picked out a rabbit, which had leapt from a ditch bank to run in the middle of the road. Feeling sorry the poor thing did not realize safety lay on either side, going slowly behind it, she set her foot abruptly to the brakes. Surprisingly, something tall and dark as a tree trunk loomed in her way. "Good gracious, Sy!" she called, stopping and rolling down a window. "You scared me to death."

"Ma'm?" The old Negro took off his hat at the sound of her white folks' voice, then came closer and grinned. "Oh, how you, Miss Allie?"

"Fine now. But you be careful walking these roads after dark. What're you doing?"

Sy raised a shotgun. "After that rabbit for a stew."

"Your appetite's improved. I saw you making a fire for breakfast."

"Ma'm?" Since no one knew how much the old man heard, and how much he pretended not to, Allie was patient. Having never been exactly right, Sy possessed what country people called native intelligence. He grew the best garden in the world, planting according to whether or not it rained the first of May, or how the moon looked certain nights. "I said, did you see the rabbit all the way from your house?"

"That rascal come from under my po'ch and I followed him."

"Know what the law car was doing in town?"

"Say you seed a law car?"

"You didn't?" Staring into his red-rimmed eyes, she knew it was worthless saying, The car went by you. "Your water passing all right?"

"It doing good since Mister Tate carried me to the doctor and I went to the horspital."

Only recently, the tall, dark figure had scared the life out of them, tapping on their bedroom window in the middle of the night. When Tate opened it, Sy doffed his hat and pronounced his full name, saying, "It's Sy Coleman. My water won't pass." Tate took him to the Whitehill clinic, where the doctor met them at two A.M. and sent him straight to Memphis in an ambulance: the farthest from home Sy had ever been; he was more terrified of that fact than coming near death. "I'm making succotash tomorrow," she said. "I'll bring you a pot."

"No'm, Miss Allie. You don't need to bother."

Then she remained, so the old man could see his way home through her headlights. She watched him enter the cabin that stood on Stewart land, both of which would be hers when Poppa died, the same as the house where she lived and its land. No one would fear dying if they thought about heaven as Sy did, she thought. Often, his tremulous, high voice proclaimed it as a place with "No mo' sickness, no mo' death, no mo' doctors' bills, and no mo' med'cine" — a place where everybody was happy shouting and dancing with the Lord. "Jesus is a good Savior," he'd say. "Now, ain't heaven a good place?"

Under those conditions it certainly would be. Now Allie concentrated more on this being the first time she'd ever offered the old man food that he'd refused.

12

ALLIE HAD A FLAIR for decorating, and much of what she had learned came from her women's magazine, *The Homemaker*. When many people said it was too bad she'd never been able to study interior decoration, she would laugh and say, what good would it have done her? Having learned from the magazine that wicker was back in style, she dragged her grandmomma's from the attic, thinking how much of it had been given away to Negroes. Following printed instructions, she painted the furniture white and covered pillows in the den with blue-and-white ticking, then worried that they looked like mattresses. After Tate asked when she was going to cover the cushions, she'd said they were covered, and added, "Ticking is in."

"In what?" he'd said.

Then she grew tired of the cold, bare look and recovered them in a blue-and-white pattern with a fleur-de-lis design and tossed around other pillows covered in a splashy, flowered material. Potted plants and ferns hanging at the windows livened up the room more; finally Allie felt she had achieved what *The Homemaker* promised, a look of being outdoors while being inside. In Itna Homa, people were used to patterns in a room that matched, and were skeptical of her ideas. After studying rooms in the magazine more closely, she realized there was something unnatural about their uncluttered, orderly look; for one thing, they never pictured any good lamps to read by. She set back into the room certain things the men demanded anyway, an old goose-necked light and a rack that never quite held all the magazines in it. She did not scold anymore about Poppa's bent TV tray on its tinny legs that stayed in front of the set, except when they had company.

One thing pleasant about growing older was her desire for fewer and fewer things. It was all she could do to think up something for people to give her for Christmas or her birthday. She had rid her closet of all but a few necessary clothes and never wanted another acquisition for the house, other than a dishwasher; even then, she'd look at her own two hands and tell herself she had one. She had finally stopped mooning over travel ads, accepting as a fact of her life that she'd probably never step foot north of the Mason-Dixon line or west of the Mississippi.

This evening as she sat before the news with Poppa, she was listening more intently for the cattle gap and Tate, later than he should be. On the set she heard talk about the astronaut, and the Yankees and the Giants and the World Series. In Washington a man said that the only alternatives in Mississippi were anarchy or law, and afterward when Deputy U.S. Attorney General Katzenbach was seen walking into a closed meeting, Poppa cried, "What chance has the South got? The Catholic Kennedys, the Jews, and the communists all siding against us with the colored!"

Soon the cattle gap rang, though afterward when the pickup stopped outside and a door slammed, its motor went on running, so Allie stood to look out. Tate was standing beside the cab talking to Willson, who drove. Tate often asked somebody else to drive, as he got worn out rattling that pickup over rough fields all day long, he said. He came inside as Poppa was engrossed in what he called a line of long-stemmed beauties, dancing in costumes as scanty as underwear. "Come here, son," he called. "Get a load of them shaking boobies."

"Hush your mouth," Allie said. Turning toward Tate to laugh, she saw him behind Poppa's chair, watching. Maybe she should have said "fucking mouth," and gotten their attention. Instead, she said, "Tate, a law car was in town. Know anything about it?"

He leaned tiredly against Poppa's chair. "It was folks from down at Parchman. Looking for one of those escaped convicts."

"In Itna Homa?" she said. Poppa leaned forward and turned down the set a mite.

"One is from here," Tate said.

Still in a false voice, she said, "Looks like this would be the last place he'd come then."

"The lawmen said where a man is known is usually the only place he can expect help."

"Maybe it's like a man who sets a fire and comes back to watch it," she said. A person comes back to the scene of the crime, she meant.

"I don't know," Tate said.

She said in her normal voice, bluntly, "Is it Elgie, Tate?"

"I'm afraid so," Tate said. "The lawmen said that back when he went to the penitentiary, a Negro could get shuttled to a camp in the boondocks and simply be forgotten. Elgie was of the old school and afraid to say anything, call attention to himself. Young prisoners now are more vocal, started talking about their rights and his. But instead of going about things the right way, and getting before the parole board, Elgie just took off with the others."

"I suppose he didn't believe in anybody after all these years," she said.

"Told folks he'd served enough time for a crime he didn't commit," Tate said.

"May didn't shoot herself from across a room!" Poppa yelped.

"Elgie said some folks in this community could have helped him," Tate said. "And he didn't mean his grandmomma. That old woman couldn't have stirred up a stink, back then. He meant white folks."

"Were his fingerprints on the gun?" Allie said.

"Fingerprints?" Tate said. "Hon, you're thinking in the present. You might as well ask if they gave him a lie-detector test, a drunk-o-meter test, or a ride in a jet airplane."

"Or a fair trial, I see," she said. Poppa turned up the set. "He wasn't even supposed to have stayed this long. Went there at sixteen and now he's — " a little old gray-haired nigger: a heap older and a heap wiser if it was him hiding at the dam. If she could not yet mention Iona, she could not mention Ralph, or what might be a figment of his young imagination. "How long did he get for shooting Momma?"

"Got life like he ought to have," Poppa yelled.

"But life is not life," Allie said. "There's parole." Then she caught Tate's eye as he nodded in Poppa's direction. His legs were jerking and his lips blue as he pressed one hand hard to his chest. He could drop dead with his adrenalin racing so fast, Tate meant, nodding. "We'd better eat," Allie said, standing. She followed Tate as he went toward the bathroom to wash up. "But Momma was definitely shot from across the room in that cabin?" she said.

"Never any question about that," he said. "Let's don't have any more questions now."

"All right. But do you — "

"I thought no more questions," he said.

"I just wanted to know if you know of other prisoners who escape and run home?"

"I don't know any other prisoners."

"But do you know anybody who does? Somebody maybe kin to one?"

Tate was in the bathroom now and yelled back, "Allie!" which meant to hush, that he was tired and wanted his supper, and peace.

He came from the bathroom wiping his face on a fingertip towel delicately embroidered with flowers. Thinking she'd reminded him before those towels were only for looks, she decided it did not matter. After he dropped the towel into her red dish drainer, she took it out in silence. She thought housewives who paid too much attention to picayune details were boring, emptying ashtrays while they were still being used, or plumping up pillows if a guest stood up and went to the bathroom. At this time of life, she wanted larger things to think about. Yet, out of habit, she wavered trying to decide whether to put the vegetables on the table in dishes, or whether to let the men serve their plates from pots on the stove? She told them finally to come on and help themselves.

"How come Willson has the truck?" she said at the table.

"That boy of his sick up in Memphis can come home. I loaned Willson the truck to go get him."

They lowered their heads while Tate said the blessing, in their small family circle joining hands. "That boy who had trouble with his leg swelling?" Poppa said afterward, stirring chowchow into his crowder peas. Tate nodded.

"He's had a time," Allie said. "Give Willson that chocolate cake I made that's in the freezer. He can take it to Dave."

After drinking off some of his buttermilk, Tate crumbled corn bread into the glass and ate it with a spoon. Watching, Allie was glad she'd broken him of doing that when company came, at least. Then she turned her attention to the wind that had risen after the rain subsided, which, rattling the kitchen window, seemed to ask, What did it matter? What company was she expecting who would criticize their manners? Not anybody she'd like to know, she thought, Emily Post included.

"Guess what happened?" Tate said. "Willson and Turner and some of their friends asked if I'd run for road supervisor in the coming election."

"Why, Tate," Allie said. "What'd you say?"

"Said when would I find the time."

"It shows the way they're thinking," she said.

"How?" Poppa said.

"They know they can't run one of them yet, but want a man elected they choose. Tate, it's a compliment."

"I guess it is," he said. When he looked afraid to grin, it meant he was pleased.

For a while no one had anything to say. Poppa got off on the subject of Mrs. Roosevelt's starting this country down its socialistic path; however, Allie cut him short, having heard it enough. "Weren't she a bird?" he said. She did not say that in this more perceptive time of life, she had begun to admire the woman, regretting all the years she'd spent snickering because Eleanor was not pretty, the standard of judgment in the South for a woman.

The kettle boiled. She jumped up to pour water for instant coffee, waiting afterward as dutifully as a waitress while the men made slow decisions about real coffee or Sanka, and finally plopped both jars to the table and settled cream and sugar beside them. She twisted her spoon, staring at her distorted image, glad to have been really pretty once, letting her heart warm whenever Tate said she was a good-looking woman still, at fifty. Though why should she not be? Allie asked herself quickly.

"Ready for that pie Tate brought?" she said. The men said they were full and would wait. She stirred her coffee with the spoon, wishing again she'd taken advantage of being young, though what would she have done differently? Maybe not have married so young, or gone up to Memphis to work? Something outside herself seemed to have directed her life, and something had: the war did. At the same time her generation had felt the world might end, and that they were making it safe forever. They were so innocent, being scared to death of parents and of all authority. A certain cigarette commercial had seemed so risqué. "So round, so firm, and so fully packed!" it went. Young men laughed, glancing at girls' chests, and the girls nearly died of embarrassment. The insinuation was all right directed at Betty Grable or Rita Hayworth, goddesses to them all. Picture shows were the only form of entertainment she and Tate had known. How proud everybody really was when Lucky Strike Green went to war! Innocent was the right word, Allie thought. She tried to imagine the old Kay Kayser Kollege of Musical Knowledge going over today. When Kay mentioned a pretty girl, saying, "Boing!" men were shocked and girls hid their faces. Only, she had to have a girlfriend explain he meant erection, Tate would not tell her. Her attitude was that it was so terrible the sponsors must not understand the joke, either.

Sprouting breasts, she had walked like a hunchback. Particularly, she could not stand the old men on the store porches leering at her, and knowing any one of them would have copped a feel if he could, giving her not only a sense of disappointment that they were Poppa's friends but also an unsettled feeling about men in general. "Anybody ready for that pie yet?" she said.

They shook their heads. Tate went on talking quietly about replacing wooden bridges linking fields, which had washed away in the strong and recurrent rains in April. The springtime had been peculiar, with people standing on the main road of town wondering at the strange dry winds, men holding their hats and women their hair. To her the winds had come from distant lands, of camels and sheiks and barren deserts; thinking of those foreign places had made her feel small, insignificant, and not cosmopolitan, the wind having traveled over so many vistas before finding her at home.

Listening to Tate's voice, she believed it his momma's fault he could not holler loud enough to bring the cows home. Laverne McCall had taken it into her head early on that she was artistic and had adopted a suitable temperament. Many of the men around her would have cured her of that, but Tate's poppa was also a passive man. He catered to her. Allie might have sympathized, but in Laverne's case felt she would have been better off, even happier, if Mr. McCall had taken a stronger stand, even shoved a little sense into her — because she went on and on making herself and others around her miserable trying to achieve an artistic prominence that eluded her. Her hand-painted china was never any prettier than that of other women, nor were the trays into which she lacquered butterflies. This was more frustrating because she considered herself socially above so many others; but country women in these parts, particularly back then, had to make with their own hands anything ornamental, fanciful. Pretty handmade things emerged from country women so seemingly plain, or without desires, that they had taught Allie something long ago about unexpected facets in human beings; like finding a diamond in a barren field. Laverne finally took up oil painting. A self-portrait by her was part of Tate's inheritance; that he burned it with trash, rather than even storing it in the attic, said more than a thousand words of hatred. She painted portraits of other people and of dogs, chickens, cats, cows, and roosters, but managed to make them all cross-eyed. After she staged a one-woman show at the Woman's Club and people left laughing, Laverne put away her palette for good. Country people who didn't particularly take to art anyway certainly couldn't take seriously a portrait of a cock-eyed rooster.

That was probably when Laverne transferred her delicate health to Tate. Deciding he was tired, she would put him to bed afternoons, where Tate lay furiously watching others at play outdoors. By the time he was old enough to revolt, Laverne really was sick; sick only of life maybe. She made him pose in a smock once and other boys spied at the window and never stopped laughing at him. He turned scarlet with suppressed rage years later when he told Allie about it: dressed like a girl and other little boys watching. Laverne kept herself sedated with quinine cough syrup, paragoric, and even drank vanilla flavoring the way Negroes did. Allie felt sorry for her. Laverne had much to offer and no knowledge of how to direct herself, and could have used a stronger man than the one she had. Laverne had wanted to lift her head above the crowd, and had had the capacity for longing, the understanding of something else beyond here, devoid in so many people, who saw not only nothing beyond the ends of their noses, but did not think anything else was there. Her medical expenses ate up almost everything. When Mr. McCall died after Laverne, his life insurance was so borrowed against, it was worthless. Aside from the portrait, Tate was left with a few hundred acres and a few hundred dollars in cash. Poppa enjoyed letting Allie know she'd married a fellow with nothing; though once Poppa was old and sick, Tate could farm well enough that Poppa was glad to have him take over his land. Allie felt repercussions from Laverne's effect on Tate, and from her own mother. She lived with a sense of two women reaching back with long arms from the grave, to touch her.

She thoughtfully tapped her spoon to the table knowing she'd not particularly like to trade places with Mrs. Kennedy, Vanderbilt, Astor — or her horse; though she'd not mind seeing how any of them lived. But they would turn up their noses at the very idea of traveling these dusty roads just to peek at her life: who'd want to bother? She felt such people might gain a great deal here, add weight to their lives, among fields and hills and people who disliked pretensions, whose taproots were deep in their soil.

"Anybody ready for that pie?" she said.

They finally nodded, and she picked up her pie knife. "I declare, Tate. I can't get over you bringing home this whole pie."

He grinned. "The Negro at the Whitehill Café was just taking some from the oven. I asked if she'd sell me a whole pie."

"You mean you could have bought just three slices?"

He nodded, yawning. "Hon," she said, "you're going to have to go to bed as soon as supper is over." How many times had she said that of an autumn evening when it was picking time?

"I just might have to," he said. He looked at his pie. "Old man, I bet you don't want any of this homemade chocolate pie."

Joining in the fun, she held her knife in the air. Poppa stared with watery, startled eyes before seeing the joke, too. "Naw," he said. "And I reckon you don't want to sleep under my roof tonight either."

There was no sting to that remark because if they were not there, Poppa would be sleeping at the Sunset Rest Home, and knew it.

"How much they ask you for the pie?" she said, sitting down.

"Four bucks," Tate said.

"Good Lord, a mercy." Her look meant she could have made a half dozen pies for that amount, but was glad for a little extravagance in their lives.

"I didn't know our ship had come in," Allie said, smiling.

13

TATE'S HABIT on Sunday afternoons was to drive around the countryside with other men to look at cattle. Allie meant to go to Oxford without saying anything to him; he would not remember it was her time to go there with flowers; then fate intervened as her personal dishwasher was going Saturday night. Her hands being wet, she let Tate answer the phone on his way to bed. After listening awhile, he said, "Of course not, Carrie. Allie wouldn't be riding over, either. You all can take flowers to the old folks anytime." He hung up, laughing. "Imagine Carrie thinking she even had to call to say your trip was off."

"Jake wouldn't let her go?"

"I reckon the woman's got that much sense herself."

Meredith was not to be taken to the campus until night. She could be at the home and back before anything happened, if anything did. While knowing enough to keep silent, she was surprised at how she'd reacted to being warned not to go — in effect told not to: she'd been riled up. Wagging a toothpick, Poppa said, "Brother, I been on one end of a crosscut saw and a Negro on the other end, but come nighttime I'm going to my house and him to his."

"What's that got to do with the price of eggs?" Tate said.

"It's got to do with genes. That's what this whole thing's about, intermarrying."

"Poppa," Allie said. "It's got to do with one individual Negro getting an education." If she said "long overdue him," that would only lead to more irrational talk she did not want to hear. She wished even to silence Tate, who was saying, "It's not really just one. They'll want to integrate the public school system, too."

"Then we're living history," she said.

"The first mistake was inventing penicillin," Poppa said.

"What?" she said.

"If it hadn't of been for penicillin, there wouldn't have been so many niggers around to start all this trouble." He stared at her with glee, though she'd almost broken him of using that word before her. She flipped her dish towel toward him, one end knotted: her gesture was not all play.

Tate said, "When you think about it, folks have treated Negroes mighty bad in the past."

She nodded, wondering why it had taken so many years for them to speak up, out. She felt terror at the idea that if you considered something too long you might lose impetus for doing it.

"The only answer to things is education and Christianity," Poppa said, startling the others. Folding his arms and widening his eyes, he laughed at them. "What're you all doing with your mouths open, trying to catch flies?" His toothpick dangled. "I'll tell you one thing. I'll never call one Missus. I'll never feel right about that. I'm glad I'm not going to live to see the end of the white race. I liked things the way they were and am man enough to admit it. If white folks have done wrong things, then we've brought all this down on our own heads. But a pushing and a shoving won't get it. Education and Christianity will. Now what's the matter?"

Allie looked at Tate. "I was just thinking how glad I am of one thing."

"What's that, hon?"

"That wonders won't ever cease." Then she looked back at Poppa, trying to imagine what else might be in his heart.

Tate's snoring followed her from the bedroom into the den, where Poppa sat aslant like a pencil. He held up one hand to the television's pale glow. "Why don't you ever wear your hair like that?"

Stopping, she stared at the girl on the set. "Because I'm not twenty years old, or anywhere near it," she said.

He seemed to moan. "I used to have me a pretty little girl with long hair like that." Did he mean her or her momma? Allie wondered. Then he said, "She went and grew up on me," and his tone was a long, shrill whining for those years. She muttered, "I reckon I did," so that he did not hear. What would have happened — could have happened — had she not grown up when she did: understood she was too old for him to come in and shave while she was taking a bath, too old for him to rub her back beneath her thin cotton nightie (though that felt so good)? An uneasiness had come into their relationship, never admitted. Poppa had managed to make her feel cheap the first time she met his dime-colored eyes after she had locked the bathroom door; even now she could feel that breathing presence, his ear against the door, his hand slowly releasing the knob that wouldn't turn, and the silence of him listening longer as she deliberately rustled her bathwater. Hadn't they milked cows longer than most people because he liked the Goddamned tits? she wondered. She asked God's forgiveness for her inner thoughts, still surprised herself that bad words popped to mind. She replaced pockets in some of Tate's worn work pants until the ten o'clock news, when Poppa exploded. "There's them hot-house flowers again! Every one of them light on his feet, I'll bet." Each time the Memphis newscasters came on, wearing pink jackets with glittery patches on their breast pockets, his irritation grew; preferring now not to listen, he fell asleep.

The commentators annoyed her, too, always laughing among themselves when the show came on, sobering when the camera zoomed toward them, as if their conversation was above the heads of their viewers, as if they were only an interruption. The ones from New York were the same way; they all acted eminent. Her feeling was the same as when she and Tate first married and had only a pickup; in Memphis she was made to feel tacky riding so high above everybody else, horns tooting because of Tate's slowness in traffic, city drivers seeming to grit their teeth and swear at country drivers who did not stay where they belonged: in the sticks. Even in a place like Nashtoba, women thought themselves so uptown and looked down on those from smaller communities like Whitehill. In both places, they looked down on women like her who were from out in the county. Chosen to represent her voting district on the Nashtoba Library Board, she was burned up when the president referred to country people. Then trying to make that sound better, she had said, "I mean people from out in the county"; either way, she meant people who had no sense. Well, everybody in Miss'sippi was a hick to Memphis people, and Memphis people hicks to folks in New York City, and people there would be hicks to somebody else, though she did not know who. She wondered whether the Negroes realized the equality they were fighting for didn't exist, or whether they would just go on fighting.

After turning off the news, she bent close to make sure Poppa was breathing. She would have checked on Sweetie, but that moment the dog stretched out her legs as if she had rigor mortis, the way dogs do, sleeping. She saw a lighter segment of sky behind Sy's cabin and knew the weather would fair-up tomorrow. Now night had a blue look broken by faint gleams from the lights Loma and Mose left on outside their stores. That a light was on at Sy's surprised her, because the old man usually went to bed when it was dark.

To stare out at the night's silence made her think again about her ancestors who settled in these hills from South Carolina. Had they thought about deciding the lives of so many who came behind them? For if they'd gone elsewhere, she'd be there now too. Proud of her plain Anglo-Saxon Protestant stock, she could not help thinking sometimes about the Indians whom they'd replaced. To get clear title to his land, Poppa had it traced back through all previous owners and found the names of Indians who had held parcels of it at one time. The deed had seemed awesome and mighty, and read in part: "Land conveyed in this deed was allotted to the grantor as his reserve by virtue of the treaty entered into between the United States of America and the Chickasaw Nation of Indians in 1834." Much of the land was no different from when the Indians had known it. As it changed she thought about the predecessors who owned it: Na-Took-Chick-Nabby and A-Pa-Sah-Che-Tubby and Kil-La-Cha. They were not familiar-sounding Indian names like those in picture shows, Chief Blue Fox or Rain-on-the-Mountain. The real ones sounded more like dishes in the Chinese restaurant in Memphis where she'd gotten Tate to go, once. Within two years of their treaties, signed in 1834 and 1836, the Indians sold their sections for two dollars and a half an acre. Didn't they call upon ancestors for advice as they did in movies? Ancestors, she supposed, could misguide you the way people around you could. Still, she stood in her hilltop house in this small Mississippi community, thinking with a quiet sense of pride of the stock from which she came.

14

EARLY ON SUNDAY MORNING, she made succotash, her fingers breaking out in prickles like heat rash after picking okra. She had studied her Sunday school lesson last night before turning out her light. Tate was studying his in the den now, since Poppa did not turn on the TV set till evening, in deference to Sunday. The sun was already blinding; in the garden the smell of damp earth warming had rushed up to smother her. There, shaded by corn, she had remembered another morning, long ago, when she had been picking vegetables after a rain, and the smell from the fecund, worm-rich soil made her move, as if in a dream, to insert a cucumber into herself. Then, drawing back, she had cried skyward, "Good gracious alive!" This morning, she had had the same impulse and came stonily inside. She wondered, though, if women of Loma's generation had the aplomb to service themselves, feeling decidedly that Loma was still a virgin.

On Sundays, she offered the men a choice between pancakes and waffles; today they agreed amicably on French toast. She sighed, putting away the pancake griddle and the waffle iron and taking out a skillet. Then, realizing that she had no cinnamon, she actually trembled, fearing their righteous indignation. Substituting nutmeg, she felt sneaky.

The bell at the Methodist church was a faint carrying sound. Since the Methodists' ranks had dwindled, they could not afford a full-time preacher and hired Brother Cooper from Whitehill to deliver an early service. He returned home for one at eleven A.M., which Baptists here snidely referred to as his "real" sermon. Soon, on the road below, cars and trucks passed carrying parishioners, the bell a magnet drawing them steadily through the breathless morning. After the men ate, she asked about the substitution. Looking thoughtful, contemplating afterward, they said cinnamon was better, though nutmeg was all right for once. "You didn't know the difference," Allie said, her conscience clear. It seemed remarkable that a grown woman was so fearful over a small matter because it concerned the wrath of men.

Tate, on his way to Whitehill for a paper, was to take Sy a pot of her succotash. Thick, angry curlicues of smoke rose from the old man's chimney, grayer against autumn's clear blue. He came out on his porch and picked up an armload of kindling stacked there neatly. Allie saw that porch clearly, as she'd seen it last evening through her headlights, when it had been as clean as a whistle, except for Sy's thin yellow hound sleeping there, tightly curled into a ring. When the cattle gap rang, it seemed some diminished echo of the Methodist church bell. She watched her pot exchange hands, Sy having come out at a fast clip when Tate drove up. Thinking his hearing had improved, she wondered sharply if she knew the truth of the matter.

They left for church, leaving Poppa to read the Sunday comics; she put Sweetie into the yard and they swapped knowing looks. "You stay here till we get home," Allie warned. "Tate," she said on the way, "everybody knows about that law car by now. I feel funny about the talk behind my back. Do you think Elgie will come here?"

"I don't, because he's been gone too long. I think he might die somewhere hiding in woods. Or, more probably, that he's gone to the family of someone he's known a long while in prison. He has no family here." Telling her not to worry about other folks, he changed the subject, saying Minnie was putting too much starch into his shirts these days. When he rubbed a finger inside his collar, she told him she'd swap the shirt for her girdle. She sat nervously, but envying Poppa's long-stemmed beauties cavorting on TV in the freedom of pantyhose. When she'd been young enough to cavort, and slim, she'd been bound by the strictures of the time, and wore a girdle, the way she always wore a hat and gloves to church. Girdles had served as a chastity belt, or birth-control pills. If heavy necking got out of hand, by the time a girl could wiggle out of all that elastic, both her and her date's fervor had diminished. It was a wonder these days more girls didn't get knocked up, as she believed the current expression went.

On Sundays, town was empty and the countryside had a special silence, canopied neatly by the wide sky, nothing breaking its openness but trees, in a community with no two-story houses, or buildings. Small snowbirds darted from the road; redbirds fluttered into mock-orange bushes at Mister Otis'; behind the church, cows grazed. Before air conditioning, when the church's windows and doors stood open, the service was punctuated by their random bellows, and by roosters crowing. While a world lay beyond Itna Homa, on Sundays Allie felt that might only be say-so.

They were late and couldn't park near the church, so Tate let her out and drove off to park beyond on a shoulder of the road. She could have walked as easily as he, but such deferences were still made to women, though she'd rather have her feelings deferred to more often than her feet. She'd always been a little different, because she could never stand sitting and twiddling her thumbs while a date ran around the hood of the car to open the door. Once they were married, Tate stopped doing that of course.

Was it nerves that made her think conversations ceased when she appeared? People seemed to sidle away to Sunday school classes after greeting her; she and Tate went to theirs. People mingled in the sanctuary afterward. There was no possibility of intimate conversations before church itself started. Preliminaries followed one another in the known routine. Brother Walker was just beginning the sermon, looking older and wise in his Sunday navy-blue suit, when the front door opened. A dropped prayer book sounded like a shot; gasps rose that ended as one faint moan from the congregation. Having timed it so that they could not introduce themselves, four men entered, strangers to this place. They were self-conscious before all the turned heads, and, ducking their own, quietly entered a back pew. Who they were was so obvious to the townspeople, the others might as well have shouted it out: a pulpit committee from another town, come to hear Brother Walker's preaching and recommend him, or not, to be called to their own church. Brother Walker's face blushed the color of his mauve tie; having lost his place in the sermon, he began it again.

The sense of fear settled into the parishioners did not desert them, while he talked on. They shot sad glances toward one another and tried to listen. When something more terrible happened, halfway through the sermon, they were already primed with the right emotions: fear and apprehension. Someone knocked on the church's front door. Stunned, everyone looked toward the pulpit, but Brother Walker and the choir, being farthest away, had not heard it. People sat without moving, wishing the sound away. The knock came again. Papers for Brother Walker's sermon shook in his hand, a deeper blush appeared on his face. He looked down at the white faces uplifted toward him, seeing them as a whole, like blooms in a flower garden.

Stained-glass windows reflecting the sun pockmarked with amber, red, and green the faces that turned toward the rear. Other people remained staring rigidly ahead, as if nothing could really interrupt this peaceful morning. A colored disc of sequins pinned to the back of Loma's head flashed brilliantly. It seemed to revolve, as if the world were tilting. "The white man's last bastion," a man said, not loudly.

Allie heard someone else whisper, "The church."

She looked back once. The pulpit committee sat with expectant faces, thinking some unusual church program was about to begin. Like everyone, she faced Brother Walker again, thinking what happened next was up to him. Settling his papers, he was about to leave the lectern. Then waving him back, John Q stood up and moved easily past knees and down the center aisle, fumbling at his waist for the holster which was not there on Sundays.

Brother Walker picked up where he'd left off and finished the sermon, then read announcements that would be forgotten today: everybody was invited to the Wooten-Thompson wedding in the church this Friday evening; Brother Bill Hooper was homebound and would appreciate cards and visits; all boys interested in Pee Wee football, see him after church.

Allie noted Tate's knuckles as whitened as her own, as he gripped the Bible in his lap. Had their own Negroes, fired up by what was happening at the university, decided to stage a demonstration? Shine their asses, as the local saying went? Should they be admitted? If admitted once, would they come back regularly? These questions had been discussed locally, already.

John Q reentered and swaggered to his seat, his expression that of the cat who ate the mouse, knowing the secret no one else did. Brother Walker concluded. Dazzling, Loma took her seat at the organ; her fingers rose and fell with authority, colors from the windows moving across her as crazily as those in a kaleidoscope. Singing voices rose:

What can make me white as snow?
Nothing but the blood of Jee-sus.

What can wash away my sins?
Nothing but the blood of Jeee-sus!

After a final and rippling flourish, Loma's hands rested in her lap. Brother Walker stood in the rear to pronounce the benediction. "... the Holy Ghost. Amen."

Pandemonium broke out afterward. Little boys tried to leapfrog pews to reach John Q. Thankfully, their parents hauled them back, for nothing warranted the sanctuary's being defiled in that manner. John Q looked haughty as a movie star, as if the congregation clamored for his autograph. Yet he told what he knew, because by the time he reached outdoors a chain of laughter followed him. The puzzled pulpit committee filed out, not a person speaking to them, or shaking their hands out of courtesy. When they drove off, one man peered out the back window and through dust a long while.

Allie was astonished that she and Tate were suddenly pulled into the circle around John Q. Being the center of attention among people who had half raised her, others whom she'd known always, it seemed she might not have liked the limelight had she known it, after all.

Laughing, John Q told it all again. Who would have knocked but old Sy! If it had to do with Sy, people were grinning before they even heard the whole story.

The old man got it into his head to return Allie's pot, also to bring her "the gret basket of vegetables" he gave her once a year in return for her cooking. He started to put the things into Mister Tate's car, then was fearful of being seen messing around one belonging to a white man. Parishioners nodded their heads. A nigger, Sy had said. John Q made it carefully known, it was Sy who said that. People laughing, still, started toward home. Only Allie thought that the old man's doing the unreasonable did not seem reasonable.

Others remained to ask questions. Suppose Negroes had come to church, and suppose they sincerely wanted to worship?

But they wouldn't be coming sincerely to worship! That was the whole point. If cameras and news folks weren't over at the university now, that Negro wouldn't be there, either.

Some people said it was simply wrong for whites and Negroes to worship together. They quoted Scripture to prove it. God made red birds and blue birds and they didn't mix; put sheep and goats in a pasture and they didn't mix. The latter made Allie bite her lips in vexation. "They shouldn't come to a white man's church any more than they come to his front door," Snake Johnson said.

Allie turned in surprise that he was at church, then saw why. Snake was accompanied by his clubfooted cousin, Fred Cullins. Fred the Body Man, he was called. The best repairman in the county, he worked at Brewster's Garage in Nashtoba, where he lived. He had come over for Snake's poker game and stayed over to work on Snake's old truck. His own wife, Rose, was away visiting her people. Fred was a thoroughly honest man, and a sober one; he and Rose were big workers in their own Baptist church. His little weakness for poker was overlooked even by those who disapproved, because of his otherwise good character. His presence, they thought, lent a temperate note to those evenings. He wore a thick, built-up shoe that gave him a rolling gait when he walked.

"Shoot," said Jake Thomas. "Negroes don't want trouble. It's the communists behind a few causing it."

"Why would they want to go to our church, anyway, when they worship so different? The Negro's still in church when we're eating supper."

"What would you have done, Brother Walker," Tate said, "if one had been knocking to come in?"

"I'd have said come on and sit down."

Allie met his eyes. "We should ask Negroes to sit on the front pew, the way most of us have been honored in their churches," she said.

The small group then broke up. People went away looking inward, the way she followed Tate along the road to their car. When as a young person she went to a Negro funeral, it was the first time she'd ever seen a dead body. Negroes, in those days, did not embalm. After the casket was opened, she was met by the smell of death, while two Negro men stood swishing flies from the corpse with undertakers' cardboard fans. Followed home by the smell of rotting flesh, there she bathed and bathed and was unable to rid her imagination of the odor. The whole thing was a humbling experience.

That was not her first time at a Negro church. She had been before, uninvited. As a summer evening's pastime, crowding into open truck beds, people once sat outside Negro churches to listen to the singing. While that was truly appreciated, hadn't those visits contained an element of snideness? "Ain't it a show!" The Negroes could not ask white people to get out of their churchyards by saying even, "Please suh." Ask a Negro if he minded white people coming? "Naw suh. Naw suh. Us be honored to have you." Such shit, Allie allowed herself the freedom of saying to herself. Sitting out in that heat, the night pulsating with insects around her, watching the preacher shouting, sometimes gyrating, till he brought some women to cry out and shake, approximating orgasm, with the congregation rhythmically tapping their feet, she had recognized one evening the wrongness of spying. One woman rose then, bent double, clutching her stomach. Pacing before the altar, she cried, "I'm so tired, Lord. Help me. I'm so tired of working." Allie never went again to listen to the singing.

A bachelor, Mose Perkins had no one to keep him in harness. Already divested of his coat and tie, he stopped to ask Tate to drive around that afternoon and look at cattle. Inspired, Allie asked him to come home and take dinner with them. Menfolks' talk would keep Tate from remembering about the church flowers; he had not outright told her not to go to Oxford.

On the way home, she ran her mouth to distract him, mentioning things that irritated men, what other women had worn to church, the color of Miss Pearlie Mae's hair, Loma's sequins, or anything else that would make Tate turn a deaf ear. Bored herself, she watched cars and trucks ahead of them. Two steep side roads ran off the main road through town and carried people away to scarcely populated countryside, dust rising behind them in clouds like her Indians' old smoke signals. The depths of these roads reminded her of the Pippin roller-coaster ride at the Memphis Mid-South Fair, where she and Tate went yearly when they were younger. Having been such hicks the first time, they arrived on a Thursday, not realizing the permanent amusement park, as well as the zoo, were closed to whites that day, since it was the one white people in Memphis gave their domestic help off.

Newly married, she could snuggle against Tate, or lay her hand on him in such a way that he'd do anything she wanted. That lasted two years. But he would never ride any dangerous rides at the fair, the kind she particularly liked. At first, she thought his refusal had to do with a country boy's natural reluctance to try anything new, the way he would seldom eat food he'd not had before. Alone or with friends, she rode the swooping roller coaster, its age enough to terrify people, and flew around in miniature planes that shot out from a center pole, and seemed apt to tump you out anytime. Tate turned greenish merely standing and watching. To taunt him would be to damage his male ego, that thing as fragile as eggs, which, once shattered, the King's horses and men could not put back together. Women tread lightly.

It gave her a permanent, peculiar feeling to know that somewhere deep inside herself she was braver than Tate. Brought up to be weak and helpless around men, she went on at the fairgrounds covering her ears and squealing when Tate took up one of those popping guns and shot wooden ducks. She would give his pitching arm an awed squeeze after he knocked down stolid milk bottles and won her bed dolls gowned in satin. Now, as she placed a hand lightly on Tate's nearer thigh, she felt how it had lost the hard, muscular tone it once had. She said, "I was looking at the Golden Agers today, thinking how I had to move up to that class when I'm sixty. It'll seem soon the way time goes so quickly."

"Don't worry about it," Tate said in his pacifying way. "Just be proud to have made it that far."

After they clanged the cattle gap, Mose came behind them. Poppa's furry-chinned fox face appeared at the den window, trembling with the excitement of two rings. Inside, Tate went to change his Sunday clothes, though she quickly put dinner on the table, keeping on even her stiff patent-leather pumps, with two-inch heels that made her as tall as Tate. During most of the meal, the conversation revolved around sports. When it turned to politics she urged second helpings, hoping to get dinner over. "Thought once the government was conservative," Tate said, taking a roll. "But Kennedy is a spendthrift. The government's going to work us to death taxing us."

"Used to be we worked ourselves to death," Poppa said.

"It's all these government programs," Mose said. "A Negro drops out of school today and gets paid to go back. But they'll never be pleased. You could give the Negro the U.S. and one-half of hell and he'd want the other half. We'll have to have a war with them because the Negroes will never stop asking."

She said, "Coffee? Pie?" only wanting them gone, before Mose's conversation brought the crisis at the university to mind. She shooed them toward the den, and pulled from pegs two identical International Harvester caps, lending Mose one of Tate's. Her dishwasher going, she raised her hands from suds. She listened to Tate's truck travel the driveway and was glad for the men's camaraderie; it warmed her these Sunday afternoons. She liked some combined male scent they brought home — mindful of cattle, sunned pastures, tobacco, pesticides, and wind. Lonesome, Poppa leaned to the den window. People here treated old folks kindly, but the men could not take him — Tate had tried. The bumpy roads rattled Poppa's bones and upset his digestive system, and he had a setback for days. He lay on the sofa with the Sunday paper; soon it billowed as he snored. One suffering handed down to Eve's daughters, but never mentioned by the Bible, was men's snoring, Allie thought.

In the bedroom, her inherited dresser had been varnished black by Grandmomma. Varnishing back then was a spring ritual like drinking sassafras tea or taking sulphur and molasses. Allie had restored the wood to its own golden color. She brushed from the surface now a sprinkling of Pond's face powder, staring carefully at herself. She was unable to break the habit of face powder, though *The Homemaker* suggested in this day it made women her age look older. She had to laugh at aging: it seemed to happen while she watched. Only down near the Gulf Coast during wartime had she once taken advantage of her looks — or nearly. Now she wondered if, when she was an old lady, she'd be glad to have been virtuous. Would she be better off with a lot of memories? she wondered, too late.

The dresser's small lamp was ruby shaded. It was as kind as candlelight. She looked longer, thinking that the last thing they would ever have money for was something like plastic surgery. Though an acquaintance in Whitehill had reputedly had her "eyes fixed," she felt a little uncertain about just what that meant. When she asked Tate how he thought Mary Jean looked, he only said, "She never was a pretty woman." What a dismissable category. She had started to say Mary Jean had other assets, important to the community: she was a good mother, PTA member, Scout leader, churchgoer — but so were a lot of pretty women. She had almost said, She's famous for her lemon-meringue pie.

For they had been at a graveyard cleaning at old Woods' Chapel. At the picnic afterward, people sang out, "Here comes Mary Jean's lemon pie," passing it along the table of planks laid over sawhorses, cloth covered. Then her own cucumber pickles were announced, coming by in a glittery cut-glass dish. When people cried, "Here comes Allie McCall's pickles," she'd had the terrible dread that those pickles were all she'd be remembered for on this earth.

All her ancestors from South Carolina, and many born here, were buried in the old graveyard. Woods itself once had been larger than Itna Homa was now. As a child, when she heard the community had gone, she asked fearfully, "Gone where?" When someone explained it simply declined and people moved off, she had the eerie sense that cotton gin, stores, houses, disappeared into thin air, that while she stood wondering about it, the very same thing could happen to all she knew. Her mother's sudden disappearance had set her up for feeling that way.

Woods' Chapel was where Poppa's own momma and daddy met, his daddy having said his first glimpse of his future bride was when she came to church in a wagonload of chairs with her family. She wore a big blue bow-ribbon in her hair. He'd sensed then that for the rest of his life she'd be the whole cheese. To Allie, her grandmomma was always a gnomelike figure in black, pushing ahead of her a worn-out mop, rather than using a cane; it was hard to visualize her as the apple of some man's eye till he died, before Allie was born. Grandmomma died, and relatives, till then only names in the family Bible, came from Oklahoma and Texas. Quite calmly they discussed Grandmomma's husband, the grandfather Allie had never known, saying, "He was the world's worst for Negroes. These hills are polka-dotted with his offspring!" She had been startled out of a dreamy world, learning she had Negro relatives, suspecting the Negroes knew the bloodline, while she lived on sadly in ignorance about everybody she was kin to.

All her lifetime, her own Baptist church had remained unlocked, until recently, the deacons voted against that. While robberies were still infrequent, people had begun locking their doors if they went uptown for a loaf of bread — Negroes stealing from one another had never counted. People didn't fear local Negroes, but rather some dropping in from Memphis or other nearby towns. Crime on the whole was spreading; whites were becoming just as bad. Annie said it for everyone when she said, "Used to was, you could go to Chicago, go to Africa, go anywhere and not lock your door." Then she returned from a visit to a son in Chicago, reporting, "Lock yourself inside and lock yourself outside. Ain't no enjoyment up there." People in the country could still think it was better, at least.

Sunday afternoons, Brother Walker stayed in his study preparing the evening service, though so few people came, some had begun to wonder if it was worth his effort. People were always on the road these days, going east or west or anywhere but to church. Now with the door open, Allie stepped inside, realizing she'd never been in the church alone. The new red runner silenced her footsteps. Colors in the windows receded with the sun's lowering. She had started down this same aisle on Poppa's arm, a bride in wartime's hurry, wearing a crepe dress with padded shoulders and a shaky orchid. They had decided to marry while Tate was home for a few days' leave, and he wore his uniform, not having with him any civilian clothes. His gray eyes had been shy but penetrating. She had turned from his watching her to stare at Loma, playing back then a piano, wearing an aqua tulle hat, which shook so, in time to the music, Allie had feared its toppling off.

She stopped now at the chancel rail, not reaching for a vase of flowers. In his study, Brother Walker was humming. The image of herself as a bride vanished, while she thought of herself as being a lot closer to being carried out of this church feetfirst. She supposed Brother Walker would be long gone, by then. She wanted in this quiet time to tell him how much he'd meant to her family, helping Tate over rough times when he despaired of farming, cheering up Poppa's long days, discussing with her the reason for the world and what might be her place in it.

Perhaps only thoughts of her own mortality took her down the hall to his study, where he hummed some catchy, old song whose name she could not recall. However, it was a dance tune, not a hymn, and she was smiling as she thought about teasing him. The hall was lined with hooks used by the Sunday school teachers, the choir, and Loma. On one, a sweater had hung so long it was misshapen. A red cap could have belonged to so many men, its forgetful owner was probably afraid to claim it. Tate had so many caps, she'd thought often of stenciling his name inside the hatbands, yet could not remember his ever having lost one. In having so many caps, did he try to change identity each time he put a different one on?

The humming was louder, and as Brother Walker moved softly about the study, his shadow loomed large on one wall and then disappeared. Just as an instinct told Allie not to enter, it was too late. Already, she stood in the doorway lightly smiling and about to cry, Caught you out! meaning humming that tune. For she had realized it was "Have You Ever Seen a Dream Walking?"

Well, I have, she completed to herself, as she stepped inside. There, Brother Walker swayed back and forth, with his fingers rakishly snapping. Atop his head was a woman's fancy hat, undoubtedly left on a hallway hook. By whom? That thought in her head, Allie stepped back in embarrassment. She fled to the sanctuary, praying that in that fleeting moment he had not seen her, feeling as cumbersome as a bear trying to get away on tiptoe. Had he seen her? The question kept time with her running footsteps, and she felt it would never be answered.

She grabbed a vase of flowers with each hand, and once outdoors heard nothing but the sound of a Negro out back mowing the church lawn, the sound growing fainter as he neared the copse of trees where she'd known John Q, or rather he her, in the biblical sense. Somewhere off over gullies and pastureland, a car backfired—in the direction where Negroes were beginning to build brick bungalows and form themselves a middle-class neighborhood, on a ridge before the hills sloped down to join the flat-running Delta, the car sounding like a popgun because of the distance the sound traveled; way beyond Mister Otis' side lot, a rooster crowed several times, a sound mindful of the solitude of all the country Sunday afternoons she'd ever known. Thus could she pinpoint exactly the starting point of anything she heard around the countryside, so intimately did she know it.

Even though church, noon dinners, and nap times were over, town was no livelier when she drove back through it. The only signs of life were cats and dogs roaming and the gleam of a cat's eyes as it hunched beneath the Grandberry store sitting on cinder blocks. Opposite it was Webb's General Mer——, the worn-out letters never repainted. When they came to town fifteen years ago, middle-aged strangers, the rumor started the couple was not married. Whites would not trade with them, leaving them solely Negro customers. How hard the rumor was on them, when no one knew if it was true. No one dared ask if they were living in sin, along with whether their bread was day old. How she could ruin Brother Walker by mentioning what she saw today, but her lips were sealed. Things could be construed wrongly by the eye of the beholder. If what she could suspect was true, Brother Walker had never harmed anyone. She knew that much, because Mississippi was like one place: sneeze here and someone might call up from as far south as Jackson to ask if you had a cold.

Her perceptions felt sharpened, and, passing Loma's store, seeing her outside burning trash, she knew Loma was gradually sneaking her store open on Sunday afternoons. Having noised that idea about, she had met with opposition from townspeople. Still, trade was to be had from strangers at the dam, camping and fishing, people who forgot matches and mosquito spray and other small items. These people sometimes turned up in stores other days, saying they had not known a town was named after the Itna Homa federal dam. Outraged locals cried, "It was the other way round!" The town had been here since Indian times, when, in the beginning, it was called Skull Bones. Two white settlers were scalped and their heads set on posts at the town limits. Everyone was grateful that somewhere along the line the name was changed to honor some otherwise unheralded Indian chief.

For the past few Sundays, Loma had been at the store, saying she'd come to check her milk, a leak in the toilet, and now that she had to burn trash from that old storeroom, Allie guessed. On the right wind she might burn up the whole town! She was glad the menfolks were talking about starting a volunteer fire department. The idea had not gotten off the ground some said, because the men could not decide who would get to drive the truck, if they raised money for one. Men went on being boys. When a carload of Negroes pulled up for gas, Loma headed alertly into the store to pull on her amber light.

Town dropped behind. She passed along the narrow road where kudzu created shadowed places, passing hillsides where whites and Negroes lived side by side, thinking of the Negro who lived near Mose speaking of their neighborliness. "He need something, he come to my house. I need something, I cut through the pine trees to his. He need my mule and I need his plow. It always used to be, if I had eggs my neighbors did, but folks getting away from that these days." Then she let her mind re-dwell on Brother Walker's borrowed hat, a crushed-velvet lavender turban with a veil studded with rhinestones. It clapped itself upon its rightful owner's head, Loma's.

She had passed a dirt side road, down which she first ever spoke to Loma. She had already noted at school that Loma's country biscuits never had even a teaspoon of sorghum to help their dryness, and had feared someday that Loma's pail would not hold a biscuit, either. One December, riding her own piece of bicycle, she saw a lonesome figure picking the year's last straggly cotton. Realizing it was Loma, she bent into icy wind and meant to pass by. Then Loma hailed her and came to the road's edge to talk. Even in those days not many white people picked cotton; to pass that over lightly, she'd said, "Fixing to buy yourself some pretties for Christmas?" Out of stiffly moving cheeks, Loma said, "Fixing to buy some for my momma." Aware then of her own privileged, childish selfishness, Allie knew the older girl taught her a lesson. Loma closed thin eyelids, exposing cold, blue veins, while her lips moved silently. Allie had said curiously, "What are you praying for out here?"

"Praying for rain. Drops of rest."

Hurrying along now, Allie thought that if Loma came to church wearing tinsel, colored lights, and Christmas-tree balls, she'd tell her she looked gorgeous, and mean that.

Loma's family of eleven children soon needed a paycheck and one less mouth to feed. She dropped out of school and went to live with old T. Z. Heiskell and his aged wife, who owned the store Loma now had. Mr. Heiskell was the happier about his new helper. Even in the store, he'd say, "Give me some sugar." Loma had to stop clerking to kiss his cheek, despite his mouth dangling a stream of tobacco spit. In her obedience, other girls, Allie among them, had felt some vague uneasiness about their own futures. After his wife died, some people felt Loma should not keep living at his house. Finally, he was bedridden and dependent upon Loma to run the store. When he died, he had left it to her, lock, stock, and barrel; his relatives tried to break his will and failed. Loma after all had taken care of him. Only the old men on the store porches said, "She took care of him, all righty." Allie had never believed those snide implications.

She wondered what speculations went on about her behind her back, knowing in this small place there were some. Had

John Q ever told anyone? She knew she was safe, though, about what went on down near the Gulf Coast. Stepping on her accelerator harder, she sped herself toward Sardis dam, having decided to cut through it to Oxford, as the government roads were so much better than the state's.

15

By the early 1940s, four federal dams completed in Mississippi changed the lives of country people. Recreational areas were unknown to them before. Now stocked spillways and lakes provided fishing. There were beaches for swimming. More importantly, returning veterans saw no reason to step into Daddy's shoes, small farming (a dying business even then). Government acres around the dam provided jobs: cutting grass, maintaining levees, tending to picnic sites and to all the needed equipment. Locals working at the Itna Homa dam told stories about federal waste that kept the community hopping mad, the newest one being that a carload of paint arrived for picnic tables and buildings and was the wrong color, and, instead of returning it, the federal foreman had a hole bulldozed and buried the cans, then sent for a new carload. All at the taxpayer's expense! It tickled townspeople, though, to know something of government business that government itself did not know.

At Itna Homa, the dam's water was of the same opaque muddiness as the countryside's ponds, but at Sardis it was silvery-blue; it rippled and glittered in the sun. Allie stopped alongside the white beach. Because of cottonmouths, copperheads, or rattlers in the muddy ponds of her youth, she had never learned to swim. She and Tate said the Itna Homa dam came along too late for them to enjoy anything but the beauty of its tended grasslands. Being raised up in hard times made it too late for them to start lolling on a beach just because the government dumped some sand. The Depression left them not carefree.

Allie had not been on a beach since Tate was stationed near the Gulf Coast. Removing her pumps, she walked in her stocking feet. Children pointed to the middle-aged lady and ran off, and several picnickers watched, then lost interest. She had a sense of freedom in this anonymity. Here she was not Tate's wife, or Poppa's daughter, or even Allie McCall representing District III on the library board. Even so, she believed the Bible's suggestion to grow where you are planted might be the right one, for she always had some identity and never suffered either complete isolation or loneliness in her community. She was surprised by letters to the editor in *The Homemaker* from women in cities, who complained they did not know who they were, and seemed alone. One writer feared no one would come to her funeral if she died where she lived, and, thinking of funerals in Itna Homa, Allie was as sorry for her as the women she read about who paid a thousand dollars, or more, for a single dress. She settled her feet in the sand and thought that even if she had gone to Memphis when young, or if Tate had stayed in the army, she would not have mislaid her sense of self. Having her past rooted to the land, she would have strength anywhere.

Life's potential, so rich when she was young, so impoverished once they settled back home, made her glad to have known something else while Tate was in the army. The Gulf Coast was the wildest part of Mississippi. They drove to Gulfport often from where Tate was stationed in Hattiesburg. In seafood restaurants they tried to make themselves order something besides the fried catfish they knew at home. Tate never could bring himself to swallow an oyster, though she bravely did once. Branching out and ordering pompano, she was startled, not having known what *en papillote* meant, when her fish arrived in burnt, scorched paper. She and Tate did not drink, but did not object to people who did — within reason. Married couples could not live on the base at Camp Shelby, so she and Tate had a room with kitchen privileges in the house of a nice old lady. They tended to run with the same kind of people they ran with at home, those who attended church and taught Sunday school. She landed a part-time job clerking in one of the temporarily rented stores that New York Jews who had come South rented during the war. She sold jewelry and pseudomilitary items.

Since she did not play cards or Mah-Jongg, or care to learn, she was lonely when Tate went away on maneuvers for two weeks. The kind of women she knew stayed at home when their husbands were gone, though many wives did not. Waking one night bleeding, and not prepared, she walked downtown to the one drugstore that stayed open late. She figured enough MPs would be around that she did not have to worry about being bothered by soliders. She worried more about being picked up as a woman straying through the night. She was equally afraid of having to buy sanitary napkins from a male clerk. That was something women of her time had not yet mustered up the courage to do. She waited outside till the store emptied of soldiers, leaving only an elderly man behind the prescription counter. She stalled for time, picking out a rat-tail comb, Life Savers, and a package of powder puffs. If only she could pick up a discreet little box of Tampax, but they chafed her insides. With her eyes lowered to her bulky purchase, she passed money across the prescription counter, glad the box was prewrapped. The clerk put only her small items in a sack.

Outside, she attempted to hide the box behind her purse. Mortified when someone called her name, she twirled beneath a pink neon sign to face a real country boy from east Mississippi, who'd adopted Tate as his daddy away from home. Learning Tate was out of town, he insisted Allie come to a party. Before she could say no, she was propelled up some stairs that reeked of urine. She knew the boy only by his nickname, Bear.

In the apartment, the few lamps had towels draped over them. So many people were dancing, she hoped the tall, lanky girl standing there with a box of Kotex went unnoticed. She told Bear she would be right back, not sure he heard her over Glenn Miller's "Chattanooga Choo-Choo" playing on a Victrola at its highest volume. Having taken care of herself in the bathroom, she hid the box in the dirty clothes hamper for the surprised owner of the apartment to find in the morning.

Bear said into her ear, "What chew want to drink, cute?" when she came back. Allie said she did not drink; he suggested fruit juice. "Yeah. Pass-shun fruit," said another soldier, dancing by with his face tucked into his partner's hair. She needed to leave, but did she not want one glimpse of a wild party? The kind she'd always heard about?

Bear brought her a glass from the kitchen, where a bare bulb hung from the ceiling. A nicked enamel table served as the bar. He insisted they dance while drinking. She spilled grape juice on her blouse, jumping to the flip side of Miller's record, "A String of Pearls." "I can't get you another drink till the nigger comes," Bear said.

Dancing close by, another boy mistakenly heard and cried, "The nigger's come!"

Soldiers moved toward the bar, till the remark was corrected. She was glad when a slow tune came on, Helen O'Connell singing "Besame Mucho." She let herself go unexpectedly limp in Bear's arms, while he plastered his wet face to her own. Everyone perspired all the time in south Mississippi, and there was something intimate about sweating all over one another. She was glad when the cry went up, "C.C.'s here," and Bear moved away from her. In the kitchen, a portly Negro in a white waiter's jacket was taking bottles out of a large sack. "He make it or buy it?" someone said. But, stopping dead still, Allie had the curious feeling she knew the Negro, his white teeth flashing as he talked to his customers.

She drank more grape juice, and tried to keep Bear from sticking a knee between her thighs as they danced. Giggling, she told him it was like playing Ride a Cock Horse to Banbury Cross. Whenever they twirled past the kitchen, she stared at

C.C. Once he realized this, he looked directly back at her. She danced on with a strange shuddering feeling, thinking she had never before looked directly into a Negro's eyes. Grandmomma fired Negro women who looked her in the face while she gave them directions about cleaning; she considered that impudent. But being away from home, and in the army, was liberating. Negro men, she suspected, were not going to come home as servile as when they left. Staring at C.C. that way, she felt as limp as if she'd sat on his lap. She buried her nose in another glass of grape juice, and did not even know when C.C. left. Why was it, she thought, the juice a sharp and acrid taste on her tongue, that white people didn't want to look into the eyes of Negroes? Where she came from, townspeople claimed there was no such thing as Southern guilt.

Bear's mouth opening smelled like the bottom of a birdcage. "How you like Purple Jesus?" he said.

"That some kind of sacrilegious joke?" she said.

"That some kind of high-falutin' mess?" he said.

"I don't know what you're talking about."

"I'm talking about whether or not you like gin and grape juice?"

She did not answer, but realized the room was spinning around while they stood still. She supposed she was drunk. An interested part of herself asked, What next? "Green eyes," Helen O'Connell sang. It was a record thought racy then, and was banned some places from the radio. The words seemed simple to Allie then: "those cool and limpid green eyes/the pool wherein my love lies/brings to my soul a longing/a thirst for love divine." Maybe she was more sophisticated than she thought. She had always resented, like Negroes, scenes of Negro entertainers being cut from picture shows in the South, Lena Horne in a slinky evening dress singing in a Negro nightclub, for instance. Negroes in the peanut gallery in the Memphis movie house might get uppity ideas! Often, they dared let out belligerent hoots when the film was not perfectly spliced, catching a half glimpse of Lena before she was obliterated. Bear's hand wandered beneath her dress. Feeling her pad grow damper, Allie knew it was not from the curse.

"Come on into the bedroom, cute," he said.

"I can't. I've got—"

"I felt," he said. "It only makes things juicier."

Since he pulled her along with him, she told herself she was not going willingly, then, short of the bedroom door, he let out a yelp and ran.

She found him leaning from a window and, cringing for anybody below, she got her purse and ran. God or Fate had saved her from herself. Gulping fresh air outdoors, she saw street lamps giving off double rings of light, dancing in buckling sidewalks that rose and fell. The town had changed. Streets once familiar no longer were. Nearly an hour passed before she stared down a block and saw her own place, where in the yard a white wooden momma duck was trailed by four ducklings, which had been lovingly carved by her landlady, Mrs. Peabody. Allie patted the momma duck's head before entering the house with tears of gratitude that she was home. She swore to the old woman this would never happen again if only she did not pop from bed to discover that her nice Sunday school teacher from the hills, with such a sweet husband, was tipsy. While she lay across her bed waiting for the room to settle, Mrs. Peabody snored below. Allie thought of her rising each morning to don an antebellum costume and drive off to escort visitors through Jefferson Davis' nearby retirement home. Then she had cried harder, having betrayed everything of value she had been taught to believe in.

16

Later, as soon as she drove from the beach, the dashboard indicator light warned her of trouble. She had sensed something was wrong with the car and had put off telling Tate, since it was picking time and he was too busy to follow her to Brewster's Garage in Nashtoba and take her back when the car was ready. If the car broke down, and she got home later than he, what was she to say? She would use those crutches Southern women always fell back on, ignorance and helplessness. When a dress bill arrived, she might cry, I didn't know. I thought ten percent off meant a lot more than that! Then Tate would get over being angry. Women would rather be honest, but men did not seem to like honesty and forced women into wiliness. Arriving later than Tate, she'd have to say, I didn't think you really meant for me not to go. He would say, Why did you think I kept talking about it being dangerous? She'd keep repeating, I don't know. I just didn't think you really meant for me not to go, letting her voice grow fainter, until Tate got tired of the argument and walked away shaking his head. He'd tell it the following day to other men as an amusing story about women.

Already, on the backseat, chrysanthemums and late roses were shedding petals, while only bright red stalks of salvia, which reminded her of Christmas, still looked fresh. Determined the flowers would reach their destination, she drove slowly to nurse the car along.

Outside the Sunset Rest Home, a Negro swiped a doorknob with a rag and gladly stopped when she asked if he'd take one basket to the men's wing. Then she parked in a lot and entered the home carrying the flowers for the old ladies. She held the flowers' faint fragrance close to her nose, as the home smelled sourly of the inmates' noon meal. Then she remembered *inmates* were in prison and that people here were called *residents;* though they were residents of a world she hoped never to inhabit. Several in the hallways gave her petulant looks, mad and jealous that the flowers were not for them.

She looked away from a small room outfitted as a beauty parlor: a hairdresser came over from Oxford on Sundays. Canes, walkers, wheelchairs, and thinning hair did not lend themselves to the usual chatter in such a place, and she was depressed passing its silence. Wondering about curling and primping going on to the grave, she finally admired the old women's spirits; also, she'd heard plenty tales about romancing, and even marriages, taking place. One marriage between a couple in their eighties led to divorce. Thinking that things between men and women never changed, she carefully skirted an old man lurking behind a potted palm, as nurses had warned he was waiting to expose himself. She felt a little inclined to stop, look, and shriek, to give the old man a thrill, thinking that having seen one man, she had seen them all.

A perspiring nurse pushing a wheelchair trudged around a corner crying, "Lift your feet." Her resident was Miss Birdy, her feet in red slippers planted to the floor, while her eyes flashed and her pursed lips secretively smiled. "Pick up your feet," the nurse shouted again, shoving with all her weight. Miss Birdy suddenly turned senile, dropping her head as if her neck were broken and trailing her arms over the sides of the chair. Allie came behind them into a stark television viewing room, where Miss Precious waited, tied by a white sheet to her wheelchair. An old man was asleep in a wheelchair turned from the set and facing one dead geranium in a pot on a windowsill. Miss Precious' wispy hair was pinned back on each side with a child's pink barrette. Her enlarged eyes seemed to swim behind the lenses of thick glasses, and found Allie shortly. The nurse departed, leaving Miss Birdy suddenly erect beneath a lacy, crocheted shawl. She gave Allie the same contemptuous look she had given her companion. Allie had taken a few Sundays to learn those looks hid happiness at seeing her, and warded off any attempt on her part to come here like Miss Pollyanna, feeling sorry. "Ladies," she said gaily. With sly eyes they watched her advance and set the flowers down, noting critically their good points and bad ones. Lightly holding her breath against the room's vague stinks, Allie said, "What are you ladies busy with today?"

From her lap, Miss Precious held up a long strand of waxy braided Wonder Bread wrappers. Beside her a carton was filled with flattened ones. "Making jump rope," she said, "for the kids at the school across the way. They come over here and sing us songs. Nurse says we got to do something for them. Says old people are catered to and get selfish. Nurse says."

Miss Birdy sniffed. "Chirrun sing because they get credit for it at school. And nurses don't do a damn thing in this place they don't get paid to do. Act like they own the place."

"The Brewsters own it," Miss Precious said.

"No, Miss Precious," said Allie, smiling. "This is one place they don't own. It's out of our county." She came toward Miss Precious' beckoning finger. Straining against her sheet, she said, "Get me out and take me for a walk."

"You know I can't do that. It's against the rules."

"There's no rule! You don't want to." She shifted her glasses and stared. "You're not nearly so pretty as your momma was," she said spitefully.

"Who was her momma?" Miss Birdy said.

Allie said, "Now, you know who my momma was."

"I certainly do not, because I don't know who you are!"

Had Miss Birdy failed so much since she was last here? Allie gave Miss Precious a startled, questioning look. She said, "Old Birdy's got as much sense as she ever had."

"I do not. I forget things."

"You do not. It's me forgets."

"You do not. You're clear as a bell. You know the past like it was yesterday."

"Of course, I know the past!" Miss Precious snapped. "I don't remember yesterday."

"Had creamed tuna for lunch," said the old man, not lifting his head.

"What did you come here for?" Miss Birdy suddenly shrieked. "What do you want?"

"Why," said Allie, fighting not to feel childishly huffy herself, "I don't want anything." At least not here, she added to herself.

The old women stared thoughtfully at nothing, while the old man raised his head to look at the geranium. Why was it let die? Allie wondered. She stared at stiff hairs growing on the chins of both women and at the hairless, pinkish, babyish face of the old man, and wanted to lash out blindly like the old women. In time, her face would grow whiskers and Tate's wouldn't. She found to her astonishment that she was rocking herself, the way some senile residents did all day long. She suddenly understood the motion's power. The rocking filled her mind. She twisted hair around one finger and let it uncoil before twisting it back again. She could sit there, doing it on and on, staring ahead. It might be restful to sit endlessly, mindless, while others tiptoed around her feelings. Then, remembering that back in high school, girls who twisted their hair were said to be sexually frustrated, she set her hands into her lap. When Miss Birdy said, "Is that your momma?" glancing at a visitor passing the door, Allie looked there before saying, "No."

Miss Precious leaned forward and whispered into Miss Birdy's ear, who said, "Oh ho," and looked back at Allie. "Anyway, sugar, you've got pretty ankles."

"Ankles ain't the same as titties to men," Miss Precious said, snickering behind one hand. "Whole town waited to see if she'd get her momma's. A blessing she didn't. Them titties were May's downfall. Couldn't resist sticking them in the face of anything in pants."

"She is more boyish than her momma," Miss Birdy whispered.

"Boyish!" Allie cried. "And you do so know my momma." She grabbed her piece of hair again.

"Do not. The woman is dead."

"I combed May's hair out while she lay in her coffin," Miss Precious said, "though it had to be closed."

"Closed?" Allie said, letting go of her hair.

"Whew! It stinks in here." Miss Precious covered her nose, glaring at Miss Birdy. Blushing, Miss Birdy said, "You're the polecat. Always thought your shit didn't stink."

"Ladies!" Allie said.

"You've got a problem," the old man said. When Allie met his cold stare, he said, "You keep doing this." He tapped repeatedly on a front tooth with one finger.

"I do?" Allie said.

"You do it all the time," he said, in disgust.

"I never knew it," she said. "I'll have to watch out. I guess I'm nervous."

"You're wasting your time," he said. Standing, Allie said, "Wasting it how?" feeling the old man had some strange sense of clarity about things, and wanting to ask, Wasting it here, or always? Tears burned her eyes.

"You ought to be at the dentist right now," he said.

She went through twisting corridors as rapidly as possible, not having given the old ladies her usual promise that she'd see them soon. At the reception desk, a nurse bounced up, pleading for her to help wheel residents back to their rooms, as the staff was shorthanded. Allie pushed forward through the circling door without answering. On the front porch, she met the Negro, who said, "I carried them flowers for you."

"Oh, thank you," Allie said.

"Where can I spend thanks?" he said.

Turning back confusedly, opening her purse, she had no change and shoved him a bill, seeing at the last moment it was five dollars. She went on to the parking lot, and circulated about as if in a maze, unable to find her car, wishing for once she'd adopted the practice of adorning her antenna with a baby shoe, or a small Confederate flag, or some other distinguishing object: like the red fox tail John Q had tied to his. On the verge of tears, she had the same sense of abandonment and terror she once had getting separated from Poppa or Grandmomma in a store; always it seemed they'd lost her intentionally. She never dared look for them, fearing Poppa's saying, God dog it, how'd you find us, you little bugger? and that she was to burden them forevermore. When they found her, they were never quite comforting enough, never understanding the enormity of her relief. Kids lost these days stood bawling their heads off. If Momma was sneaking away, she'd be mighty embarrassed; then treats were given them to relieve their traumas, while she'd been afraid to cry out, fearing Poppa's thumping thumb to her head, as children in those days were to be seen and not heard.

It seemed a fateful, kindly accident when the car turned up. She gasped when someone touched her arm, as she was about to get in. "Don't be scared," said the Negro porter, when she whirled. "Here." He tucked the bill back into her hand free of her purse.

She stuck the money out again. "Go on and keep it."

"No'm." Pointing to a lighter coloring in the sky, an arctic reflection that was the town lights of Oxford, near the university, he said, "The Negro peoples are being uplifted tonight," and loped off.

17

SHE DROVE AWAY feeling the car limping, and wondered if she'd find a filling station open on Sunday evening. *The Homemaker* had predicted the future would be a world called unisex, bringing to her mind images only of animals and bicycles. Such a world would be boring if men all became sissies, but in it she might know something about automobiles. Lifting a hood and poking here and there, men performed miracles. In countryside unlike home, the hillsides here being red, she admitted to herself that she had left home hoping for adventure, though probably it was unrealistic to hope something outside herself would change her life.

Still, was it not natural for people feeling distressed to bank on outward things, chance, whim, or superstitious symbols? Had a black cat crossed her path now, she'd have turned and gone another direction. She had chosen a back road because breaking down on the new super meant she could stop at Stuckey's where a uniformed, competent attendant would fix the car in a hurry, while she deliberated about buying a sack of their divinity with pecans. She'd have lost the debate and eaten a whole sackful, hating herself afterward. Her entire moral life seemed made up of such small decisions, except for Bear — and that decision was taken from her hands. Always, she had been so law-abiding. She quaked if her dime was about to run out in a Memphis parking meter. She had never exceeded a posted speed limit. While she and Tate voted Republican in national elections, in local ones they often canceled out one another's vote. Yet she was among early birds at the Masonic Hall, voting, along with farmers going to the fields, feeling it her duty.

A gas pump rising out of the late dusk seemed a lit, giant lollipop in a Hollywood fantasy. She pulled up to a shellacked yellow pine store, a jerry-built affair, with a sign saying "*Open.*" She was always suspicious when a store had to advertise the fact. The window displayed miniature toilets that were ashtrays with "*Drop In Anytime*" on their raised lids; and flimsy Confederate caps for kids who no longer knew much about the Civil War, except that it was caused by meddlesome Yankees — people with rapid speech who pronounced all their *r*'s, who visited Miami and said they'd been down South, who could not pinpoint the state of Mississippi on a map, people who lived in towns that all ran together, and who said that Southerners said *Nigra* to be derogatory, when it was only their speech pattern: when they wanted to be derogatory, they said *nigger.* A barely jolted bell tinkled as she entered a shellacked and antiseptic interior without any country-store smells. Something about its emptiness and clinical atmosphere sent warning shivers down her spine, but she went to the rear where a curtain of flour sacks stitched together partitioned off living quarters. Possibly the store was run by Chinese misplaced from the Delta, the only people she knew who lived in their groceries. Yet it seemed unlikely those quiet people would be playing some caterwauling music so loudly. Her nerves were on edge from it. Having shaken the curtain, having called "Yoo hoo" repeatedly, knowing no way to make herself heard, she finally yanked the damn thing aside.

She stared first at tight, hard white buttocks, and then into the startled eyes of their owner, blue ones nearly obscured by a golden beard and shaggy hair, watching their look change into amusement. "Hep you, ma'm?" the boy said. Reaching for a striped grease-monkey's suit lying on a chair, stepping slowly into it, he slithered the zipper only waist high, leaving exposed more curly golden hair. "Please excuse me," Allie said, trying to be casual. "Something's wrong with my car. I hollered." She nodded toward the phonograph. "A red light won't go off."

"Your fan belt. If you come a ways, car'll have to cool off before I can look at her." He raised a beer can. "Have a brew?"

"No thanks. But you can fix it?"

"Depends." Leaning straight-armed to a table between them, and bringing himself closer, he kept his look of amusement. Allie raised a hand to a pulse beating in her throat. "Sure you don't want a brew?" She shook her head, knowing she reddened. He knew she could have slapped that curtain back, or turned away, and that she'd taken a good, long gape and enjoyed it. She stared past him, glad when she could look in the direction his finger pointed, at a bulky cube on the floor. "Sure?" he said.

"That a little icebox?" She tried to keep her voice steady.

"Refrigerator."

"I meant," she said. Her voice rose disastrously, but she waved away with a jerky hand having slipped into the past, a habit she had with some words. What matter, though for certainly the boy could tell how old she was by her face. As if to shrug those years away, she let her shoulders rise and settle, and found herself obeying. For, as he still pointed, she went to the refrigerator for a beer, asking into the coolness what on earth she was doing. When she was old enough to be his mother, why did she tremble with shyness before him, and how could his eyes make her feel funny, when he was young enough to be her son? Would women like her, trained to be submissive, always feel so toward any male not actually a child? She could not open the beer and handed him the can. "There you go," he said, with a grin. She had difficulty taking the beer, since he clamped fingers down over her own. It was hard to believe he was making a pass. At me? At my age? After so many years, wasn't it understandable that she felt excited? Though, absolutely, she realized he'd make a pass at a female gorilla, if one walked in — he was that type. Beer dripped from her chin when she drank hastily, hating the taste.

Why wasn't she free of being reduced this way, having lived thirty years with a man and heard him take a crap and a leak, knowing one's humanness: once so filled with the idea that men belonged on pedestals. First hearing Tate toot in the bathroom on their honeymoon, she'd jerked off her ring, staring at the small diamond as if it were fake.

The boy straddled a chair, talking endlessly about the nature of fan belts, while she thought about his hard-on when he'd first turned, and that it had nothing to do with her, but was the nearly permanent erection of youth. Wistful, Tate said recently it'd been so long since he went around with a hard-on all day, he'd forgotten how it was. Now the boy's would not leave her abashed mind's eye. She wondered what Tate used to do with his, for she'd said no too frequently, regretting it now these lonesome years later. For girls like her, sex had been associated with wrong: how were they supposed to change overnight because they stood up before a preacher? The boy realized she was not drinking and said, "I got some Three Feathers and some 7-Up, if you'd rather?"

She hated saying no thanks, when he wanted to please as

obviously as a wiggly puppy. "Let's check the car now." She stood up.

"Drink your brew, then we'll see. No hurry."

"It's late. I'm afraid of getting lost."

"You're not going to get lost. I'm going to tell you exactly how to go wherever you want to."

His comforting air made her sit down again and pick up her beer. Flattening his can with one hand, he sailed it to a wastebasket filled with similar ones. With two strides, and an air of surety, he crossed the room. Watching, Allie thought of the difference in this generation, and how hard it was to believe so many men in Tate's actually came through the war still virgins. The VD propaganda movies had scared the bejesus out of them, Tate'd said, describing one where a soldier went into a bar and saw an ugly woman, and how she evolved into Dorothy Lamour after he'd had a few drinks. When the next shot showed him in the medic's office, hangdog and sick, the moral was clear. The boy set another beer in front of her.

"What's the story?" He sat backward in his chair again, his eyes fixed to her knees. Finding them so tightly clamped they seemed stuck by perspiration, and that her hemline parted after her row of stout buttons, revealing them, she meant to tuck the folds together properly, then changed her mind. She swung a leg and let be noted one of the ankles she was known for. "Story?" she said, a little mystified. Why had she chosen the pattern for her matronly brown dress, except that she had always dressed too conservatively? "I have no story." She met his eyes when he looked up at the sound of her swishing stockings. "I just took some flowers to the old people's home. I've got more than car trouble, since my husband didn't want me to come near the university."

"Jesus God, that mess!" He got up and kicked his chair away. "Your generation sucks! It's your fault." He squashed his beer can between his palms and flexed his arms. "You sold out all those coming behind you, is what you done. So washed out from the Depression you don't have enough balls not to give in to niggers. Let me ast you something. A nigger ever taken anything away from you?" He gave her no time to answer, shouting, "No! But I got a brother will be in the first graduating class with niggers if they integrate the schools. They're already saying they'll call off graduation. You know how important that is to a kid."

She lifted her beer. "Why call it off?"

"He'd be embarrassed to walk down the aisle with niggers, in front of Momma and his aunts and uncles!" His eyes reduced to pinpoints. "Let me tell you something. In ten years it'll be my generation running things. Then you'll see a switcharoo. Integration been crammed down our th'oats and nothing to say about it. Wait."

"Could we turn down the Victrola?" she said, looking about the little quarters and thinking the boy would never run anything.

"Stereo?" As he went toward it, she again waved a dismissing hand and repeated the word after him. "You don't like the Beach Boys?"

"Not if that's them," she said.

He battered his chest with a steady fist. "Rah-rah for your school. That's what they're singing about. Sounds corny, but it gets me here. I wish often I hadn't of quit school." His lost look made her wariness of him vanish. She felt similar feelings could bridge an age difference. "What's your life like now?"

"My life's beat," he said. She thought, So young? watching him with sympathy, as he closed his eyes and silently sang out of a wet mouth with the record on the Vic — the stereo. She felt isolated with him in this service station on a back road, in his barely lit back room, not as if they were shipwrecked together but rather abandoned by everyone who had loved them once. A horn had a hollow sound down the road, though something told her to listen more closely — that there was a commotion. By the time she listened to herself, however, the sound had vanished, and the country night returned to its great silence, penetrated only by frogs and crickets. She had been thinking, in fact, about changes in the countryside and its people; people adapted to new ways more easily than would have been guessed. She let her eyes stray to the boy's crotch and his huge thighs as he abruptly stood and sailed another flattened can to the wastebasket. His eyes meeting hers had their same amused understanding as he remained wide legged and said, "Ready?"

"No." She made herself take another bitter sip, watching his tall figure move away again with great striding steps. Being able to adapt to new ways meant maturity, and the times were not so virtuous as they once were. Was she truly wrong to have one extramarital adventure before old age set in?

From behind, the boy drew her up by the armpits, as if she were weightless, and, turning her around, set his boozy-smelling mouth to hers, pulled back, and said, "How long was you going to set there and not make a move?"

"Till I left," she said, laughing. "Boy, I've never done anything like this." Out of the family way, as the local expression went. He lifted his eyebrows and smirked: he'd heard that one before. He began undoing her buttons, frowning at each one and becoming clumsy as Tate had when fumbling with her clothes. She wanted to laugh; she wanted to stroke his hair — he was absorbed like a child with the cloth book that teaches them to lace shoes, tie knots. She finally looked at the wall beyond his right ear, growing more and more excited and terrified the farther down he went. On a wall shelf sat several healthy green plants with leaves so shiny he must have coated them, and close by was a yellow box of the same plant food she used. She was moved by his wanting something to care for. She vicariously lived his loneliness as he tried to make the ugly back room some kind of home.

"You ought to get a dog," she said.

"Huh?" He was not listening. He was pulling her shoulders bare, her dress off her back, while she stood frozen still. She lifted her feet as if they were fragile and stepped out of her clothes. Then she dug her nails to his hands and absolutely refused to take off her underwear till she was under the sheet. He stared with puzzled eyes, saying, "Everybody's got their nutsy thing." He got naked himself.

She wanted to laugh that he saw no reason for her not appearing naked in front of all his youth and strength. She felt scared enough about wearing a full-length sateen slip with a zipper along one side; it must seem as old-fashioned to him as Grandmomma's homemade straight cotton ones had to her. She was glad the zipper pulled in her waist, glad that her figure was not stout middle-aged, but she was not twenty, or thirty, or forty either. Underneath the top sheet, she finally removed her slip and girdle and stockings and dropped them all to the floor. He watched, shaking his head. She hoped he had not noticed the girdle. His interest seemed mainly on her being undressed. Once she lay down he held gently his large purple thing. She was afraid for a moment he was going to masturbate; but he only wanted to show her, pleased again as a child. "Got something for you," he said.

Before she could answer, he had his mouth on one breast. She had to jerk her chin out of his way. Aren't I entitled to this? she thought, staring at the ceiling, waiting for a great rush of pleasure that never came. Who are you? some other self kept asking. It seems ridiculous you're here, the self scolded. She shrugged. Lifting one arm in a limp way behind his head, she looked at her wristwatch and guessed this was about the time Miss Precious and Miss Birdy were having their evening treat, fruit juice in fluted paper cups nearly the size of a thimble. Oh, what is ahead? she wondered. She closed her eyes and felt the need to nourish and to care, whether she were any more moved or not. When she looked again at the top of his head and at his thick hair and the curly beard round his ears, she pressed him closer. With her fingers clutching his head, she caught sight of her little diamond, as if it were trying hard to shine through. Then Tate's face swam through tears in her eyes, and Poppa's, and old men huddled on the store porches shaking their heads. Finally there were the four white stores of town and their gas pumps, with the Baptist church not far away from the copse of woods and the pastureland where buzzards still circled so knowingly after all these years.

All that vision vanished when, after several hard tries, he finally pushed inside her. She did not know if she should apologize — even the very first time it had happened with John Q had not been as difficult as now. Wasn't he surprised a woman her age was hard to penetrate? He seemed satisfied and, with eyes as blue as a doll's closed, rocked as if on a horse. She was glad his eyes were shut, for there was no way she could not grimace against the pain, or keep from gritting her teeth until her neck ached, shocked by her own terrible dryness. Quickly, she opened her eyes when he stopped, relaxed her pained expression. The boyish eyes peered down. "Hey," he said.

"What?"

"What's your name?"

"Betty. What's yours?"

"Just call me Buster. That's all anybody's ever done. I just am a Buster!" He rode on. She wondered how long it was going to take, why he couldn't finish. Never had Tate taken so long.

"Flip," he said.

His hands gentle, turning her so lightly, she found herself backside up in surprise, her nose squashed to a pillow. She was fearful at once about how her butt looked to him. What was to happen? Her nipples were sore from not having been used in so long, and were like raw blisters against the rough sheet. She pulled to her elbows to protect her breasts and stared into the pillow in wonder at making love backward. She drew up gradually onto her knees, feeling the degradation of being an animal, but finding she liked the position. Had Tate not known about making love this way? If she could tell him, suggest it, could they resume lovemaking? Did she really care? His suspicions would certainly be aroused. She smiled thinking of telling him she read about the position in *The Homemaker*, where she found out so much else.

"Flip," he said. Over she went, like a bubble floating through air. All the guilt this was going to lead to was worth it, she decided.

It was amazing these interruptions did not make Buster lose his erection; he was in her front or back the instant she turned. Tate lost it if a dog barked outside their bedroom window. She tried to remember the first time she'd left their bedroom door open to hear Poppa if he called out. Unable to recall the exact time in her marriage, she saw herself saying nothing as she opened the door, as Tate lay in bed. Some small expression had crossed his face so quickly she had been uncertain of it, though imagined there had been a faint grimace: a grimace of acceptance, of years having passed. What changes would come into their lives when Poppa was gone?

Even lying flat, her legs had begun to shake. She was exhausted. On her knees, her trembling arms trying to hold her weight, she could not go on much longer. But be a quitter? Why couldn't he finish? Finally she looked up at him again, knowing that she had to stop. "Would you like to finish?" She meant that as a hint, but it was lost on Buster. "Otherwise, I have to go to the bathroom."

He appeared to think, then nodded to himself. He slid out. "Go on, so we can keep at this longer."

She sat on the edge of the bed and waited for her legs to stop trembling. Then, reaching for his grease-monkey's suit, she wrapped it around her body to run in front of him to the bathroom. Was he watching? When she looked back he was staring at the ceiling and lighting a cigarette.

She supported herself into the bathroom by grabbing hold of the washbasin. Lowering to the toilet was difficult because she shook. She sighed deeply and leaned against the toilet tank, glad for its moistness, coolness, and mostly to rest. Why couldn't he finish? Maybe he was a pervert? She was crazy to have got into this. She clamped down on her knees to make her feet stay to the floor, her legs still shaking. Her urine felt hot: it chafed rather than relieved her burning. Her chaste former life seemed so sane and precious. If only she could leave without seeing him. Light came from a mermaid atop some shells, whose breasts were outsized and painted with phosphorescent red paint. How long could she wait and stare without his thinking something had happened to her? She pulled herself up finally. Finding blood was a shock; years and years seemed to file past. It was not funny to try to think of herself as young and virginal again. Instead she was furious that her body had behaved like this, when she had this chance, when there should be triumph that a young boy wanted to go to bed with her: no matter who he was, she couldn't be awful-looking, at least.

Buster was as she'd left him. He began again. "Flip," he said, at intervals.

She was finally at her wit's end. One more rub along her raw insides and she would have to scream. "Can I ask you something?" she dared. He stopped and gave her a still look. "Are you having a hard time finishing, or don't you want to?"

Something like a spasm crossed his face. He seemed about to speak, then only a darker look came into his eyes before he began again. It was obvious her question was too stupid to answer—she knew that now herself. Simply, he was unbelievable and she too dumb to appreciate him; some knowledge about life seemed to have escaped her, not knowing before people made such love. His voice was low. "I bet you've never had much, Betty. Bet there's been only your husband, me, and maybe one other fellow. How long since you last had it?"

Protective of Tate, not wanting to be felt sorry for, or to admit there'd been no other fellow, she said, "New Year's Eve," thinking that not so considerable a time, and remembering how she and Tate once celebrated it.

Buster saw things differently. "That long! What's your old man do, stroke the bishop?"

She answered truthfully. "I have no idea."

"Well, what'd you like? I want to do something you'd really like."

"I can't think of anything. Is there something you would?" She was a little fearful.

"It's not me hadn't had it since last New Year's."

"Eve," she said, smiling.

"Come on. Tell me something you'd like."

"I'd like for you to — come."

His cheeks puffed out. Afterward, she meant to leave. But Buster pulled her against him and lit another cigarette. Surprised that companionship came along with random sex, she wanted to see this affair to its end. Later, she would think about what to say at home. "I wish I hadn't of quit school," Buster said softly. "This here life's lonesome. My daddy run out on all us. My momma went from bad to worse. Wasn't her men that bothered me though. One day I came into the house and she was in bed with my oldest sister."

"My Lord," Allie said. She grabbed his thigh and was glad to find she could still be shocked; it had been a long time.

"Listen, if you want to stay all night, you could."

"Thanks, but I couldn't." She pictured facing him in the morning. And knew staying meant she'd sleep in her makeup.

"Now, tell me what's your story," he said.

Sketching briefly the years with Tate, she thought how dull they must sound. She might make Tate some wounded war hero, but could think of nothing interesting for herself. Then she spiced up her life a little by telling about her mother, without concluding that she thought the guilty Negro was hiding across the road from her own house, now.

"At least I know what I seen," Buster said. "You've never figured out what you really do know. Boy, do you know something. Standing right outside that cabin when it all happened. What happened after you heard the shot inside? Said you heard it."

"I thought maybe it was a backfire on the road."

"Bullshit," he said. "I bet you was standing there wondering what your momma was doing so long in there with black boy. Don't say again, teaching him to read! Kids know things."

"Like, I knew she was teaching Elgie an awful lot of times how to read?" she said slowly. Maybe too hard and too fast? "But I grew up with old men sitting round store porches and snickering about everybody. I chose to believe they were wrong, and that people were good. Only, it usually turned out they were right about what was going on. In fact, they really never guessed at something so bad, somebody wasn't doing it." She tried hard to think back. "If I did know the next minute it wasn't backfire, I was too young to guess somebody was being shot. Gunfire was just part of my existence. Poppa and Elgie were always shooting round the house at birds, or at pigeons in the barn, or at squirrels and quail. I never was afraid of guns, or of Negroes either."

"White folks weren't, back then," Buster said. "Niggers were just scared of each other. Too bad that day's ended." He threw back the cover and yawned. "It was just a black son of a bitch. I wouldn't worry none you did nothing about a accident."

"Accident?" she said, leaning up.

"Hell, I thought that was what you was saying. Never mind. You said you didn't believe he'd have shot her on purpose. Sounds like you liked black boy yourself."

"I was five," she said. "I loved him. He'd always seen after me. Taught me to shoot at tin cans. Taught me a lot."

"What the hell, they got rid of the motherfucker. Took the attitude if he hadn't of done it, they could think of a lot of things he might be going to do. So, get rid of him while they could."

Had he chosen *motherfucker* on purpose, or only used a common expression? "Momma was yelling at him. White women didn't yell at Negroes. I jumped up and down and couldn't really see anything. After the shot, Elgie ran fast and took off over the pasture. It was, Buster, as if the whole town had just been waiting. Because men on the store porches came running. On the road where the pasture ended, two white men stopped in a truck. Elgie ran headlong into them."

Buster laughed. "That was it, man!"

"That was it," she said quietly.

"Forget the past, it don't hold nothing for you."

She could not let it go, Allie thought. Not all of it. Now, she would leave. Then Buster tweaked one of her breasts, and she settled back for a little longer. "You always been that flat?" he said.

She glanced toward the bathroom and the mermaid's red glow, supposing she deserved anything. The remark stung, innocent though it was. Repeating, "Flat?" she pretended to laugh.

"Yeah," he said. "Flat."

"Why? What do you want?" She could guess.

"I want you more pointy. Haven't you ever been more pointy?" He fashioned a tepee with his hands.

"I suppose when I was fourteen," she said, getting up.

Still in ignorance that it was age, he said, "Well, I suppose you've just got what you've got." He went to urinate loudly with the door open.

When he came back she was dressed, but had one bare leg. "I can't find one of my stockings."

"Look for it," he said.

"I have. Everywhere."

"Look under the bed."

She said, "I did," but, feeling helpless, got on her knees to look again. Then she was stunned, and did not believe the weight on her back. She waited in silence for him to remove his foot; afraid to look around or speak. He pressed her almost flat. "Grovel," he said, pressing more. "Let me see you God-damn grovel, Betty."

She was afraid to do anything but obey. She looked under the bed and then under the skirt of an ottoman. Buster lifted his pressure, allowing her to go on her knees to feel under the rug's edge, to search under a far chair, knowing these places impossible for the stocking, but not knowing what else to do. "Crawl. Crawl," he said.

"Buster," she said, in a pleading way as she had several times, with no response. "Please. Let me look in the covers."

She could feel him thinking, remembered how his blue eyes had a startled look then. "Jesus," he said, laughing to himself. He let her up.

She rose and rubbed her aching knees. His back was to her, as he changed the record. She thought it better to say nothing, not tempt him to start up again. Just as he turned around, she felt a lump in her girdle and reached up and drew out the stocking, feeling foolish. "Jesus," he said. "You are crazy." She did not feel like saying the thought was reciprocal. She held the stocking and walked out stiffly. "Please see about the car."

At the door, waiting while he went out past her, she put on the stocking. Buster stood as if bathing himself in delight in the pale glow from the gas pump. Only she worried because he was naked. "You're lucky," he said, coming back in. "It's just a small outer belt, or I couldn't do her." He whistled with his head under the hood, his backside gleaming. "Got-cha," he said, wiping his hands. She went out and paid what he asked, wondering how you said goodbye to a stranger you'd had sex with. She found out: you said the conventional. "Come back to see me, hear?" Buster said.

She found herself saying in a polite voice, "I had a nice time," the way Grandmomma had taught her to do after visiting. She got into the car, and Buster hung through the window.

"Can I tell somebody?"

"What?" she said.

"Can I tell some friends?"

"No!"

In astonishment, she forgot he was naked. "Please," he said. "But why?"

"Because my friends all think I'm kind of like spacey." He drew a circle at one temple with a finger. "They'd never think a nice, respectable married woman forty years old" — and plainly something registered on her face, because he said, " — forty-five" — and something registered again, because he lifted a hand and said, "hell, fifty-year-old woman would come in here and hop in the sack with me. I won't tell many. I won't tell but one. Just one friend. Please. Don't you have one friend you'll tell?"

Feeling lonesome about it, she said, "No."

Standing without a stitch on and wiggly and eager still as a puppy, he said, "I'm not going to tell your name, that your car come from Brewster's Car Sales in Nashtoba, like it says on the bumper, not your license plate, not nothing."

It would seem to deny a hungry child one tiny cookie that wouldn't spoil his supper. She said finally, "All right."

Those moments he'd been so domineering, shoving her to the floor, proved her private belief that men did not very much like women. Wouldn't those blue eyes get wide if he knew she'd had no orgasm; though truthfully that was not Buster's fault. She glanced back to see him standing at the pump, buck naked and waving her down the road.

18

REARVIEW MIRRORS tend to be flattering. Meeting her flecked green eyes as she looked back at Buster, Allie wondered if she could pass for forty-five. Suddenly the answer seemed unimportant, since her age had not mattered to him. Despite her guilt, she had the disturbing feeling again that having upheld morality so long, she had missed out on some living.

With no illumination but the moon, the night seemed closed in on itself as tight as a bud, or a tick, or a drum, and to be as dead as a doornail. All the old clichés applied to Negroes came automatically to mind — black as the ace of spades, and black as a raven's wing. Black as pitch? she thought lamely. If the car crashed and she died, the stars would remain fixed and the moon's face go on looking amused. She felt like a minute bug scurrying for cover. When she was with Buster, she had wanted Tate, though his lovemaking had never been so good. More importantly, when Tate rested, it wasn't to ask her name, but to share a mute sense of affection when their eyes met; that was worth far more than any orgasm: between them they acknowledged a backlog of mutual associations.

Affection was harder to come by than passion, or love even. People fell out of love, while affection could last. Love was talked about too easily. Women left stores in town and said I love you instead of goodbye. At Christmastime, *The Democrat* published in Nashtoba printed letters from children to Santa. More and more the letters began, Santa, I love you. A list of toys followed. The children were being taught to manipulate with love — warm up the old man first, kid. On TV's inane quiz shows, the host often signed off by crying, I love you, folks! From the audience they shrieked the same back to him.

Against the steering wheel her small diamond was shadowy. She had not let Tate buy her a larger one. Once she had walked into an engagement party and found the girls all comparing their rings; the size of their carats had seemed to determine how much they loved the men who gave them. A feeling like melting was called love, when it was often only physical attraction. Try to tell someone you held them in affection, though, and the words were apt to stick in your throat. The other person would probably be embarrassed. Her and Tate's moods often matched. Without a word, he'd dig out an album of Confederate songs. At the end a man, supposedly General Lee, said "I bid you an affectionate farewell." Then she and Tate sat shamelessly crying; neither would have been moved had the General said, I love you men.

When she reached the road's dead end, the night was alive

again with a commotion similar to the one she'd heard back in the filling station. Pickups flew past, their beds filled with screaming young men, and cars loaded with them passed. She remembered Governor Barnett's inflamed speech to a crowd at a football game the previous day. The fool had sent all the rabble-rousers in the countryside to the university tonight. If trouble came, President Kennedy meant to send in additional law enforcement. The morning paper said he'd recruit men from their normal duties as prison guards and border patrolmen; they were the scum of the earth to start. Didn't he know that? Decent folks would share the blame for all this trouble. Because when outsiders looked at Mississippi, they didn't differentiate between different kinds of people in the state — everybody was a red-neck. So we go on being the whipping boy, Allie was thinking.

Suddenly a familiar maroon truck overlaid with silver passed. From the antenna John Q's red fox tail flew its length. She would have cried out to him if he could hear her.

Never before had she understood the Catholic practice of crossing yourself; now one hand made an *x* on her chest, touching faintly the sore tips of her breasts. The closest she'd been to a Catholic church was passing the one in Nashtoba. She knew little more about Catholicism than what she'd learned from old movies on TV. Feeling the need for something beyond her usual religious experience, she said aloud, "Holy Mary, Mother of God." Openmouthed, she wondered why Mary had no prominence in her own Protestant religion, or any female saint. She considered the kind of men she knew would not pray to a woman. Did Catholic men, or only other women?

After the last car passed, she turned in an opposite direction and headed back through the lonesome dark area of the dam site. She'd never had gumption to mention feeling dubious about the virgin-birth theory, to say men wrote the Bible and had to believe in Mary's purity, the way unconsciously they had to believe in that of their own mothers. What man conceived of his mother's having fucked to get him?

Jesus was always pictured as too frail, tubercular, and effeminate-looking for her taste. Tate's momma had not helped the image when she gave such a portrait to the church. A kid had sneaked in and drawn on a pair of gold-rimmed spectacles; the picture vanished from the sanctuary. Even then she'd wanted to ask why Jesus could not look hale and full of wry humor the way country people really were. Finally, she passed through the countryside feeling she could not call on anyone substantial for help tonight, except a mysterious force found in nature, called God for lack of another name. Saints, candles, statuary, genuflecting, and other trappings of religion would have to stay where she found them: in old movies with Bing Crosby, Spencer Tracy, or Pat O'Brien. Always, she was mystified as to why Catholics carried their problems to nuns and priests, because the last person she'd think could help her was someone who'd never lived with a member of the opposite sex.

For once, she drove faster than the law allowed, slowing only to cross the old bridge over Grey Wolf River. Mosquitoes in the bottomland were supposedly as large as horseflies; hearing their humming, she could believe that. The road dipped as she drove toward town. Then her headlights picked up the fuzzed lights on store porches, the stores blacked out by night. Allie drove quickly past her own driveway. A pickup was pulled sharply to Loma's steps, as if it had crashed into them. Snake Johnson, weaving past his weak headlights, suddenly fell to the ground. She got out. She was sickened by the sight of four dead dogs lying crushed in the road; tire marks could be seen across the bodies.

"Who's that!" Snake cried.

She let out her breath. "It's Allie." Stepping forward, she had a hard time not kicking him. "Mongrel. You're the one that ought to be dead."

He rolled over and sat against a cinder block. He said through spittle, "I didn't kill none of them dogs, woman. I almost smacked up my truck trying not to run over them again."

"Snake," she said, "you could have killed people. You should never drive through town so fast."

"I didn't done it! If I had of I'd have gone to bed by now."

There was truth in that. "Did you see who did?"

"No'm."

"You didn't see somebody leave Cottondale ahead of you, Snake?"

"No'm."

"Somebody you don't want to say, is what you mean."

He got up to reel toward her, and putting out her hands protectively, she supported him; he righted himself, while she held her breath against the stinks of vomit and whiskey. Tiny tears appeared in the corners of his eyes. Weak tears, as weak as his knees.

"I'm a dog lover myse'f," he managed. "Go home and keep your mouth shut."

"Shut, my foot," she shot back. She went over, crushing her hands together at having to look at the three worst mutts, one hardly recognizable as a dog, cadavers already, having no meat on their skeletons to start. She realized one still breathed, not that the dog's poor crushed sides moved, but one eye, as the dog lay on its side unable to move, had a winking eyelash with a huge mistrustful pupil that dared her to come close. "Snake, this one's still alive. Put the poor thing out of its misery."

"That thing'll die by itself."

"You can't leave these dogs here for kids to see coming through here in the morning. Now, shoot this one. We'll drag them all off to the gully behind Mose's."

"I'm draggin' my carcass to bed."

She met him at his truck door, swung open. She stood as close as she could to say, "Somebody drove through here aiming straight at these dogs. It was a game. You know it was probably Quad Brewster."

"It could have been niggers. It could have been somebody on a motorcycle. It could have been any bunch of hooligans from around here."

"Shoot the dog," she said.

He moved to get into the truck instead. Allie shoved him, sending him sliding down his truck door to the ground, as blank and mindless as a tackling dummy. She took his shotgun from the rack and got shells from his glove compartment, where she knew they'd be kept. After loading the gun, she looked around to see him kneeling, pulling himself up at last by the truck door, and not quite knowing what was going on. She reminded herself to be brave. She took a dose of air into her lungs and walked with solid feet to the center of the road, where she put a shot through the dog's small head. "Were you afraid to do it, Snake?" she said, turning back.

"I'm sick already," he said.

"You're going to be sicker if you don't get your gun back. You're not getting it back until we toss these dogs out of sight of town."

He stared at her with hatred. She imagined no woman since his momma had told him what to do. After he picked up the first dog by its hind legs, she replaced the gun in his truck and carried the dog she'd shot in the same way. Snake brought the other two; they sailed out of sight into deep grass. She knew the buzzards would be there early in the morning: saw them against the blue sky sailing and sailing.

Behind her, Sy's cabin seemed to follow her home, as solidly as a large stranger, for hadn't someone briefly appeared on the porch, in the dark, who was not Sy: someone who seemed to be watching to see that she was all right?

On the way home hadn't she seen a car coming straight toward her, whose headlights suddenly disappeared from the road? She had without really thinking about it assumed the car had gone down a side road — but at that point there was none. She knew too late it had turned into a cotton field, its headlights doused, waiting until she passed.

19

For some time country people had been slowly learning the new vocabulary of prosperity. Now, they froze rather than canned. They talked of boating and water-skiing on the government dam, and more recently of sailboating, something of a marvel still as local people stood on the dam's banks wondering how the boats skimming the water like giant moths were steered; of course the word *segregation* had been known always, but by now *integration* was on the tip of everyone's tongue.

Standing at the den window, Allie watched a small exodus of cars, people heading out to work in Memphis, or to nearby small towns strung along Highway 51. Here, nationally known businesses had built branches that manufactured records, children's underwear, shirts, elevators, and other objects with well-known names, so that everybody was tickled to have them settle in this part of the world. The number of people departing for the day grew every year: their motors, as they roared out too fast, unsettled the former quiet of the mornings. Watching, she thought how strange it was to think about commuting from here. She could never have guessed how life here would come to be, certainly not that she'd step outside when things were wet with dew and have fumes from traffic along with the smell of pasture grass reach her nose.

She thought back to a more flowery time when *The Democrat*'s society editor wrote up her wedding, wishing her much success on the sea of matrimony. She had not thought that could mean troubled waters. Now, she decided not to speak to Tate about Iona. Even Jesus forgave the adulteress the first time. If Tate had had a fling, she thought it had been only once. She was now guilty too, but did not feel especially gleeful. If the scale was balanced, it would not tip again in her favor.

Late that Sunday night, she sensed a difference between them when she crept into bed. The whole house seemed to reproach her: lights had been left on for her convenience. She could not remember ever coming into the house in the small hours and having the men already asleep. Surprisingly, the supper dishes were washed. Left to drain, they were as direct a reproach as if Tate stood there confronting her. She did not take time to cream her face, but put on her nightgown. She lay in the bed's contours she had shaped over thirty years; Tate lay in his own. With his back to her, he seemed unapproachable. For the first time she could not say, Hon, I'm home. He might only sit up furiously and want to know where she'd been. She looked at moonlight on the ceiling and knew that in the morning there would be no wiles, that ignorance and helplessness were lost to her as crutches.

She could not sleep and thought of milestones in her life. She had had nothing to do with her mother's death. John Q's molesting her had happened because she did not know how to stop it. Fearing embarrassment, she had kept quiet about the whole thing. Marriage was the largest step she had taken. But that had come about through a certain amount of pressure: Tate's insistence but also wartime. Probably, the temper of the times was the most important, for girls were not supposed to do anything but get married. She had attended Mississippi State College for Women for two years, compelled to wear only navy-blue clothes, as if this were penitential punishment. Though what good did college do a woman? people wondered. She might get ideas as uppity as a Negro going North: ones that would do her no good in the long run. If the fiasco with Bear had come to something more, she knew that back then she'd have confessed to Tate. No matter how she begged forgiveness, a breach would have been created in the marriage, and she'd have been called a loose woman. That incident would not have happened if she had not been innocently given liquor. So she had gone to bed with Buster willingly, and on her own. She had not felt pushed into it. All my life, Allie thought, I've had to react. I never did much on my own. The boy seemed to affirm her identity. He could have been anyone, anyone at all. She had done something that made her think suddenly, This is me. That was something I simply wanted to do.

She had not been unfaithful to Tate. She had only been faithful to herself after so much time. It was a good feeling, even if she felt ashamed too. She would not have gotten involved with someone where love might be concerned. She would never run around back roads like some other women, meeting men in their pickups. Facing down Snake, she had felt brave and had taken the reins in her own hands. Now she had to face as well the void in her life that being childless had meant. Closing her eyes, she let the fact surface. In earlier times, it had been a mark against a woman not to have children, and no one ever considered that it might be her husband's fault. No doctor she consulted ever suggested that Tate be checked, although the idea had occurred to her. Men had seemed to shield one another. She had known that if Tate were proved at fault, his masculinity would have come into question. She had preferred to take the blame.

Having assessed her weaknesses, she felt strong.

She slept late and did not hear the men get up. She was startled to turn over and find the bed empty; last night had not prepared her for that. She dressed and went into the kitchen. Poppa ate cold cereal before TV. Tate would have told him some story about her being late that pacified the old man. Tate sat drinking coffee and said nothing when she came in. Realizing how seldom they argued, she expected things to go smoothly. Tate's habit was to say nothing when bothered, and he kept stirring his coffee. She leaned to the sink and said, "I went to Oxford."

He halfway looked at her. "I'd have called John Q to say you were missing but he'd gone, too, when the emergency call for law folks went out."

"I was safe. There was no trouble out where the home is. I was late because my fan belt broke. Had to stay at a filling station a long time waiting to get it fixed." She had never told Tate anything but a white lie before and promised herself never to again.

"I said for you not to go, Allie," he told her directly to her face.

"Wasn't it something for me to decide for myself? I'm grown. When I came back, Tate, four dogs were dead in the road, and Snake there stumbling drunk. He said he didn't do it. I believe him, or he'd have run home right away. It had to be Quad Brewster."

"If it was, it's nothing for you to be messed up in. That's John Q's business, or menfolks' at least."

"Not if John Q or menfolks don't do something about it."

He got up and took his cup to the sink. She moved aside. "It's nothing you have any business meddling in," he said.

"I don't call it meddling."

"Allie, don't be hardheaded. Don't try to run somebody else's business. That's always been your shortcoming."

"Why, whose have I ever tried to run?"

"Mine," Tate said.

"When!"

"From the beginning. Maybe you've wanted to forget. You were always trying to push me into being something more than I wanted to be. Maybe more than I was capable of," he said, catching her look. "But I never wanted to rent out somebody else's land. I never wanted to farm more than what I was left with. You made such a fuss, I went ahead and farmed the old man's"—and he nodded toward the den. "I wanted to rent it out, too."

"It seemed to me you wanted to shun responsibility," she said. "You just never have been able to shoulder much, Tate. You've made far more farming it for yourself—well, I mean there's been good years and bad, but on the whole, more than if we'd rented that good land to somebody else. For them to get richer."

"I've never wanted to be rich."

"There was never any possibility that you would be!" She was sorry for having said it.

He said, "I know you've always felt if we didn't live in your poppa's house, we'd have had a shack. But that wasn't so. And living with him has been rough."

She agreed.

"What you don't see is you can be as sharp-tongued as him sometimes," he said. "I had Momma always telling me what to do, then you. I'm tired of womenfolks telling me what to do!"

"Well," she said, laughing a little, "you certainly didn't always do what I told you." She was glad to see a flicker of amusement, and pleasure too, cross his face. She was rather surprised by a strong set to his chin, pleased herself. She had been quite wrong-minded never to realize there were resentments on his part in this marriage; it gave her a hollow feeling. Wishing further to clear the air, she said, "I don't think you realize it's been hard on me that our sex life dwindled away."

"Did you never stop to think," he said, turning clear eyes on her, "that you played a part in that?"

She said, sorrowfully, "I certainly never meant to." When he looked away from her, she knew there was no way to repair the damage. "I won't tell you any large things to do then. I might still ask you to burn the garbage when you forget. I suppose you're going to get shut of Poppa's land sooner than you have to retire, and rent it out?"

Tate carefully bit into a piece of melba toast.

"Well then, Tate, don't tell me large things not to do either. You can keep on asking me not to leave my knitting in your chair."

Tate took another bite of toast before saying, "Other women are content, why aren't you?"

She told him what she knew to be the truth. "They're not so content as you might think. By the time they're my age, most housewives spend a good deal of time alone. And they are lonely."

Then Tate put the rest of the toast in his mouth and went

out, after shrugging; because women's problems usually came down to being their own.

Even though she'd fantasized sometimes about being alone, she felt like apologizing to him now, for the idea of rejection hurt, the idea that her husband had not loved her all along as much as she had assumed. Crossing the den, not speaking to Poppa, she watched Tate leave. She and Tate would go on in mutual affection and love, though there was now, and probably always would be, a great hurt between them. Still, she could not imagine either one packing up and leaving the other one, when they had been together for so long.

20

"WHY'S YOUR LIP all stuck out?" Poppa said. Milk dribbled from his chin. She looked into his imp's eyes and at his evasive grin. Suddenly, he doubled up his little dukes and fought air. "Go ahead and hit me," Poppa said.

"Hit you?"

"I can read that mad look you got on your face." His head swiveled; his voice grew louder to reach her retreating back. "Caught it from Tate, didja, about sitting up so late with old Brother Hopper, sick? You got me to look after. You don't need to go running round nursing sick folks for the church too, less you're a do-gooder like—" His spoon dropped with a tiny clink to the floor, and Sweetie began to lick it.

She came back and picked it up when the dog had finished. She made her voice quite firm. "Like my momma? Tell me something more about her, for once." Now, there was something brand new in her voice.

It registered on Poppa. Briefly it flashed through her mind to wonder what she'd do if he said nothing: bop him on the head with the spoon?

He said, "She was this kind of woman. Always had to have as a dog one of them pretty little fellers with a tail curled up so tight over its back, its hind feet wouldn't touch ground."

She pictured her momma in dressy clothes, her face haughty because of her tits, a flighty lapdog at her heels. Allie suspected she and May Stewart would have been worlds apart. She'd not have liked the woman much.

She reached out to straighten a flimsy, babyish strand of hair atop Poppa's shiny little pate. He dodged and cried out, "Get away, woman. Can't you see when a man's busy! No. Because a woman don't have sense enough not to bother a man then." She hid her smile. Actually he was pleased by her touch. "I couldn't breathe in the night," he said, petulant on purpose. "You let me run out of Mentholatum. And me and Sweetie ain't had a piece of candy in a week."

"All right," she said. "But Mentholatum's not the answer to your breathing problem. You haven't been taking your heart medicine, have you?"

He drained his cereal bowl of its milk. No sense standing here and looking at him and warning him again that the doctor had said he could go out like a light without his pills, anytime. She had sometimes watched him take them, but felt her real duty was to go on reminding him. She reminded him again. He seemed so much at her mercy she said she'd go to the store after picking up a little, and putting in Monday's load of wash. Minnie wandered in at random for her one day a week; they were good enough friends that it didn't matter. Minnie knew what to do without being told.

Allie walked to town, the buzzards solemn behind Mose's. Sy came around from his outhouse pulling up his zipper; usually, he looked toward the road for company. Today, his chin tucked to his chest, he did not notice her wave. Once, when white people wanted to know what went on at a Negro's, they walked through the door and looked. Much had changed. How much more was coming? She had to speak to John Q today about her suspicions concerning Elgie.

Inside Loma's, talk was of the rioting on the Ole Miss campus last evening. In contrast, the death of dogs not even someone's pets seemed a subject that could wait; John Q ought to know about that first, too. These things on her mind, having come here expecting to meet him, she was surprised by his Monday morning absence. Till noontime the store was crowded with people going in and out. A Memphis salesman lingered and read (once the Memphis papers arrived) that the riot was considered the most serious constitutional crisis experienced by the United States since the War of Secession. People told of phoning relatives in Oxford, hardworking decent folks of the middle class, who'd waked up this morning as stunned as the rest of the world. They had slept peacefully in the town near their university without knowing what was going on; yet blame would be on them. Rabble-rousers had come from everywhere: red-neck kids from every little local college in Mississippi. They came for the sheer hell of it. Beer bottles had flown. In the store, everyone was proud that John Q'd gone over on the side of law and order. While he might run his mouth aplenty, when it came down to the wire that was where his interests lay. He would not go against the government once it had spoken, as it had; neither would anybody else standing here, or anybody they knew. What had come, had come. They were all shocked as the salesman read about a major general of the army standing at the base of the campus statue of a Confederate soldier and urging on the rioters. "Insurrection!" he'd shouted. No wonder the kids tore up everything. The army had already sent him off to a federal insane asylum up in Kentucky, where he belonged.

The bell tinkled, admitting Mister Otis. He gave one of his usual greetings. "You all standing round in here looking like white folks." The others looked back so quietly, he sagged, as if knowing that in laying that egg his day was done. "Go to bed and wake up and your known world's gone," he said. "Hit a Negro now and I reckon he could hit you back." Beneath Loma's watchful eye he slipped a bag of popcorn from between metal claws, as she wrote on her charge pad.

Mose had remained a strangely long time, his bald spot purple under the lighting, his store meanwhile unattended. Sauntering in, he'd said he'd come for a pound of bacon, as a customer had phoned for some in an order she was picking up. He had none; rather than causing her an inconvenient side trip to Loma's, he'd buy it. He and Loma often did this, making no profit, as he'd have to sell the bacon for what he'd paid, but each was afraid of sending customers across the way, fearful they'd not come back. Though why did he keep lingering, Allie wondered, with the bacon in his hand, with plenty of folks to talk to in his own store? Loma had opened as usual at six A.M., to catch folks on their way to the fields. Since then, when not busy with a customer, she was painting her old storeroom. Why paint, if she was only cleaning out its trash, as she'd said? Allie thought Mose was not there really to buy as much as to snoop, as curious about what his competitor was up to as she was. Despite paint on her face, Loma stood drinking a Coke while she rested, looking bare and brisk without her swinging earrings, wanting to spare them her paintbrush.

The salesman went on with the paper, reading about the three hundred people who were injured, and the two who were killed. "A Frenchman," Miss Pearlie Mae repeated, clearly awed by a foreigner being killed on her native soil, so far from home. What a soul in torment till he could rest where his bones had come from! Her eyebrows drawn on with a sienna-colored pencil rose and fell, while she mourned for his poor family, and, watching, Allie could not help remembering how Miss Pearlie Mae's cousin once confided the old lady had hair nowhere on her body. "I mean nowhere!" she'd said. People around here, she thought, knew such intimate things about one another, whether they wanted to or not.

"That poor jukebox repairman from right near here," Loma said. While they mourned him, being local, with even more compassion, they made no distinction when they agreed he'd had no more business being there than somebody from a foreign country. They felt no one had belonged on the campus but university people and the Negro, including the federal government, which had taken disciplinary action out of the university's hands.

"Seems like states' rights are as obsolete as the surrey with the fringe on top," Mose said. "The Constitution's been torn to shreds. Southern folks don't take to being shoved around. We're too hotheaded. Us hotheaded Southerners would have seen that Negro got an education if he'd truly wanted one."

The others, saying nothing, meant Amen. "The South's the most patriotic part of the country," Loma said. "We'd all salute the flag anytime it went by." All turned to the road as if there were one, though Miss Pearlie Mae had not heard clearly. Jumping up to peer out, she sat back down looking mystified.

"Once we were drifting toward centralized government," Mose said, going to the door, "and now we're being swept toward absolute federal control. The Supreme Court, what's that?"

"Stooges in black robes," the salesman said, mightily; the others seemed to applaud.

"The battle ought to a been in Cuba, anyhow," Mister Otis said, popping his cellophane bag, which seemed a signal, for busy folks all departed. Jake Thomas muttered something about socialism, a word cropping up often in their new vocabularies, as often as integration would. The salesman came out of the storeroom shutting a tape measure back into its holder like a snail's shell and whispered to Loma before leaving. Allie selected the jar of Mentholatum with the least dust, watching him drive off in an electrical truck.

"I declare, I don't see how folks could behave so bad on a Sunday," Miss Pearlie Mae said.

Timing was important, Allie thought. Hesitant, she wondered, had she waited too long for John Q to pay attention to her suspicions, with so much else on his mind? She bent to the open paper and said, "Sunday's a good day for something as momentous as this. Here it says the real issue is whether the rule of law can be flouted and dishonored at home, in the United

States. Because here we are trying to promote law in other nations, and this riot makes us lose face."

But "Momentous" was all Miss Pearlie Mae said, her quivering eyebrows making clear she thought that word a mouthful.

To no one's surprise, Negroes had shunned the stores today, and only a few had passed solemnly through town. Town, though, at this moment should have emptied of everyone, people heading home for meals, women to their program. Then Loma's phone rang. While she stood talking excitedly, Mose ran out of his store to halt those in the road who were leaving. Loma came running from the phone. "John Q's never come home from the riot," she said.

Queen of the May once, Betty May Dobbins, née Spraggins, was now what Allie's day help, Minnie, called a settle-aged lady. Having five children and happy with motherhood, she was a practical woman, whose great breasts were no longer so noticeable since the rest of her had rounded, too. She kept to herself the knowledge that John Q had been glimpsed around back roads in his pickup with a waitress from the Whitehill Café, letting the infatuation pass over her as well as other suspected ones. Those days were over. Not because John Q had more sense, but because he was shy about when he could or could not get it up, and how hard it'd be and how long it'd stay. He was simply settle-aged himself.

In any case, an overnight disappearance would still be improbable, since there was not one excuse he could possibly have for staying gone overnight, living where and as he did. His absence meant trouble. Betty May had phoned the sheriff, who talked to the law in Oxford. No one had anything to report, including alerted game wardens at Sardis dam, who'd scouted roads as well as small cabins there for rent. The maroon truck overlaid with silver, and sporting a red fox tail on its antenna, seemed to have vanished.

Poppa's morning was busy and happy, as he had to answer all the people phoning Allie with the news. She wondered how many calls he'd missed by not being close enough to the phone to hear it. Tate would not be home for lunch, as he was in line at the gin with his cotton trailer and had a long wait. Poppa looked peeved. Some rackety woman had phoned, and her message was not clear. "I-o-n-a, though," he spelled out. "I got her name right. Said she was phoning from a pay phone at the dam. Wants you to hep her with her boy a game warden's after. How come she's calling you?" He looked in from the den.

Allie clattered pans in the kitchen, not knowing how to answer him. She muttered something above her own increased noise, letting Poppa think he was simply not hearing. She wore the exasperated expression he saw from her and Tate often, which said if they had to repeat everything to him again, they'd croak. He went back to the set. This afternoon the Woman's Club had its regular meeting, so Iona would have to wait until tomorrow. There was no reason to leave home at night except to go visiting. She'd just come from Loma's; if she did not go where she said, Tate could find out by chance.

That night he came in fuzzy with lint. Having no news, he feared in John Q's case that did not mean good news. A rimmed moon over the pasture seemed under water. Allie looked out. "Rain tomorrow?"

"I'm afraid so." Tate stretched out at the supper table. "October's on us." His exhausted, tense expression reflected the worry of farming; Willson and Turner did the hard work. Tate's temperament had always been wrong for his profession. "You ought to go to bed," she said. Soon he did.

Beside him later, she leaned across and kissed him on the cheek. He woke a little and tried to pat her, but his hand fell to the bed. Tonight was cool, so they turned off the air conditioning, and she was glad for opened windows again; though the weather could zoom up to a hundred by tomorrow. She felt pain over her talk with Tate, still. Things were the same between them on the surface, their looks only a trifle evasive sometimes.

Beyond gully land behind their house, on a hill, a dog barked at the house of some Negroes named Walker. Soon it was answered and barkings began to ring through the countryside, echoing from way off. She smiled, waiting for what she knew would come, the softness of a Negro's voice calling through the dark for the dog to hush. A cow disturbed gave a single deep bellow, silencing locusts, the moment ominous in its blankness until they started up again. What was it she had wanted in former times, when she wished to live in a city, with restaurants, picture shows, neighbors, and shops? Allie turned over in her bed thinking how young and foolish she had been.

21

TUESDAY MORNING, squeezing last into the post office again, she ran into a conversation about the person she was going to see. Letty Brown leaned on the network of little mailboxes, talking about the pitiful white family who'd sprung up down the road from her, the kind the community seldom got. "I can't tell whether that woman hangs out new wash every day, or's had the same one up a month," she said. "Now the game warden's onto one of her boys for shooting squirrels at the dam."

"Game warden?" said Ardella's husband from his breakfast table. "Stool pigeon is more like it. Worse law we got."

"None of us on the road cares about the squirrels," Letty said. "But he's shot some of our milk cows with buckshot, saying he's after snakes and frogs. I had been going to speak to John Q about him."

"John Q wasn't — " then Billy John Roberts hushed his own mouth and swallowed. "I mean, he's not — "

"— isn't good about talking to folks," Ardella said, leaning toward her bar. "Let's do be hopeful till we get bad word."

"It looks mighty bad," Ardella's husband said. "If it's as bad as we think, there's not another educated fellow in this community who'll run for constable. The election on our necks."

Allie left as Billy John was saying, "John Q might not have been, or isn't, the best in the world. But he's better than nothing, or was."

Iona scattered all the little kids behind her after opening the door, promising candy if they were good. Once inside, Allie stepped around several wet diapers; she shooed away a weak-eyed kitten sniffing one. To discourage the kids scuffling at the half-closed door to the next room, she snapped off the television they wanted to see, without asking.

"Ralph in school?"

"I reckon he is. You want to sit down?"

Allie decided against a chair missing a caster, and a soft one where the kitten had wet, and regretted sitting down on a small couch for two. Having no springs, it lowered her in an unlady-like position to the floor, her knees nearly meeting her eyes as they rose. Iona perched herself on a crate to say the game warden had given her a warning. Next time it would be a summons, and she'd have to pay a fine or Ralph would go to juvenile court.

"I would hate to see him started on that route," Allie said. "It might not end."

"I was wishing you'd get your constable to see him. He might scare the fool out of Ralph."

"We don't have a constable now." Allie worriedly explained about John Q.

"No law?"

"There's the high sheriff in Nashtoba, or one of his deputies. That's not like having somebody in town. They're for what the constable here can't handle. The sheriff will have to appoint another constable soon, if nothing's heard from John Q. If he's dead, which I fear might be the case, an interim appointment will be made till the upcoming election."

"Inter —?"

"An appointment meanwhile. Speaking of that, what have you decided?"

"I don't guess nothing."

Allie thought of possibilities for Iona: a factory job, but they were scarce. Then a baby-sitter would eat up what she earned. Couldn't she go home?

"These chirrun run Momma crazy. Her women friends flat out wouldn't come to the house to play canasta. I couldn't move back."

"Memphis?" However, Iona agreed with her that living alone in a strange city with kids would be too hard, and the city getting so dangerous. "Do you have any particular skills?" Allie's little sarcasm was lost on her opponent.

"I worked in a ten-cent store onct."

"No hope about your first husband?"

Iona showed her dimples. "He'd take me. But it's tough hoeing to get yonder with no money. I couldn't write and ast for so many fares. I'd been thinking about showing up at the door. Seems like he wouldn't turn us out."

"Showing up's the best idea," Allie agreed. She must figure out how to learn the facts. Wasn't it human nature, or the female's anyway, to want to know if another woman had slept with your husband? Even steven or not, she wanted to know. Tate might think her outspoken, but she was shaky now. She felt defenseless and yet quite able to claw the kittenish face opposite her, good and hard. Iona sat praising Texas, then took an opposite tack about her brother. He never had come round to help her, she said. "The longer you live," Allie told her, "you'll find you can't depend on many people besides yourself."

"You and Momma! Just alike." Iona stared appraisingly.

Iona's momma rose to Allie's mind's eye. "Is that right," she said, smiling thinly. Like a very old woman, she tried to push herself up from the sofa. She needed to take her own advice to Iona. On TV, when detectives gave the third degree, they shot out a lot of questions and buried their most important one in the middle of them. "I guess you could take a bus from Nashtoba to Texas, couldn't you?"

"Yes'um. Have to transfer some."

"Got any idea of the cost?"

"I was thinking on a hundert dollars. The kids have to eat ever stop."

"How'd you like my husband?"

"Which 'un is he?"

Her throat filled. Allie swallowed as she answered. "For his age, he's handsome. Five-nine. Not tall and not short. Dark hair, pretty gray eyes. Drives a blue pickup. Might have brought candy?"

"On a Sunday?"

"Probably, if he was here."

"Fellow owns a store in town come onct. Another one waited outside. They 'as in a blue truck."

"Mose?"

"I think it was. Wanted to use my phone, said. Looks like he'd knowed I didn't have none. The kids was making such a fuss he just gave 'em the candy and skedaddled."

"He's a bachelor. Not used to noise. The other one didn't—" She broke off.

"Didn't what?"

"Come in?" she said, at last.

Iona put her fingertips over a smile. "No'm. But Ralph sure been looking for him again. He let Ralph drive his truck up and down the drive while he was waiting. Like to tickled that kid to pieces. Reason I seen the other fellow, I had to go drag Ralph out."

That was so much like Tate, Allie thought, smiling to herself. "So, Ralph knew his name and where he lived?"

"I reggin. Because Ralph now, he's going to ast you a bunch of questions ever time."

"Ralph does need a man's influence." She caught hold of the sofa's arm. But why take a chance on its being Tate's? "Texas sounds like your best bet, Iona." She managed to take her checkbook from her purse, and to hold it on her knees and write. Iona kept saying she couldn't take money. Allie finished writing as Iona concluded she didn't know when she could send the money back.

"No need to," Allie said, in her airiest manner. Handing over the check, she thought it took a good bit out of her October food allowance. She'd have to make casseroles, which Poppa and Tate complained about, thinking something was being put over on them when food was in one dish and covered with cheese or biscuits or bread crumbs. Well, she could endure their being mad for a month over what they considered gooey female food.

Iona fluttered the check like a fan. Then she reached out a hand and gave Allie a tug upward. "How come you gimme this?"

Allie straightened out her skirt, saying, "I had one reason when I came, and another now that I'm leaving." She pushed through the door to the porch, thinking how relieved she was, foolish or not.

"He did have pretty eyes."

She turned back to Iona behind the screen.

"Who?"

"That other fellow." Iona's dimples flashed.

When Allie arrived home after twelve, Poppa was roaming the kitchen with his punctual stomach growling. He had set out a can of tuna. The curved fish on the iridescent green label seemed to look at her with the same belligerence as Poppa. She shoved the can aside. Supper tonight would be tuna covered with cream of mushroom soup and crushed potato chips. At least she'd know what she was eating, though the men would complain they didn't.

Poppa said Tate had come home for a time, and did not know when he would be back. All the able-bodied men in town had formed a posse to look for John Q; farmers had gone off and left the fields to the Negroes and even Mose had gotten somebody to keep his store. Poppa had watched from the window as they left—it had been like a long parade. "Most excitement round here since folks came through recruiting for the Spanish-American War," Poppa said. "We don't have any law in this town now, or a white man left worth killing."

The thought made her look out the window toward Sy's, goose bumps along her spine. Yet she went on feeling someone on that porch had watched protectively when she stood out there at night with Snake Johnson, facing him down. She realized Tate's gun was missing from its rack on the wall. On the top rung, an old beloved Purdy of Poppa's had been resting since he last used it, years ago. Now, she felt resentful of him sitting there with his nose stuck into a drama on TV, and said, "Didn't there used to be a third gun on that rack?" She remembered being small and looking up at the guns over her head.

Poppa yanked at the paper napkin tucked under his chin as a bib, but choked anyway. "Woman, let a man eat."

She lowered her voice. "What happened to the third gun?" After cramming food into his mouth, he spoke finally. "Your momma took it." She waited. "It wasn't no account," Poppa said.

"Took it where?"

"I told her if she took it anywhere, she better carry it to Memphis and get it fixed first."

"What was wrong with it?"

"Safety was bad."

"She didn't take it to Memphis?"

"I don't know what the woman done." He yanked the napkin completely away and threw it to the floor. "She never listened to me." He belched loudly, peering sideways at her. Then pressing one hand flat to his chest, he meant she was giving him indigestion, or an attack of some kind. She'd better watch out.

"She never took it," she said softly. She bent carefully for the napkin and stood with it, imagining her mother stepping out the back door with the gun's muzzle pointed toward the sky, as she'd have been taught, even if she'd never done anything before but dust one, while behind her came flouncing some smart-assed little dog without its feet touching the ground. She longed to rid herself of the inward picture of her mother handing the gun over to Elgie, as she must have.

Men in the posse who had taken dogs began coming home first, since it was the dogs' suppertime. Pickups went by on the road below at a fast clip. When none stopped in town, even though people stood around waiting, she knew there was no news. Dogs steadied themselves in the pickups' beds, their fur ruffling in the breeze. She saw them soundlessly barking, though she heard nothing with the doors and windows closed. The tuna casserole had grown gummy sitting in a warm oven before Tate arrived; the cattle gap seemed hardly to announce the truck. He hung his cap on a peg by the door, without saying anything, so they knew the news was bad. It was only by the grace of God that John Q had been found this time of year, when the leaves were still on the trees. More likely wintertime would have had to come before his truck could have been spotted nose-dived into that sluicing bottomland along Grey Wolf River.

"He had to have been traveling," Tate said. He struggled to take off his boots, and she helped him. "I never knew John Q to be a fast driver."

"He never has been," she said.

"Used to drive like a mud turtle when I went to the woods with him to hunt," Poppa said. "He was young then, too."

Tate said he felt sad, thinking how many times they had crossed and recrossed that bridge without finding John Q, searching every side road and dusty, weed-choked cow path a truck could get down. There he was all the time, so quiet. Well, if it was God's grace it had taken the form of a crop duster. This was a method of poisoning too expensive for most hill-country farmers, though occasional springtimes those who got up enough money wanted to spend it that way. One of the flying duster pilots had fashioned himself a runway out of a pasture near the Brewster Gin in Whitehill. It was lined and lighted too with upright old tires painted a luminous white. He kept in a tin hangar one of the little planes almost as flimsy as the kind children made out of plywood. Off-season for dusting, he took the plane up for what he called acrobatics, though to those on the ground, his twistings and turnings seemed little different from his farm stunting. He skimmed treetops, and flew so low his wheels touched the tops of plants, riffling them till it seemed they would shred. He even flew under telephone wires. Few country people were real bettors, but none would have put down a theoretical plug nickel on the chances of a crop duster living out his lifetime. They always ran into the road to watch the plane, stopped what they were doing in the field while he rose straight into the air like a dove hit by number-eight shot, and then spiraled down the way a dead bird did, only so far he had straightened the plane out every time.

This evening, Silly Billy, as he had painted on the plane, had returned from his pastime, coming down low over bottomland, following the yellow river's winding curves. He knew what the men on the ribbons of road below were searching for, and dipped his wings, in a sad way, to let them know he had found it. In tangled underbrush and among trees that were some of the countryside's last woods, he had caught sight of gleamings like quicksilver, and after landing told where the truck was. From the air, he could see a swath cut through the underbrush, though on the ground it seemed all to have closed up behind John Q, leaving no trace of his whereabouts. Stopped by a tree, the truck was half buried in mud. John Q had gone through the windshield, so that when they found him some of the men did not want to look.

They felt better knowing that even if someone had been on the road behind him, John Q could not have been saved. The coroner and ranger from Senatobia guessed he died instantly. The ambulance had taken him. Early tomorrow morning Fred Cullins would come with the tow truck and haul out what was left of the pickup, just to junk it. No one wanted it there as a rusting reminder, when the leaves had turned and gone.

Tate went on compulsively as if he had to tell everything. When the men reached John Q, his eyes were wide open and boggling. When he was first moved, his arms flew wide as if asking somebody to save him, or love him. The men took off their hats and stood in two rows, while John Q was carried out on a stretcher between them. Bourbon was in the house from when Allie made fruitcakes, and for emergencies that seldom came. Saying this was one, she fixed him a couple of jiggers in warm milk, though Tate was shy about drinking even that much.

He still did not sleep for a long time, and neither did she. He talked in a whisper about those who had gone off the bridge; none of their reasons applied to John Q. Now, the weather was not bad, and John Q did not drive fast, and he was not a drinking man. The last thing that could be said was that he did not know that bridge was coming up before him in the country dark.

22

THE FARTHEST AWAY of John Q's kin was a daughter Martha, at Ole Miss. In spite of the reason, her momma was glad to get her away from campus for a few days. There had been another flare-up after a short calm: a few troublemaking students had thrown bottles at federal troops. On Wednesday, the papers reported that one student had said hello to Meredith in one of his classes; another one had exchanged notes with him, using a professor as an intermediary. One student interviewed on a newscast about Meredith eating in the cafeteria reported, "He drank him a glass of milk for breakfast," but missed reporting that no one sat with him but his federal bodyguards.

Meredith publicly stated that he was lonesome and did not understand why everybody was mad at him. "That shows he don't have sense enough to be in college," Poppa commented, watching the newscast. For him, though, the real guffaw came later when Meredith was asked where he was during the riot. He said he'd gone to bed and slept through it. "Now, if that's not just like a colored man," Poppa cried. Tate and Allie worked frantically, holding his arms above his head, patting him on the back, when he seemed apt to choke. He sat a long time pressing his chest as if to keep his heart there.

John Q's funeral would be on Thursday, and townspeople had little time to go elsewhere to shop. The storekeepers kept to themselves being pleased with the flurry in business; everyone would take food to the Dobbins' house. The most beautiful item was a Lady Baltimore cake Annie sent Miss Betty May. All her available space was taken up with hams, fried chicken, homemade relishes and pickles, stuffed eggs, homemade breads and biscuits, all varieties of cakes and pies, casseroles of vegetables or macaroni. When Allie stopped in with a pie, she wondered if the term *groaning board* had not originated with Southern funerals.

Throughout Miss Pearlie Mae's adult life, she had been the local correspondent for *The Democrat*; she still wrote in the embellished prose of another day. While the residents regretted it, they'd rather let outside folks laugh than hurt the old woman's feelings by having her replaced. She read her obituary over the phone to Allie, crying as she began: "The Death Angel has visited our community and called John Q Dobbins to his heavenly home." Allie told her it was fine.

On Thursday afternoon, when she entered the old cemetery out from town, Allie felt that perhaps a death angel was one of the unseen presences around. The graves lay in shade. Sunlight filtering down through giant oaks and old cedars cast running shadows on headstones, some lying flat on the ground, others cracked, many belonging to people no longer known to anyone in these parts. Way off in one corner were a few graves belonging to Negroes, buried there by whites in another time. Their position in a far corner marked them, as the graves had no headstones. She noted people no longer were afraid of bad luck if they stepped onto plots, and did not think that disrespectful any longer. For many years, Poppa brought her here on

Mother's Day to put down flowers. Then, without explanation, he said one year they were not going. Sometimes she came alone to visit, without grief anymore either. Tight-lipped now, she passed the edge of her mother's grave; her eyes roved the name and dates and the single, cold granite rose, beside the distasteful words Poppa had had carved: *Why me, Lord?* Today, she wondered who was supposed to be asking that question. Her mother? Or had Poppa been asking himself why he had drawn May as his wife?

So much, like the simple service itself, was the same as always. As long as she could remember, the spindly iron fence around the cemetery had been rusted orange; the gate creaked; when mourners arrived and shut car doors, the cracks echoed over the hillsides. Acorns and twigs snapped beneath feet. Finally, when the casket was lowered into the ground, the levers made the same grating sound as over the years. Brother Walker's voice was hollow, reading the words he always chose. In the distance hunkering Negroes held shovels, waiting for the service to end.

"'. . . and hath given him authority to execute judgment also, because he is the Son of man. Marvel not at this: for the hour is coming, in the which all that are in the graves shall hear his voice. And shall come forth; they that have done good, unto the resurrection of life; and they that have done evil, unto the resurrection of damnation,'" Brother Walker ended. Then each of John Q's family threw a handful of dirt into the grave.

"Amen, Brother," cried Mister Otis, in the old-timey custom he used in church too, which irked Brother Walker.

Others remained a moment in respectful silence, before people began to file out. When she said, "Ouch," Tate whispered, "Sorry. I didn't mean to grab your funny bone, but you were about to walk over your momma's grave."

They went out last, as Tate was a deacon in the church and it was his assignment to lock the cemetery by wedging a stob of wood on a rusted chain into a hook on a gatepost. She put her foot back into one pump, loosened when Tate grabbed her. It had been quite childish to want to trample that grave, she admitted to herself. "I wonder why Loma wasn't here? I've never known her not to close up for a funeral. It won't set well with people."

"Mose offered to bring her. She burst into tears and said she couldn't stop painting. Had a deadline to get the place ready."

"Ready for what?"

"Mose said he couldn't bring himself to ask her." They went along behind the others to the road, Tate taking her arm more gently. "It seemed not having the casket open in church that we didn't really say goodbye to John Q. It gave me a lonesome feeling, like he went off all alone," he said.

Tate had been too young also to remember about her mother. She said nothing. Catching up then, she let her heart go out instead to John Q's daughter Martha, who hung onto her mother, her heart-shaped face streaked with mascara. As they passed, she was saying, "Oh, Momma. Don't you understand anything?" She blew her nose on Betty May's handkerchief. "Homecoming at Ole Miss is part of the very reason I went there! Now it might be called off in my freshman year."

"Honey, everything we do these days has to be done with the approval of the powers that be," Betty May said.

"You got it, Betty May," said Billy John. "Honey, I heard on the radio coming over here, Robert Kennedy is going to decide whether the game's on or off. Might not be."

Martha said, "Oh," not looking comforted.

"The stronghold of Southern democracy has been bursted wide open by the Kennedy family, the handpicked Supreme Court, and the minority group called the N-double-A-C-P," said Mister Otis. He leaned against a car to get his breath.

"Why Otis," Miss Pearlie Mae said. "That was just momentous!"

He put an arm around her waist, and they walked on away.

"Meredith has offered, though, to leave town for the weekend if it'd help things about Homecoming," Ardella's husband said.

"Sounds like he could have been a good Negro if the communists hadn't gotten hold of him."

"Momma, how do I look?" Martha said. "Do you have a mirror?"

Betty May had borrowed the Baptist church's coffee maker, which, after rumbling like a small volcano, produced coffee for all those who came by after the funeral. Excited by the crowd, Miss Pearlie Mae flitted about like a dirt dauber, not exactly lighting anywhere. Passing close to Allie, she whispered behind one hand, "I so hate for a death to come, they always come in threes."

"Oh, that applies only to movie stars, or famous folks at least," she said.

Miss Pearlie Mae shook a positive, shimmering headful of red hair.

With difficulty, Allie and Tate made their way through the crowd to the table, snatches of conversation reaching their ears. "Well, with ten thousand federal troops staring them in the face over at the university, the folks had to realize they couldn't buck the federal government."

"That'll do it."

"Patriotism? A fellow on TV said that was the last refuge of a scoundrel."

"Why, they shouldn't let people say such things!"

"What the mass media does is teach people to be afraid."

"People in this state need education before they need culture, even if we are world conscious now. We never have had Ivy League education in Miss'sippi. We're never going to. What's needed here is technical training. Folks got to make a living."

Because they were in John Q's widow's house, people did not talk about another matter as important to their community. Who would let himself be appointed temporary constable? Who would run to be elected?

At the table, Allie could not help being pleased that her pie was already gone; while pretending not to, the women kept their eyes on whose food vanished, and whose didn't, and went home talking about it.

As if holding court, Martha stood surrounded and telling stories about campus life these past few days. ". . . then a boy ran along behind him yelling, 'I smell a gar.' Another boy said, 'A cigar?' The first one said, 'No! A nee-gar.' Only I don't think Meredith heard them." No one listening allowed more than a little twitching to their lips. Martha said, "A professor begged me to go on and go to class with Meredith, instead of boycotting like most students. Said I'd be passing up a—I mean, an, historical opportunity." When she happened to look around and see Allie, Allie nodded to the girl.

"Opportunity's not supposed to knock but once, is it Otis?" Miss Pearlie Mae said, a hand on one of his cuffs.

"I don't know'um. It's just a good thing all this didn't happen in the springtime when young folks' sap's already risen."

"Jake says what's really bothering everybody," Carrie Thomas said, "is that in the past the behavior of the Negro was predictable. It was a constant thing. Now we don't know."

Deciding they had to see about Poppa, Allie and Tate were about to leave, when several men motioned him to the front door. A feeling of summer still clung to the outdoors; there was a faint smell of freshly cut grass. Mosquitoes hummed in ditch banks, a faraway sound. From the depths of the ditches moonlight escaped, lighting a silvery plain; gullies, ridges, hills, pastures, and fields were indistinguishable from one another. Coming out of the house, Allie had something of the restless, run-down feeling she once had emerging from afternoon picture shows in Memphis. Back then, the twilight streets after the movie's shimmering darkness had seemed lesser and plainer. Shops and buildings took on the gray hue of the sidewalks, and people all seemed poor and grim. Now, the men gathered together and were suddenly silent, maybe feeling the night's enormous pressure, hanging heavy with stars. Billy John suggested they move away from the house, as if that would help something; their footsteps on crushed gravel were not so loud as the insects singing in the night, giving it a throbbing quality.

The men wanted Tate's advice. Would it seem disrespectful to John Q to go ahead with the meeting scheduled at the Masonic Hall tonight about buying a fire engine? Tate's opinion was that John Q'd had a bee in his bonnet about being fire chief. So, if the vote went through, they would make him an honorary one. When the rest of the women came from the house, the men decided the women should go home, and menfolks to the hall. Tate took Allie's Chevrolet, since it held six, and she went with Ardella. "I can't think when we've left Poppa alone so long," she said. "He wouldn't admit it, but I think he's scared there by himself. I've been leaving Sweetie outside when we're gone."

"Maybe pretty soon, if he catches the house afire, you'll have a chance of saving it. I don't think the Whitehill fire truck ever got here in time to rescue anything."

Saying goodnight, Allie stepped out by the porch light, Sweetie leaping and gyrating in welcome. She rubbed her head, asking why Poppa hadn't left any lights on. Then, inside, she saw he'd gone to bed without intending to, that he'd come into his room for candy, and sleep had somehow claimed him. He was in his pajamas though. She took the wrapped candy drop from his fist and set him straight under the coverlet. Without lights, the house was covered up with moonlight. She left it that way, undestroyed, and went to bed by that light, too. Only first she stood and looked at Sy's dark cabin. A light went off at Loma's and she stole across the store porch like her own thief, and left.

To anyone looking at the house, it would seem Allie and Tate were still gone, with her car not there, and the porch light burning to welcome them.

23

QUAD BREWSTER woke early. He turned into his pillow wanting to sleep again, then roosters crowed in Sister Belle's yard, near the kitchen. If they were not hers, he'd kill the bastards. Sitting up, he threw one pillow against a window. Sleeping was hard enough. He sat up dizzily and shook his head to clear it of the nightmare. The roosters went on crowing. He could cry when he thought of other times. Why was he put in this position?

He never wanted to remember. At his upstairs bedroom window he looked down between columns at Negroes in the pecan orchard below. They were swathed in head rags, with hats and clothes of grays and browns, the same indistinct colors as tree trunks; they were all on their knees, where they belonged. He could at last laugh. The trees had been shaken for the first time of the fall; the Negroes scrambled around for nuts beneath leaves.

If it hadn't been for the damn nigger going to Ole Miss, he wouldn't have the nightmares. *Look what the nigger did to me!* he thought. The whole state of Mississippi seemed at fault. He'd only gone to the riot like everybody else, for kicks and fun. Moving into his bathroom, in the shower he turned on only the cold water. When prickling cold stung him, he opened his mouth to silent cries; he thought them maybe pleasure, he thought them maybe pain. He was of different minds too about that country constable signaling him out of the crowd. Even the other kids were impressed. Yet he always had to think about the family, what others before him had done. He had to plant a pecan orchard. The one in front was started by Great-granddaddy, the one across the road by Granddaddy, the one behind the house by Daddy. Always there was family talk about whose orchard yielded most. Better get started on yours, Quad, Daddy kept saying. In ten years my trees'll be past their prime, and yours should be coming into maturity. Maturity, Daddy repeated, squinting his eyes, the closest he came to chastisement. Quad grinned and shut off the water.

Momma ordered her thick towels from Memphis. Quad knotted a corner and thumped his feet till red welts rose. The damn constable's face went out of his mind; the voice remained: "Son, anybody from your family's the last person ought to be here with these rabble-rousers. You go home or I'll call your daddy myself." Picking on him. It was a kind of flattery, but he got tired of the family. Your daddy's son . . . blah blah blah. Law and order. Obey the law. He heard him yelling inside that truck while he and Richard rocked it. He ran a hand over his face and decided he did not need to shave.

He met himself head-on in the full-length mirror on the door, not wanting to look. He covered his few pubic hairs, red-gold-white like the hair on his head; at school the jocks teased him in the locker room. When's something going to happen down there, Quad? they said. They must talk about him behind his back. A prostitute did not mention his bareness, and girls he dated never let anything happen below the waist except a little finger fucking. His daddy would die of embarrassment if he asked him whether having no body hair was inherited. Daddy's only fact of life had been that some girls were not nice. Quad wished for nerve enough to meet them: he could not face a prostitute a second time.

He dressed in crisp clothes smelling of Sister Belle's ironing; they felt warm still. Sunlight lit up amber in all the polished preserved furniture. Nothing was ever out of place, and everything was done for him. He felt angry that nothing swelled in the leg of his seersucker pants; always it was a matter of pride to keep Momma from seeing his bulge. Ever since that country bumpkin flew off that bridge, he'd not even been able to come by masturbating. Jeesus Christ. When he stroked, he saw himself meeting up with that maroon truck again as he headed home, and he chased the fool over those country roads as a joke, and maybe bumped his fender. He did not remember, and if the truck flew off the bridge because of that, he was innocent. Because he did not remember. Momma talked about alcoholics on her side, saying whiskey made all her brothers go crazy. That past had nothing to do with him; he could handle drinking.

From the landing he looked down the carved stairway, its Oriental runner thinning. Momma said years of use by the same family made its being threadbare valuable. Out a fanlight window he saw the Negroes again, crawling around on their knees. They were laughing and jostling one another and he envied their being brainless and without responsibilities. He did not want to plant an orchard, or work in a bank, or a cotton gin. He thought he would join the foreign legion and be like Gary Cooper in *Beau Geste.*

The clothes crackled as he moved; he could smell Sister Belle's homemade starch. At school, he had been stunned at the number of red-neck kids who washed and ironed their own clothes, had always done it, had families that didn't have twelve bucks a week to hire even one nigger to do their housework. The bannister smelled of furniture polish. The houseboy, James, was standing on a ladder and polishing the crystal chandelier; the prisms blinked and occasionally tinkled against one another, making James blanch and look toward Momma's room. She seemed to keep telling him to polish it so she could take to bed.

In hues like the prisms, shot through with color, scenes came back. One morning he woke in slow surprise and thought of that truck; it came up out of his subconscious. If he was too drunk at the time to remember what happened, then he was innocent.

He flew past James, sliding down the bannister. He pretended not to hear, as he was not supposed to hear, James grumbling, "Too old to carry on thataway." Quad went *heh heh heh*, not really laughing.

"Morning, Mister Little Quad," James said.

"Morning." He yelled toward the kitchen. "Morning, Sister Belle. Coffee in Momma's room."

She came through the swinging door in her run-down shoes

and blue uniform. "You going to eat some breakfast, Mister Little Quad."

"All right." He liked to give in to her mothering.

The dark Oriental rugs silenced noise. Like the heavy antique furniture, they helped make the house dark. Marble tops of tables shone whiter. He stumbled past twin love seats covered in wine velvet and past the abundance of *objets d'art* Momma collected that made the house a museum, or a mausoleum, he thought: past cabinets displaying beaded watchcases and pincushions made by Indians. Always, he had to think about being from the first white family to buy land in Nashtoba (1836). Windows looked out onto pine trees and cedars of Lebanon, and one pine had come stropped to a buggy that brought his ancestors from South Carolina, here. A paisley shawl covering the music room grand piano had been worn by one of the women. The past was a trap.

Outside, old Leander talked to a hand mower he pushed. "Whoa," he said. He was from the past too and would be retained till he died. He cut away English ivy from brick walls, thinking it weeds. He sheared away the bottom branches of magnolias, for his mower to fit beneath. The trees had a surprised shorn look, like country kids back in grammar school who got haircuts by having a bowl turned over on their heads, while scissors went around its rim. George was on a tractor dragging limbs from the orchard. Katie was running a vacuum in the den; he glimpsed her uniformed butt moving past the door. By day, the niggers took over the house. When Momma was not in bed she played bridge or went to committee meetings.

"Oh, darling," she said, stretching her arms. She greeted him day by day as if she had not seen him in years.

"Momma." He smelled her scent of lilacs, touched her cold cheek. He tried not to look at the soft long sides of her breasts where her gown parted, where her pink lacy bed jacket was open. He knew that he hated her, he knew that he loved her. He did not know which he felt most.

"Son," Daddy said. Whenever Momma was in bed, he sat in attendance. He would go to the bank late. "How are you going back to school?"

"Oh, does he have to go?"

"Cornelia," Daddy said. "He's home more than he's there."

"Well, it's such a terrible school, I wish he didn't have to be there. We should have sent him to a school in Virginia. Memphis people all go to school in Virginia."

"Cornelia, he barely got out of high school."

Quad put his hands in his pockets and looked past them out a window. In one pane the names of those who had lived in the house were etched in with diamond rings. He squinted at his own. He hated their talking over his head as if he were not there, or were a small child.

"Nearly failing wasn't Quad's fault," Momma said. "That teacher Miss Wooten was jealous. I'll never forget her look when I came to school in the back of a Buick, with James driving. She resented us, and took it out on Quad because of what we are."

"I'll find a ride. I'm going to tinker on my car myself. I might find out what's wrong."

"Just take it on down to Fred," Daddy said.

"No. I mean, I will. Next week, if I can't stop that humming myself. I've got it locked in the garage. I don't want somebody on the place going in there."

"Oh, nobody would touch your car, darling," Momma said. "No one will have a better one at Ole Miss, will they?"

"He's not into Ole Miss yet." Daddy sat, balancing his coffee cup on his knee.

"But he will be." Momma smiled.

"I should be hearing," Quad said.

"I hope your grades are up," Daddy said. "If your grades aren't up, this is the last car I'm buying."

"Oh, Thaddeus," Momma said.

Daddy smiled. "Of course, they've taken in the nigger—"

"Oh, Thaddeus." Momma giggled.

"The NAACP fixed up his grades, though," Quad said.

"Maybe you could go to Virginia after two years at Ole Miss," Momma said. "This little time at State is just to be wiped out of our minds."

"Why should he go to Virginia? He's going to live in Mississippi. He needs to go to school in the state where he'll live and work, to have contacts."

"Virginia's so lovely in the spring," Momma said.

"Here you is, Mister Little Quad. You eat this breakfast." Sister Belle brought his tray. She had it fixed up like Momma's, with a cloth thin as tissue paper and a camellia from the yard in a vase; he wished she could see the difference between masculine and feminine. She took away Momma's tray. "Thank you," Momma said.

"Thanks," he said.

Sister Belle stood shyly in the door. "You all wanting anything else?"

"Mister Quad's going back to school," Momma said.

"Aw naw."

"He's got to go sometime," Daddy said. "I can't throw away money."

"Oh, Thaddeus. It hardly costs a cent there. Darling, when you go to Ole Miss you've got to go to Memphis for a new wardrobe. A blue blazer with gold buttons would be lovely. A camel's hair coat."

"Nobody wears camel's hair coats," Quad said. He dreaded all she would buy.

"I'll order one," she said.

Daddy stood up and put on his hat. "They've taken in a member of a race that can't learn at Ole Miss."

"Don't talk like that," Momma said. "You say things like that at the dinner table as if James and Katie can't hear when they're serving."

"They're not supposed to be listening," he said. He grinned at Quad, and he grinned back. It was one of the few times his daddy showed spunk. "Goodbye, son."

"Daddy." He stood and they shook hands.

"Did you have enough, darling?"

He held up his tray and nodded. "Sister Belle will get that," she said. He put the tray down. "Do you need money, darling?" He nodded. "Look in my purse. But don't tell Daddy." He kissed her again, and took away the lilac smell and the soft feel of her flesh. "I'm having a hard time explaining to Daddy where my allowance is going," she said. Quad looked at her helplessly. "Never mind," she said.

He went back into the hall where James was climbing down from the ladder. "Mister Little Quad, you got any that twenty dollars you owe me?"

"I'll have it next time."

"You done said that the last three times. I wonder could I get it off Mister Thaddeus, and you pay him?"

"No. I don't want Daddy on my back. You either. I'll get the money."

James looked sulky. However much you loved them, when they looked sulky you wanted to smash them. He looked back down at James from the landing outside his room, surprised that he had asked him for the money, surprised by the look on James' face. It made him feel uneasy. He felt uneasy when his parents talked about Ole Miss; he didn't see any point to college except to pass time. He had hated the barrage of questions they asked him when he went there for an interview. "Is it your parents' desire that you go to school here, or yours, Quad?"

"My parents'."

"I thought so," the Dean had said.

Fucking smartass, Quad thought, lying on his bed. His daddy could buy and sell that whole school; his daddy had hinted around about making a contribution toward the new gym, or to the library. He didn't know how that had gone over. He reached for his phone and called a little cashier at the bank and asked her to lunch. She said she couldn't go.

"What do you mean, you can't go?"

"Just what I said."

"You want some extra time off I'll get it for you." He couldn't, and hoped she did not take him up on that.

"I don't have to go out with you because I work in your daddy's bank."

She hung up, the little red-neck bitch, when he was trying to do her a favor. He called Richard. "Have you ever not been able to come when you're beating your meat?"

"Hell, no."

Quad was silent.

"I had a piece last night. Date with Ellen Jones' Memphis cousin. Sucks you like a piece of candy. Fucks like a rabbit. On the first date."

Quad could taste his breakfast. "Is that right?" He thought Richard was a pathological liar, but was not certain. "Tell me the details later. Come on over and let's drink beer in the pool house till time to head back."

"O.K. But if I was you I'd get those wheels fixed. Quick."

"Yeah?"

"Yeah. I wouldn't leave it around in the garage any time."

"Maybe you're right. Come over and drink beer and we'll drop the car at Fred's on the way back to State."

"How about boilermakers?"

"O.K. I'll tell Momma I'm leaving when you get here. Park behind the pool house. She'll never know we spent the afternoon there."

"Quad, one thing. Control yourself. After a few you—"

"Yeah. Yeah." He hung up shaking: something did happen when he drank; he didn't remember anything. But he never thought he drank any more than anybody else.

He and Richard kept the record player low and drank a few boilermakers. The niggers knew they were there. He had the feeling James was going to blackmail him, or something. Ever since the joker went off the bridge he got crazy sensations. Richard said, "What about this not being able to jerk off."

"Oh hell, man. I was kidding."

Richard told about the Memphis cousin. "She was a nice girl, too. She goes to a private school up there."

Quad got up. "Yeah. Private-school girls suck and fuck on the first date?" Why did Richard luck out, or was he lying? The mail had run. He saw the carrier's car shooting down the road, through a haze of dust. He went down between the pecan trees, aware of a lot of white eyeballs and black eyes peering at him from around trees. The poor klutzes were still on their knees; they had smudge pots going and the smoke whirled past, making him sneeze. He saw James coming with the family's mail. He knew James realized he was drunk. Quad accepted his letter and read it.

Richard spilled his drink. "What the hell, man?" He stared back with wide eyes.

"They took the fucking nigger. They didn't take me!" Suddenly he saw his hands at Richard's throat, and saw his teeth marks on Richard's cheek. He couldn't believe how quickly the place turned blue.

"Christ on a crutch." Richard had pulled away. "I'm splitting."

"No, man. Wait. I'm sorry. I've got to go, too. We'll drop my car at Fred's. I'll get the nigger-loving bastards, someday."

24

IN HIS HOUSE in Nashtoba, Fred Cullins said, "John Q never did know which side of a fence to empty a boot. But I declare, I never expected him to meet so sorry a end." He had gotten home from the body shop and washed up and put on some clothes not much more respectable-looking than the ones he'd had on dirty, but they were comfortable. He might as well be talking to himself. When Rose got her mind on one thing it was hard for her to think of something else. She was cooking.

"Poor soul," she said.

He could not stop looking at the picture with the obituary. "Death Angel"? He believed he had heard it was that little red-headed woman who wrote up for Itna Homa, like it was a hundred years ago. The picture was taken in the forties. John Q stood busting his buttons, posing beside the first bale of cotton ginned in the county that year: his. Why had they used such an early photo? He figured because John Q'd never had reason to have another one in the paper, or one taken in a studio. He had to feel sorry, looking into that younger man's eyes, who had no idea on this earth how he'd end up years later. He always had thought that way. Something about the whole business made a rabbit run over his grave.

"You ought to have gone to the man's funeral." Rose had her mouth full of hairpins as big as horseshoes, and was trying to talk, pinning up her hair at the back of her neck again. No sense repeating he got tired of hairs in his food. It took a minute to figure what the woman was saying, then he said, "How come?"

"You did business with him."

"I can't go to the funerals of all I do business with." He felt the way she was looking at him, and did not look back. "Wouldn't get no work done."

"You'd a gone had it been some poker player." Her mouth was free — too free. He watched from under his eyebrows while she held a pork chop on a fork and let grease drip back into the skillet. Each drip she seemed to be talking to him, still. She had to squint when she looked around, even against that weak ceiling light that didn't do a thing for the kitchen but light up a spot above itself; she batted her eyes when she faced out toward the lean-to where an orange bulb was supposed to keep away bugs. Moths were dancing all around it. She brought him his plate. "What channel?"

"It don't matter."

She brought her own plate, and looked at him where he waited, his arms around his plate and his fingers touching at the top. He hadn't been thinking what he was doing. She said, "You better get holt of that plate now before it gets plumb away from you." They had to laugh at the same joke, and his same habit. He reckoned it came from back in the Depression when he didn't know whether he was going to have anything to eat. She sat down and punched the set at the end of the table. By the time she'd said her blessing, and him Amen, the picture and sound had come up, and neither one the way they ought to be. He'd tinkered with the damn thing as much as he could—he knew they needed a new set the way Rose said they did. He ate some mashed potatoes logged down with gravy. "I don't like to ask for no more time off than I have to."

"That's what I thought." She smiled at him as if she'd just answered one of those fancy questions on TV. She cut up her chop with little teeny strokes, being polite. But her knuckles came up with gravy on them, which she sucked off.

"I didn't ask for time and that's that," he told her.

"That is right," she said, her tongue on her knuckles. "The funeral's over with."

"Ask for time for it and something more important might have come up."

She nibbled some gristle. "People in these parts lenient about funerals."

"Mother. I didn't ask." He had not meant to bang the table so hard that the dishes all jumped, and a little bowl of dessert slid toward him. It was the peach cobbler she made fresh, but so thick with cornstarch it was hard to get out with a spoon.

She looked at the table. "Been there twenty-five years. Will be day after tomorrow." She spoke to the set, telling it all to some elderly woman on it.

"Mother." He put his arms around his plate again, but this time felt tired. "I just understand cars."

"I understand that." She put her hand on one of his and patted it a long time. "It's just that after so long there, you ought to speak up about what you want. You're the best man they've got, don't forget." Then she stopped patting and her eyes looked like a sleepy bird's, not quite closing. Her ears had gotten sharper as her eyes got bad. Then he heard the car coming up the driveway, gravel scattering like the sound of a light rain just beginning to ping the windows, or the roof. Headlights came past the window, a horn tooted quick and sharp seven times—shave and a haircut, six pence. "Go see who that is."

A rubber cap was missing from one of her chair legs; the aluminum end set his nerves on edge scraping the floor. She got to the door as if ahead of herself and caught hold of the doorframe to stop. She looked out. "It's a car, all right," she said.

Fred looked at a fellow on TV who was running his mouth about Meow cat food, and imagined they commiserated with each other; in fact though, maybe he was a little better off.

"It's a drunk. You reckon we ought to call John Joe?"

"Don't bother the sheriff 'less he starts something."

"Who you thinking it is?"

He looked at the food on the end of a toothpick he was using. "I'm not thinking it's anybody; I'm not thinking."

"Fred, turn down the television."

"I'm not fixing to turn down the TV."

"It's Mister Brewster's boy out yonder ahollering," she said.

He got himself sideways off the chair, and turned the set off. That white eye in the middle of it took longer than usual to go away. He watched it thinking it was like that evil eye he'd been reading about in the bathroom this morning, in his *Horror Story* magazine. This time, the white eye wouldn't leave, and made him think it was laughing about going somewhere he didn't know, and a better place than where he was. He stood there riled up, and said, "What the Sam Hill does he want? What's he saying?"

Rose said as if she were far away, "I thought he said tell the crip to come on out here, old woman. But he couldn't have."

"Naw. Not even a college s.o.b. would say that. Been telling you your ears going back on you too, old woman."

She said the way she always did, "Pot calling the kettle black. Old man. Don't go out there, Fred. He's drunker than a coot."

"Mother, don't tell me what to do."

"Better'n somebody half your age," she said.

Nobody knew how it was for him to go across a long blank place, like this kitchen of theirs, with nothing to grab hold to. He'd never told anybody. He would be glad to reach the kitchen door. His foot was tired by evening time in that built-up shoe, but he had to keep it on; he listened to his worn-out felt houseshoe on the other foot flopping against the linoleum, hating the sound. Hated it because he'd listened to his daddy's old worn-out felt houseshoes flopping around the house the whole time he was growing up, the old man never having made a dime. Never had made a dime because he never had done no work. But *he* had. Yet his life hadn't turned out the way he expected. The railing to the steps down from the lean-to wasn't no account either; he'd sturdy her up soon, now. He knew how he looked in that boy's lights hobbling down the back steps. That lean-to smelled of cat pee when he'd told Rose a cat box would seep through and once you got that smell into wood you couldn't get it out. But she went on picking up every stray she saw. He only blessed Jesus there wasn't one mewling back behind him tonight. Still, when he limped toward the boy he imagined the smell followed him and that the boy was somehow going to think it was him, his old clothes, or his old dumpy, weak-eyed wife. He hated the boy making that thought about Rose come to mind when she was a good woman, just a bad cook. The house behind him haunted him with its window air conditioners sticking out like ugly warts. Once he'd spent all that money and installed them, folks told him it'd be cheaper if he'd had the house centrally air-conditioned instead. So what should he do? he thought, stepping along grass that suddenly needed mowing. The boy's face came toward him, looking like a new-boiled, unpeeled shrimp, that shiny. His own chin needed shaving twice a day to keep it from being blued, stubby, like now. But who had time for that bother? When Fred reached the boy he felt a day late and a dollar short, the way he always had. Shit, them Brewsters had a man-made lake and what they called a recreation house that was bigger than the house he lived in full time. How could you win?

Womenfolks said Quad Brewster was so pretty he should have been a girl. His eyelashes were black and thick and stubby as if he wore that goo on them some women did. He could bless now Rose's eyelashes that were the same no-color as her eyes. Someday, though, the boy standing no taller than him, this Quad Brewster, would be called what his daddy was, short and stocky. It went through Fred's mind what they said Quad meant — something about him being the fourth Thaddeus Wharton Brewster, though he never had gotten the connection, exactly. Quad had a piece of shrimp-colored hair falling on his forehead. He reached out a hand. Fred jerked one out to shake, but the boy only shoved the hair away, as if warding off flies when his hand went through the air, and Fred stepped back, as if shooed. He tried to put his hands into the pockets of the baggy sweater Rose had knit, but the pockets were too small. He found a place for them by running them over the seat of his pants. Rose shouldn't keep the air conditioners so high he had to wear a sweater this time of year, anyhow. Down at the end of the driveway a car was waiting, but why? A cigarette was flipped through the driver's window and sailed and disappeared like a fizzled-out little sky rocket.

"Your friend's motor skipping a beat," he said. Quad kept looking at him, so he said, "What can I do for you this evening, son?"

"Now, I'm glad you asked that question, Fred." Quad rocked on his heels, only maybe he was staggering. "I need your help. By the way, good evee-ning." He bowed.

What a jackass; and him at Quad's beck and call because he worked for the boy's daddy. "What's on your mind, son?"

"Need your help. Had me a little run-in with my car. If Daddy finds out, my riding days are liable to be over."

Fred doubted that. "I'll be glad to fix the car for you if you'll come to the shop tomorrow."

Quad Brewster stood straight. "You don't get the picture. I want it fixed on the q.t. Don't want to bring it to the shop. I'm going to pay you for your little silence."

"I don't want to be paid for silence. I get paid for work. I can't fix your car here, anyway. Tell you that before I know what's the matter. I don't get many calls to fix Ferraris out to my shop."

He let the boy laugh.

"I can imagine," Quad said.

Fred looked over his shoulder at the garage, built in the thirties when the house had been. He'd meant to get it fixed up better than having two poles propping up one wall. Hadn't been something he'd thought about in a long while, till now. He could not make himself look around, knowing how the letters in black, "Fred the Body Man," looked, home printed and wobbly; he wished he never had gotten up on a ladder one time and opened up for business. "Out there,"—he did not look back—"I mostly do tinkering for folks, fixing toasters and mixers and electric razors." Seen through the boy's eyes he knew his hobby looked like some pitiful attempt to make a little money. No reflection on what Mister Brewster paid him, either. He coughed. "I can do a little work on a car, son. But not much. Not one like yours."

"I want the car fixed quick, Fred."

"Bring it to the shop tomorrow."

"Can't you get the picture yet? I don't want to bring it to the shop. Not tomorrow, or anytime." Quad stepped away. Suddenly in his brown loafers bright copper pennies shone in slits; it was the damnedest, silliest, sissiest thing Fred Cullins had ever seen. He had to look again. Then the boy's face that ought to look young looked hard, in the direct glare of his headlights. "I don't want to get short-tempered with you, Fred."

"No need to. I'm a reasonable man."

"So I thought. I want the car fixed here. You like your job, Fred?"

"You fixing to lose it for me?"

Quad started smiling; it seemed he might never quit. "The old man wants me to take an interest in the car business. Suppose I saw something round the shop that didn't look right? You far from your pension?"

"I didn't think so. Drive your car into the garage and let me look at what you want."

He pulled the old bolt and yanked hard to open the door. The boy got in and drove the car inside. The only light was like a plate, the light going upward, and it made the place all full of shadows. Hard to see. He never had thought before about getting another one, until now. He got his droplight.

"It's only a little fender work," the boy said, getting out. "No reason for all this fussing."

"How'd you do that to your fender?" He stood up and held the droplight toward the boy's face, watching it.

The boy's face lit up like a Halloween pumpkin, grinning while he talked, his teeth pointed as a gar's. "Had me a little run-in at the university."

"The night of the riot?"

The boy hiccuped, or pretended to, and winked. "Ran into some damn red-neck—" He stopped. "Oops."

He took back his light. College folks were always the same, always looking down on the other man who'd had to make it on his own, and they were harder to get along with in the shop than regular folks, too: had their heads full of book learning, but never had real sense—common sense. "Where's your car been since then?"

"In my garage, if that's your business. You know how it is, Fred. Get a little too much moose juice, and get into a little scrap, and you got to lay low awhile. You know?"

"No. I don't know. I might play me a little poker, but I'm a teetotaler, myself. And I don't know nothing about red-necks' business, either. Except what I hear, like them tearing up at the university. How come you was there?"

"Down at State, we didn't see why the boys at Ole Miss should be having all the fun. Had to have a look." He stepped back acting playful, and put up his hands. "I know. I know, old man. I didn't have any business over there."

"That's right." He said it in a way the boy's daddy never would have. "Well, you need you a new fender. I don't carry them out here, or at the shop in town, either."

"Then order one. From Memphis, or wherever. Special order it. Just fix this one so's I can drive it into my garage and leave it, and anybody glancing at it won't notice the difference. People be glad to have me off the streets."

"The county roads, too, from what I hear." Fred looked at the fender closer, ran his fingers over it. Not knowing exactly what to say under the circumstances, he decided to whistle and keep looking and feeling with his fingers. Then he stood up. "Got yourself all bunged up on your passenger side."

"What difference does that make?"

"I don't know." But with a worried heart, he thought he was beginning to. "You need a new fender, and a new tire. This one fixing to blow. It's ruint. All you had to do was pull her out from the fender, and it wouldn't have got cut up. You must'a been in a big hurry, son, not to take time to pull your fender out from your tire."

"I'm not much on cars except for driving them." Quad's breath smelled like beer and was warm, blowing on his face.

"Look in that clutter on that table, son. Get you that tire iron and straighten out your fender. Then drive on away. Come to the shop tomorrow."

"I want the dents out and it painted here." The boy yelled, as if he'd lost his mind.

"Fred?"

Rose's voice sounded closer than it was, back there on that old lean-to porch smelling like cat pee. He could see her with her glasses fallen forward on her short nose, without looking. "Tell your old woman to go back in the house."

"Go back in the house, Rose," he shouted without turning. "Where's the other fellow?"

"What other fellow?"

"The one you sideswiped. Or he you. Didn't you call the sheriff? Ought to find the other fellow easy, if he's anywhere round here. He'd have yellow paint scratches on his driver's side fender."

"I don't see what the side has to do with it, yet. But what other fellow? I hit a tree."

"Oh?" Kneeling on the dirt floor again, Fred made himself busy looking at the fender. He did not want to know just what everything meant, how it fit together. But he said, "Well now, son. You shore found yourself the only red tree in the county. Leastways, I calls it red. Smart fellows on the showroom floor calls it maroon." He watched the boy carefully. "That red tree left you some of its scratches on your passenger side, all right."

"What the fuck does the side have to do with it!"

He tried to dodge, but looking up saw only the halo of ceiling light and the tire iron in the boy's hand swinging right around in it; then he felt a sudden sharp thump to the side of his head. He thought how mad Rose was going to be. It was a surprise he could think at all — a surprise that he was not looking at Quad Brewster face to face any longer, but from somewhere way below him. The boy's eyes came down toward him, like big black knotholes. Quad was saying something, but Fred lay down to sleep thinking there were a whole lots of things he'd meant to do that he never had done: one of those things was to get Rose that fur coat he promised her when they married, since he had told her he wasn't going to settle for a fur collar. He would like to curl up and sleep, but a doorbell kept ringing, and he couldn't think of a one around here.

"Jesus Christ, Quad. Did you hit him with that?"

"He gave me grief. I don't like grief."

"You're crazy drunk. Crazy when you're drunk. That other one you said was giving you grief only said go home and obey the law. Even when we were rocking him in his truck that's all he said. Then you had to follow —"

"Shut up! I told a lie. Did you see me? No. You were sleeping at home like a pansy. It was a lie. I went home, too."

The other one was crying. "Is he dead?"

Fred's head was lifted like a ball separate from his body, then put back into the dirt without hurting him at all. Felt kind of gentle-like. A surprise. The warm beer breath blew on his face again. "Fred, if you don't want more trouble, fix the car, hear?"

There were no footsteps on the dirt garage floor, yet he knew they were going off. Running. Then he heard the sound of gravel being trampled, and later the motor with that little ticking going away. He kept listening, but there was nothing else. He felt sorry for himself, left back here lying down like he was. He guessed he ought to get up. In a little while he was on his hands and knees and looked into the Ferrari's fender till it stayed still, then he sat up and touched around his head. His hand in front of his face had clots of blood in it. He waited a minute before saying, "Blast that college son to hell. I done lost me a ear."

Pretty soon, he was outside. There was a sapling bound to an iron pole with a piece of sheet; the iron was cold even in this weather. So, he was headed toward the house all right, because he knew just where in the yard that sapling was: had put it there. Yes sir, he told himself. Then he said aloud, "He can drive that car right back out of there, the way he drove it in. That's my whole part in this, keeping it overnight." He walked on a little toward the house; then he felt like baying at the moon. He'd fix that sum'bitch's car, because he didn't know what the boy would do if he didn't. Me a growed-up man, Fred thought.

He touched his head, feeling he was listening to himself hard! *What I'm saying is this: something been bothering you all along about that truck of John Q's, from the time you towed the heap out of the bottomland. It come to you there was something funny about the fender underneath all that slime and yellow mud, and it seemed like you knew it was all scratched up, and it wasn't just trees and brush had done it, even if you didn't know the scratches was yellow, too. Nobody but Fred the Body Man would have sensed it. Cuss his luck.*

If only he could stop her screeching before Rose ever started it. But he had no more'n got his foot in the door than she began, waking the dead. "It's only a ear, Mother," he told her. It was hard to see her with the blood running down. He found her hands and held them flat together and put his forehead close to hers, just so's he didn't touch blood to her. He waited till those far-off colored eyes of hers turned more blue, looking into his. The pupils were like a cat's coming from the dark to the light. "Mother, stop that hollering like I told you to do. You're not calling John Joe, the doctor, not nobody."

"Why'd he do that?" she said finally, when she could. She held her wrists after he let go. She floated backward and forward. He said, "I'm going to take a shower. You got some whiskey left over from your fruitcakes?"

"Are you going to drink it?"

"All you got," he told her.

He was finding the door, when she bent down to the cabinet under the kitchen sink, and said, squatting, "I don't call it left over, I just call it whiskey for next year's fruitcakes."

He went on. Inside the shower, he heard her calling over and over could she come in, and turned off the water. He wrapped a little towel around his head like a turban, one of the ones she called a hand towel, and put a big towel on like a skirt, so she could come in. She'd never wanted to see him with no clothes on. He told her to come in. Her apron was pouched out, like she was pregnant: holding the whiskey under it so she wouldn't see it, he guessed. Embarrassed. Bleed to death, and she was embarrassed. He had to jolly her up some, so tried to sway back and forth, but his head hurt too bad. "Remember how the past potentate did the hula at that last Shriners' party we were at?" She nodded, pleased. His coming up from Mason to Shriner was the biggest thing that had come along in her life in a long time: kept her busy fooling with the woman's half. He couldn't remember the name tonight, but Rose stood behind him in most things he undertook to do. He was seeing the past potentate's rolls of belly fat when he did the hula, then stopped his own dancing because of the pain. He drank as much whiskey as he could stand at once.

"This all?"

"You going to drink some more?" Her mouth and eyes looked as large as doughnut holes; her whole face got bigger. She said finally, "I've got that rum from that rum cake I made." All at once, she blushed so bad, she looked like a young pretty girl again, covering her mouth to titter a little bit, the way young girls do. She was still afraid some of the Baptists would find out, still hadn't gotten over how she dared to buy the rum. "Bring it," he told her.

"It never was nothing but a pint," she said, reassuring herself.

When she came back, he was sitting on the closed lid of the toilet. She looked at his black bag with his instruments for doctoring on his cows when he could—no sense paying a vet when one breeched at birth—as he was dusting it off. He put some of the strong, shiny black thread in his mouth and held the big needle to the light, then she got the message and said, "You're not going to sew that ear on yourself?"

"No'm." He took the thread out of his mouth. "You are. Now, Mother," he said, "I tried to see round in the mirror how to do it, and I can't." He got up and pulled her forward again, as she seemed permanently glued to the backs of her heels. She came a little forward. He took the rum out of her hand. The whiskey in his stomach was doing him some good, driving out the thoughts in his head as well as the pain. He drank some rum and spit into the sink.

"I can't," she said.

"Yes, you can. You know why?"

After she shook her head, he said, "Because there's not nobody else to."

"I can't," she said.

"Look at it like this, Mother. Remember those pretty little rag dolls you used to sew and carry to the Mid-South Fair? Won you a blue ribbon one time. Now, just pretend I'm a doll."

"You're real, Fred."

"Mother. You rather have me stand here and bleed to death like I'm fixing to do?"

He knew she would when her tongue formed a funnel in her mouth, and the tip showed between her lips, that look of being busy she got. He could hear her breath whistling along the funnel while she sewed. Her hand went way out into air pulling the black thread, her eyes following as if she wasn't sure where the thread might be going, before coming close to his head again. It wasn't more than some little bitty stings, he told her, drinking the rum in between stitches. Then the scissors snipped close to his head, as if he were having a haircut. Afterward Rose sank to the edge of the tub, her hands holding it. "I might be sick."

She hung her head into the toilet bowl, but nothing ever came but the dry heaves, her face turning splotchy and her eyes bugging out, till she stopped having them and said she'd get some lemonade in the kitchen. He lay down on their bed for the pain to throb into the pillow; then she was sitting by him, in the room without much light. It seemed like their courting days. "Tell me what happened," she said.

"I caught my ear in that old wringer washer of yours. Washing my overalls after work. You always had told me to be careful of that thing, hadn't you?"

"I never had known you to wash your own coveralls."

"Mother. Use your imagination. Things like that happen. Remember the time Miss Edie Burton caught one of her long old titties in hers."

"Hush your mouth, Fred," she said. "I think men could go to talking dirty after a little communion wine."

"More accidents happen in the home than anywhere. I read that. It's a national known fact."

"You going to tell me what happened, or not?"

"Not," he said, sleepy.

"I could be the one reported the boy."

"Not if you want me to keep my job, Mother. Be a shame not to finish paying our notes on this house after all this time, or to lose my pension."

"I don't want that boy not to get what he deserves."

"How about something you deserve?" He lifted his head. "How about that new electric washer you been eyeing in the Sears catalogue so long? Time we need it after this bad accident in the home, with the old one."

She was thinking hard, her glasses turning toward everything in the room, blinking by themselves. She started tracing around and around a big polka dot on her dress with her forefinger, then looked at him over the glasses. "What about the dryer that matches?" she said.

He lay down. "We'd have to see."

"But, Fred. What was it he come here wanting you to do?"

"Nothing, Mother. Nobody was here tonight. Understand?"

25

TOMORROW WAS Friday. That was her last conscious thought before falling asleep, while looking at moonlight flowing into the farthest corners of the bedroom. She had a lot of mismatched dreams, before a clear one about John Q standing in Loma's only a week ago. She pointed to the calendar and told him that a week later he would not be here. She knew she did not like her dreams.

Sleeping, she kept asking herself why she did not want to wake up. And told herself she was tired, that there had been enough for a while. The part of herself that did not want to wake up had to find some solution, then, to noise about to wake her — someone talking. It had to be Tate talking to Sweetie, though it did not sound like him. She forced her head to the edge of the mattress and looked down to see a spot darker than shadow that was Sweetie sleeping in her usual place. Allie opened her eyes wider, as if her eyes were listening. The conversation made them want to close, it went on so steadily, low, like bees humming in clover in summertime. It came from Poppa's room: someone besides him was there. She did not remember getting out of bed, only that she was running out without her robe or slippers. Suddenly the floor furnace grating in the hallway was cutting her feet, making them burn. She stood a minute, making sure she had her bearings.

As quickly as Poppa woke every morning, he told Allie and Tate he hadn't slept a wink, believing that himself. So they stopped telling him how his snoring bothered their own rest. Afraid of his having an attack in the night, after leaving the bedroom doors open, she gave Poppa a bell also, in case he might need her and not be able to call; the bell did not work out. Poppa would set the clapper ringing just to make certain Allie would hear him. Having leapt across the hall, she'd find him lying there and grinning and timing her by his alarm clock; soon he fell back asleep, while she was awake the rest of the night. Though she told him the fable about the little boy crying wolf once too often, Poppa failed to apply the moral to himself and only wanted to know if she knew some more tales.

Sometimes, after saying he'd heard the hall clock strike all the predawn hours, he would raise his voice and cry, Dong! for every numeral overheard. They cut him short at six, since they were up by then and knew if he slept, or not. Tate countered on occasion by saying, Oh, is that right, old man? What time in the morning did the rain start?

Rain? Rain? he'd say, and tell them with an honest, straight face that dew had filled up the birdbath last night, or maybe he did doze for a second. A second? Tate would say. It thundered and lightened half the night. Maybe he dozed a few minutes, Poppa would say. Tate would ask if he heard the limb break off the big oak by the house? This, of course, would be the night Poppa had despaired and taken one of the sleeping pills the doctor had given him.

Sleeping under air conditioning made his bones ache, so he always opened a window at night. Maybe thought he was dreaming when someone spoke to him in his old four-poster, a head through a window: maybe heard nothing till the words brushed his face.

She made certain of her bearings in the nighttime house, while her feet itched from the grillwork. Even still half asleep, she had recognized that it was a Negro's voice talking: she had heard some of the words; they came clear as if from somewhere in the back of her head.

"Mist' Zenos, wake up. Talk to me, Elgie. How come you done me like you done? Song at Parchman they sings. Goes, 'I'm settin' down here on Parchman farm. I ain't never did nobody no harm. . . .' "

Then she came in. To Elgie she might have been a ghost, her nightgown wide, full, and white. She said his name. Before she spoke, he was gone. His hair had looked whiter than even the moonlight. She had seen only that — the top of his head disappearing, saw it with the same sense of shock, surprise, wonder that a star was viewed, falling, slipping past sight as one wondered if it really had been there, at all: a ghostly white pate, a ghostly star.

She looked out the window, half seeing him as if he were a shadow dodging trees, bushes, and circlets of flowerbeds outlined in white stones, which looked now like traps yawning for his feet, in white shoes with flapping tongues. He was gone.

"Poppa?" She went to the bed. He was not sleeping, yet she wanted him to be. How much easier just to say, Go on sleeping. She did all she could think of, quickly. Bending, she put her own rounded mouth to his open one, but feared she sucked breath rather than gave it. Suppose she were scaring him to death? Drawing back, she pounded a rhythmic beat on his chest with fists that seemed inadequate, though he was dead. She knew that. Possibly was it too late before Elgie came here tonight? How many times had she expected Poppa to die, and been told to expect it suddenly, this way; yet none of that made it any easier. A sense of guilt ran through her, that it was over. She would not, she saw, ever be free, after all. He had been part of her life too long. She began to cry. Passed over, he called dying. She hoped he was safe. His eyes in the moonlight were dime colored. They matched those above him, glassy, glazed, bluish, looking back at her from the mounted deer head above the bed, the one taken in the woods that day a friend thought a bear was a nigger in a fur coat, and Poppa had gone on laughing for years.

He smelled of Mentholatum from the nightly rub to his chest; the room smelled of apples which he hid, as if from himself, to give the room their scent. He seemed a child lying there in cotton pajamas buttoned to his chin. Poppa, after all. Her fingers were wet with tears, too, when she put them out to close his eyes: tight against this world.

26

POPPA'S FUNERAL on Sunday seemed repetitious after John Q's, following so close on its heels. People were kindly but could not really mourn a man his age who'd died peacefully in his sleep—supposedly. Allie told Tate the truth and she knew he thought it only hers; they had all the rituals of burying to take care of, so she said, "All right. I'll wait a few days. But no longer. Then I'll smoke Elgie out of the cabin if I have to. You'll help me do what I have to?"

With tightened lips, Tate told her not to be so antsy: not to have ants in her pants for some reason lost on him, he meant, not believing anything but that she was following some imaginary red herring in a mystery concocted in her head. "It's for the law," he said stubbornly, and meant to be pacifying, but she felt the disconnection to him that was new, still.

Across Poppa's grave, Miss Pearlie Mae's eyes in a face flushed with apprehension clearly recalled what she'd said about death coming in threes, only turned pale. She would be thinking that at her age the next death could be her own. Allie tried to concentrate on Brother Walker's familiar words and forgot to smile back reassuringly. Someone had remarked this would probably be Brother Walker's last funeral here, as he had been called to a larger church. Doffing his hat with due respect to the bereaved, Billy John came up after the service, hating to bring up the subject now, but the community had to form its own pulpit committee. Would Tate serve on it? Leave Allie alone for the next few Sundays? he was asking cautiously. She nodded approval. Suddenly, she wondered why women were not included in the search for a preacher, when they gave more time to the church than men. Why were they expected to clean the sanctuary, prepare meals, and leave the kitchen perfect after various functions, but never were asked to pass the collection plates or pray before the congregation? Tate went with other men to make plans, while she looked ahead to the house stripped now of Poppa's personal effects, most given away to Negroes, some burned, only the old Purdy left in its place, and his worn gold watch suspended on a small stand under a glass cover. Beneath a canopy of oaks, acorns thinly cracking from her footsteps, pretending to listen to others, she thought that for the first time she had a guest room: she would furnish it to her own liking, with ruffled curtains and a flowery spread. She saw Tate look suddenly like an old man, bending with his hand fashioning a trumpet to one ear as he said repeatedly, "What?" in a voice loud for him. Something outlandish suggested by a pulpit committee?

Thinking of Poppa she wondered if the dead were resentful that the living so promptly went on with their daily tasks and with thoughts of the future, when they were hardly out of sight. Laughter among people as they returned to their cars jarred her, and seemed inappropriate. As she neared her own car, people with solicitous faces opened up a pathway, leaving her again to a limelight not of her own making, as had happened when Sy came to church. She fought for the subdued look appropriate to next of kin, when her eyes caught a glitter and went up a pair of sheeny black pants and past a stringy black tie to look into Snake Johnson's arrogant, doggy face. Tate got into the car. Instantly she cried, "What's Snake doing wearing John Q's gun and holster?"

"I just heard. He's the new constable."

"No!"

"Endorsed by the high sheriff so highly, the board of supervisors approved him."

"John Joe's lost his mind?"

"John Joe probably got tired of looking for somebody to fill John Q's shoes. Folks suppose Snake volunteered. Though something strikes us all as fishy about the deal. Even though Snake and John Joe are kin somewhere way back down the line."

"They're not close enough kin for him to move Snake up from doormat to constable," she said.

"I reckon nobody expects politicians to be honest," Tate said.

"Why not?"

Tate shrugged. "Maybe there's nothing funny about it, since John Joe asked others."

"But who? Who'd he ask?"

He drove along in his cautious way. "Now that you mention it, I don't know. Nobody mentioned being asked." He braked ahead for a dog crossing the road, and spoke slowly. "Always has seemed strange John Joe's elected when not a soul you know's going to vote for him."

"Elected," she said. "Who in this world's going to run against Snake?"

"That," Tate said, coming to a complete halt before turning

in over the driveway, causing those behind to stop short, "is what you call the sixty-four-dollar question." Suddenly, she thought he had not called her hon in quite a while. "If John Q didn't have an opponent in the August primaries, I don't see how Snake can be anything but a shoo-in in November." He very carefully turned off the air conditioner before the ignition.

Poppa had lived in the county so long many people had known him all their lives, and felt it their duty to come to the funeral. Only Poppa would not have been surprised by the number, or thought anything about how many people had to introduce themselves to his daughter. To her they were only familiar family names in the area, without personal identities. Allie was as pleased as Poppa would have been. Glancing all around the house, she was glad the many flowers gave it a cheerful air rather than the depressing one of a funeral parlor; both sides of the church and its rear had been lined with floral offerings. The house might be a huge flower shop, and the arrangements all for sale. They seemed a bit wasteful when the flowers would die so soon. A new, strange thought came to her: there was something a bit archaic about funerals. She had not liked Poppa's waxed-looking figure on display. Always before, hearing of cremations, she'd felt something drop out of the bottom of her stomach, had been repulsed. What did it mean that she no longer considered it such a bad idea? Minnie had shined with spit, she suspected, all the inherited cut glass, but its polish was perfect; the restored oak dining-room furniture shone, and the table with her momma's heirloom lace cloth looked lovely; tall tapers of a morning-glory blue melded away finally into the blue of dusk. The only unpeaceful mishap was Fred Cullins knocking over a candle into the centerpiece of chrysanthemums in a wicker basket, and singeing it before the candle could be stood upright again, helping himself to lime-sherbet punch but spilling most of it on his sleeve.

Short little Rose's eyes looked like silvery tadpoles, swimming around behind her glasses, with worry. She told everyone Fred was taking too many tranquilizers because his head still throbbed from his cut, and he was taking aspirin to boot. People in other rooms assumed he fell because of his imbalance in his rocking shoe. Several people whispered they thought the man'd been drinking. "Shoot. Fred!" said another voice. Fred had come in for a good ribbing about catching his ear in his wife's washer. The ear was an ugly sight with those crisscrossed black stitches. Melinda Morris said it made her too sick to eat. Ardella wished he'd worn that old cap he always wore backward in his shop. When Rose got him out at last, it was noted she took the driver's seat. Watching Snake outside seeing them off, Allie thought it would be a cold day in hell before she'd mention Elgie to him or to John Joe.

Suddenly, Miss Pearlie Mae squealed, "Loma, that's uptown and no place to park!" Allie joined the conversation to hear at last Loma's new use for her old storeroom. Itna Homa was to have a Laundromat, causing Miss Pearlie Mae to squeal again, "Uptown and no place to park!" in admiration.

"Surely, you're not going to let the colored use it." Carrie Thomas had made her own statement.

"It's mostly the colored who don't have their own washers and dryers," Loma said. She looked at certain ones. "You let them carry your clothes home to wash and iron. The clothes lay around on the Negroes' beds. They probably wear them."

Several women laughed. Allie thought of Poppa's aversion to penicillin and said, "The time's long past when there was a reason for separate facilities."

"Water in Laundromats is plenty hot," Letty Brown said, a little unsure how hot. Loma had a set look: she had not kept store so long for nothing. She knew women would wear down at the inconvenience of toting everything ten miles to Whitehill; even though the two facilities there were still segregated by some unspoken, but mutual, consent.

"Four washers and two family-sized dryers," Loma said. "In what the Maytag salesman says is tawny beige. Decorator colors." Loma was proud. Then her freckles stood out when her face became frightened. "Only he says everywhere he's installed some, they've been jammed and jimmied. People use screw-drivers trying to get out money, and put in slugs. I've got to make mine pay for themselves before I start repairing them." She looked even paler, thinking about it.

"Got the constable at your back door," Letty said dryly.

"He'll be the first there with the screwdriver," said Ardella. "This community's come to a sorry sight."

"Has not," her husband said, coming up and hearing only the last. "Got the fire department off its feet. Final plans'll be made tomorrow evening. Mister Otis is donating his old barn for us to keep the engine in. We're setting up the main committee to get started on the academy. We're growing."

Everyone was gone. Tate was carrying food back to the kitchen. Ardella stood last at the door. "Sugar, I know you can't go round the public yet. But everybody else will be at the meeting tomorrow night. We'll put you on a committee."

"No." Allie spoke so quickly she frightened herself. Too much else was on her mind. She only told Ardella it was too soon. The lawn emptied of cars, and her heart raced, while she thought of the evening ahead.

27

THE TIME HAD COME and she was no longer afraid. Her nervousness disappeared as they talked, though she heard herself answer faintly one of Elgie's questions. "Tucker telephone? No, I don't believe I ever have," Allie said.

"The Tucker telephone is worked on a hand crank," Elgie said. "You going to have to 'cuse me, Miss Allie?" She bobbed her head. "They tied those two 'lectric wires to a man's testicles and then crank that phone and it had its own 'lectric circuit, don't you see?"

They were in Sy's. And memory, not the stuffy cabin, was making Elgie sweat. "It not likely you would have heard of that phone, Miss Allie," Elgie said. "Them young prisoners down to the farm didn't know nothing 'bout the old ways, either. Good old days wasn't so good there. Gov'ment in-spectors come in though and have changed things. Before that it were a rough go."

"I imagine it was." Allie felt the government's eye on every sparrow, like God's, as well as inside this little cabin, too.

They had talked a long time in the larger of Sy's two unpainted rooms. The smaller was his kitchen, with a wood-working stove perched atop bricks and an old chifferobe tilted into a dark corner. A table stored his armful of supplies. On the floor was a heap of browned plastic gallon milk jugs, tied together by rope; now they held Sy's water supply, which he drew from a spigot outside Loma's. In the second, larger room, a full-length cedar swing hung on iron chains from the ceiling. Sy sat there looking into blue flames jumping in a gas heater. He wore indoors or out an old brown felt hat of Tate's with a black grosgrain ribbon, now shredding.

Sy heard Elgie's explanation of the Tucker telephone and pulled the hat straighter. "I say," he said.

Elgie continued, "I went down yonder young and feisty. Told myse'f they could break the other man, but not me. That natural-born how young peoples is."

"They sho is," Sy said.

"I commenced running off, don't you see? Ran outen them fields ever' chance I cotched. They got tired settin' them dawgs after me." He laughed. His teeth were not so white as she remembered them, Allie thought.

"Tell you 'bout them blood dawgs too," Elgie said. "They likes folks. That how come they keeps them on them long leashes 'stead of the dawg running free. Dawg come up on a prisoner by itself and would go on off wif you. Be me and him. Dawg don't keer who he go wif." They all laughed.

Then Elgie wiped his face with a handkerchief. "Used to was, down yonder a man could get hongry, too. Had aplenty food don't you know? But last man or so in line liable to get a big rat served up out of a vat with his supper. Lemme tell you too, it wasn't no better for the white man than the colored man. There just was mo' of us colored. Still is."

"We have got some of the worstis folks," Sy said loudly. "I have had white peoples do me better than my own peoples, yas suh." She looked at Elgie, meaning was Sy serious when he spoke like this, or saying it for her benefit, because she'd never known? But Elgie was too deep in his own thoughts. "They cured me of running with that phone," he said.

"I guess they did," she said. Sy nodded.

Elgie wiped his face again. "It have all improved one hundert percent. The young peoples coming in now, they different. Went to calling me a Uncle Tom. See, but they hadn't seed all I had down on that place. Folks don't just disappear no mo' like they used to done, or turn up dead in the field. Man be black and blue and doctor stand there and tell the free world he died of sunstroke. Didn't nobody care back then. I was one of the oldest numbers they had down there. Didn't have no family to come speaking for me. Some folks come and visited awhile but dropped off, 'cause that's human nature, don't you know? I was still wearing my old ringarounds from back in the time I come there. Clothes didn't matter to me. Young peoples told me to take them things off. I was made trusty and commenced wearing these white clothes they gimme. Even if it hadn't of been a Tucker telephone, after time had passed, my running days were coming down."

"I know what you mean." She smiled.

"Naw'um. You ain't old. You be's a nice-looking woman, Miss Allie."

"Why, thank you. But you're not all that old either, Elgie. And not stepping forward and letting the law decide things is wrong. Run on from here to Chicago? You are old to go there and start over alone." She leaned toward him.

"I rather be a lamp pole in Harlem than a rich nigger in Miss'sippi," Elgie said.

"Things are changing," she told him.

"You listen, brother," Sy said. "White is right."

"Sy, that's not a popular idea anymore," she said.

"Ma'm?"

She shook her head.

"Brighter day ahead," Sy said. "That what the preacher have said. Told all us the white man have had the state of Miss'sippi. He going to have to calm hisse'f. Got anything on his mind and going to have to hold it back. Education have been held back. Now the young peoples going to get what they deserves."

"If anything can lead me to God that is it," Elgie said.

Earlier she had chosen Elgie's own nighttime and dodging route here. She had to bide her time only once, hugging a tree, when a truck passed on the road below, somebody late for the town meeting. She had crouched in the ditch, knee-deep in goldenrod and thin spiky wild blue asters, and then darted across to Sy's door, the dog on the porch knowing her and only lifting its head and then its tail to thump the porch. Sy cried out, "Who 'at?" as instantly as she knocked, hardly audible—though the town beyond was as silent as a tomb, as darkened, and the wide road seemed paved not with yellow dirt and gravel, but smoothly, with solid, moon-colored stone. Sy's great cedar sighed, and she smelled its fragrance. The quick silence in the house was broken by scufflings, for, once she'd said, "It's Miss Allie," Sy had no excuse not to open the door.

"Yas'um, yas'um," he said, opening the door and excusing his taking so long. "I was fixing to take me a bath." Beyond his tall thin figure she did see a number-three washtub in the middle of the kitchen floor and pots heating on the potbellied stove.

"Sy, I've come to see Elgie."

Nothing in the wide, dark countryside seemed to shine like the whites of Sy's eyes as he stepped backward. She might have socked him. She pushed easily past and saw an empty cabin and said right off, "Come on out of the chifferobe, Elgie."

Very strongly, the cabin smelled of kerosene Sy used to wash down his walls to rid himself of spiders, despite Tate's warnings. "Oh," said Sy, rather late. "How you, Miss Allie?"

The chifferobe door creaked open as slowly as in a mystery story. After Elgie stepped out, she told him of her long-held suspicions and also that she knew he did not kill Poppa, that the doctor had said for ages Poppa could go out like a light, anytime: so he had. Probably, it was for the best because he certainly had nothing ahead of him.

The chifferobe smelled inside of camphor and old things, and had a scent mindful of clothes dried outdoors, on windy afternoons, in rain or sun. Would amenities go on even beyond the grave, she wondered and imagined the Devil and the Lord saying, How you? for Elgie said, as if they had met yesterday, "How you today, Miss Allie?"

"Fine. How're you?"

"He doing all right," Sy said. He led them into the larger room where they all chose seats. She and Elgie stared at each other shyly the way they probably always had, bound together by shared experience and yet set apart. "Last time I 'members us together, you know when it was?" Elgie said.

She tensed before remembering her last memory was not his.

He went on. "Mist' Zenos he carried us to Nashtoba. Carried us to see a big old snake they had in *The Democrat* window. That rascal was four foot long and four inches wide and had six rattlers and a button."

"Get on out of here," Sy said.

"No, I remember," she said. "We went another time to take that funny sweet potato I dug. Remember? You had helped me make my first little garden. The potato had grown round some baling wire. You couldn't get that out without ruining the potato, but it was edible. They wrote it up in the paper as a freak vegetable and I worried that would hurt the potato's feelings!"

"I 'members that 'tato too," Elgie said.

"Wasn't just children interested back then in a freak sweet potato and a snake in a newspaper's window. Everybody came to see them. Didn't have much else to do, or much else to see out of the ordinary. Those things were hot news," Allie said.

Elgie's face darkened. "I 'members something else about that day, though. A man come by in a pickup with two-by-fours sticking out its rear. Come close to the sidewalk as he could trying to knock me off. Did that on Saur'days when the town was full of colored folks. That was they sport."

"They sho done it," cried Sy, laughing in a gleeful way without his eyes changing from a solemn expression.

"I never did think the white peoples was serious fools, though," Elgie said. "Went down yonder to the pen, a boy, and used to sit and wonder, If hell such a big place, how come it ain't full of white peoples? All I knew was that the white man was in control of everything in the United States. He know everything first. Long as he know everything first he goin' stay in control. You can't beat the white man. You can't beat him with a short stick."

"Preacher say time coming you can," Sy burst out. His round fearful eyes nearly hidden by his hat glanced toward her.

Elgie spoke as if she were not there, glancing into space, testing her. "You has to feel sorry for the po' white trash. Don't have nothing but to kick a dawg or a Negro. Outside everything. They must be the most lonesomest peoples in this world."

Sy slapped both knees. "Preacher say white man have had this state. But when a man arrested from now on he going be arrested like a man. Yas suh! They going to talk to you and treat you like a man, not going to whup you up. Miss'sippi going have to open its heart and mind, preacher said. Yas suh!" he went on saying to himself awhile.

She said, "Elgie, where was I that Saturday? I don't remember the truck incident."

"Naw'um, you had gone into the drugstore to get each us a comb of cream. Mister Zenos he had done give us bof a nickel. Nigger, he can go into the white man's drugstore and spend his money on all he got but his food."

"Young peoples, they going to change that all too," Sy said, stuffing hands into his pockets and stretching out his shoes toward the flames. "Time got to be here, Elgie, there wasn't no young peoples round here. Ain'ts that right, Miss Allie?"

He looked up. She said, "It was right. Nothing for them to do around here till these little factories started coming in."

"Yas suh," Sy said. "Got them little fact'ries in here or all the young peoples they be from here still."

"No future for any of them in farming," she said. "Negro or white."

"All their daddies could do was tell 'em, go on." Sy looked at them steadily. "Young peoples want that right now money."

Elgie laughed. "Ain't never had much of that farming cotton."

"Not in these hills," she said.

"Not nowhere," Elgie said. "Living high on that credit in the Delta just like us always done."

"Tate says farmers are like camouflaged tanks," she said. "Everybody got a house and a pickup out front and a tractor and so on, and don't anybody own any of it."

"Can't blame the young peoples for going," Elgie said, rubbing his hands together. "But coming back now?"

"Sho is," said Sy. "It be lonesome when they gone. They tells me the young peoples be lonesome too, gone off. Say water in they eyes when they start off from here, and there when they see these hills again. Get off from here and don't know who they is, see? Then they raise up chillen off from here and those chillen sho don't know. Don't know they own peoples. That sad."

"Well," she said. "I guess the government's just daddy to everybody now. Elgie, did you learn a trade in prison?"

Elgie turned around. "Learned how to chop cotton." His laugh was short. "Knew how to chop cotton when I went down yonder."

"I reggin," Sy said.

"Chopping cotton about played out, so I went to driving a mule to haul garbage. Knew how to drive a mule when I went down yonder, too. Did some garden work, but my knee went to bothering me bad. What else I'm going do? A man my age ain't got no education, he too old to ketch up."

"What about Momma? Didn't she teach you to read?" Having had a hard time mentioning her mother, she sat back pressing her arms to her ribs.

Elgie swung a flyswatter a long time, Sy's eyes roving back and forth following it. Something settled in himself and Elgie sat back. "I'm going be honest with you. She was sincere at first and teached me a whole lot more than I'da learned in that colored school. I learnt my letters good now. But that spelling, it come hard. If I could have kep' on though, I believe I could have learnt. I believe I could."

She leaned over. "At first, Elgie?"

He stopped swinging the flyswatter. "Ma'm?"

"Momma, you said, was sincere at first."

Elgie studied Sy. Sy studied the toes of his shoes turned up at the ends of his long legs. "What did you mean?" She made her voice demanding, yet the other two went on about their silent business: looking off from her. Finally Elgie put a finger in one ear and rang as if to shake out water and then stared at the finger, reading some message, it seemed. "At first?" she said.

"At first, us started out in y'all's kitchen." Elgie looked at Sy, who felt the gaze and said, "Tha's right." As neither would look at her, she began to feel slow rage.

"You be sincere with me," she said.

"Y'all had a good cook back then." Elgie reared back to stare at the ceiling above her head. "I forgot that woman's name."

"Maggie," Allie said.

"I 'members that girl," Sy said agreeably.

"Elgie," she said.

"You 'member her, Sy? That woman could cook!"

"She sho could cook," Sy said.

"Ever' time I come into that kitchen that woman had something good to eat. Had gingerbread, cookies, corn pone, puddin' —"

"Elgie," she said again.

"Say you eat her cooking, Sy?"

"I eat a bunch of that woman's cooking."

Not intending to, she found herself crying, the tears like long streams of cold, silk threads along each side of her nose, and, reaching around, she had nothing to use as a handkerchief.

The men looked at each other uneasily. Sy brought her his roll of toilet paper. "You sho be sweating too," Sy said. "Yas'um, you can sho sweat some, Miss Allie."

"Not used to these old hot houses," Elgie said, turning down the heater's flames a little.

Feeling she hardly could breathe, she broke off a long piece from the roll, tried to smile, thanked Sy, and hid her face behind the paper a moment and apologized. Then she stopped crying as quickly as she started and said, "Elgie, please just tell it all straight out," wearing what she hoped was a brave smile. In answer, he moved his bottom lip enough to show its inner, whiter part. "You started out in the kitchen," she said. "Then what?"

"Started out studying in y'all's kitchen. Then went to studying out in Mammy Lou and my's cabin."

"That was Momma's idea?"

"I reggin." Elgie watched the flyswatter move slowly.

"You know it was," Allie said. "Where was Mammy Lou?"

His sigh was a long one of remembering and love. "Mammy Lou," he said.

"You know whether or not Mammy Lou was in the cabin, Elgie."

"What does you think, Miss Allie?" He looked up.

She clenched the paper in her hand into a wet, small ball. "Where'd she go? Momma told her to leave?"

"Told her? Mammy Lou was a ole colored woman didn't

have to be told something like that. You knows how things was."

"Where did she go?"

"Stay in the yard, or go uptown."

Of course, she thought, remembering the little woman under a shade tree in a straight chair that never seemed uncomfortable. She moved only to spit snuff, her pert, wrinkled face monkey-wise. Had Mammy Lou approved?

Elgie said, "Now, I'm going tell you the truth. I didn't want no kind of nothing like that."

Like what? She wanted him suddenly to lie; wasn't it natural to want to protect her own mother? Yet May Stewart was not simply a foolish woman, but a bad one with self-serving motives, who did not care about involving helpless people in trouble, so her eyes told Elgie to tell the truth she almost knew.

"I begged that woman let me alone. Told her she ain't going start nothing but trouble. Ast Mammy Lou what I ought do. She say I best do like Miss May want. Or she might put us off that place. I couldn't do nothing but take keer Mammy Lou."

"She couldn't have," Allie said. "It was Poppa's place. His daddy's before that. He said your family, like Sy, could stay on his land as long as you wanted."

"Us couldn't be sure. You don't know how a man going do over something a woman says. Don't know he going do like his daddy tell him, when that man in his grave."

"And done been in it," Sy said.

"Miss May, she might have turnt Mist' Zenos round 'gainst us."

"I doubt it, though I see it would depend on what she said. Might have been something that would make Poppa have to act against his own grain. I guess you were scared."

"Colored peoples used to that," Sy said. "They all the time scared. Lived in fear back yonder in them days."

"Fear is something the white peoples just learning," Elgie said.

"Tell me what I'm afraid to hear, then," she said.

"I don't see no sense in it," Elgie said.

"Well, there is! If I'm to help you I've got to know."

Before he could protest, she went on. "I am going to help you. You'll promise me to stay here till I talk to a lawyer and find out how to go about it. If it all begins to look hopeless, then run. I'll help you do that too. You can go to Chicago first class. I'll scrape up the money for a plane ticket. Go ahead, Elgie." She leaned forward and placed a hand for a minute on his knee.

"It hard to tell." He bowed his head. "It like something I dreamt." Then he stretched out in Sy's stance and, sometimes looking at the fire, said, "She were like a 'squito. Hardly know whether that woman really touched you or not. Think she put her hand on my leg, or arm, whilst I was reading, but it so light it be gone and I could think it hadn't of happened. Same like when she pass back of the cheer. I would think she touch me, but next minute she be looking at me from yonder in a corner. It would seem like she couldn't have did bof things, rub up against me and be yonder looking at me sweetlike too. Then when she went to putting her hand on mine to hep teach me my letters, I couldn't fool myse'f no longer."

"What did you do?"

"I kep' on being smart enough to play nigger-dumb, what I done. Try to inch off from her and she get mad. Finally ast me if I don't know what going on? I say, Yes'um, you trying hep me learn my letters. She say, 'Oh, Elgie.' I kep' on staying like a stone and not getting any learning in my head. Too scared. One day she put her head in her arms down on the table and commenced to cry. Now, that woman cried some. I had to feel real sorry for that white lady."

"I've never imagined my mother crying."

"She cried that time. Said the white peoples all thought she did a lot of things she hadn't did. Said she just liked to kid around with the mens. There was no more to it.

"Said Mist' Zenos don't care nothing but about his farming and hunting and give mo' time to his pointers than to her. She wanted somebody show some affection to her, and her to him. Said what she wanted was hep train me like she'd hep her own flesh, but had done gone and—"

"What?" she said.

"—and lost her head." Elgie looked ashamed.

"I wonder if that was the truth, though?" she said. "What happened on the . . . last day?"

"I have dreamt that day over again," Elgie said. "She had done gone finally and got im-patient."

"Did you ever suggest not having lessons?" she said.

"Sho I did! She wa'n't having no truck with that. Then that day I believe that woman had been into something."

"You mean like whiskey?"

"Yes'um. I believe she had been into Mist' Zenos' white lightning, 'cause she just different. Was out of her head. She come up and start—"

"Yes?"

Elgie filled his lungs. "Start unbuttoning my shirt. I got off 'cross the room and told her I ain't having nothing do wif nothing like what she want. Told her Mist' Zenos liable to kill me."

"I'm sure she said he'd never know."

"Yes'um, that sho what she said. Then she crying some mo' telling me she ain't supposed to come begging. Who I'm think I is turning her down? I told her I ain't turnt her down, but she had to get holt of herse'f and go home and she'd be glad. She say she ain't never glad to go home, can't stand home. I told her go on somewhere with some white peoples then, 'cause she ain't going do nothing but get me and Mammy Lou in trouble. Finally she commenced calling me names, black ape and all them other names the white peoples had."

"They sho had 'em," Sy said.

"Poor Momma," she said. "Hard on a woman to have to beg. And what were you doing?"

"Still standing up yonder against the wall across the room from her like I had been doing. She suddenly yank up the coal-oil lamp on the table and chunk it at my head. That the honest God truth about what happened. That lamp hit that old double-barrel shotgun of Mist' Zenos' she had done gimme. Didn't have no hammer and the safety all wore out. I didn't have me no white man's gun rack, had some nails in the wall and the gun setting on them. It swung right off the wall and the butt hit the flo' and it fired, is what happened. Not a white person would listen. When I say, 'You think a colored boy going shoot a white lady?' they all said, 'Naw.' They think she had the gun on me for trying to mess wif her, and I knocked it away and kilt her. Or that the bestest idea any of 'em had."

In a minute, Sy said, "I got to get this Garrett out my mouf," and went into the other room and opened the door to spit. Standing too, she moved stiffly behind him and breathed in muggy night air; in that instant Allie saw frondy things moving in the wind and the dark/light ripple of grass down Sy's front yard and across the road in her own. As she stood in the doorway of the cabin, Elgie stood tiredly too and pulled the string attached to the light bulb overhead. More string stretched from the swing's iron chains held a shallow pan of water beneath the bulb. Bugs batted the light and often fell into the water below it. In the room she heard only the faint gasping sound of the gas jets, then suddenly a *plink*, and afterward, silence, while she thought of the bug drowning. When Sy came back, the dog was with him, and they all sat and watched it twist around and around, nose to tail, trying to decide how to lie down; finally it sank down with a sigh. She had read the first page of a church bulletin lying on a rickety small table:

> Charming sight to see the halt, the blind, the lame and the old in big numbers standing round and receiving help from this Christ-like Government. Long live the Government.

She stopped reading, not only because Sy and the dog came in.

"You didn't see me outside the cabin that day, Elgie?" she said.

He said, "I didn't see nothing but that fast-moving sky. Didn't see them white mens either till I come right up on 'em, standing and waiting. One of 'em said, 'Got your heart in Dixie, boy? But trying to git yo ass out?' "

"They told Poppa later they had stopped because any nigger moving that fast had to have done something wrong."

"Yes suh," said Elgie, clapping his hands. "Not a serious fool among 'em."

Sy swung slowly. He looked at a picture of Jesus torn from a magazine and pinned crookedly to sheetrock covering what had been his fireplace.

"I can't trust white peoples. Don't trust 'em no farther than I can see 'em. And I'm near-sighted myse'f," Elgie said.

"But you trust me to find out if I can help you? You'll still be hiding if you run to Chicago. How have you stood this life so long?" She looked about the cabin.

"Git out and roam around at night," he said. "Git aplenty exercise and sleep in the daytime. Just got to be keerful on nights when Mister Snake have his old poker game. Now, looka here, Miss Allie. The biggest source of fear for the white peoples have always been reality. Not a white man or woman going to act like they believe Miss May done something wrong. The white woman have been on her ped'stal a long time, long time. Can't change ever'thing overnight 'cause one colored boy going to the white man's school. How come they all so worried 'bout that? He just trying to add a little color to the place." They all laughed.

She went to the door and listened to night sounds and opened it only wide enough to slip through. She said, "Elgie, stay and give me some time to help you."

"How you going hep me, Miss Allie?" he said.

28

SNAKE JOHNSON's Friday evening poker game went wrong from the beginning, and he could only blame himself for it. While it was not the usual policy to invite strangers, he could see no harm since none of the regulars could come except old Otis and Fred. Right when the strangers stepped into his trailer, he told them this was a sober game, though what they did after it was over was nobody's business but their own. Right there in the beginning too, Mister Otis told them, "Take the stopper out of Snake's peach brandy and it'll knock your eyes out."

"Peach brandy!" the newcomers yowled, like hyenas.

Being also from a dry county, they arrived with their whiskey tucked down into their boot tops, then laughed about that when they found out they were playing at the constable's. Before supper, the regulars stuck to drinking his homemade scuppernong wine, but the strangers had their dander all up and wouldn't settle for anything but some knockout peach brandy. The regulars would fleece anybody who just sat in for an evening, strangers or not, though once these dudes got into the peach brandy cheating them was so easy it wasn't much fun. Rube Galloway was a red-faced tractor salesman who stunk up the trailer all evening with a dry two-bit cigar; the other was a bleary truck driver who'd just come back from the Gulf Coast and had no sleep. He mumbled his name was Dink. Nobody bothered about his last name. Snake would wonder about it sometime later.

They were sour too about having to play poker before supper, even though Snake said his stew wasn't ready. They made him nervous. Going to check on the food, he glanced into a mirror over his sink and dashed some Vitalis on his hair, flattening it with his hand. They got mad again when Snake told them the stakes were nickel ante and quarter limit. "Hell's bells," Dink said.

"Some play with us are on Social Security," Fred said, not

looking at Mister Otis. Snake nodded. It eased the conscience of all the regulars not to play for more than anybody could afford. Snake caught Fred's eye and reached over the table, putting a dollop of peach brandy into the strangers' fruit jars, so they never noticed the cards flashing in Fred's quick hands or that the card he dealt Mister Otis off the bottom of the deck turned out to be a winner.

"How far's this place Cottondale you was talking about?" Rube said eventually, stretching. "Ain't that the place you said the poontang is?"

"I thought you come here to play poker," Snake said.

Rube chewed his cold cigar. He narrowed his eyes against cigarette smoke from the others and said, "Didn't know I was driving here all the way from out east to play Spit in the Ocean." His narrow look meant, With a cripple and a senile old man.

Snake smiled and watched Fred riffling the cards. "Don't anybody here who plays have money for high stakes," Fred said. Mister Otis who had the least money bowed his head toward his cards.

"Seems like my mind's just gotten off onto poontang," said Rube, draining his Mason jar. Dropping some cards, he had a hard time fitting them straight into his hand again.

"Count me out chasing poontang," Mister Otis said. Only the newcomers snorted.

"Can't you get poontang any night in the week?" Dink said. "What's the matter with your old woman?"

"She's blowed up with them pinto beans again. I hate making it over that swole up belly," Rube said.

Dink snorted. "Jesus, I thought you was finished making kids."

"I thought so too," Rube said. "I was ready to quit after the first young'un."

"Well, she didn't blow herself up with them pinto beans." Dink toasted Rube with his Mason jar, as Rube said, "Can't hep it if I don't shoot blanks, boy."

"Itn't your oldest still a baby?"

"Naw, hell. She's twelve."

"When a apple gets red it's ready to pluck. When a girl gets twelve she's ready to fuck."

Rube stood up.

"No offense," Dink said. "Just talking about women in general."

"You come here to play cards, now you going to play some cards," Snake said. "Fred, you come back here and set down." But Fred went on to fill up his fruit jar with wine; Mister Otis had asked earlier when he'd started drinking. Fred had barked, "Lately." Rube got up for more brandy and Dink went to pee out the front door, so Snake took that time to ask, "You having some trouble with your old woman?"

"Rose hasn't said nothing that got to me in twenty years," Fred said.

"Then how come you took up drinking?"

"Told myself I might be missing something. Wanted to see." Fred smiled crookedly.

"If I had it to do over with, I wouldn't start," Mister Otis said, wiggling from his boot top a new deck of cards. He passed this under the table to Fred. The others sat down again. "Y'all come here to play some poker, now let's play some poker." Snake ran his hand over his head and wiped it against one sleeve.

Rube sat down saying, "Shine, shine save pore me. Get mo' pussy than your eyes can see." He grabbed Mister Otis by the shirtfront. "Sir, pussy is good and so fast, if you can't swim you'll drown your mother-fucking ass."

"I know it," Mister Otis said.

"Son, you feeding the kitty?" Fred said.

"I'm folding," Rube said. He dozed, or pretended to. He opened his eyes when the old school clock on the wall struck the time. "Quarter to five," Rube said. "I 'as between them thighs."

"What happened at quarter to fo'?" Dink said.

"Quarter to four and we was on the floor." Rube looked at his new hand. "Two bits."

"Fold." Mister Otis got up. Dink said, "Old man, you're leaky as a faucet." Mister Otis covered his crotch and glared. "You'll be too when you're eighty-one," he said.

Snake got up with his fruit jar and went over for more wine, and to check on his supper. He peered into his mirror and decided on a little more Vitalis. He waited for everyone to play another hour, then said, "Supper's ready." The clock struck. "Quarter to six," Rube said. "My dick took sick." They stood at the stove. Snake whispered to him about some poontang he'd had down in Cottondale. "Had to fight her girdle off. Kept saying it weren't in the way. Reckon her head was dyed. Because you know where them gray hairs was at." He was thinking, My dick took sick.

He picked up the lid on his kettle, and Dink stuck his head over the pot. "What's cooking?"

"House specialty." Mister Otis shuffled up. Fred covered his face at the card table.

"Brunswick stew," Snake told them.

"You call it magic, but I call it love." Rube whistled under his breath. "I've never saw anybody cook squirrel with the head and tail on."

"It's meat," Snake said.

"And the eyes," Dink said.

"They cook out." He dished up their plates full. The strangers wanted to know what else was in it.

"Anything Snake got in the house," Mister Otis said proudly. He carried a plate to Fred, telling him to sit up. Snake told them what he could remember. "Coon and chicken necks and Irish taters and some turnips and some creamed corn left and—"

"Neb mind. Sounds like hog slop," Dink said.

They didn't have to eat it, Snake thought. Rube was singing again; the clock struck. Dick took sick, Snake kept thinking. "Quarter to seven!" sang Rube. "Her stomach started swelling."

Snake told them when they finished eating to scrape the

plates out the front door. "Wild dogs eat up the garbage. Put the plates in that there dishwater."

Rube poured whiskey. "Anybody else want something to wash down that supper with?"

"Mister Otis, you don't need none of that." Snake watched the old man take a jelly glass half full, and he kicked Fred slightly in the shins, but he took a glass too. "Deal them cards," he said. "We come here to play some cards." He didn't need to worry though, because Fred was a card-playing genius. Not seeing straight, he dealt the regulars the best hands.

"You ever tried to earn a living dealing cards?" Dink said, in a low voice. Snake felt hairs on his head rise up.

"Quarter to eight. The doc was late!" Rube sang.

"No," Fred said. Snake told about the woman from the Delta who came after Fred with a pistol once because her husband showed up every Friday evening without his paycheck. And then thought maybe he ought not to have told it. When Dink said nothing, Snake's hairs lay down.

Finally, Rube chimed in with the clock again, singing out, "Quarter to nine, the baby was crying," then threw all his cards over the table and said, "I don't know what it is, but me and him ain't won a hand tonight." Dink gave him a disgusted look. "At quarter to ten, I rather be fucking again," Rube said.

"Got your plow cleaned," Mister Otis said.

"Old man, you couldn't do nothing else but pee tonight, anyway," Dink said.

"I don't never play to ten," Mister Otis said. Getting up, he held to the table. He put on his black-and-red plaid lumber jacket. Snake had to help him put his arms in straight.

"You going to make it home all right?" he said.

"Sho," said Mister Otis.

"You think the weather's done turned cold?" Rube said, looking at the old man's jacket.

Mister Otis looked purple. "My blood's thin, and yours'll be too." He put on a red-leather deer-hunter's cap.

"I'll drive you," Fred said. "If you wait till I go to the bathroom." He knocked into the table standing up.

"I can walk better'n you can drive tonight," Mister Otis said, watching. He pulled the cap's flaps straight down over his ears till they fit about his face like a horse's blinders.

Dink got up. "Let me leave you all with this one," he said. "What comes of a cross 'tween a octopus and a nigger?" He waited for no answer. "A eight-row cotton picker that runs off watermelon juice. Harty-har!"

Snake thought that pretty funny. Following after Mister Otis, he said, "I got to take a leak, too. Come on outdoors, Fred. Ain't nobody cleaned that bathroom in more'n a month."

Mister Otis must have been seeing cross-eyed, because he lifted both feet high to step over the aluminum strip at the trailer door, as if it were a foot high. Snake had to laugh again. Outside smelled like fresh-cut hay from Brown's pasture all down back of his own acreage. He stepped to the cinder block below the door and looked back to see if Fred would make it all right. He reminded him to be careful walking because of all the large green husks shed by the walnut tree. Some year he ought to pick some up himself. But he just told niggers or anybody wanted them to come get them; they were like large balls of mold. He called to old Otis to take it easy. The old man turned and waved once and headed on toward the road guided by the light on Loma's porch, which helped get him on home, too. Fred was spraying the black-eyed Susans that grew up volunteer alongside the store and several orange petals flew to the ground. Snake sprayed the side of the store itself, since Loma always complained about the stains on the planks. The trailer door was open. He looked back toward the other fellows and felt mad again about the different tone they'd set to the evening. Quarter to five, he thought, I 'as between them thighs. He watched his water pockmark Loma's planks. He'd never get all that rhyming out of his head this evening, he'd bet: between them thighs and my dick took sick. Fred had moved on a little closer to the road, and Mister Otis had just brushed past a clump of cattails as tall as he was, which in the autumn of the year were as red as flames.

Snake told his brain to rest from all that rhyming in his head. He was ready to speak to Fred about the strangers when he saw Fred listening to the sound of a car coming fast; a car swerving and sliding, producing that soft juicy sound of not being able to stop on crushed gravel.

He heard a thud that sickened him. Because no other sound on earth could be mistaken for what it was. A body being crushed by the fender of a moving car.

Snake ran and Fred hobbled toward the road. They saw the old man in a dreadful dance reel straight along the length of the car and spin off its rear, to leap into air before he fell softly to all fours and lay down.

The car's oil pan dragged dirt as it shot down into the ditch beyond the McCalls' cattle gap. It ran along awhile as if on two wheels and then righted itself and flew on down the road, fishtailing, the taillights one red streak being swung from side to side that way. Twice the horn had honked, as if the driver fell against it. He burned rubber out of sight, the tires squealing.

"Did you see that!" Fred said. He hobbled on.

Snake caught up easily and told him to his hurt ear, "I didn't see nothing, Fred. And neither did you. You know whose car that was well's I do."

They bent over the heap of clothes in the road. "This puts me in a hell of a mess," Snake said.

"You ain't in as much mess as the old man is," Fred said, blubbering. "Oh, Jesus Christ. Why me? Why him? Why anything?"

"He's dead, Fred." Snake watched his cousin's eyes bat back and forth as if he were going to faint, and cautioned him, "Get holt of yourself. A growed man don't need to let hisself go that way. A old man's dead and that's that."

"I got to tell. Rose told me to tell. It's my fault. My fault."

"Ain't nothing about this your fault." Snake shook him roughly. "And you ain't done nothing in this world yet Rose wanted you to do, 'cept buy her a new washing machine you wanted." He kept shaking him till Fred's eyes stayed still in their sockets, and looked at him. "Now, you get aholt of yourself and keep aholt. Shit. The whole town's coming."

Fred sank to his knees and began to crawl in the road. "Get up, asshole. Everybody's coming." Then seeing what Fred was trying to do, Snake went toward Loma's and picked up Mister Otis' red hat. "Here. What you want with it?"

Fred went on blubbering. He tried to set the cap back on the old man's head. "He's all right," Fred said. "He just fell down. Had too much to drink. Get him up and help take him home. You'll be all right in the morning, Mister Otis."

"God fuck it," Snake said, grabbing Fred up. He slapped him hard across the face. "You ain't giving way when all these folks gets here. You hear?" He slapped him hard again. "We seen nothing but them fishtailing taillights. You remember that." He pressed thumbs to Fred's windpipe. "I got my trailer and ten acres. You got a wife and a nice house and a hundred Charolais and a hell of a lot more'n me to lose, telling. I ain't backing up no fool story told by a drunk, either." He pressed harder. "A old man's dead. He had a good enough life." He released his hold, allowing Fred to turn his head in the vise made by his hands. "The whole fucking town," Snake said.

A light had come on at the post office. Now Ardella and her husband were running up the road in their nightclothes. A light shone from the McCalls' where one of them was waving a flashlight and waiting for the other one. Brother Walker was headed down the parsonage walk and his car soon started up. Lights from houses farther along were dim, tiny dots that seemed to grow larger as the road filled with other twin headlights, and the single round lamps of motorcycles. All in all it could have been a carnival going on, Snake thought.

One long terrible minute passed before anybody arrived, some crying and some yelling.

Fred had said, "Maybe you didn't see it. Maybe I didn't see it. But the Negro did."

"Nigger. What nigger?"

"One standing in the ditch yonder watching. Watching us watch, too."

"Could you tell anything about him?"

"He was old. Not the old man living up in that cabin. I know him."

"Oh." Snake felt relief. "If he was a coon, we don't have to worry. If he had been a black now, it might be another matter." He wiped spittle onto his sleeve, and stopped laughing when the first folks arrived. "A old man's dead and that's that," he said.

"I envy the bastard," Fred said.

29

WOMEN STANDING in the road decided not to tell Miss Pearlie Mae that night. The old lady could have one more peaceful night's sleep and perhaps pleasant dreams. Yet, once home, Allie tossed around in bed and let her tears stream. She wondered how quickly Miss Pearlie Mae's phone would ring, one or two of the women having decided the promise was not solemn enough to outweigh the thrill of being first to tell her the news; the worse it was, the better for gossipers. Miss Pearlie Mae's prophecy had come true: death came in threes.

All the lights and the noise in the road had disturbed the cows, and several went on bellowing after town was quiet. She lay trying to identify their calls; whether they were for reassurance, or companionship, or whether a calf was separated from its momma. If so, Tate would get them back together when he came home, or they'd be awake and listening to the two consecutive bawls all night long. Not that she expected to sleep anyway. Though probably she'd be like Poppa, and telling a tale if she said she did not sleep at all.

She dreamed and told herself she was dreaming, was aware of both her sleeping and waking self. Soon Allie's whole life would seem to take place in that twilight, as she encountered people she'd known only casually and never expected to have touch her life. Itna Homa and its surroundings would come to seem a place she was exploring for the first time. She would watch everything with the sensation that nothing happening to her was real. Frequently during this time, she dreamed of being in a room where a bat with great spread wings flew and soared and brushed walls trying to escape, as she fought up from sleep. At the bedroom window she heard sudden light tappings, too faint for Sweetie's old ears to hear. Elgie stood outside. He wore Sy's old hat that had been Tate's, the brim turned down all around. "Got to see you," he said, black against the blackness.

She motioned toward the closest door, to the kitchen, and went to meet him there, by only the light falling in from the bedroom where she'd turned on a lamp. He came in. "I seed Mist' Tate's truck go off."

"He's gone to the coroner and ranger's. It was old Mister Otis who —"

"I seed it all. How come that have to happen to this colored man?" Elgie whipped off his hat and swung it against his knees.

"Saw closer than from your house?" she said. "Who ran over him?" Waiting, she saw the flounced kitchen curtain move in and out the slightly opened window, with the same steady, quiet breathing as their breaths.

Elgie raised a hand. "Yes'um. But you tells me first. How you going hep me, Miss Allie?"

She told reluctantly how little she knew. "I asked around but had to do it cautiously. I found out that the logical procedure would be to tell the constable in our own —"

"Yeah'um. You going tell Mist' Snake, and I'm 'posed to go free? I be free all right. I be one dead man."

"What're you talking about?"

"I'm talking 'bout folks yonder in the road washing away that poor kilt man's blood, and I'm going tell what I knows? What the first thing going happen when the law knows where I'm is?"

"You'd have to let Mister Snake take you back to Parchman."

"Mist' Snake ain't carrying me to no Parchman to git me out again."

"It wouldn't be his say-so. I suppose they'd come after you instead if he called them to. But you did escape and have to go back before anything can get started about getting you a pardon."

"I don't wants no pardon for something I ain't did. Got to kowtow to the white peoples then?"

"Why, I don't know what it is called to be set free for something you didn't do."

"Called a pardon. 'Cuse you for doing what you ain't did. Going to leave some doubt in folks' mind, still." He sat down in a chair opposite so close that their knees touched. "Come to tell I be leaving out. If you could see clear to just some bus fare, I be paying you back soon's I kin. You going hep me, drive me up to Memphis where I can cotch that bus without seeing nobody us knows."

"You'd never have to pay me back," she said, touching his knee lightly. Stalling for time, she could think of nothing to say but, "Please don't leave yet. I just haven't thought of the right person to help us. Can't think who I truly trust."

"You can't hep me. You can't do it. You just a woman with a good heart."

"Tell me what you saw. Maybe there's more reason for you to get help." As they sat close at the table, her floating self observed them as they were many years ago, sitting there playing Rook or eating something Maggie had cooked.

His hat brim circled around in his fingertips. "If I gots to tell, how come the two white mens that saw, too, don't gots to tell?"

"What two white men?"

"Mist' Snake and a mans with a funny shoe."

"Fred Cullins?" she said. "He's a good man. What happened?"

Once he told her, she said, "I'm not surprised it was Quad Brewster. I think I knew it was. But, Elgie, I think he must be crazy, not mean. Killing a human being is a different thing from killing a rooster. Or a dog. Or four of them. I don't think he sees the difference."

"Lots of folks in this world like that."

"Can't do anything about them. Can about him. Are you going to help?"

"Who going take a colored man's word?"

"The law," she said. Then she saw how naive that was, because the law had not taken the word of Negroes in the past. She had seen some of that injustice, but never felt it before—because she'd always felt safe and secure with the law: she was white.

He did not look impressed. "What've you got to lose?" she said. "You'd be back in prison either way. Unless you did keep on running." But he might be free in Chicago, and suppose the law did not take his word, here, and he only went back to prison, with her responsible? "I hate to say I've learned law from TV. But when I watched *District Attorney* with Poppa, there were always deals. Maybe you could get free for testifying?" Why was she asking Elgie?

"The law round here don't wants to know what I knows," he said.

"Oh, I don't know a damn thing, Elgie," she said abruptly. "But I'm going to find out something." She was hot and flushed, staring at him somewhat happily. "Would you by any chance like something to drink?"

"Mammy Lou, she sho turn over in her grave, then."

Time had stood still for him, though their known world was on the brink of change.

"Elgie, there's something strange about Mister Fred. It's not like him to hide what he knows about someone being murdered. Not even with the Brewsters concerned. When he came to Poppa's funeral some people thought he'd been drinking. It was passed off as tranquilizers. Fred acted too peculiar. Maybe something happened to him first?"

He sounded as if he were humming. "Git the white mans to testify, and I might."

She stared. "Well, we certainly couldn't get Snake Johnson to, so that leaves only the one." Wandering to the door, she looked into the den to quote. " 'Fear no man whate'er his size. Colonel Colt will equalize.' Snake thinks, now, he's up to anybody with that gun on his hip."

She did not hear everything Elgie said. "Sy say peoples starting to come back home again from up the country. Say it ain't no life for me up yonder in Chicago at my age anyway, cold as it git. What you think?"

"About what?" she said.

"What I'm just said."

"I'm sorry. I didn't hear."

"What on your mind right now?"

"I was thinking you didn't have to tell me what you saw. That you did it because you have a conscience."

Elgie watched his hat coming against his chest. "What the other thing you thinking, Miss Allie?"

"That Snake Johnson has to have an opponent in November."

Preachers she knew said they preached because they had a call. She always took that with a grain of salt, and to her mind came some image of a man wrestling with God in the sky, speaking to him, an old biblical picture. Having heard no patriarchal voice herself, having confronted no burning bush, she had only her own voice telling her to do something about justice. To have a clear conscience, and because it seemed the only honest thing, first she had to speak directly to Snake. She met him one day outside Loma's, her arms full of groceries, and asked, "Snake, you didn't see the color of that car?"

Parting stained teeth, he spit tobacco juice to pink wildflowers growing at the porch's edge and would have pushed by, but she stood in front of him. His cap beak nearly poked her in the eyes; he looked from beneath it and squinched them. "I told what I've saw."

"Them fishtailing taillights." She sang his song before he could. "You saw Quad Brewster hit Otis."

Fright flashed across his face, twisting it. She thought his look as ineffectual as the threat from the poor, mistrustful dog lying in the road, which had lifted weakly a portion of its upper lip to snarl when she came close, knowing its own impotence. This was her first intimation that Snake knew of his reputation in the community, and that he cared. It's my kind too that he hates, she thought.

"Supposing ain't knowing."

"I didn't say supposing."

"Ma'm?" About to clean a fingernail with a match end, he quit to squinch the hard eyes again.

"Someone else there told me."

"Fred?" The laugh was a snort through his nose.

"No."

"Some old nigger works for Tate?"

"He doesn't have anybody but Willson and Turner, anymore." She felt fearful even mentioning them. "Why did you guess a Negro?"

He blustered saying, "White men don't sneak round roads at night."

"It wasn't Willson or Turner. They'd have told."

But she could tell Snake knew a Negro had been there, and he'd said "old." "You want to stick to your story, Snake?"

The little pink flowers received another blow. She shuddered. "I ain't got but one, honey," he said, a little cockiness coming back.

He switched tobacco to his other cheek; it gave him time to study her, peaked cap brim shading his eyes. Allie watched his thoughts settle, and smiled at him.

"Go home. Git your supper on."

"Where I belong?"

His smile appreciated her. "That's ever' bit what I meant. And tend to your knitting whilst you 'as at it."

"I'm warning you."

"Of what?"

His green-gold tooth flashed as he went by. He looked back at her from Loma's steps, his face still heavy with hatred of her kind, those born with a silver spoon, to his way of thinking.

Blood was not thicker than water between Fred Cullins and Snake; it was poker only that ever drew Fred to his cousin's trailer. Standing on Fred's lean-to, holding her breath against the smell of cat pee worsened by damp weather, Allie let down her umbrella, tapped on the door's glass pane, and saw Rose already coming, like a small agile bear. She seemed to be appraising the air when she looked out. "Who is it?"

"Allie McCall."

"Child, I couldn't see you against the grayness." She laughed at herself. Allie expected her next words to be the usual ones, Come on in, and felt awkward meeting a flat, stilled expression.

"I'm not collecting for anything." She was lighthearted, but thought she'd hit the nail on the head.

Rose nodded, her expression still that of a country woman suspicious by nature.

Allie said, "I've come to talk to you about Fred."

Rose's eyes dilated. "Fred's to home. He's bad sick. I'm busy now tending to him." She tried to block her kitchen being viewed.

"Brr," Allie said. She meant the dampness. "I'm sorry to hear that. Can I come in?"

Beyond Rose was a silent, steaming teakettle and one cup set out; blue crocheting was set aside; company seemed lacking.

"If you've got something for Fred to fix, leave it. I'm telling you though, he's plumb jammed up."

She pushed the door open wider and passed Rose, whose head

lowered. Her eyes traveled the route of Allie's feet. Allie was determined to make herself speak absolutely to the point. She would not prattle about the weather, or the good special advertised on the family-sized box of A & P tea bags by the stove. Wanting a cup of hot tea to fortify herself, she dealt head-on with that. Not waiting for an invitation, feeling Grandmomma's horror, hearing her say, Why, Allie! she said, "Could I have some tea?" and added, "Please," hoping Grandmomma better satisfied.

Rose was surprised — Rude of Allie to ask, her face said — and properly as hostess, unwilling one that she was, she said, "Would you like some tea?"

"Yes." Allie sat at the table and took the cup of hot water presented and dunked her tea bag and watched Rose do the same, before saying, "Rose, why has Fred started drinking?"

"I didn't know nobody knew it," Rose cried out. Allie was startled when Rose's tears came so furiously. As soon as she got up and put her arms around her, Rose leaned sobbing to her and said, "Are you going to tell everybody?"

"I think a lot of people know it. They only wonder why, too."

"They'll be saying it's my fault. Any man goes to drinking, it's going to be his wife's fault."

She was aware that moment it was not Rose's fault, that Fred had a separate reason and that Rose knew it. So she hugged her harder to mean she'd help her, if only she'd tell her why. She leaned away to say, "Rose, I've got reason to believe Fred saw who hit Mister Otis."

Rose's glasses fell to the end of her nose, her mouth opened, and her hands groped without finding them. Then Allie went back to her own chair.

"Rose, drink some tea."

"I reckon he couldn't carry something like that," she said. Her cup wobbled while she sipped tea.

"Do you believe Fred would keep quiet about it?"

"I reckon he might, now."

"He's changed?"

"Yes'um."

"Is he really sick?"

"He's drunk. Been drunk three days. I can't keep on acalling him in sick. Folks coming day and night, and telephoning, wanting things he's supposed to be fixing. I can't keep on covering up for him. Can I?"

"No." Allie saw her go fearful at having told so much.

"You want some cake?"

"No. I want to find out what's the matter with Fred. Why he started drinking before Mister Otis was killed, even."

"What'd we do if we was to lose this house, his pension, everything?"

"A boy being wild and driving too fast is bad enough, but I know as well as I know Fred saw it that Quad Brewster hit Mister Otis."

"He . . . did!"

"We've got to make Fred tell that. What about at Poppa's funeral. Wasn't he drinking then?"

Rose nodded, her tears starting up.

Allie went around again, hugged her close, and put her face against the wet one. She took the teacup out of Rose's hands. They stayed pressed close, hearing rain burst open on the windows and let up, until finally Rose stopped crying. Would she tell?

"He can't go on like this, Rose. He will ruin himself."

"No'um, he can't. I can't, either."

"I know you want to help him," she said softly.

"I've tried."

"Maybe I could help you. You're not alone, you know."

"Oh!"

"You tell me now."

"I'm afraid." She brought both their hands against her face. "Will everybody have to know about his drinking, and about his not telling?"

"If you want Quad to get what he deserves. And Fred will

be admired for having told. I find it hard to believe the boy might go scot-free, don't you?"

"After all he done."

"What all do you know?"

"It was him bunged up Fred's ear. One night he brought his crazy car here for Fred to fix. He hollered and yelled out there in the garage, terrible. Then Fred come in the house with his ear all hanging off. Wouldn't tell nothing about why that boy done him thataway."

"Why didn't Fred want to fix his car?"

"He didn't mind. But the boy was wanting him to fix it here. Fred can't fix a car like that out to our house." She felt Rose had more to tell that not even Fred knew.

"Why do you think that was, Rose?"

"I can't get the straight of it in my head." She looked around with a face of fear, breathing so hard her eyes disappeared behind steamy glasses. "I did something Fred didn't know about. I went out yonder and looked at the car. It only had a bunged-up fender. I went and did it after Fred told me to mind my own business. Did it when he was asleep. After he woke up, he locked the garage. But I'd already been out there, and I never told." She thought of herself in awe.

Imagining Rose's heartbeat, Allie knew that a world had opened up when she had disobeyed Fred.

She had to see this to its end. Sitting in the kitchen with its removed air, rain at the windows, Allie thought how it would be easier to tend to her knitting. Snake coming to mind made her more determined. "Quad couldn't have been afraid of his daddy," she said. "When he flipped over that convertible he had, Mister Brewster only got him this new car. Had so many cars, it's a joke. Why would he have worried about a fender, Rose?"

"Ask Fred a question and he told me to hush. Got mean. More he drinks, the meaner he gets. A mean drunk's a whole lots worse than just a plain drunk. I've got right scared of him. It was just a dented-up, scratched fender. He hit something."

In a moment, Allie said, "Can I try talking to him? His wife is usually the last person who can get anywhere with a man drinking."

"Fred's not going to like it." Rose meant, What would happen to her later?

"I think Fred'll be glad when everything's off his chest, or he wouldn't be drinking. Snake, now, feels free as a bird. Fred's not like that."

"He talks on in his sleep. Can't rest at night, is another reason he's trying to dope hisself up."

Without any more words, they got up. She went behind Rose to a closed door, nodding when she said, "Sssh." The whole bedroom stank of whiskey. His bottom sheet was pulled loose at both top corners, as if he had clawed them loose. "Can we open a window?" Rose went over to one window and lifted it slightly, letting in some fresh air, a gentle breeze carrying small rain; these things made the man on the bed seem more unreal. The man was not free of his guilt even in his stupor, not with those sheets, and with a tic in his cheek, like a pulse, even while he slept. Rose pulled the chain of a floor lamp by the bed, as if she were timid. "Fred, you got company." Her voice was neutral, making of this any day, this time, only an ordinary call, the way it once might have been. Allie felt sorrier for Rose than before.

They watched him look up slowly, try to sit up, fall back again, and finally plead, "Turn off the light."

"We want you to tell us something first, Fred." As he reached to pull the light chain, Allie bent for him to see her, bent into the light. It fell warmly on her hair, as she watched him dumbly staring, while she told him to get off his chest all that was worrying him so much.

"Who . . . is . . . that?"

"Allie McCall." Her voice sounded crisp in contrast. She stepped back for him to see her.

"Rose, what'd you do? Bring somebody else in to help you bitch?"

"Fred! Language."

She told Rose not to worry.

He tried to lean on an elbow, and missed, and fell back to say, "What's a man got to do to get peace in the house he's slaved all his growed days to own?"

"Tell us what you know," she said.

"Tell her about the Brewster boy bringing his car here, Fred." He put fists to his face like a baby crying in a rage no one could understand; they watched him helplessly. "I told you to bring me some food, Rose," he whined, "before I lie here and starve to death."

But Rose looked stubborn, shoved her glasses up on her nose, and said, "I brought you food. I brought it three times. You wouldn't eat, and I'm not bringing it again."

When he said, "Rose," though weakly, her lips thinned out into a tiny, whitened smile of pleasure. He said, "Turn out the light." They watched his pained face, knowing that he'd lost even her minding him, and wondered how that had happened after so many years; they watched him lean to do it himself, stop, and stare at the chain, knowing the light would only come on again, and there they'd be, waiting still. He dropped back.

"Get out. Now. I'm sick of being bitched at."

"Fred! Language."

"Rose, it doesn't matter," she told her again.

"Fred, Rose says Quad Brewster brought his car here to be fixed, and hit you. What's happening? What's all the secretiveness about?"

"Rose is full . . ." He dug his fists tighter to his eyes.

"Why did he want the fender fixed here?"

The fists left his eyes, leaving them reddened in rings, staring at them.

"I didn't say nothing about a fender."

"I did. I told her. I saw the car when you was asleep."

"All them red scratches?"

"I've told you a hundred times and I'm telling you a hundred and one, Fred. That color is called maroon."

"Maroon?" Rose's face suspected nothing. Fred's was perspiring enough to drown him. Allie could think of nothing but maroon. She said the word again. "Maroon?" She saw that dark country road, and the bridge lit up in the moonlight, and John Q staring into his rearview mirror, knowing who it was coming along behind, probably realizing at the last minute what the other car was going to do. She wondered how long she'd see that image; how long she'd dream about it. "Are we talking about John Q's maroon truck? Did the boy hit—I mean, push him off the bridge?"

Rose made a sound that was a little cry, and went forward and grabbed Fred by the shoulders, and he lay willingly, smiling with the relief of it, while she shook him up and down to the pillows.

"How could you go to church, how could you sit there praying, listening to somebody preach about God, and keep on sitting there without telling anybody all this?"

She dropped him, and pulled back terrified by what she had done. He only lay there with a crooked smile, then covered his face to the world, and sobbed without control, the way a man does when he finally cries before others, and is not ashamed.

They watched until he stopped, and crossed his arms over his face, his elbows up. Then Rose walked over and pulled his arms apart. She held them by the wrists on each side of him and bent to his face to say the cruelest words she could.

"What kind of man are you?"

She had to give Fred Cullins time to come around to his normal state of health. Would he be honest? Rose said he would get sober; she promised her that much. The rain brought on two days of cold, the temperature dropping into the forties. People seemed hushed, fearing an early winter and a killing frost, which meant that cotton late to mature would never fill out. Afterward, warm weather came back, the soaring, clear blue skies of autumn. People wore lightweight fall clothes. They talked frequently of the weather, in charge of their livelihood;

though all along they never stopped talking about the bridge, and the number of deaths it had caused. Heavily laden cotton trailers rumbled across it too fast, wearing it away, and came back empty, swaying crazily from side to side. It was last year that a Negro, hitting sixty, let the rear end of his trailer swipe part of a railing, caving it in; that section had never been replaced. Then another winter, a white man hit ice on it and spun around and went off the other side, taking that railing with him; now that John Q had taken away another section, the bridge had no railings that amounted to anything at all.

The subject came up at the Woman's Club. Members wanted to know why they could not spur the menfolks into doing something. Someone suggested that maybe they would when ginning was done. But then soybeans had to be harvested. And afterward the men were busy taking their cattle to auction. By that time, Christmas would be here, then everyone was busy with that season. Maybe January or February, when it was laying-back time? Allie said, "Why keep waiting?" standing to address the president. "Legislation moves slow enough. Why lose three months sitting around talking and waiting?" Those months menfolks would want to sit and rest or tinker with equipment to get ready for rowing up again. "Why don't we do something?" Allie said, as the women nodded. They put their heads together.

That was a Friday morning; they meant to accomplish something over the weekend. What they called on Allie to do on Monday morning was most important.

She put her hand on the telephone, thinking for the first time of not having to worry about Poppa overhearing; then she gave her information to the operator, with a sense of daring.

She waited, feeling again the smallness of her community, awed by the presence of fields, pastures, and hills, so dependent on government directives, and so far removed from the urban place where they were presented. She felt that even more listening to her operator with a thick Mississippi accent speak to other voices with different accents. She told herself she would never reach the party she wanted — he would be too busy; she'd be put off with some excuse.

Her introduction was country. People who went off to important jobs often forgot their humble beginnings. For two summers Tate had played amateur ball with a boy named Richard Murphy — Shine Murphy, now a representative in Washington. On his first campaign, he spoke from the flatbed of a crepe-paper-festooned truck outside Fred's Dollar Store in Nashtoba, and then in a pasture near Whitehill, with some hillbilly country singers to entertain. Little boys celebrated the Fourth of July with firecrackers, sending frightened cows rambling into the audience. However, she and Tate had gone both times to hear him. Shine had remembered Tate, shaken hands, and said how well thought of he knew Tate was in the county; he appreciated his support. After all, a county was a county to a politician. Once Shine won, Tate had received a mimeographed letter thanking him for his support. At the bottom, Shine had scrawled, "*One good ole boy to another — thanks a lot!*"

She considered herself lucky when a secretary put her through. "You and yours doing all right?" he said.

She assured him they were, answered his questions about how the crops were doing, and said she was calling about something important to the county: a bridge. She explained its danger, and the need for a new one. She felt hesitant about explaining how the women had gone to work on getting one. All her past taught her that men laughed at, and were irked by, womenfolk meddling in what was considered men's business: running anything outside the home. So, she spoke rather sternly in a half fright when she said that women had carried petitions to all the businesses in Whitehill and Nashtoba. She raised her voice explaining that all the *businessmen* had signed them — they wanted the new bridge because their businesses were suffering. People chose not to go over the old bridge when they did not have to; there was a way to circumvent it by driving through the federal dam, which took them up to Memphis, instead.

"With Christmastime coming up, you know how concerned all the merchants are feeling," she said.

"Is that so?" he kept saying.

"Small businesses are having a hard enough time around in this part of the country," she said.

"The same as everywhere," he said.

She explained that they did not need new railings, but a new bridge.

He laughed, saying that could hardly be done by Christmastime.

She laughed too. "I'm not expecting a miracle," she said.

In his chuckle, she heard something that said he was still good old country Shine, so, drawing a deep breath, she told him everything, though she was not herself completely in favor of what some of the women had taken it into their heads to do. Women from the largest nearby towns, as well as smaller ones, and living on rural roads in the county, had banded together and decorated the bridge with crepe-paper streamers and balloons, then marched up and down it with signs. They stopped everybody crossing it, getting them to sign the petition for a new one, including those who could only make an *x*.

He was laughing.

"They created so much commotion, Channel Five up in Memphis heard about it and sent a camera crew down. They were on the news. That of course goes out over the whole Mid-South area. A lot of people who never heard of that bridge before know about it now. They'll be watching. Everyone is saying that with Ole Miss integrated, the public schools will follow, and that it's likely we'll be having a lot of new voters soon, too. That is, the drive to get the Negroes voting will be stepped up. A great many of them use that bridge, naturally." She felt downright cagey.

He was not laughing, saying, "I see," every so often.

"You could certainly carry this county for anything you ever ran for, if we got a new bridge."

"I've heard complaints about it, of course," he said. "I know a little about it. When the federal dam in your area was built, with that bridge in the floodway, control of it was given over to the state."

"The state says it doesn't have money for a new bridge. That route's been explored long ago."

"That's what I was going to say. The state doesn't have money for a new bridge."

Typical of men, she thought. They always wanted to tell you the thing themselves.

"Take some legislation," he said.

"Everyone here is saying they would want the bridge named after you, if we got a new bridge."

"Have to have some legislation to return control to the federal government, so federal money could be used," he said. "It'll take some time, but I think it could be done."

"Shall we call it the Richard Shine Murphy bridge?"

"I think we'll let Richard Murphy do," he said. There was a pause, while she thought he was smoking. Or writing? "Well, Allie. Is my word good enough for you ladies, for now?"

"Yes it is. Thank you."

She hung up shakily, and leaned to the phone a minute, laughing at herself, at how she felt a part of the powers that be, as if she were there in Washington, doing business.

And laughed with the women who said if only the news had reruns, so they could see themselves on TV again.

They seemed to have won.

30

SHE RARELY NEEDED to go to Whitehill or Nashtoba. It felt unusual then to be driving out from town, around the twisting, hilly countryside, where kudzu made the road banks dark, and trees sometimes overhung, touched, and shaded deep low places, yellow banks rising way above her head, until low places seemed spooky. Remembering her best friend Minnie's tales that headless ghosts walked them, she was glad to come out into sunshine, atop again, to ride on past infrequent houses and flat fields that seemed friendlier. Now she dipped and rose and flew along, thinking about going to see someone else she'd known since childhood but whose life she had never expected to twine with hers.

Ward Grierson lived out near the bluffs where Negroes were beginning to build their community of new houses, close to one another, so that it would seem a city block if the roads were paved. At the end of his steep driveway, his homemade sign — two planks nailed together in the shape of a cross, the horizontal one with *Justice of the Peace* printed in black crooked letters — was nearly swallowed up by kudzu. The road to his house led off a main one and was not much more than a soft lane of yellow dust. Her own dust traveled everywhere, and so dusted the windshield she had to turn on her wipers to see.

She should have phoned for an appointment, she realized. A justice of the peace came to her mind as someone who held weddings at midnight, an idea that came from old picture shows, or who occasionally confronted a beer drinker or speeder. Now, at his house a full-scale wedding was just breaking up, with an air of such gaiety she felt lonely, parked and watching, and jealous of all the fun. Negroes of all ages came outside and threw rice at an elderly couple, emerging last. All the girls and women wore soft dresses in pastel colors; all the boys and men wore white carnations. Dogs penned behind Ward's joined in by barking. She waited in her lonesome car for the wedding party to drive away, swallowing themselves in dust.

His watery old man's eyes lit up with appreciation that she had come — for him, she was Poppa's girl, the daughter of his old coon-hunting pal from long ago. Behind the house the black and tan coon dogs went on wildly barking at her, until they quieted at last underneath the house. Inside, a tall heater with a stovepipe going out a round hole in the ceiling so filled the room with heat that she looked in wonder at Ward's high-domed forehead as cool as a cucumber. She took off her sweater. At his insistence she took the softest chair.

"I need your advice."

She told what she suspected without mentioning names. Bristly silver, short hairs seemed to stand straighter on his head the longer she talked; afterward he cupped one pawlike hand over the other one and cracked his knuckles.

"Lady," he said, "you've got to come in here telling me you know something. Not that you think you know."

"Well, I think the people who gave me information are telling the truth. I didn't see those things happen, either Mister Otis or John Q killed."

"Then you got to get on those people's heads. Make them testify."

She felt grim, while his old man's pink cheeks looked even pinker, until he seemed a fragile concoction of spun sugar; yet his frame was strong, and his hands, for seventy; the man he once had been was still evident.

"You can understand why the Negro is reluctant. He's old and is of the old school. He can't believe better days are ahead of his people." She did not say that he had escaped from prison, knowing Ward would guess it was Elgie. And he'd get on her head till she told where Elgie was hiding, too.

Ward leaned to her. "Bring me a signed affidavit, lady. I'll arrest the person who kilt them both. It's the same person, I take it?"

She nodded.

"What can I do now?" he said, cracking his knuckles and waiting for the only answer she could give him: Nothing.

"That's what I wanted to know. I guess the answer is nothing, unless the witnesses testify." She let her uncertainty fill her voice. "One might be on the edge of being carted off to the asylum at Whitfield. Then his testimony really wouldn't amount to anything."

He spoke adamantly, seeing how uncertain she was. "You got to get on his head."

"I've tried," she said. "My hands are tied. Only his wife, or his own conscience, is going to make him come forward." She felt eager to know which one, if either. A good man gone bad; the words came back from some old blues song. Ward's wise, warm, country man's blue eyes opposite seemed to be dissecting her thoroughly. She moved uneasily, wondering about his final appraisal, wondering if he found her lacking.

"The Negro will testify if the white man does?" he said.

"I think so." She added, "I'll get on his head."

He said in an expressionless way, "Not but one family in these parts folks are ascared of, Miss Allie. Didn't you think I'd know who you were talking about?"

Allie spoke truthfully. "I must have."

"There's nothing I can do without the affidavit."

"Who should I see next?"

"The district attorney. He wears shining armor. He's got immunity. Got five districts to look after. Don't have to be ascared of nobody. But the district attorney can't do nothing either on hearsay, lady."

Sighing, she said, "I'm tired of feeling so helpless." She got up and began to walk aimlessly.

Ward spoke in a musing way behind her. "It don't surprise me none a-tall it was that boy. John Q stopped him some. The boy only thought it was funny to get fined out here in the country. Liked to brag about it. John Q never was tough. But I talked to him tough. Might's well have been talking to them dogs out yonder."

"John Q never spoke to Mister Brewster." Allie thought to herself: I don't have any right to criticize what somebody else didn't do. She turned. "I guess Mister Brewster would be like talking to the dogs too." Ward nodded.

He said, " 'Course, Snake Johnson's not going to stop the boy even if he was to run over Snake's foot."

"Well, he'll probably do as much as John Q did."

"Hell. Excuse me, lady. You got a lots to learn."

She turned and sat down with an expectant face.

"Where you think Snake's aiming to earn the most of his money? Why you think he's bothered to haul hisself out of that beer joint in Cottondale long enough to say he's constable?"

"I thought to be a big shot."

He cracked his knuckles and went on looking at her. "That might be some of it," he said. "But hell. Excuse me. It's the beer joints nearby in the Delta paying him not to stop the boy, not to stop nobody speeding through the county drunk. Because where'd they get drunk at? Those beer joints. They don't want to ruin business." He laughed. "You got you a lots to learn, lady," he said again.

"I've never had any idea. But John Q?"

"Oh, now, you know he didn't done it. Snake's the one playing into their hands. Don't quote me, lady. Any more'n I'm going to quote what you've told me. There's other places Snake's making money too. He's taking it from several general merchandise stores around this district. One's out toward the dam, one's 'tween here and the Delta. The other's going on out toward Redmud. All of 'em selling beer out the back door now and paying Snake to let them do it."

"And the sheriff recommended him to the board of supervisors!" She felt more the fool at Ward's howling laugh.

"The high shuriff? Lady, you do have you a lots to learn. Him and Snake's in it together." He held up crossed fingers. "Thick as thieves because they are thieves. The constable picks up the bootleg money for the shuriff. The bag money. That's how John Joe come to be for Snake. Knew he could trust him." He winked.

"I can't believe this kind of thing's going on in the community where I've lived so long."

"Not the kind of thing gets talked about in front of the ladies."

"A lot more interesting than what does," she said, smiling.

"Bet if you look out you'll see Snake ain't sleeping so late these Sunday mornings. Where's he going so early? Not to church. And he ain't looking for speeders or beer drinkers or drunks early on a Sunday. No'm. That's when he's making his rounds. Going round to all the stores and collecting the shuriff's kickback for illegal beer, bootlegging, and moonshining going on. Him and John Joe splits it."

She leaned over her knees toward him. "Ward, somebody decent in this community has got to run against Snake Johnson."

"Why don't you do it?"

She pulled back, looked at him with a shocked face, and had a hard time speaking: "A woman couldn't be constable."

"Why not? Is there a law against it?"

She could only whisper. "No, but—"

"I don't want no buts about it. Don't it sound ladylike enough for you?" His twinkly eyes laughed at her.

Had she only been whistling in the dark about wanting to change her life? "You know men around here wouldn't vote for a woman."

"There's a lots of men around here who'd vote for anybody besides Snake. You're in the right place at the right time, is what it amounts to."

"There isn't much chance of finding a good male candidate?" she said.

"About a snowball's chance in hell." He leaned toward her now.

"You know the kind of Christian home folks we got around here would vote for decency before they'd vote between pants and a skirt. You're on the side of the right. I wouldn't have suggested this to the average woman walked in here, you understand that?"

She searched his face to see if this was some empty compliment, but his eyes were quite steadily looking at her, into her. She wavered. "You mean because I can shoot a gun?"

"That's one thing. The fact that you're riled up about this case enough to try to do something about it is another plus. Out of eighteen hundred votes in this district, I think you'd have a good chance. You know what you're lacking now?"

"A lot of things."

"Nerve," Ward said.

"Seems like I'd need more than that." She asked herself, Am I seriously considering this?

"That's a great big part of it, lady. That's how lots of folks have gotten to the top. You already have vim. If you got this case to court, you'd have it made."

Uncertain she could do even that, she again got up to walk about.

He watched her. "Most men wouldn't be where they are without a woman," he said. "By the time women get to be your age, they're a lots of times stronger than their men. They've learned a lot taking care of a family for so many years."

She suddenly stopped. "That's true about middle age. Still, a woman couldn't overpower many men physically."

He pulled one leg across the other one, stiffly. "A woman with a gun can kill a man as easy as a man can kill a woman, can't she? You need you only three common things: Mace, a blackjack, and a pistol."

"Oh, Ward," she said.

"Oh, Ward." He mimicked her, shifting from his masculine way of crossing his legs, putting his feet daintily and primly side by side, his ankles touching, taunting her. "Now, listen. You got you more than a high school education. We never in the history of the community had a constable that had that. The voters will be impressed. You've got women working, now, in all these factories around here. These days the menfolks are watching their womenfolks go off to work, too. Those factories are hiring more women than they do men. Women doing men's work in them, or what used to be called men's work. It's harder than being constable to make that hundred a week, and bring it home. Women putting food on the table, and not just cooking it. And you will do the right thing, and not just walk around sporting that badge. That's where Snake can't beat you."

She tried to imagine telling Tate, and imagined things he'd throw up in her face. She said at last, "I don't think men would believe a woman could get out on those dark country roads at night and ride."

He looked peeved. "Lady, you can get out and ride with the best of them, if you want to. They've got women matrons in the prisons and jails. They're in danger. Women riding these roads back and forth to work are coming over them at night in the wintertime. I told you what you need. Nerve. Women do good under stress. Better than menfolks do. Think about this countryside: it was all frontier once, back when the South was the West. Back when your own people come to these parts. Back in the old days, wasn't women Indian killers, spies, and scouts?"

She thought about Meredith at the university and his solitariness. She felt that word intensely. Its sound so much connoted its meaning. Even if the idea hadn't originated with him, if he had been sent in by a body, the NAACP, and if he'd come in a chauffeur-driven limousine, protected by submachine guns, he was still that one alien individual, alone, breaking ground, eyes on him, hairs standing up on the back of his neck, left finally always to his own thoughts.

"The traditional way of looking at women never has been the right one," Ward said. "Country women have always been made of strong stuff, or this part of the world wouldn't be settled, yet."

She smiled. "I guess if a man of your generation thinks I ought to run, other men might too. I guess my own thinking is more stereotyped than I realized. I feel myself still Allie McCall, the little girl brought up by all the rules. Yet something inside me sure has been struggling to come out."

"Yes," he said.

She ran back to one more possibility. "Maybe my just announcing I was running would make some worthwhile man come forward, just to stop me?" Her eyes pleaded for him to say that would happen.

"I don't know who it'd be this year. What we could hope

was that you'd set a precedent. Make it an office that respectable people would seek. A lots of new people coming this way, moving down here from Memphis, coming down from the north with these factories. Looking for space to live. Young folks moving in. Put an example in front of them."

He got up as Allie put on her sweater. "I'd have to think about it." He stretched. "I shore hated it about old man Otis. Since it happened on a county road, the highway patrol can't get into it unless the shuriff asks them to. Like I said, even the district attorney can't do nothing on hearsay." He put an arm around her shoulders. "Bring me that affidavit, lady." They walked toward the door.

She laughed. "Well, if we lose our interim constable, you can be certain John Joe wouldn't ask me to be the next one," and stopped.

"Snake Johnson's the one you're after! Lady, you get busy." Ward said he never had believed that story about the taillights; he bet nobody else did.

The dogs rushed from under the house, barking. She strained to hear him.

"I've found out something else in my long experience too."

"What's that?"

"If there's reward money, most of the time somebody'll come out of the woodwork who seen something."

She watched Ward pull out a thin wallet and extract a bill: a lot for him. Ten dollars.

"There's you a starter. Now you and the church ladies get busy, you hear?"

She said, "I hope I won't disappoint you." *Or myself*. From the yard, she had to strain again to hear him over the noise of the dogs.

"What?"

"I said you got one thing else to remember."

"What's that?"

"Snake Johnson's fighting for his bread."

She went back over the roads, scarcely seeing them, instinctively took the right turns, seeing everything through a haze of her own. *I wanted to do something. Now I have.* Part of her wished that none of this had been started. But the faces of those she had talked to came back sharply; the faces of those she had looked at on the news: James Meredith; the astronaut whose name she could not remember. When she went into her own house and sat down to comb her hair, she considered herself in the dresser mirror. At fifty, she did not think she could pass for much younger. Her skin was dryer, yet her eyes seemed as eager as a girl's. At her age though, excitement was rarely possible; there were too many calluses.

When Tate came in, she was still sitting with her silver-backed hairbrush. She watched him. He was becoming a little round-shouldered. They had been polite to each other for so long. But politeness was not the same thing as truth: neither was it so painful. They were envied as a couple, they got along so well. Yet she could not tell her husband the thing closest to her heart: she wanted to be constable.

"Tate, we don't talk about ourselves enough. The other day seemed the first time."

He blanched at the idea. Then his face took on its new set look that not only surprised, but worried, her. Tate possibly could be mean, and she had never once thought so before in their whole existence together. Which then was better, their old silent compatibility, or the new openness she had forced? She tingled with apprehension just as he started to talk.

"All right, then," Tate said. "You're stubborn. As stubborn as your Poppa ever was. You kept those set ideas about what I should be. Stopped saying anything, I'll grant you." (His eyes did harden as he watched her shrug almost imperceptibly to mean she'd given up on him. The gesture had been spontaneous. She regretted it. But her apologetic look could not erase it.) Tate seemed to make himself soften.

"Allie, I never wanted to be anything," he said. "In a game, somebody's got to lose. Why not me."

Outraged, she began brushing her hair with sharp strokes.

Tate considered a moment her hair flying about, not perceiving the reason. "I have felt so much criticism from you," he said. "That you stand at the window and watch me leave here thinking I'm keeping folks in the road from getting where they want to go." Allie clenched her jaw not to say there was talk in the community about no one wanting to get caught behind his truck.

"I don't stand at the window watching you leave." She put as much warmth as possible into her words. She watched him from the distance of one who liked to win, and wanted to admire his attitude that he did not care if he lost.

"I," he said, "laugh sometimes at those folks having to get somewhere so fast. I bet half the time it doesn't matter a dern if they get there five minutes later, or maybe at all."

The whole slow sense of time in the countryside in olden days rose up in her; she felt impatient just remembering. Tate perhaps noticed her clenched jaw. "Well, I cut back on cotton and went to soybeans ahead of some of the other fellows, and you weren't sure I should. Till the bigger farmers did it, then you saw it was the right move. When I decided to cut back on soybeans because we had a surplus of them once folks switched from cotton and went to raising beef cattle, you weren't sure it was the right move. Till others did it too."

She turned. "You were right."

Tate relaxed back to being himself. "Shoot, folks working themselves to death in Nashtoba just to belong to that little country club. What do folks like that get out of life?"

She looked at his familiar face, wondering why, once he made two good decisions in farming, he could not have made others — gone on ahead. In the dresser mirror, she studied herself. Unable to help that thought, the important thing was not to say it. She'd like to belong to that little country club, too.

"Allie, I just never have wanted to shine my you-know-what."

"I know what," she said, smiling in the mirror at him. Your ass, she said to herself. "I guess I've always wanted to shine mine." It seemed such a simple desire. "I want to before it's too late."

Tate, studying his fingernails, picked up a file from her dresser. "I thought at this point you'd get rid of some of your nervous energy."

She whirled on the dresser stool. "You mean after the menopause." Her infuriated tone seemed to linger in the room. Tate dropped the file into place on the dresser. "That has nothing to do with anything! I'm talking about drowning and wanting to save myself," she said.

Puzzled, he said, "Can't you keep busy with your womenfolks' things? You've got your church work. The Woman's Club. Maybe you ought to teach Sunday school again. Or maybe you could teach at the academy when it opens."

She felt so much sorrow suddenly: felt that she could cry for the whole world.

"We're going to need you ladies, too, to help us raise money for the fire department," Tate said. Unknowingly, he quirked one dark eyebrow and gave her a crooked grin; these, in combination, back in their early days together had just about knocked her flat. A reminiscent quiver of desire went through her, vanishing as quickly as Tate's look. You ladies, she reheard him saying. She got up. She wondered if physical desire had left her altogether.

"Other women manage to keep busy, Allie."

"I'm looking for meaning, not just something to keep me busy," she said.

He went on enumerating again. "There's a canasta club in town. Why don't you take up the piano? Get with one of the sewing bees."

"Bees. Do they still call them that? I thought it was clubs," she said, hollowly. She faced him. "I could take up painting!"

Tate muttered, "Momma was a different situation."

"Was she?" Allie said. "I've wondered. Maybe she wouldn't have had to drink vanilla flavoring under different conditions. Or I could take up crewel work." She continued in her false voice. "Make a patchwork quilt. I know women here who don't do anything but needlepoint pillow covers, then put them into drawers. Can't give them away because everybody's already got a house full."

"Well, we all reach this age," Tate said, starting toward the kitchen. He would have whistled, sticking his hands into his pockets, but she interrupted.

"Tate. Somebody decent has got to run against Snake."

"I know that," he said over his shoulder. "But let's stick to one subject now. I'm tired."

"It is the same subject, Tate." Her tone caused him to stand still, facing opposite her. His shoulder blades tightened. Then to Allie's whole astonishment, the past rushed up over her again. Her own voice came out almost like a girl's, pleading. "Tate, you run," she said.

He could relax and turned around smiling: Was that all? his face said. "Shoot, woman. What's the pay? Four bucks for every arrest?" He was ready to laugh with her, knowing she was not really serious.

"A couple of hundred dollars a year," she said, tightly. "You could take kickbacks, if you're like Snake. There's a dollar for every jury summons you serve." She found herself still pleading.

Her seriousness about his running was beyond him. "It's a mess," he said, about to turn away again. "Everybody's too old or sick or no better than Snake."

"We have got to have somebody with the interests of the community at heart," she said.

"I know that," he said, irritably. Tate was hungry. "But who?"

"Me."

She might have been waiting for a blow. Cold perspiration dotted her upper lip. Tate was going to laugh, then he read an expression he knew. "I never thought I'd go through something like this with you, Allie."

"I am not going *through* anything. I'm going to run, Tate."

He took one quick step toward her. "You'll make a fool out

of yourself, woman! If you don't care, think about me. Can't you see me walking into the Whitehill Café and having every man in there snickering?"

"Put me in a pumpkin shell. There you'll keep me very well."

Would it be exciting to have him hit her? she wondered. Was there something sexual about that? Suppose they fought and tussled like people on TV: would they end up like them, in bed?

Tate had changed his mind several times about what he was going to say. "Allie. Do you think you're going to ride around these dark country roads chasing drunk Negroes?"

"Yes. Drunk white folks too. I can handle a gun and can learn to use Mace, which I'm told knocks you down like a chunk. I can serve a summons. I can fine fishermen drinking beer at the dam. I'd have a blackjack and could use that."

"Where'd you get all this information?"

"From Ward."

"Gone around talking behind my back again. Messing into the menfolks' world." Tate had never forgiven her for calling up Shine Murphy: like all the townsmen, he felt the bridge had been their business, despite the women having been successful.

"It was Ward's idea for me to run. I know that'll surprise you. It did me too. There are precedents. When the sheriff in Clarksdale was killed, his wife was appointed and ran on her own afterward and won. I'll bet Mister Otis would say if somebody can land on the base of the Creator's moon, a woman can be constable. All kinds of things nobody imagined." Tate however was not going to be lighthearted about this.

"I've got a deacons' meeting at seven. I've had enough talk. Is some supper ready?"

"There always is." She went past him abruptly. "How about helping and speeding things up." She was still being lighthearted, but to her surprise, he stepped in, stood like a stranger, and finally found the right cabinet with glasses for their iced tea. Having turned on burners, waiting for the food to heat, she looked out at the pasture; she could not help gritting her teeth, listening to the tinkle of his spoon stirring sugar, going around, knowing the exact number of turns it would take, that it would end in a hesitant stop before he hit the spoon against the glass to knock off drips.

Tate hunched over his plate and ate methodically. "I've got to get there a little early."

Hands on the wall clock seemed never to move. Allie thought of the number of Green Stamps she had saved to get it, and how routinely she did so many small things she did not want to do. She had not openly complained much in her life and did not ache over the unobtainable or frivolous. "You've got plenty of time," she said, watching him eat so fast.

He glanced at the clock too, with the hands that seemed not to move. He was hard up for conversation to bring up a subject he did not want to discuss with her. "The Brewster boy's reported his car stolen," Tate said.

"Stolen when?" She had his answer on the tip of her tongue, and hadn't needed to ask.

"The afternoon Mister Otis was killed," Tate said. "Says he left his car on the road with the keys in it. He went to inspect one of his daddy's fields bated with sunflowers, to see if any dove had come in. Says he thought a friend who owes him a practical joke had taken the car. Now, he thinks it's been stolen."

Allie thought cautiously that the boy had probably hidden it himself. Would this mean that for the first time in his short life he thought himself not above the law? It seemed like, what they would call on TV, a crack in the case. She pled to God that the Brewster boy did not go free. She wanted to believe in some mysterious guiding force. Tate was so bothered about her news tonight, she'd better not talk about her involvement with the boy. There seemed then nothing of importance to say: only the small clatter of silverware and dishes broke the silence; to talk trivia would be what he often referred to as women running their mouths. He pushed back his chair, at last.

"There's ice cream for when you come home," she said.

"Cherry vanilla?" He guessed his favorite, without much interest.

She nodded. Tate slouched as he carried his dishes to the sink, the first time ever without its being suggested to him. He went out for his cap on the peg in the den.

"I won't be home till around eleven."

"I'll be asleep by then," Allie called, like a promise.

31

WHEN ALLIE CAME HOME in the evenings now, the wild flowers of autumn along the roadsides had a white cast, and the bare fields had a rained-on look. Though fall was approaching, soybeans and cotton were still being harvested. Cattle were on their way to auctions, rattling along the roads, often bellowing in their frightened, sad way. Nearing November, hogs were butchered, and the air was frequently pungent and blued with wood smoke: the hogs were lowered on slings into troughs to be scalded before having their hair scraped off. People were busy, too, in their gardens, planting winter greens, turnip greens, kale, collards, and onions; and everywhere men were killing squirrels.

As an avowed candidate for constable, Allie traveled frequently near Nashtoba, so was made treasurer of the reward fund. She often stood in Brewster's bank to deposit reward money women raised from cake sales and other functions. Reading backward the name in gilt letters on the front window, she felt guilty about trying to convict the heir while transacting business at his father's bank. It was sad that a family line could weaken as the Brewsters' had. With a rotten apple like Quad it would virtually end; if he had progeny, none of them could ever again hold up their heads in pride, the way the Brewsters once had done. The genes seemed to have played out. Quad's father did not have the ability of the two previous Brewsters, who had acquired everything and sponsored so much building in the town: the local junior college had a football field named after them. Mr. Brewster III's greatest astuteness was to realize he had little. He rented out his farmland, got a good manager for the gin, hired smart heads to run the bank, men who would retain the Brewster image of being hard-nosed in business, while he remained a figurehead. Local people felt Quad would never fill even his father's insubstantial shoes. Mr. Brewster was known to realize that now, too. Did he blame himself at all? everyone wondered. He never had the guts to stand up to Quad or to his wife; she was the one who had spoiled the little tin god. Summertimes, when Quad was a boy, his daddy put him to work in the fields, tried to make him a regular fellow, wanted him to hoe and tote water, but at noontimes, it was reported, the family car showed up with a chauffeur who spread out Quad's lunch (luncheon?) on a white cloth, separate from the Negro workers.

Why hadn't Mr. Brewster put a stop to all that? Allie wondered, studying him in the bank; gumption had been refined out of him perhaps. Maybe lacking gumption, Quad had to drink. If he had been a harmless drunk, people would only have felt sorry for him. A few people now knew he had caused two deaths, but everyone knew of his reputation as a liar and a cheat and that he had broken the hearts and spirits of quite a few vulnerable young women who trusted him. Several had had frightening experiences with him when he was drunk; had been tossed out of his car to the loneliness of a dark road, had his hands held threateningly around their throats. That he would come to a bad end had been predicted quite awhile. When Quad bragged that his only ambition was to be a playboy, people here said, "In Nashtoba, Miss'sippi?" and laughed. Had the boy no sense of reality? What would happen if the Brewsters lost their money and he had to make his own living someday?

Driving on out through the countryside now, she wondered if, in the scheme of things, there were simply worthless bad pennies? God's plan seemed more mysterious than ever. All around the county she had visited general merchandise stores, leaving her printed cards on their counters, with her name and the office she was seeking. In each she chatted and had a soft drink and shook hands with customers. She went to remote houses and stopped along road banks and walked into fields. She mentioned the missing car to people who were most apt to spot it in bottomland or woods.

She drove today to the new chicken factory with the idea of talking about the car more than about voting, as the workers were largely Negroes. The stench of the factory met her a long way ahead. When she turned in, Negroes were unloading large crates of live chickens from trucks, wearing blood-spattered, wet clothes and hip boots. Women particularly took her cards with a childlike and delighted air; many said they were already making a collection from the general stores. They had no idea what the cards represented, what voting was all about. Some took them with an air of bitterness, some with respect; they appreciated the white lady coming around and ruining her good shoes in the water, with the implication they would be new voters, sometime. Voter registration drives for them were rumored—the communists coming down here to rile them up, whites felt. But right now it was hard for them to register. One question registrars asked them was, "How many bubbles would a bar of soap make?" White folks laughed about that. Allie had made up her mind not to have anything to do with the academy, intending that as a small silent protest, like Brother Walker's refusal to laugh at jokes about Negroes. Having left the community, he had been replaced by a nice young man whom people were never going to accept. They resented him as if it were his fault Brother Walker had left. While towns-people knew they were being uncharitable, and ruining the young man's life among them, they'd not change. Unjustness was often on her mind these days — its existence in small ways and large all around her.

Doors and windows to the factory stood open. Through them she could see chickens, tied by their feet and hanging head down, passing by on a conveyor belt, feathers flying. The whole area was raucous with their squawkings, but also with the laughing and joking and hollering among the workers. This factory was one of the few places paying minimum wage. Jobs were sought. So terrible was the smell, and the guttings so nasty, that many Negroes boasted about coming to work drunk. They brought stories to town about a man losing a leg out here, about nicks and cuts, and their blood mingling with that of the chickens. Once a woman almost severed a thumb; as she shrieked and jumped, the thumb was pulled off by an overhead suction meant for guts. "Look in the store packages for thumb if you buying gizzards," the Negroes often warned.

To look into the Negroes' faces now, having lived among them all her life, Allie thought of them in a new way; when all was progress, they lived almost like a past generation. How have they lived? Some of them could not tell you one times one, or do anything but make the smallest change when they made purchases; they were so much at the mercy of others. How have they lived? she asked herself another time. She felt tearful when Buster's words came to mind — "In ten years' time my generation will be running things. You just wait!" She wondered if she and Brother Walker were right in thinking that integration would in many ways drive the races apart. Solemn as she shook hands with everyone, she drove off thinking about breaking a precedent: what a small thing it had seemed. She had shaken hands with Negro men. She had been touching Negro women all of her life.

In Nashtoba she went into the truck stop for lunch. She sat down before realizing that ashy-faced Fred Cullins was at the next table. He supposedly was on vacation from "a recent illness." He gave her a frightened grin; she tried to keep accusation off her face. Rose had said he was no longer drinking, but his system had not recovered. She let her eyes ask him, When are you going, Fred? He pretended interest in conversation at his table.

"Spent over a thousand dollars on poisoning this year. With cotton late I'm just hoping to break even," a man said.

"Small farming amounts to surviving. That's all. We've survived," another man said, after a moment.

"American ingenuity always works its way out of a corner," the first man said.

"Everything's politics in Washington. All politics. It don't have anything on earth to do with what the farmer's real problems are. The politicians all make compromises that aren't feasible —" The words were broken off when something like a whirlwind came through the truck stop door.

Just before, a waitress was refilling Allie's coffee cup, whispering that she didn't live in Allie's county, but hoped she won. "That Snake," she had said, heaving a buxom sigh. Her coffeepot overflowed Allie's cup, as Rose burst in. She brushed past tables, bumping elbows of diners, sending paper napkins swirling to the floor, and went straight to Fred.

She noted Allie in surprise. Opening her mouth as if to speak to her first, Rose looked back at Fred. He half stood and then sat down. The men assumed a domestic argument begun at the breakfast table had followed him, tracked him down, cornered him by the window. They looked embarrassed. Each face reflected, What if this had been my wife!

"So, Fred," Rose said, crossing her arms, "how do I look?"

All appraised her. He said in his lowest voice, "You look fine, Mother."

Rose touched with pride the neat bun at the back of her head. Her glasses shone with spit and polish. Her dress was the one beyond Sunday's best, saved for special occasions that did not materialize, and for Shriners' affairs. Having a party aura, fitting becomingly, the dress made Rose prettier. Her face did not match her gray hair: it was touched up with rouge and lipstick. Above her bun sat a straw hat, so firmly in place, it alone did not shake with agitation.

She shook a finger in Fred's face. "I'm going to DeSoto. I don't know when I might be back." She hissed. "I might stay up there in a motel — all night." Her hands slipped over her hips in a suggestive way. Despite her age, despite the grayish Rose all were accustomed to, the men envisioned what any woman could offer, and looked interested.

"Mother," Fred said.

"I might not ever come back. I didn't even leave you anything cooked to eat."

"Mother, go home. Let's —"

"Home," she said. "I can't share one with a man like you anymore, Fred. A man knows what you do." She looked at the others. "Suppose they knew! Like Allie does." As she nodded at Allie, their eyes connected.

Allie saw little, gray-haired Rose differently. Eyes snapping behind her sparkling, but muddling, eyeglasses, Rose had grown. Allie did not regret the softer, sweeter Rose that had vanished. It was better to sacrifice a little of that self to have more backbone, spine, she thought. Fred sat, his lips parted.

Slowly the other men had begun to resent Rose. A woman making a spectacle of herself was bad enough, but Rose had not only disobeyed her better half, she was acting as if Fred were not that. She had embarrassed him before his peers. He sat in shame. Finally, the men busily asked for more coffee.

Allie crossed to the cashier and extended her money wordlessly. Like Rose with Fred, she was no longer the person Tate had married. Men like Tate and Fred were uneasy with change; she did not fault them for that. They could not help wanting things static, any more than she and Rose could help changing.

Allie waited for Rose. She was saying, "Mister Brewster phoned home for you, Fred. Said he didn't want to bother you while you were having your vacation. But he did, didn't he?"

She snapped her fingers in the middle of the table again. "And you hop," she said.

The faces of the men all sagged before this woman's authority. Rose said, "Some hunters found the boy's stolen car. Way out in some woods." Her voice was full of derision. "Just the way somebody would really dump it off who stole it. The tires were gone, and it was stripped. Somebody knew just the right things to do. Mister Brewster wants you to tow it to town." She grew more harsh. "Tow it, Fred," she said. "Tow it right to the very middle of town, why don't you? Leave it by the courthouse steps for everybody to see." Again she snapped her fingers beneath the noses of all there. Several of the men shook their heads to mean the woman ought to be put away somewhere. The others smiled as if in sympathy. They began to dig out nickels to place beneath their saucers, eager to leave the scene now. Rose straightened the hat that was not crooked.

"Hop, Fred. Mister Brewster's a-waiting on you. I'm going to the district attorney." Fred paled; the others looked mystified.

She met Allie at the door. From the moment Rose mentioned DeSoto, Allie had known where she was going, and why. They smiled, understanding so completely that they were ready, at last. And that they needed the support of one another; they linked arms.

A commotion stopped them. At Fred's table a ketchup bottle fell over as he stood. He came on as quickly as he could. "Wait," he called.

Rose's dry hand gripped Allie's arm. "It wasn't me that shamed him into doing it," Rose whispered. Allie was about to agree; then Rose said under her breath, "Was it?"

Nathan Bedford Percival was not in his office. They arrived after a twenty-mile trip through the twinkling autumn country side, north toward Memphis. His scarlet-lipped secretary was startled. She blinked at the threesome who entered, unannounced, without an appointment, the man with a greasy cap on backward, a grayish woman dressed to the teeth—and Allie wanted to laugh searching for some way to describe herself. She came up only with an earnest look.

"The district attorney is not here," the secretary said. Then she looked sorry for them. "He's around the square, drinking coffee and talking. You'll have to look. Except at five he'll be in the furniture store watching TV and having a stirrup cup."

Allie called, "Thank you," as the door closed. They rushed around the square and into each business and found him finally at the counter in the darkish drugstore. The weather was still hot. In the little time they spoke about seeing him, a brief harsh storm came up: drops pelted the grooved tin roof jutting out over the fronts of stores, like the hooves of a thousand maddened little horses. Suddenly the afternoon was a luminous green, and then a softer glow. When rain stopped as suddenly, the world seemed to have been punished. Old men had remained on benches under magnolias and turned to watch as the four of them ran across the square.

He seemed young to be district attorney, lanky and not yet filled out. That was part of being her age: schoolteachers, dentists, firemen, policemen all seemed too young; the bright side was that Percival was filled with enthusiasm for the case; he did not act world-weary.

That afternoon he said the credibility of the witnesses might be the whole case. "A person's quality counts, reputation, and demeanor on the stand. What motivates a person to get up and say x, y, or z?" He looked at Fred over folded hands, one long finger speculatively on his nose. Fred had a hard time these days looking back directly at anyone; he was still hangdog.

"I just have to tell the truth," Fred said, watching his cap go around between his knees.

". . . the law must see both sides." As Percival continued to talk, Allie couldn't help thinking about Elgie's side; she could understand his refusal finally to testify: there'd been too much time, to remember, to ruminate—to rusticate, as Sy called it. She was quite horrified at the anger that rose up in her: though wasn't it natural? She heard herself saying things she'd been weaned on — "A nigger'll turn and kick you in the end" — it was impossible to forget what you'd always heard, only possible not to believe it.

The hearing was held in Ward Grierson's small house. The dogs were heard to grumble often under it. Ward dominated the room; active, he appeared larger. Quad Brewster shrunk his head into his collar and seemed diminished, a turtle about to hide. His lips remained on the verge of smiling; he might charm them out of all this grown-up behavior yet. He wore a conservative dark-blue suit, which was a replica of his daddy's and would have come from an expensive Memphis store, too. But he was a child playacting. He spoke seldom, having nothing to say. Had nothing to say because his mind was empty, Allie thought. He understood racing a car through the countryside, dating girls, having a good time. He would never grow up; he both vexed her and made her sad for him. Ward's face looked stronger, a country man's good one.

Ward began. "This is no trial," he said, avoiding the boy's eyes. "It's a preliminary hearing. I'd like to get it over with quickly." He did not look at Quad's parents either.

Quad said what he had to in a low voice. He was respectful. His lawyer would have primed him. "No sir, I remember nothing. I don't believe I hit Fred. That is, it doesn't seem like it, because I don't remember any of it." He admitted to being drunk that night. If he had hurt Fred, he certainly never meant to. He began to half cry, to blubber a little. His mother's eyes welled up then. Everyone was against him, Quad said; he knew that now. He had enemies, people who wanted to get him. People were jealous. His eyes kept turning toward his mother. She sat trying to baby him from across the room, but her face showed fear. Ward leaned back and let the boy talk. "I went up to Fred's. I remember that," he said. "Because he's the best body man around. Everybody knows that. I needed to have the Ferrari tuned. Maybe I acted up, being drunk and all. I get impatient. Daddy's always saying that. But I didn't think I did anything mean. I never meant to."

He looked appealing, the little boy in his daddy's clothes. He stuck to his story. What else could he do? Allie thought. Squirming in the heat, he was boxed in. She stared closely at the handsome weak face; he was not a man, but he was not a boy.

It did not last long. An hour later, Quad Brewster was bound over to the grand jury, and trial date was set. Quad sat dumb in his chair. When everyone rose to go, his mother's eyes glistening with tears, he sat still, waiting for it not to be so. His pale eyes at last looked into emptiness. From their corners, tears appeared and ran down his cheeks unchecked. He sat like a small boy ready to bawl because somebody bigger had taken something away from him, Allie thought.

On the trial's opening day a crowd stood outside the courthouse. It was old and a bronze plaque on one wall had a poem by a late and local poet, from that simpler time when people went to see a snake in a window; when to people hereabouts the poetry was the highest kind:

They do me wrong who say I come no more
When once I knocked and failed to find you in.
For every day I stand outside your door,
And bid you wake and rise to fight and win.

Dost thou behold thy lost youth all aghast?
Dost reel from righteous retribution's blow?
Then turn from blotted archives of the past
And find the future's pages white as snow.

Art thou a mourner? Rouse thee from thy spell!
Art thou a sinner? Sins may be forgiven.
Each morning gives thee wings to flee from hell,
Each night a star to guide thy feet to Heaven.

Couldn't it offer comfort yet, Allie wondered, if sophistication were lobbed away? She had tried to rouse from her own spell. Today she heard whispers: "There's the woman running for constable from Itna Homa." The present constable was stuck with his story about them fishtailing taillights; if Fred proved his version, Snake would be up for a perjury trial. Percival had said, "Miss Allie, if we win I can come down hard on the sheriff. You'll get Johnson's interim appointment. After that, you're on your own. I think you'll be a shoo-in in November."

Hearing herself talked about, her ears burned, though she did not have red ones like several women standing around who'd just stepped out from under dryers. Every beauty shop in the countryside had opened earlier this morning to accommodate all the women wanting to get fixed up before the trial. Mary Lou, the judge's wife, passed. A local woman whispered, "She was in Pandora's Beauty Box this morning. She forgot to lower her voice after she got out from the dryer. Thought she was whispering and called the judge and told him, said, 'You cover your rear!' "

Everybody laughed. They speculated on her meaning. Mary Lou Morton was scared of her husband making the wrong decision about leniency or punishment, because she wasn't sure how those men he played golf with out to the Nashtoba Country Club wanted him to decide. She and the judge were social climbers of the worst kind. Mrs. Morton knew the politest shunning in the world came in little country clubs in small towns.

Most merchants had begged off jury duty since this was their busiest season. Farmers were slowing down and the jury consisted mostly of them, except for a few retired men. Culled from the district attorney's five districts, some of them were almost strangers to the town, and the Brewster name. "Reckon they'll ever have women on a jury?" Miss Pearlie Mae whispered. A man behind them said loudly, "God dawg, I wouldn't want one on a jury even. Can come up with some devilish things, a woman can." No sense mentioning whether Negroes would ever serve, Allie thought.

"All rise." Judge Morton in black accoutrement seemed to flow into his seat. Allie considered herself judging him. Everyone was on trial. She sat down wondering if the judge did not realize it was common knowledge that he'd been caught parked in a car with a teenaged girl in the part of Sardis dam restricted to the public, and that it was hushed up because of his position. She thought of her unease just glimpsing a police car in her rearview mirror, when she was not exceeding the speed limit. All here had senses of guilt.

"I'd be scared out of my britches." Miss Pearlie Mae's lacy gloved hand touched Allie's ear. Rose Cullins took the stand.

". . . after the accident your husband's usual character changed?" Percival asked gently.

Rose nodded. Her stiff round hat remained upright. Allie thought Rose had hesitated for a moment, as if thinking about the two accidents, as she was: Quad could face only one charge; Percival assured them that if he was found guilty on this one, he'd be found the same in John Q's case, which would come next.

"Fred has always been an upstanding citizen in this town," Rose said.

"Provided well for you?"

"I had everything in this world I needed, and then some."

"Paid his bills?" Percival's voice urged her to continue without him.

"Yes, sir, paid his bills. Every one on time. Every Sunday morning he was in that Baptist church school and church afterwards without urging. He was always in the car first tooting for me to come on. He liked his work at Mister Brewster's. He liked working out to our garage, fixing things. The Devil makes work for idle hands. Fred's never were. All the way to our house I could hear him whistling out in the garage." Suddenly she slipped so far forward, Percival sprang to catch her, as if she were fainting. Rose made a little announcement.

"Anybody that's got anything out to our house to be fixed, Fred's caught up. Everything's ready now."

There were sounds of relief; Judge Morton asked for quiet.

Percival addressed the jury. "Fred Cullins was a man we might all envy. A man without material wealth by some standards. But a happy man. A man whose wife was happy. Simple people suddenly on a stand to testify to their involvement in this crime and what led up to it. Without any motivation except to tell the whole truth. A man whose entire life has been changed by circumstances outside himself. Yet who has willingly come forward after a period of natural and normal fear, a man who was — as his wife's testimony describes him — an upstanding citizen until . . ."

Having stepped down, Rose paused by Fred. He sat at the prosecutor's table. She wished to touch, but Fred would not look up. Her faltering question in the truck stop was resolved, Allie believed: Fred would have come forward. Fred was shying from Rose's testimony about having everything she wanted; in the rush back from DeSoto that first afternoon, when unmatured cotton blooms had folded into their evening's tight pink buds, he'd looked out the car window as if not to listen when Rose had whispered, "Fred, I never did care about that fur coat." Rose told her privately about the promise later. Allie guessed it still ate at Fred, since the coat seemed farther from possibility than ever.

He took the stand. Fred held to the railing of the witness box with one hand, his knuckles whitening as he was sworn in.

"Could he repeat that?" The young court stenographer stopped what seemed her mindless silent typing.

"Fred Cullins." He gave his name again.

"You're going to have to talk in a voice that loud, Fred," Judge Morton said. Fred breathed in and said in nearly a correct tone, "All right."

Percival led him quietly through their rehearsed answers. Rose moved her own lips, like someone speaking behind a prompter. There was finally an air to the questioning of Percival tugging a toy that moves as required. "Lived here how long?" he asked.

"Born and reared," Fred answered promptly.

"Church affiliation?"

"Baptist."

"Immersed?"

"You bet your boots."

Fred's credibility as a witness was easily established. The jurors heard he was a local boy and a self-made and religious man; however, Allie sensed there had been too much talk around the county now: how he set right there whilst his wife blessed him out in public. What kind of man are you, Fred? Allie thought, with compassion. Perhaps she ought to ask, What's this done to you; what kind of man are you now?

Rose Cullins was crying.

When the defense lawyer, Ben Wray Hood, went forward, all the whispering about Fred's answers and behavior stopped; everyone was thinking exactly what Ward Grierson muttered: "Yonder walks the poorest white boy ever raised in river bottomland."

"Mr. Cullins." Ben Wray wrapped his arms behind himself, and he seemed unable to think of a single thing to ask this witness. Fred looked embarrassed. River rat: sentiment was against the defense, yet Ben Wray'd worked his way up too and settled in the Delta, smart enough to know that where folks had the most money they were more apt to need criminal lawyers. People were mad because the Brewsters had felt nobody in north Mississippi was good enough to defend their brat.

"How close at the closest point were you to the scene of the accident?"

Fred repeated what he'd told Percival. "About twenty feet."

"The car was traveling at a high rate of speed?"

"Yes sir."

"Do you have any impairment of vision?"

"I wear glasses —"

"Did you see the license plate? Can you describe the person driving? Do you know it was a male? Did you see any facial hairs?"

Percival leapt up objecting to the line of questioning, the witness being deliberately intimidated.

"Sustained."

"Exception!" Hood cried.

"Noted," said the judge automatically.

"No," Fred said.

"How'd he remember all that?" Miss Pearlie Mae whispered against Allie's ear. She said, "The answers were all the same."

It was particular to Delta lawyers to dye their hair silver-white and to have it marcelled; Ben Wray looked like a Southern gentleman lawyer of the old school. He often touched his tight little waves.

". . . yellow Ferrari?"

"Yes sir."

"You were wearing your glasses?"

"No sir, I—"

"Forgot to put them on."

Rose turned to whisper, "He doesn't wear glasses all the time!" Those nearby said, "Shush."

"I've got some reading glasses and some for distance—"

"You forgot them that night?"

"No. I wasn't fixing to drive."

"I've been under the impression all this time you were leaving that poker game," Ben Wray cried.

"I was leaving but—"

"You said you were not!"

"I was, but—"

"Were you leaving or not leaving, Mr. Cullins?"

Fred swallowed. "Leaving. I'd stepped out first to—"

Rose's little hat finally shook. Language, Fred! Allie imagined her saying so clearly.

"To relieve yourself?" Hood smirked toward the jury

Fred nodded.

Ben Wray said, "There was a lot of drinking that evening. You said the deceased was drunk. Define that!"

"Define?"

"Drunkenness, man. Was he reeling? Falling down? Passing out?"

"He was just old man Otis when he'd had a few," Fred said, in a sad voice. "If you know a fellow . . ." His voice trailed away. The court stenographer jumped up and shoved the microphone toward him.

"Thanks, honey," Judge Morton said and winked.

"Mister Cullins, let me redirect your attention to the road, then. A general store on one side helped obscure your vision. What about the cattails on the path's other side?"

"Cattails?"

"Don't you love nature, sir? How many times have you been to that trailer? Aren't you aware of cattails taller than a man's head? Taller than yours?"

"I thought I saw clear of them."

"You thought?" Hood said. "Thought?"

"I saw the car hit the old man."

"In what light? The moon's? Were there lights on at those stores? Big bright clear lights? Wasn't it a dark night?"

"Objection," Percival called. The automatic responses came again.

"Sustained."

"Exception!"

"Noted."

"Will you answer the question, Mister Cullins."

"Which one?"

There was some laughter and much sympathetic shuffling about. Hood said over the noise, "What lights were there?"

"At the stores there were bulbs to keep away bugs. There was some moon. And the trailer door being open made light."

"How many drinks had you had?"

"I wouldn't know how to count."

"You lost count?"

"Didn't anybody count."

"Not how many shots you had?"

"We were drinking scuppernong wine."

"Oh, then. How many wineglasses full?"

"Wineglasses?" Fred said.

"You didn't keep account of that either?"

"We drank out of fruit jars."

Ben Wray repeated that, laughing to himself. Most spectators heard someone whisper clearly: "As if that river rat don't know all about it."

"All evening?" Ben Wray said.

"We did drink some whiskey after supper." Noting Ben Wray's expectant expression, he added, "We used shots."

"When was your last drink before the accident?"

"Just before I went out to piss!"

Fred realized his mistake, and fell back. Rose began to cry again. The women from Itna Homa agreed to leave with her. Everyone had had enough for one day.

"Is that boy going to be brought to taw?" Miss Pearlie Mae asked when they stood on the courthouse steps.

"Maybe when Quad's on the stand tomorrow things will look up," Allie said. "Though Mister Percival thinks he'll say anything to save his own skin." And she looked out as they drove on home through the dusk. He had also said it would be an open day on corruption if the boy won.

They drove into town feeling their tails were tucked. On the main road people stood around cars and pickups listening to highlights of the trial from Nashtoba's local radio station. Now those with firsthand information went into the stores and attracted crowds. Allie wanted only to go home. Backing to drive away from Loma's, where she'd dropped off the women, Allie saw Sy inside the Laundromat. He was aware of her car. She crossed the cattle gap knowing Elgie would hear the trial was not going right. Thinking of her promise to drive him to Memphis for a nighttime bus to Chicago once the verdict was known, she felt helpless about his going. He would not let Sy contact anyone else to take him, believing the law would come back here; that it would break down any colored man who'd helped him. The way the law could always break us colored down, he'd said.

Elgie determined to believe that things were the same. If only she discussed her marriage with him, she might convince him differently. You and Mister Tate! he'd say in disbelief. She had never expected any difference after all this time, she would say. So, couldn't Elgie believe that changes came to pass?

32

THEN ELGIE WAS going with her, and she had believed it all along. She wanted to dance all over the kitchen. Sy made no comment, but if Miss Allie was happy, then he was: his round dark eyes said that much. It was not quite daylight. At Loma's and Mose's the tin roofs sheltering their porches seemed shutters allowing the stores to sleep.

His hat riding high atop his head, Sy had passed their bedroom window. Tate was just lifting the shade, and said, "The old man must be sick again." Light frost covered the ground, and Sy's breath was quick starts of smoke as he came to the back door, not stopping to tap at their window. She knew he was not sick. Though he swung, by their connecting rope, his browned plastic jugs for water, they were an excuse, because he got his water outside Loma's. She dressed quickly and arrived in the kitchen, where Tate and Sy stood talking. "He's going," she said, a flat statement.

"Say you come after him anytime. Elgie ready," Sy said. At the sink, filling the old man's jugs, Tate tightened his shoulders, and even his back seemed grim.

She gave Sy coffee and left him holding the steam toward his face. Tate came back to the bedroom with her. "I'd better go with you, or there'll be more mess."

"Me driving alone with Elgie?" she said, tartly. "We will not be intimidated." She shared that bond a moment. Roosters were crowing, and Tate looked out. "It doesn't matter now what time you carry him, Allie."

"Why, you're right," she said, dropping her coat. "I hadn't thought he's going to be seen anyway."

He went back to drink coffee with Sy. They were jollying one another along: the words *marbles* and *cotton* reached the bedroom. Her impulse had been to phone Elgie, and, stopped short, she found it again so difficult to believe in this day and time. Minnie, others like her, were still using outhouses when men were going to the moon. Why were they not more resentful? Aware of resentments on her part, she thought them difficult to live with. She could not undo the past. Things already said could not be taken back. She saw no point in asking forgiveness when the feelings persisted. She wished Tate were more aggressive; he wished she were more content. As if she could break down a certain barrier, she said, "Tate, come on to the trial today."

"Why?" he said. "After two days I feel I've been there, I've heard so much. I wouldn't even have wanted to look at that boy yesterday. I'm better off anyway cutting my hay before it rains." Sy nodded.

She went to the telephone and called Percival, shortly after dawn.

They met at the courthouse several hours before the trial was to open. Percival ushered them downstairs and into a janitor's closet, having bribed to get it awhile. There was a window at ground level, and the narrow space was filled with the smell of a disinfectant that made her sneeze. Elgie wore Sy's old hat that had been Tate's. With the hat worn so low, she told him, he was more conspicuous. He took it off in the half-light, to shake hands with Percival. He was wearing the same denim coveralls that had been Sy's when he was a larger man. There was one old armchair; Allie sat down to give the men more room. In the narrow space, Percival seemed sky high. Elgie seemed shorter and rounder.

Percival went over and over everything with Elgie, pacing back and forth. "That boy yesterday had all the motivaton in the world to give false testimony. Fred had nothing to gain but peace of mind. That's not enough to convict Quad. There hasn't been any way yet to prove he wasn't where the state'd like us to believe. You saw clearly through the windshield?"

Elgie nodded. "Saw when that car hit the ditch and he fell over the horn. It was a young white man."

Percival said, "Three friends of his took the stand yesterday to testify they often drove his car."

"This one had a headful of light-colored hair," Elgie said.

"Surely it's Quad," Allie said. "I could convict him on those pretty eyes suddenly looking like a weasel's, so shifty. Even exposing his twenty-six traffic violations didn't mean anything?"

"All that showed was that family influence has kept him out of court before."

Up high, in the courthouse steeple, the clock struck. Percival checked his wristwatch. "There's some obvious questions I'm not going to ask you on the stand, Elgie. I'm hoping the defense will kill itself with the truth." He waited a moment. "I'll have to turn you over to the sheriff on the escape-warrant charge."

"I figured something like that," Elgie said.

"You'll be here in the jail for now. After the trial it's Parchman."

"I figured like that too."

"Then why are you here, Elgie?"

"I done figured on that." He laughed. "If I have pride I thought I best lay it aside. If I has fear, best lay that aside. I figure it that the Negro peoples always have wanted to make a contribution. Now Mister Meredith going to the white man's school got hisse'f a opportunity. I figured this my opportunity to do some little thing to hep my race get out the rut it been in a hundred years."

Feet passed or loitered by the overhead window and dabbed them with daylight, or shut it out. A small Negro boy peeped down between his knees and laughed and ran off. Then they listened while the clock chimes played a few strands of "Nearer My God to Thee" before the hour struck.

"I needs to tell you a little story," Elgie said. From a back pocket he took a light tan hand-tooled wallet. It had raised initials: L.G.H. "Make these here down to the prison." He waved the wallet toward them. He slipped out a small piece of nickel tablet paper so worn its folds parted and it had an oiled appearance from age. "I done had this here evidence for a long time," he said.

Percival almost smiled. "Evidence?"

"Yes suh. Agin some more of the Brewsters. It been on my conscience too. Agin Mister Quad's granddaddy this here. How you say the white peoples thought about him, Miss Allie?"

"Well, he was a pillar of the Baptist church, and of society."

"That man pulled the wool over ever'body's eyes. Had me a uncle that lived on Mister Brewster's place back then. Mister Brewster, he had stills all over that land. Paid the colored to keep them going. He bought that white lightning by the half-pint. Come election times and he be delivering it to white peoples all out in the county. Then election day he sent all these cars out to carry them folks to town to vote. My uncle, he drove for Mister Brewster. Now the colored figured something wrong going on 'sides his whiskey-making."

Percival said, "Yes. That's what's called influencing the vote."

Elgie looked satisfied. "He come to this tenant house next to where my uncle was cropping for him. He be ever' time figuring all out on this tablet paper 'bout how many half-pints he'd need. So my uncle, he just slipped him one of these papers with Mister Brewster's writing on it one time, after he left. Mammy Lou, she kep' it and then me. Well, the colored have always said give the Negro a opportunity to stand up and be a man and he going to stand up and be a man. I had to study on it a bit more." He glanced at Allie. "See, trouble 'bout this state been it's too race conscious. Your race can't climb long as it is holding me down."

Percival slipped an arm along Elgie's shoulders; they moved on toward the sheriff's office. "Told myse'f if the day have come when I can stand up, then I better stand up or it's goodbye."

Outside the office they could smell cigar smoke; it seemed to ooze around the door cracks. "I have to apologize," Percival said.

"How come that, Mister Percival?"

"It crossed my mind just once the reward money might be involved."

Allie laughed, then Elgie. "What I'm going do with five hundred dollars in Parchman? Buy me a lots of cigarettes and whiskey. I don't use nary one."

Percival pressed his arm harder around Elgie's shoulders. "Either way I'd have done what I'm going to do. But I don't want to tell you now. Because when you go on that stand you can truthfully say nobody promised you anything for coming here today."

"They sho ain't done that."

"See you in court." Allie found she still whispered. "I was going to say don't be afraid, but I am."

"When you be's in quicksand and get out into some other kind of sand, it still is better. Don't worry none, Miss Allie."

In the crowded courtroom she was waiting when Percival came in and spoke to Judge Morton, who then rapped his gavel and said there would be an hour's delay in the trial's opening. "The state has new evidence. Everybody go get some coffee." He got up and went out.

Among the spectators, Mr. Brewster held out a hand to his wife. She stood. Miss Pearlie Mae's light gloved hand brushed Allie's ear. "I think the whole thing is, that's a family that doesn't pray together," she said.

Talk began in back, and reached from row to row; heads

turned. Then Ward Grierson leaned between Allie and Miss Pearlie Mae. "There's an old Negro in the sheriff's office who Percival's talking to. They're saying he's the reason for the delay."

An old man had turned to listen. "Pshaw," he said, turning back again.

33

PERCIVAL HAD BEEN disappointed in reports from a forensic laboratory in Jackson. Having Elgie waiting, he rushed through questioning a technician. Ben Wray repeated him almost exactly.

"Mister Ramsey, you say weeds caught underneath the Ferrari don't necessarily come from Itna Homa, or even this county?"

"Yes sir. You got those same weeds anywhere in Miss'sippi."

"What about mud found on the car?"

Mr. Ramsey decided to smirk. "I think all us country boys know that old yellow mud comes from a heap of places around this state."

Percival hopped up to cross-examine. "We've heard that the deceased at the time of his death was wearing khaki pants and shirt and a wool plaid jacket. Any of those materials caught on the car?"

"No sir."

"Any material at all?"

"Yes sir."

"Would you tell us the kind?"

"It was denim. I'd say it came from the work reinforcement along the seam."

He was excused. Percival went to his table, carefully not looking at his opponent. Again, Quad Brewster wore the dark-blue business suit like his father's. He kept peeking at Ben Wray and then writing busily in a little notebook in front of him. "Playing lawyer," someone remarked.

"Call my next witness, please," Percival said.

This time when the bailiff went out, there was a general rustling in the court; everyone craned to watch the door open. The delay and the talk about a mysterious Negro in the sheriff's office had caused suspense. There was a general air of disappointment when a gray-haired older Negro walked in, looking exactly like ones spectators lived among. Miss Pearlie Mae began saying something, and Allie said, "Honey, don't talk now."

It had not occurred to her that she would cry. She took a deep breath, realizing something on her face caused Miss Pearlie Mae to stare more closely, afraid to speak. The unknown past overwhelmed her, while that which was known threatened to undo her. She accepted quite simply that this might always be true. No matter how often she was told to forget, she was a person who chose not to wipe out memories, but to live with them.

Taking a deep breath, she said to the home folks around her, "That's Elgie Hale." He passed her with a slight nod in her direction, and went through the gate before the witness stand, as his name was called. "Why, Allie," was all anyone could think to say. She could understand that. Then she let herself begin quietly to cry.

". . . your name?" Percival said.

Elgie repeated, "L. G. Hale."

"L. and G.?"

"Plain L. and G. That what my momma named me. But white folks all the time telling me I had to have a name, so I just spelled that E-l-g-i-e."

Ben Wray folded his arms and rolled his eyes toward the jury. Percival, his head down, went on looking as if this minor testimony was as important as any Elgie had. Ward Grierson's surprised breath was still on Allie's neck. Only a handful of people here from her community remembered Elgie, or even the name of the Negro accused of killing her mother. Percival went on in the same way. "Where were you living at the time of the hit-and-run death?"

"I lives in a little house belong to old Sy Coleman in Itna Homa. It set right up over the road where that poor man was kilt."

"Were you in the house at the time?"

"Naw suh, I was walking in a ditch. I stopped and couldn't move when I seen them lights coming at him and me bof, seem like."

When Elgie finished, Percival stood with bowed head a moment; he then gave up his position.

"Now, Elgie." Rocking on his heels, Ben Wray nodded at him; he might have known Elgie forever, might be calling him uncle in his kindliest voice. "You were just out walking around at night?"

"Yes suh."

Again, Ben Wray glanced toward the jury, smiling a little — surely they thought the old man as funny as he did. Then suddenly he whirled toward Elgie like a dog about to bite.

"You say you were close enough to get a look at the driver. How close?" His voice had a hollow sound, as if it came from his chest. Allie found Miss Pearlie Mae's hand in her own. "How close?" the defense cried again. How close, nigger? rang out so clearly in his voice people shifted uncomfortably. Elgie stared at him a full moment.

"This close?" Ben Wray held his hands wide. "This close? Or this close?" narrowing them. "How many feet away? Twenty? Thirty?"

"Mought have been about six."

"Six?"

"Six feets. Mought have been a little bit less."

Ben Wray slapped his hands closed. He shook his head. A smile spread across his face. "Now, I don't think you know just how close six feet is, Elgie. You didn't get hit less than six feet away?"

"Yes suh, I did."

Percival wanted to laugh. Ben Wray stared at the witness.

"You got hit, Elgie," he said finally. "You went to a doctor."

"Naw suh."

"Got hit by a car. But you didn't go to a free clinic!"

"Naw suh."

"You got hit by a car. You don't go for medical attention. You never said a word to anyone. We're to believe that?"

Allie sat forward, waiting for the question Percival wanted.

"Why didn't you tell somebody before, Elgie?"

"I be escaped from the penitentiary and been hiding."

Those from Itna Homa who knew the truth did not move and sat with silent and self-important looks, but the rest of the courtroom was filled with motion. The sheriff walked about looking as if he wanted to be congratulated, photographed; people jumped up to ask him questions. Judge Morton demanded silence. The defense glared at the district attorney, and then spoke. The stenographer looked up. Judge Morton told Ben Wray to speak louder. "What were you offered to come here, Elgie? Immunity?" Ben Wray managed.

"Suh?"

"Were you offered freedom to come here? A pardon?"

"I weren't offered nothing. I come to tell the truth because it be pressing me down not to. This here where that car clipped me, too."

Elgie suddenly stood up and offered his own leg as evidence. He set it to the railing before the witness box and drew back one pants leg. Jurors craned forward. From her seat Allie saw on the old man's thin bony leg a large white healing scar. Everyone behind her pressed forward to look. The cut was certainly recent.

"A lot of things could have made that." Ben Wray began to enumerate them.

Suddenly, Percival pushed forward. "Your honor, if I might interrupt." Nothing could have stopped him.

He snatched down Elgie's pants leg so quick, he almost lost

his balance. "My Lord," Percival said. "My Lord. Elgie, were you wearing these coveralls that evening?"

"Yes suh, they all I gots."

"Come here, Mister Ramsey," Percival cried. Even Judge Morton looked excited. "You got that swatch of material?"

Mr. Ramsey got up from the front row. It was only a few steps before he was measuring his piece of material from the Ferrari with the work reinforcement along one seam of the pants Elgie wore. While pulling up his pants leg to show his scar, Elgie had revealed too a large patch of a lighter denim.

"Ooooo," said Miss Pearlie Mae. Allie laughed outright. There was a hushed moment before people began talking. She watched Quad Brewster and his parents when Mr. Ramsey spoke.

"The piece matches," he said.

34

A HANDFUL OF PEOPLE attended the sentencing six weeks later. Allie chose a seat in the back of the courtroom; she wanted to be as far away as possible.

Quad seemed alone when Judge Morton motioned him to stand. His mother was not able to attend. Rumor said she was under sedation. Mr. Brewster looked as if he would not hold his head up in the streets again. As she had before, Allie had the uneasy sense that something about Quad was like a weasel. His pale hair was slicked down and shiny, and his eyes darted from side to side. Ben Wray Hood had had the starch taken out of him, and hill-country people were pleased that the smart Delta lawyer had not whipped them.

Judge Morton regretted Quad's age. "But through gross negligence you have caused the deaths of others. Have you anything to say, boy?"

Quad hung his head. Something in his gesture was too appropriate, too perfect. Any remorse he felt was for himself: everything had been done to him. Conscience was left out of the boy. "They," whoever "they" were, had done him in; in his own mind he was innocent. All this could be read in Quad's acting. "I never meant to —"

"What was it you said, son?" Judge Morton had to lean one ear in Quad's direction. Or had he heard? Because Quad turned his sweet appeal even on men; the judge studied those soft eyes.

'I never meant to harm." Quad shook his head. "I think I'd be better off not going to the penitentiary," he whispered.

Judge Morton sat back, his sympathy lessening. He tapped his gavel in an absent-minded way. It was obvious that he, like everyone in the courtroom, thought of all Quad Brewster had been given to start in life, and of what he had done with it. Those who'd scratched dirt for a toehold could know resentment, but now they considered themselves superior; for Quad they knew only pity.

"Quad, power and position is not a free ticket to criminal activity," Judge Morton said. Quad received twenty years each for his part in the deaths of John Q and Mister Otis, to run concurrently.

People believed the boy had not meant to cause either death; neither had he curbed his willful drinking, when it made him absolutely crazy. In saying goodbye to Allie, Percival said he believed much of Quad's story: it had been a game chasing John Q after the riot. If he had not meant for the man to go off the bridge, and he went, was that his fault? Quad childishly had asked. Probably, the boy would go on thinking himself wronged. The two talking felt little hope for his rehabilitation; they had to regret even that he'd ever be free. Having hit Mister Otis by accident, Quad raced away out of fear and a lack of manliness. "It's a breath of fresh air in this courtroom that he's found guilty," Percival said. "That Elgie could speak up." All who overheard nodded.

Quad then came outside with the sheriff, saying, "John Joe, you've known me all my life."

"I know it, son. I'm sorry. It's the law." John Joe clasped Quad's wrists with cool bracelets connected to a chain about his waist. Despite his words, there was satisfaction on the sheriff's face, as there was on the face of everyone watching.

However, when they started home, those from Itna Homa were not jubilant. There was something too awesome about the punishment of an individual—about incarceration. Ward did say, "A rich man's son is something new for that country prison farm. I hope he doesn't get special treatment." All stared from the car windows, with their own thoughts. Allie thought the scenery fit their moods; things were beginning to seem lackluster in November, without the sun's brilliance in their hot seasons.

They drove past a sign that welcomed them back to Nashtoba; it was decorated with two white sycamores, an Indian sign for rest for the weary. This was the town's centennial year. Overhead a banner stretched across the road billowed, its words reading "*Indians to Industry*"; Indians were so celebrated now when once they were driven away. While industry had saved this part of the country, it took away too its particularity, Allie was thinking. However, that was progress. She thought of Elgie's saying, "White peoples had the colored when they was furnishing us." With Negroes working in factories they were dependent on themselves. Everyone in the car sighed with relief when Nashtoba fell behind, laughing at themselves for the country people they were. They breathed freely at last only when Ward turned off the highway altogether, for them to breeze along the narrow road home, between fields now almost bare, and pastures that were browned. They were solemn again only crossing the rackety bridge over Grey Wolf River, where locusts hidden in willows continued their age-old, unsolved warnings.

Allie liked winter, the house snugly closed up, and the things that belonged to cold weather. She considered though that hei life had changed. She had forgotten to plant her narcissus bulbs early enough to flower for Thanksgiving. The wintertime scene created here such a different world, too. Instead of making it a green jungle, dead kudzu hung everywhere, browned skeletal reminders of a time passed. To her mind suddenly came a line from a poem Grandmomma used to quote her. Allie realized it had been with her for some time, and surfaced now. "He will justify you if you will it." So it had happened. With Quad sentenced, her election was assured. Her mind ran on to something lighter. Ward turned toward her, saying, "What's up, lady?" when she laughed.

"I remembered your saying you'd have starved to death from lack of fines if Snake had stayed constable," she said.

"Dern truth," Ward said.

Miss Pearlie Mae leaned forward from the back seat. "Allie, we're so proud of you. You stuck your neck out and didn't get it chopped off."

Allie nodded her appreciation. She found she could say nothing. Perhaps all achievement, all success, cost something? Always, she had counted on the stability of Tate's love. Now she had to question not only the love but whether it were foolish to count on anything remaining as it always had been. How deeply, too, did she really love Tate? Wasn't there mixed up in it simply the need for a woman of her time and place to have a husband? She had lost something to gain something; it was always to be so, she thought. Sternly, she reminded herself she was constable, that that was what she had wanted. Suppose Tate died, she'd have to get along without him. . . .

What would he do without her? He could date somebody like that pretty young stenographer in the courtroom. The idea outraged her! She saw herself alone as only growing grayer and planting narcissus bulbs to flower early. She returned then to the satisfaction of knowing that she had accomplished something she had set out to do, which had meaning.

Unexpectedly, Miss Pearlie Mae scrunched up to herself. "You know what just tickled me? That smarty lawyer thinking the boy ought to get off because all his momma's garden club wrote letters of recommendation!"

Everyone laughed. "You know us country folks have always had more sense than folks in towns," Sudie said.

"Country folks never had a high horse to get up on," Ward said. "Around here we've just always been extra poor and struggling to make a living. One reason nobody like the Meredith Negro came along till now. Folks always been too busy to think about integration. Now that we've got more leisure and more money, we can give thought to it. A lots of folks are still going to go round yelling 'Time — time — time.' Hell, the time is here. Excuse me, ladies."

Allie said, "I never expected that hotshot lawyer from the Delta to use such old-fashioned persuasions." She raised an arm and imitated Ben Wray Hood's oratory. " 'He's a good old boy who got in with the wrong crowd. He let drink drive him. I need not remind you that his family, great landowners, settled Nashtoba, and of all their endowments. Right now there's the hospital. It's long been the dream of this county that its sick won't have to go to Memphis.' " She wound down.

" 'Had to live in the shadow of generations of illustrious forebears —' " Ward began and halted. "As if that's a handicap. Hell, all it done was give him a free ticket through life. Excuse me again."

"Can you imagine a free ticket to anything?" Betty May Dobbins said.

Ward said, "Born with a silver spoon in his mouth and spit it out early. The rest of us ain't never owned one. Yet we want to be law-abiding."

"Quad said he was sorry. He thought that would get it," Miss Pearlie Mae said. "Always had before. Poor thing."

"He needed a stick of stove wood burning up his britches a long time ago," Betty May said.

" 'Punishment not for its own sake, but to reaffirm society's values,' Mister Percival said. I've got to agree with the man," Ward said.

This late in fall was called scrapping time. Having gone through the fields repeatedly, cotton pickers now went back in desultory fashion searching bolls that opened in their own good time. Along the roads, signs read that hay was for sale; stacks were seen in barns, or in pastures, the hay's faded yellow the color of the grass, and not yet the flat brown that would soon make pastures nearly indistinguishable from fields.

Ward let the women out at Loma's. The Laundromat was filled with young Negroes; it quickly had become a place to congregrate. Farmers were idle at this season and hung around town. Allie spoke to several. The other women scattered to the different stores to discuss Quad's case. She felt watched going up the short hill to Sy's — to Sy's and Elgie's, she reminded herself. Miss Pearlie Mae had carefully divided the reward money. With his half, Elgie was building himself a room onto Sy's. Fred was starting a savings account for Rose's fur coat. He would continue on at Mr. Brewster's; sympathy for Fred was too high for Mr. Brewster to fire him. Besides, he was flat out the best body man around.

When she approached, Elgie snapped his chair's front legs to the porch: he had been leaning against the house. Sy's old dog opened its eyes and swiped the porch with its tail as usual and went back to sleep. Wispy smoke curling from the chimney blew along the open porch. She asked Elgie what he thought of Quad's sentence: twenty years on two counts, to be served concurrently.

"Be out in about seven years."

"Is that enough to stay? Is that fair? I feel bitter, because nothing will bring back the ones who're dead. You certainly have a right to feel bitter, Elgie. Percival said you plainly and simply got lost in the paperwork down there." She took a deep breath before concluding. "I remember his saying, 'What value does tomorrow have if we can't take the word of a Negro.' "

"I 'member that." Elgie buried his face a minute. "No sense worrying yourself to death about the past." He looked up.

"I agree bitterness doesn't help," she said.

"God going to look down on the peoples for what they done," Sy said, listening from the doorway.

She and Elgie smiled at each other. "I'm so glad Mister Percival let you testify, expecting nothing, not knowing he would waiver your escape charge and cut your sentence to time served. Didn't tell you he'd go back and look into your original case and conviction, too."

"Said I got grounds for appeal," Elgie said. "That sho got me. Said I got 'em 'cause I didn't have no lawyer back yonder. I reckon I didn't."

"The governor's going to come through with that pardon, I'll bet. Mister Percival thinks so."

"Then I believes it too. I sho be glad to take that pardon for what I ain't did."

She looked across the road. Seeing Tate and Mose outside talking, she waved that she was on her way. It was near suppertime. "Elgie, I can't tell you what it's like to have you here again, like old times. To see you and talk to you when I want to. Only, we don't want the old days, do we?"

"No'm. Ain't got them, either. It all coming along like you said."

"It's all changed," she said rather wistfully, looking across the road again.

35

"SHOOT." Mose spoke as she came up the hill. "Miss'sippi's a territory ruled by the federal government. Next, they'll be telling storekeepers they can only serve red-headed customers on Thursdays. You know anything as prejudiced as the NAACP? How come it's left?"

She said nothing because he was talking to Tate. He only nodded. Mose was leaving. "Cars'll be running all night again tonight." He stopped short and looked embarrassed.

"Nobody's slept this week." Tate spoke in a flat, even tone; neither man looked at her.

She wanted Tate to. "It's always been like this the week before an election. Cars sound like hornets singing all around these roads at night. Noise is worse on the main road," she said. Tate kept his profile toward her. Men like these had to get over her victory, she thought. There would be no shoo-in at the last minute to replace Snake. She could not help letting her excitement and satisfaction outweigh Tate's opposition.

Mose looked off. "Well, you're lucky. If somebody was running against you, you'd be out chasing votes in the dark, too. All this night riding, electioneering, and buying votes. Always somebody going to sell theirs by moonlight."

"That'll change if the community gets large enough to have more than one balloting box," she said. "Nobody will be able to tally who everybody votes for."

"Town's going to get that big." Tate spoke toward its traffic on the main road. Mose said happily that was O.K. with him, and drove off. She watched Tate's back uneasily as he went to see about a sick calf. Then he came in and busied himself getting washed for supper. She waited till they sat down before finally asking her question. "Tate, did you ever have an affair with a woman named Iona?"

His mouth opened. In that instant, Allie thought of whole truth and how she might not have known it over these long years. Why had she so innocently trusted Tate when she had lied sometimes?

"That was a woman Mose went to see," he was saying. "I let him drive and just rode along. Was like visiting the old woman in the shoe. He never went back." His voice grew cross. "No. I never did, either."

Hearing again his new tone, it crossed her mind again, too, how seldom he called her hon, anymore.

"How'd you know her?" Tate said.

Allie explained about Ralph. Repeating the boy's conversation, she nearly said something new and frightening to her—

Ralph said he knew where you lived. Catching herself back, she said, "Ralph said he knew where we lived." That was so much more normal to her life. The singular was alien, uncomfortable, and lonesome when you'd been part of a couple as long as she had. She tried to smile. "I wouldn't expect you to tell me if you had an affair."

"Then why'd you ask?" he said.

It caught her off-guard, because she'd expected him to be humorous, and something too deadly serious had been in his voice. For the rest of dinner, they talked casually about happenings in the community, in a wary way. She felt unsure that she'd ever again know what was beneath Tate's surface, as once she'd felt certain. Seeming more aggressive, would he stay this way? Or slip back to his old personality? She hoped he would, and hoped he would not. She felt a little excited by his change, though resented it too. Had their relationship been more comfortable when she thought herself the more positive one? Or had she only felt so because the relationship had been the way it was for so long? Surely, she truthfully had always wanted Tate to be the stronger? she asked her reflection. Beyond the kitchen window was the blackness of the pasture.

She went to bed ahead of him, perhaps with more behind the idea than that she was really sleepy. Wasn't she glad when Tate's ideas about farming had turned out to be right, the two times he'd had new ones? Yes. Of course. She turned into the pillow, remembering how she had thought it was going to be a new beginning, with him stepping forward at last. Then it had not been.

Tate would return to his former self; only hidden anger would continue to lie beneath. Before, she had not known it existed, hadn't known that they lived with it — she expressed hers. Probably, they needed a knock-down-drag-out fight. But for Tate's nature, one would be disastrous. He would interpret it as their inability to get along.

She had meant to sigh. Tears flowed into her pillow instead. She sobbed aloud unintentionally, wishing she could plain bawl.

Only, unlike some little lost calf, she had to figure out everything for herself.

Tate was in the doorway. "Can I help?"

She sat up and looked at his silhouette. "Tate, I don't want another husband." (Not even a fairy-tale prince to whisk away all problems?)

"I never have wanted another wife," he said. "One's enough."

Was he smiling? joking? She could see nothing of his face but shadowed contours, and what she knew were his moving lips. There rose up again that sense that men did not much like women, or marriage; they sensibly married, needing a housekeeper.

She lay down, saying, "No, you can't help. Thanks. I just needed a good cry." She longed for Sweetie, too feeble to be able to jump up into bed now. She felt Tate's relief, as he turned more quickly than she would have thought. She had wanted him to come sit beside her affectionately, even though she'd said he did not have to. She felt despair at his turned back, as he left. Why not cry out to him? Because he needed to come on his own, she thought.

She hoped Tate came to understand her new strengths. He had his own attitudes though, which she saw better now. She respected them. In the same way, she would respect him if he left her some day.